Land of Hope and Glory

GEOFFREY WILSON

HODDER

First published in Great Britain in 2011 by Hodder & Stoughton
An Hachette UK company

First published in paperback in 2012

1

A CIP catalogue record for this title is available from the British Library

Paperback ISBN 978 1 444 72112 6
Ebook ISBN 978 1 444 72111 9

Typeset in Minion Pro by Palimpsest Book Production Limited, Falkirk, Stirlingshire

Printed and bound in UK by CPI Group (UK) Ltd, Croydon, CR0 4YY

Hodder & Stoughton policy is to use papers that are natural, renewable and recyclable products and made from wood grown in sustainable forests. The logging and manufacturing processes are expected to conform to the environmental regulations of the country of origin.

Hodder & Stoughton Ltd
338 Euston Road
London NW1 3BH

www.hodder.co.uk

For Helena, for everything

Prologue

Harold Neary flinched at the first crack of a musket. A bullet whined past in the dark. Then another. But Harold spurred his horse on towards the line of soldiers who stood ahead in the gully.

Tonight he would kill Rajthanans. Nothing would stop him.

The Sergeant Major – riding beside Harold – drew his scimitar and shouted, 'Charge!'

Harold and his eight other comrades lifted their swords too and roused a cry somewhere between a cheer and a shriek. They thundered down, the musket flashes rippling before them, the bullets thickening.

Harold gripped his scimitar tight as he rode. His heart flew, but there was no need for fear. God was on his side.

He thought of his brother, who had died fighting the Indians – the Rajthanans. Those heathens thought they were so high and mighty, the lords of England, but Harold would teach them that they couldn't lord it over him. When he'd served in their army, they'd shouted at him, flogged him, practically starved him, but he'd survived. And while he still had strength he would slaughter as many of the bastards as he could.

Cloud covered the moon and in the faint light Harold could barely see the scattered row of forty European soldiers – only their faces and hands stood out. Their fingers, like fireflies, darted to ammunition pouches, lifted cartridges, slammed ramrods down barrels. Grey powder smoke drifted along the line. Behind stood Rajthanan officers in silver turbans that brightened at each firearm spark.

And further back rose the bone-white tower of the sattva link, shining slightly against the black background of the hills.

Bullets hissed around Harold. With a metal scream, one struck a scimitar. To Harold's left, young Turner cried out and jerked back off his horse.

Turner. Down. That left just nine riders.

'Steady, men!' the Sergeant Major shouted.

Harold glanced at his commander. The Sergeant Major was a big man with broad shoulders and thick arms. In the grey light his face was like battered tin: his nose crushed, his ears mangled and his shaven head pocked and dented by old injuries.

He was a great man, the Sergeant Major, and one of the toughest soldiers Harold had ever met. It was the Sergeant Major who had convinced them all to don peasant clothes and take to the hills. It was the Sergeant Major who had taught them how to fight the Rajthanans, how to burst out of the wilderness and attack before anyone knew what was happening, and then vanish again as quickly as they had appeared.

Harold would follow the Sergeant Major anywhere.

The enemy were near now. The Europeans stopped firing, clicked the catches on their weapons to release their knives, and formed a line of pointed steel. Their faces were set hard beneath their blue cloth caps and the brass buttons shone on their blue tunics. Harold had worn a uniform like that for three years. He'd fought for the Rajthanans just like these men. But no more.

The Rajthanan officers screamed for their men to hold steady.

Harold remembered hearing the news that the Rajthanans had murdered his brother and then he was shouting so hard his throat ached and the sound seemed to blot out everything else, save for the wind whipping past and the undulating movement of the horse.

He swerved and aimed for the nearest officer. For a few seconds he could see his opponents in great detail: wide eyes, teeth, nostrils. It was like a dream.

Then his horse jumped and the soldiers dived. He swung his blade, hitting nothing. He couldn't see the officer. He heard hooves nearby colliding with heads and chests. Scimitar chimed against knife-musket.

And then he was through. He glanced about, and saw that none of his comrades had fallen and their pace had hardly slowed.

'To the tower!' the Sergeant Major bellowed.

Harold wanted to stay and fight, to get his first kill, but he had to keep up.

The windowless, two-storey tower loomed ahead in the narrowest point of the gully. A twenty-foot-high brass rod topped the pointed roof.

Away to the right, a set of tents came alive. Soldiers stumbled out in their underclothes and almost fell over as they pulled on their trousers. They came running up the slight incline in their nightshirts, baying like dogs. Harold could make out snatches of what sounded like Andalusian.

The Sergeant Major shouted to Harold and pointed towards the tower. Harold followed his leader over to an arched entrance and leapt from his charger. He released a sack hanging across the back of the horse, then humped the heavy weight on to one shoulder.

The Sergeant Major glanced at him. Harold grinned, patting the sack. Within that cloth was something worth more to him right now than gold.

Powder.

The Sergeant Major went first up the circular stone stairway, drawing an ornate, multi-barrelled pistol from his belt. It was dark, save for a trace of misty light from above.

Harold breathed heavily and his heart whispered in his ears. He shook the long hair out of his eyes.

Near the top of the stairs they paused. Above them was an archway, out of which floated the faint light.

'Anyone up there?' the Sergeant Major called. 'Give yourselves up and we'll spare you.'

No response.

Harold heard shouting and pistol shots outside. His comrades would be fighting off the soldiers. There wasn't much time.

They advanced up the stair.

With a sudden high-pitched cry, an Indian officer charged through the arch, stumbling down the first few steps. He fired his pistol straight at the Sergeant Major. The hammer clicked—

Nothing happened – a misfire. The officer's face dropped.

The Sergeant Major smiled, his pistol cracked and smoke blurred the stairwell. The officer's left cheek flared open and spat blood against the wall; the white row of his teeth was visible inside the wound, as though he were smirking. He fell forward, clattered and jerked on the steps.

'Good shot, sir,' Harold said. Another heathen dead.

The Sergeant Major grinned, his eyes quivering in the dim light. 'Any more up there? Give yourselves up.'

Silence.

They crept up the remaining steps. The Sergeant Major pressed himself against the stone wall, then swung into the entrance, holding the pistol before him.

Nothing happened.

He looked down at Harold. 'There's no one.'

Staggering under the weight of the sack, Harold ran up the stairs and entered a stone-walled room lit by pale yellow lanterns. To one side, on top of a pedestal, stood a spherical wire cage, within which squatted a metal shape that looked like a creature dredged from the sea. Numerous crab-like claws hung from its sides and a mass of mandibles and feelers covered its head.

Harold stopped dead and made the sign of the cross. That thing was one of the Rajthanans' devils. Avatars they called them.

The Sergeant Major stared at the device and rubbed his hand over his shaved head. He shot a look at Harold and nodded.

Harold took a step towards the machine, noticing a copper cable leading from the thing's back, across the floor, along one wall and up through the centre of the ceiling.

The avatar moved. One claw scraped along the bottom of the cage and a feeler lifted.

Harold hesitated. He'd heard the Rajthanans fed these beasts on human blood. Whether that was true or not, he'd like to see them all smashed to pieces as soon as the Rajthanans were kicked out of England. The country was in the grip of black magic and only the crusade would free it.

'Hurry up,' the Sergeant Major said. 'It's harmless.'

Harold swallowed. He stepped up to the pedestal and heaved the sack to the floor. The avatar moved more rapidly, scuttling about in the cage and snapping its claws.

Harold pushed the hair back from his eyes, struck a match and lifted the fuse sewn into the side of the sack. He looked up at the avatar, which was now scratching frantically at the bars and making a clicking noise, as if it knew what was coming.

Harold smiled and lit the fuse. The flame settled into a red glow that crept up the hemp cord.

'Let's go,' the Sergeant Major said.

They charged down the stairs and came out in the middle of a melee. Only six riders remained – one more had fallen. At least fifty soldiers ran about the horses and jabbed with their knife-muskets. The riders slashed left and right with their scimitars and continually circled to avoid being struck. Pistol shots rang out intermittently and Harold caught the sulphurous scent of powder smoke.

Two soldiers lunged with knife-muskets as Harold came out of the entrance. The Sergeant Major skipped to the side and dashed his opponent's head against the wall, but Harold moved more slowly. He saw the gleaming blade rush towards him and strike him in the shoulder. His arm went cold as the knife grated against bone. He gasped and fell back against the tower, the knife still stuck firmly and the soldier still holding on to the musket.

Harold locked eyes with the European soldier. The man's face was twisted with battle fury and he was panting so hard Harold could smell his stale breath.

'Bastard heathen,' Harold managed to say, and spat in the soldier's face.

Then the Sergeant Major roared and punched the man on the side of the head. The soldier stumbled sideways, his round cloth hat flying off. The musket slipped out, tearing an even greater wound in Harold's shoulder.

Harold shivered. He could see the Sergeant Major kicking the fallen soldier in the face, but the scene was becoming blurry and strange.

He had to stay awake. He couldn't let the heathens beat him.

'You all right?' The Sergeant Major was suddenly standing before him.

Harold nodded. Sickness welled in his stomach and his arm was like ice. He shuddered and stumbled, but the Sergeant Major caught him and helped him up on to the nearby horse.

The Sergeant Major then swung himself up behind and fired his pistol in the air. 'Knights, ride!'

Harold felt the charger galloping. He slumped forward against the animal's mane and clung on as tightly as he could with his one good arm. His six remaining comrades bounced along to either side, stray musket and pistol fire flying after them.

Something was wrong. Grimacing at the pain, he looked back and saw that the tower was still standing. Had the fuse gone out? Had the heathens found the powder sack?

Then the top storey of the tower blossomed into a red and yellow flower that lit the whole valley for a moment. A baritone pulse rushed out and rippled through his bones. Chunks of stone whistled in the dark and soldiers scrambled for cover. The horse stumbled slightly, but didn't fall.

Harold smiled. That was for his brother.

The Sergeant Major lifted his fist in the air and gave a defiant cheer. The other riders joined him.

But their celebration was cut short by the sound of shots from the darkness off to the left. Around a dozen horsemen were riding from the camp and bearing down on them.

'Hurry, knights,' the Sergeant Major shouted, and they spurred and slapped their horses onward.

They turned into the trees at the end of the gully and the horses scrambled over an embankment. Then they sped on through the mottled gloom of the forest. Branches and leaves leapt in front of them. Shrubs appeared and disappeared like clouds of dust. The horses whinnied and rolled their eyes.

Every jolt sent a wave of sickness through Harold and he could hear himself groaning.

After what seemed a long time, they came out on to a grassy slope. They zigzagged up, the horses skidding and kicking up clods of earth. They took around ten minutes to reach the summit, where they paused and looked down.

Harold blinked. The cloud had lifted now and he could see a wide sweep of the countryside rolling away in great folds and buckles, like the ocean at night. The knots of forest, indistinct valleys, open hills and heaths were all powdered by the moon.

'Down there,' hissed Smith, pointing to the line of trees they'd left earlier.

Harold could just make out the enemy cantering along beside the woods several hundred feet to the left.

The Sergeant Major snapped open a spyglass and followed the horsemen for a moment. 'Must have lost us in the forest. Don't think they've seen us yet. Come on.'

They turned and galloped down a short slope before reaching a further stretch of trees. They followed a track that wound through the undergrowth, leaves slapping against the horses' sides.

Harold felt himself slipping away, then shook his head and managed to pull himself back.

After a few minutes, the Sergeant Major called a halt, dismounted and walked to the rear of the group.

Dizzy with pain, Harold looked back over his shoulder and watched as his leader sat cross-legged on the ground, rested a hand on each knee and closed his eyes.

The Sergeant Major breathed slowly and deeply. Apart from the rise and fall of his chest, he was still. The sound of insects swirled and an owl hooted in the distance.

Then Harold noticed the faint, sweet scent of incense – the smell of sattva, that mysterious vapour the Rajthanans used for their machines and avatars and unholy powers. He was leery of it, as he was of all the Rajthanans' devilry, but the Sergeant Major had some skill with it, and Harold had grudgingly come to accept that it had its uses.

Sometimes you had to fight black magic with black magic.

Harold's comrades shifted in their saddles – they were just as nervous of sattva as he was.

The Sergeant Major blew gently and a strange breeze seemed to emanate from his body and flow back along the path with a hiss. But it wasn't so much a breeze as a warping of the scene itself. Tree trunks, branches and the leaf-littered ground all rippled, as if reflected in a pool of water into which stones have been cast. Slowly, the horse tracks on the path disappeared, as if sinking into the earth. The twigs and small branches that had snapped as the horses passed, regrew. The wind rose in strength and then faded, the whorls and eddies subsiding. All evidence that the riders had been there had now vanished.

The Sergeant Major stood, chuckled and rubbed his hands together. He walked back to his charger and said to Harold, 'You still with us?'

Harold tried to speak, but couldn't form the words. He grunted as he fought back the vomit stinging his throat.

'We'll get you back soon.' The Sergeant Major mounted and looked across at the riders. 'Well done, knights. Our land is in darkness, but our crusade will bring light. God's will in England.'

'God's will in England,' the others said in unison.

As they moved off, Harold felt as though the night were thickening and suffocating him. If he drifted off he was sure he would die. And yet he had to stay alive to keep up the fight against the Rajthanans.

The pain in his shoulder seemed to be the only thing he could cling to – he concentrated on it, sensed the swell and ebb in its intensity. But even that was fading now.

He had to hold on . . . but he was letting go.

PART ONE
THE TRACKER

1

DORSETSHIRE, 617 – RAJTHANAN NEW CALENDAR (1852 – EUROPEAN NATIVE CALENDAR)

Jack Casey crept through the trees near the front of the house. It was after nine at night, but it was summer and the sky still suspended trails of blue within the darkness. He could see the lantern beside the front gate and make out the new guard, Edwin, leaning against the wall beside it, picking at something in the sole of his boot.

Jack stepped on a twig, which gave a loud snap. He froze.

Damn. He was out of practice.

The trees rustled in the slight breeze. Faintly, he could hear people talking back in the house, the tinkle of glasses and the rattle of plates being cleared away.

Edwin didn't react at all.

Jack shook his head, then advanced, hardly making a sound now – he hadn't completely lost his touch.

Edwin was still oblivious to the approaching danger. Jack stood poised in the darkness, just a few feet away from the lad, then stepped out. 'Bang – you're dead.'

Edwin jumped and fell back against the wall. 'Christ! You nutter.'

'If I was an intruder, you'd be lying there dead and I'd be on my way to the house.'

Edwin sniffed. 'But you're not an intruder. There are no intruders. Nothing ever happens around here.'

'And that's the danger. It's quiet. You get lazy. Then – pow – you're dead.'

'You're mad, you are. We're in the middle of the country. There's no one around.'

Jack smiled darkly, his weather-beaten features creasing more deeply. He had a triangular face that seemed to emphasise his eyes and his craggy brow. His eyes were narrow and pale, the irises almost white in the dim light. His long hair was tied back in a ponytail, and he wore a brown, knee-length tunic that was spotlessly clean.

'That's what you think.' He looked about as if there were enemies in the trees. 'There are thieves and vagrants. You get bandits in the hills.'

'Bandits? How often have they tried to get in here, then?'

'They know we're here watching. If they come, they see us and go on to the next farm. But if they see us dozing, that's when they'll strike.'

'If you say so.'

Jack shook his head. He was too soft on the boy. That sarcastic attitude would have been beaten out of him within one day in the army.

'Did you hear about the Ghost?' Edwin asked. 'Struck again last night. Knocked out the sattva link to Bristol.'

'That so.'

'They can't stop him. He's there one minute, gone the next. I heard he's a sorcerer.'

Jack snorted. 'Don't you believe everything you hear down the market. The Rajthanans are a lot stronger than you think.'

Edwin looked sideways at Jack, then spoke more softly. 'Word is, the rebels will win.'

'Watch your mouth, lad.' Jack glanced over his shoulder. 'The master hears you talking like that, he'll fire you. If you're lucky.'

'I'm not scared of him.'

'Well, you should be. You're talking treason. You'll get yourself reported to the sheriffs.'

Edwin looked down and scuffed the ground with his boot. 'It's still true.'

'The Rajthanans rule all of Europe, and a lot of other places besides. You really think a few mutineers in England can beat them?'

'They've got London now, and the whole south-east.'

'Once the Rajthanans have built up their army they'll smash those mutineers to pieces.'

Edwin muttered something inaudible.

'Listen, lad. I'll give you some advice. Forget about this Ghost or the mutiny or whatever other rubbish is filling your head. There's an order to things and there's no point in fighting against it. Some people rule, others follow. That's the way of it. The Rajthanans rule here and we follow. Now, you look sharp and keep your eyes peeled. And don't you dare fall asleep.'

Edwin bowed with his hands pressed together, as if Jack were an army officer. 'Namaste, great master.'

Jack rolled his eyes and walked off into the darkness to continue his evening rounds. Edwin had no idea what he was talking about. The rebels might have won a few battles, but that was only because there were hardly any foreign troops in England – there had never needed to be. Now the Rajthanans were bringing in French and Andalusian regiments, and even soldiers from Rajthana itself. Once they'd built up their army in the south-west they would crush the rebellion. It was as simple as that.

He followed the stone wall for a few feet, went through a gap in the trees and came out on the front lawn. Before him stood the house. It was two storeys high, more than a hundred feet wide, and built in the style of a Rajthanan palace with miniature spires and domed towers. In places, lacy detail in bas-relief lined the rust-coloured walls. The leaded-light windows glowed and cast a series of bright blocks across the grass.

Through an arched window, he could see the dining room, where silver thalis and bowls glinted on the table. Dinner had just finished and Shri and Shrimati Goyanor had risen and were gesturing for their three guests to join them in the drawing room. Shri Goyanor – a short, plump man – wore his usual beige tunic, while his wife stood tall and elegant in an emerald sari. The children had probably already been sent to bed. Servants in white were busily clearing the table.

Shri Goyanor was obviously in a good mood – he beamed and rubbed his stomach as he spoke. He was a good-hearted man. He could be sullen, but then so could anyone. The main thing was that he always kept his word, and Jack valued that. It was like in the army. You trusted your officers because they treated you fairly, and in return you would lay down your life for them if they asked you to.

Jack went on around the side of the house and past the line of palm trees that Shrimati Goyanor insisted on trying to grow. He met Tom, the nightwatchman, coming the other way.

'Evening,' Jack said.

Tom raised his lantern and nodded back. He didn't speak much and Jack approved of this. Tom was a reliable man, who'd been at the house for eight years – almost as long as Jack himself. During that time Jack had never caught him shirking or sleeping on the job, although perhaps he did like a drink a little too much.

'Keep an eye on Edwin,' Jack said. 'Don't let him leave that gate.'

'Aye, I'll watch him.'

Jack continued to the back of the house, where only the light from the pantry trickled across the lawn. Ahead of him, the four acres of the gardens were almost pitch black. Off to the right, behind a row of bushes, stood the wall of the servants' compound.

'Jack.'

Sarah, the head cook, appeared from the pantry and slipped across the grass towards him.

He cursed under his breath. He'd been avoiding her. He'd slept with her a few nights ago, but that had been a mistake. Now she seemed to think there was something between them.

She stepped out of the shadows and looked up at him. She was pretty, with brown hair that fell in thick locks past her shoulders.

'Haven't seen you around much,' she said.

'Been busy.'

'Big night tonight. The mistress's been in a right state.' She waggled her head and imitated Shrimati Goyanor's thick Indian accent. *'I told you never to use garlic and onions when we have government officials to dinner.'*

Jack smiled slightly.

'I'm dead tired now, though,' she said. 'Got another blessing in the morning too, first thing.'

Jack knew that all cooks had to be blessed regularly if they were to prepare food for the Rajthanans. The Rajthanans had a lot of strange ideas about food and drink. It was something to do with their system of caste, which they called jati. The higher jatis wouldn't take food from the lower jatis, and no one would take it from Europeans unless they were blessed. Jack had actually seen a dying officer in the field refuse water from a native soldier to avoid being polluted.

'If you have an early start I'd better let you get on,' Jack said quickly, turning to leave. Maybe he could get away before things got difficult.

'Jack.'

He stopped and turned back.

Her face was serious now. 'What's going on?'

'Look, I'm sorry if I gave you the wrong idea—'

'I see.' A glint of moisture appeared in one of her eyes. She looked off into the dark gardens. 'Like that, is it?'

'You know the rules. Servants can't be couples. We'd get fired.'

'No one would find out.'

'We can't risk it. Anyway, you could do better than me. Get yourself a good man. Get married.'

He meant it. He wasn't well, not since . . . his accident. Sarah didn't know about his injury and he didn't want to burden her with it. She should have a strong man who could take care of her . . . But there was more to it than that. If he were honest, the memory of his wife, Katelin, still held him back.

'Have it your way, then,' Sarah said, with an edge of bitterness to her voice. She turned to leave.

'Wait.'

She looked back.

What could he say? 'It's for the best.'

She huffed, spun away again and marched back to the house, her long dress swishing about her.

Jack scratched the back of his neck. That had gone about as well as could be expected. At least it was over now. Part of him wished he could just give in and be with Sarah. She was a good woman. But it would never work.

He pressed on into the darkened grounds, crossed the small stone bridge over the brook and continued into the formal garden. Oblong-shaped, ornamental trees stood in rows beside ponds that reflected the moon. Lines of white orchids and lilies swayed in the breeze. He smelt the cool fragrance of flowers and moss. The wooden gazebo, half buried by vines, brooded in the centre.

Beyond the garden was a series of hedges and then the orchard. He walked between the apple and pear trees, smelling the sweetness of the growing fruit.

About halfway through, the hairs suddenly stood up on the back of his neck and his skin rippled. The air seemed to tremble with a strange energy. He'd been expecting this.

He stopped and sniffed. A faint, but familiar, scent encircled him. It was like a mixture of sandalwood, musk, saffron and rosewater. Distinctive, yet impossible to describe.

Sattva.

A powerful stream coursed through the grounds here, and he sensed it every time he walked through. He was sure no one else in the house knew about it. Only he had the sensitivity and training to detect it.

He took a deep breath. That smell reminded him of the past, back when he'd still been able to use his power.

A movement off to the left disturbed him. What was that?

He crouched, peered into the gloom, listened intently, searching the surroundings for signs. Tracking came to him instinctively – he'd learnt the skill from his father from the moment he could walk.

He noticed the movement again – a quick swish near to the ground. He sneaked forward and paused, partially concealed by a tree trunk. Despite the warning he'd given Edwin, the only intruder during all his years as head guard had been a vagrant boy stealing fruit. He waited for several minutes and then a red-brown streak shot between the trees and disappeared – a fox. He gave a small chuckle. He'd thought as much, but it was always best to be cautious. The old army training, the old reflexes, would never leave him.

He slunk to the end of the orchard – leaving the sattva stream – and reached the stone wall that marked the perimeter of the property. Beyond the wall lay miles of fields belonging to Shri Goyanor – the nearest neighbours were five miles away.

He walked beside the wall until he reached the iron gate that was the only back exit to the property. He checked that the bolts were secure and then, satisfied that everything was in order, set off back towards the house.

As he crossed the bridge, he started to feel out of breath.

He stopped on the other side and leant against a willow tree. He tried to catch his breath, but his chest felt tight and sweat formed on his forehead. This had happened several times recently. What was wrong with him? Was his injury getting worse?

He shut his eyes, and after a minute his breathing eased. That was better. He opened his eyes again and went to move on.

Then he felt a thump in his chest, as though someone had kicked him. His ears rang and white spots spun before his eyes. He fell against the tree and sat there, hunched. He was choking. He tried to call for help, but he was too weak even to do that. Blackness passed over him and he fought to stay conscious.

'Jack!'

He opened his eyes. Sarah was crouching over him with a lantern in her hand.

He blinked. He felt better – he could breathe again and the pain in his chest had gone.

Sarah crossed herself. 'Thank the Lord. You had me worried there.'

He sat up against the tree. 'What happened?'

'You tell me. I heard this choking sound and I came down here and found you out cold.'

'Ah. Think I fainted. Haven't been feeling too well lately.'

She frowned. 'You should see a doctor.'

'No need for that.' He struggled to his feet. 'Just a touch of the flu.'

'Flu, my foot! At the mission hospital—'

'I said, there's no need.'

Her eyes flickered. 'You're bloody impossible.'

'Don't make a scene.'

'Don't make a scene?' She raised her voice and turned as if calling out to the house. 'Why, you worried the master will find out about us?'

'Sarah—'

'Think you'll lose your job?'

Jack winced as his chest tightened again and his breathing became laboured.

She paused for a second. 'Jesus. You look terrible.'

He waved her away. 'I'll come right in a moment.'

'You'd better get back to your room.'

He was too weak at that moment to disagree, and he let her walk with him to the compound and past the small white-walled huts of the other servants. By the time they reached his hut he was feeling a little stronger.

She followed him into his room, despite his protest. He lit a lantern, revealing his plain cubicle. A sleeping mat lay on the floor, a few blankets folded neatly at the end. His spare clothes, also neatly folded, sat on top of a crate in a corner. The stone floor had been carefully swept and washed.

'Why don't you lie down?' she said.

'I will . . . in a minute.'

'Here, let me get this.' She bent to move a carved wooden box that was sitting in the middle of the sleeping mat.

'No.' He slammed his hand over the box. Then he saw the surprise on her face and his voice softened. 'It's just something personal.'

'Touchy, aren't you?'

He sighed. 'It's just some letters. From my daughter.'

'Your daughter? I didn't know . . . you're a dark horse, aren't you? How old is she?'

'Fifteen.'

A suspicion moved across her forehead. 'What about the mother?'

'She died.'

'I'm sorry.'

'It's all right. It was eight years ago.'

'Do you see her often – your daughter, I mean?'

'Twice a year, at the most. She lives in North Dorsetshire. It's expensive to get there.' It was less than a day away, but neither he nor his daughter, Elizabeth, earned much. 'Sarah, you've been very kind, but I should get some rest.'

She nodded. 'You see a doctor, though.'

'I will. Just one thing, if the master finds out about . . . what's happened, he'll think I'm not fit to work.'

'I won't tell anyone. So long as you see a doctor.'

He half smiled.

'I mean it,' she said.

He gave her a nod as she left. He had no intention of seeing a doctor. He'd always been able to control his injury and this latest attack would just be a temporary setback.

He was sure it wouldn't happen again.

He shut the door, lay down on the mat, put his face in his hands and massaged the skin. He opened the wooden box and took out Elizabeth's latest letter. He looked at the lines of curling ink, tracing the marks with his finger. He couldn't read the words, but he could recall them. Whenever he paid a letter writer to read one of her letters, he would listen intently and memorise as much of it as he could.

Dear Father,

Thank you so much for your letter. I am well and everything is coming along fine. I have been promoted to chambermaid. It is hard work, but more money. My mistress expects a lot, but I am doing my best. She seems to be pleased with me so far.

You said in your last letter you are worried about me. I know you think I am too young to go into service, but I can look after myself now.

You know I have always had to do things my way. You used to call me 'wilful'.

God keep you, Father.
Elizabeth

He put the letter away and closed his eyes. As he drifted off, he pictured Elizabeth the last time he'd seen her – seven months ago, at Christmas. He remembered her standing outside in the cold, waving goodbye to him as he left on the back of a horse cart. She shivered and her nose was red, despite the thick cloak she wore over her shoulders. She looked so small and frail as he pulled away, dwarfed by the fields of luminous snow.

'It's very concerning,' Shri Goyanor muttered. 'Very concerning indeed.'

'Yes, sir.' Jack was standing in Shri Goyanor's study with the morning light falling across his employer's desk. There had been a disaster just before dawn. A servant boy had been caught drinking from the well reserved for the Goyanor family, which meant it was now polluted and would have to be reconsecrated.

'How could this happen?' Shri Goyanor asked without taking his eyes off his newspaper.

'The well isn't guarded. I can put someone outside it, but we may need an extra hand in that case.'

As far as Jack was concerned it wasn't his fault. His job had always been to stop anyone from outside the grounds getting in. Shri Goyanor had never said anything about the well. But Jack knew better than to point this out. Shri Goyanor was his commander, and you didn't question your commander. Nor would it do much good if you did.

Shri Goyanor sighed, pushed up his spectacles and poured himself a glass of water – Jack recognised the label on the bottle: 'Ganges Finest'. The family had been reduced to drinking expensive imports. Shri Goyanor took a sip, then stared out of the window at the central courtyard where two gardeners were bent over, cutting the lawn with shears.

Jack waited for a response. He wanted to ask Shri Goyanor for the rest of the day off so he could visit the mission hospital in

Poole, but he knew he had to time an unexpected request like that carefully. He'd had two further 'attacks' and Sarah had been pestering him for days to see a doctor. He'd finally agreed it was worth a try. Now it was Friday, the only day the hospital was open to new patients.

The floor felt cold through his hose – as usual he'd taken off his boots before entering the house. He glanced at the walls, seeing the row of plaques that were apparently awards from his employer's jati, the 'Traders and Farmers in Europe'. Next to these hung small, faded portraits of important family and clan ancestors, including a picture of Babuji Gupta, the founder of the jati, who had settled in Europe more than 150 years ago, as Jack understood it. The old man – with a huge white beard – smiled as serenely as a Christian saint, as if he could foretell how successful his community would be.

Shri Goyanor continued staring at the lawn.

Eventually Jack gave a small cough. 'Sir, if I may . . .'

Shri Goyanor stirred from the window and looked at Jack. 'Yes?'

'I'd like the day off to go into Poole.'

'Today? That's quite unusual. You need to give some notice.'

'I know, sir, and I'm sorry about that. But I have some urgent business. It won't affect the guard roster.'

'Urgent business? Very unusual.' Shri Goyanor looked down at the newspaper, shook his head and then rapped the page with his finger. 'Look at this. Brighthelm's fallen to the traitors now. I don't know . . .'

'It's terrible, sir.' Jack had already heard rumours that the port city had been taken. This was just the latest in what had been months of bad news. First, reports had come in of English regiments turning on their Indian officers, then of London falling, of the massacre of Rajthanan women and children at Westminster, of further cities falling. Now most of the south-east was controlled by the rebels, under their leader, the so-called Sir Gawain. Even

King John had given his support, although many said the old man was either senile or under duress.

'I don't understand,' Shri Goyanor said. 'I don't understand it at all. What's wrong with those soldiers?'

Jack stood in silence. He knew it was best to let Shri Goyanor talk until he'd expressed his views fully.

'Well, I dare say it'll all be over soon enough,' Shri Goyanor continued. 'The army will sort it out, of course. I just hope they get on with it quickly. At least we won't get that kind of trouble here. I mean, the sentiment of the people around here . . . it's different, isn't it? I've always said that.'

'I'm sure you're right, sir.'

'Yes. The sentiment is quite different. We won't have any trouble. Even this . . . this Ghost, or whatever he calls himself. He might be on our doorstep, but people won't flock to him. I'm certain of that.'

'Yes, sir.'

Shri Goyanor turned the page of the newspaper and studied it for a moment.

After a pause, Jack said, 'Sir, about Poole . . .'

Shri Goyanor looked up again and blinked, as though Jack had appeared out of thin air.

'I need to go into Poole today, sir,' Jack repeated.

'Oh, yes.' Shri Goyanor gave a long sigh. 'Very well, if you must.'

The doctor's eyebrows shot up when Jack pulled off his tunic. Jack had expected this reaction. His torso was covered in a patchwork of pale lines and knots, scars from numerous bullets and blades.

'I was in the army,' Jack said.

'I can see.' The doctor – a young Rajthanan wearing a brilliant white turban – walked around the table to stand beside Jack.

They were in the main hall of the Poole Shiva Mission Hospital. Behind Jack, slumped on benches, were the sick, the injured and the dying: old men weak from cholera and sleeping on the streets; worn mothers with screaming babies; peasants from the country covered in dust from the long journey into town; people whose faces were marred with pox blisters; people shivering, coughing, sniffling. The sharp smell of urine and faeces was stronger than the scent of burning incense that rose from numerous brackets about the walls.

Those patients who were currently being attended to sat in a row before a series of tables, behind which sat the doctors and nurses. And behind the doctors, at the back of the hall, was a huge stone statue of Shiva that reached almost to the ceiling. The god sat cross-legged, with two hands in his lap and a further two hands holding a trident and an hourglass-shaped drum. A cobra coiled about his neck and reared up beside his shoulder.

The doctor examined Jack's scars slowly, finally stopping at the thick, red burn mark in the centre of his chest. The doctor prodded the mark with his finger and Jack flinched.

'So that's the sattva-fire injury,' the doctor said.

'Yes, sir.'

'Nine years ago, you say.'

'Yes. Got it in an accident. On the battlefield.'

For a moment Jack remembered the fierce blue fire and the searing pain. In the heat of battle he'd got ahead of his platoon and a sattva-fire ball had fallen short. It had burst on the ground and a bolt of the stuff had screamed through the air and struck him.

The doctor leant forward to look at the scar more closely. 'Don't see this sort of thing very often in England.'

Jack nodded. England was peaceful – at least it had been until the mutiny. Only soldiers like him who'd been posted overseas were likely to get hit by sattva-fire.

The doctor drew back. 'It'll never heal. There'll always be a trace of the fire in you.'

'Yes, sir.' Jack already knew this. The army doctor who'd first treated him had told him. The injury would always be there, but he could learn to live with it. So long as he didn't try to use his power, he could lead a normal life, even stay in the army.

'I'll just check something.' The doctor picked up a brass ear trumpet and placed the cold metal in various positions on Jack's chest. He furrowed his brow, straining to hear.

Finally he put the trumpet down again. 'I'm afraid it's not good news.'

The sounds in the hall seemed to echo louder and the smell of incense grew stronger.

'What is it, sir?'

'The wound's spreading. The fire has reached your heart.'

'What does that mean?'

'Your heart is being weakened. It'll get worse as the fire spreads. Eventually it'll be fatal. There's nothing that can be done about it.'

Jack swallowed. He was suddenly conscious of his heartbeat, that regular pulse tapping away on the left side of his chest. 'How long have I got?'

'That all depends. You could have a few years left, in fact, if you can learn to live with your condition. But you have to take care. Any strain on your heart and it could stop completely.'

'What kind of strain?'

'Anything that increases your heart rate: physical exercise, a sudden shock, any form of excitement.'

Jack nodded as he considered this.

'I'm afraid that's all I can do for you.' The doctor returned to the other side of the table and began writing in a notebook. 'You can go now.'

Jack pulled on his tunic and bowed with his hands pressed together, as if praying. 'Thank you, sir.'

Outside the hospital, he stood on the edge of the narrow street and watched the crowds go by. Horse and bullock carts clattered along, scattering chickens and geese. Three-storey buildings with wooden frames and wattle-and-daub walls leant over the road, as if about to topple over. Dogs skulked down alleyways. He smelt excrement and rotting vegetables.

His wound was spreading – the army doctor hadn't told him that could happen.

Ah well, what did he expect? Karma, after all, had caused the accident, because of what he'd done, the mistake he'd made. Obviously he hadn't paid his debt in full yet. When his time to go came, he would accept it. There was no point fighting fate.

He was, in many ways, lucky to be alive at all. Many of his comrades had died on the battlefield. Now he was thirty-nine – not a bad age for a soldier to reach. And the doctor had said he could live for several years yet, so long as he took care of himself – which was exactly what he intended to do.

He wandered down to the seafront and leant against the low wall, beyond which lay a short stretch of rocks and then the expansive bay. The sea was blue marble beneath the sun, and on the far side of the bay were wooded hills and islands.

He glanced along the wall to the left and about a mile away he could see the jumble of blackened buildings, stepped terraces and jetties that formed the docks. Two military transport ships were in the port, their chimneys smouldering amidst the cross-hatch rigging. They would be bringing in more troops – every week more arrived.

The mutiny. It seemed to seep into everything these days. It would bring nothing but misery to England. Shri Goyanor was right: the sooner it was over, the better.

He rubbed his face with his hand and glanced inland to the high, red walls of the new town, where the Rajthanans lived in their orderly streets and mansions. The enormous golden towers of the Vishnu temple glistened in the sunlight and cast a warm glow over the surrounding buildings.

He couldn't help but marvel at the Rajthanans. With their grand buildings, their avatars and mills, and their knowledge of sattva, they seemed a people blessed by God, even though they didn't even worship Him. The mutineers were fools to think they could defeat the might of Rajthana.

And the rebel leader was the biggest fool of all. He called himself 'Sir Gawain', as if he were a knight from King Arthur's day, but apparently he was just a little corporal with a big mouth.

The bells of the old cathedral rang Nones – three o'clock – in the distance. He thought of Elizabeth, standing in the snow, waving goodbye. What would happen to her if the worst happened to him? He brushed the thought aside. She could look after herself now. But he would make sure he saw her more often. He would save harder for the cart fare. He would go without the little luxuries he bought from time to time: a pint of ale, chewing paan. He didn't need those things – he just needed to see his daughter.

And he would write more, many more letters. He still had time.

He left the sea wall and hurried along the muddy streets to the market square, which bustled with stalls, traders, farmers, pigs, chickens, goats and all manner of other produce. People haggled, shouted at each other, ate, drank and listened to minstrels singing along to lutes.

He went to the stall of his usual letter writer, but found a different man behind the stand – a Mohammedan with a thick blond beard and a white skullcap.

'Is Master Beatson around?' Jack asked.

'He's sick.' The Mohammedan waved his hand dismissively. 'I can help you.'

Jack paused. He didn't trust Mohammedans. He'd served with them in the army – most of continental Europe was Mohammedan – but he'd never liked them. And it was even worse for an Englishman to follow Islam. England was a Christian country, and had been ever since the last English Caliph had been defeated two centuries ago. Everyone knew the story – after centuries of conflict, the old Moors had eventually conquered Europe and ruled in England for 200 years, but an army of English knights had rebelled and forced them back over the sea to France, or al-Francon as the French called it. England had been free then, but had been mired in wars between dukes and barons and a series of kings. Peace had only been restored when the Rajthanans arrived a hundred years ago.

'I'd like to send a letter,' he said.

'One shilling,' the letter writer replied.

'A shilling? It was only ten pence last time.'

'That's the price.'

'I'll give you eleven.'

'No, no. The post-cart price has gone up. It's one shilling. That's it.'

Jack felt his heart beat faster. He was becoming breathless, or maybe he was just imagining it. He had to calm down. No point getting worked up over a few pence. 'All right, then. One shilling.'

The letter writer took out a pen and some paper. Jack tried to concentrate on what he wanted to say, but a woman pushing a wheelbarrow of parsnips bumped into him and cursed. He closed his eyes for a moment and pictured Elizabeth standing in the snow.

'Dear Elizabeth,' he began. 'Thank you for your last letter. It was good to hear from you . . .' He paused. It was so hard to know what to say sometimes. 'No, change that. Make it: "It was wonderful to hear from you, as always." How does that sound?'

The letter writer shrugged.

'I was pleased to hear about your promotion,' he continued. 'You deserve it. I hope you're still well. It's summer now. I know how you like to see the wild flowers on the heath. Do you remember how your mother used to take you out to the fields? You used to make daisy chains together.' His voice became hoarse and he stopped for a second. His throat was tight. He wished Elizabeth was there with him now.

'Anything else?' The letter writer tapped impatiently against the paper with his pen.

'Yes.' Should he tell Elizabeth about his heart? 'I am the same as usual . . . No, make it: "I am well." No . . .'

The letter writer grumbled as he crossed out what he'd just written.

'All right, say this: "I am in the best of health. Never been better. May God give you grace, Elizabeth. As always, your loving Father."'

The sounds of the market faded away for a second and the ground seemed to drag at Jack's stomach.

'The address?' the letter writer said.

'Sorry.' He tried to concentrate. 'The address. Yes.'

He gave the Mohammedan the address of Elizabeth's letter writer. And he imagined Elizabeth standing in a market in North Dorsetshire as his words were read out, those scratches on the paper forming an invisible connection across the miles, across the towns and fields and heaths and downs, bringing him and his daughter together for a moment.

It was a long ride back to Shri Goyanor's property. Normally the journey from Poole would take an hour, but the mule-cart driver made numerous detours to drop off staples at farmsteads along the way. After two hours, Jack was still sitting with the other passengers in the back of the cart, his feet hanging over the side and jiggling as the wheels bumped over the uneven road. The pile of cabbages behind him formed a relatively comfortable backrest.

At one point they passed through a sattva stream, and he shivered, a tingle shooting up his spine. No one else in the cart seemed to notice, but when he sniffed he caught the distinctive smell.

He looked out at the countryside and imagined the invisible stream tangling and coiling across the fields, through the large mansions and between the stands of trees. These streams wove their way across England – across the whole world, in fact. Sattva was everywhere, in everything, to some degree. But it tended to clump into veins of differing strengths that stretched for miles above, through and under the ground.

'Hold on back there,' the driver called out and the cart juddered off the road and stopped beside a ditch.

What now?

Jack jumped to the ground and walked around the side of the cart. He could soon see why the driver had pulled over. Coming towards them along the road, surrounded by billowing dust, was a column of troops and horses. It looked like a full battalion, maybe more – at least 1,000 men.

The other passengers climbed down and stood beside him, watching as the army approached. The yellow dust reached them first, engulfing the cart and turning the day foggy. Boots stomped in unison, kettledrums pounded, and soon the first men emerged from the haze: European soldiers in blue tunics, round caps, loose breeches and puttees. Most of them had thick beards – they looked French to Jack. Their Indian officers rode alongside on horses, barking occasional commands.

Next came a battery of light artillery – twelve-pounders in European reckoning. Horses drew the guns on two-wheeled carriages, with ammunition carts attached behind. Swirling designs encrusted the pieces, the muzzles fashioned into grinning serpent heads. Wheels ground at the dry earth, thick chains clinked, and Jack smelt animals and oiled leather.

Then a contingent of elephants swayed through the murk, the great beasts covered by quilted caparisons and pulling carts and large siege guns. Mahouts sat astride the animals' necks, driving the creatures forward with hooked sticks. A sergeant sat further back on one of the beasts, holding aloft the regimental standard – a flag tapering to two points.

Finally, a loud wheeze came from the rear of the column and

a cone of smoke rose and mingled with the dust. The scent of sattva grew stronger. Several of the men standing beside the cart sniffed and muttered to each other – even they could smell it now.

Something was smelting sattva. Something powerful.

The last of the elephants lumbered past and a cloud of steam and smoke swirled across the road. Another wheeze, then a shrill whistle . . . and then a dark shape, larger than an elephant, solidified in the haze.

The onlookers murmured.

A monstrous form of black iron studded with rivets crawled into view. It looked like a giant lobster interwoven with hissing pipes and pistons. Smoke frothed from beneath its carapace, and its feelers lifted and swayed as they checked the air. It paused for a moment, then it gurgled, the sound like bubbles under the sea. A jet of steam shrieked from its side.

The onlookers all gasped and jumped back. One man slipped on the edge of the ditch and stumbled to the bottom.

A man near Jack crossed himself and whispered to his friend, 'A demon.'

But Jack knew this was no demon. It was an avatar, a living being wrenched from the spirit realm and bound to the machinery of the material world. Most Europeans feared these creatures – considering them the work of the Devil – but Jack was used to them.

This one surprised him, though. He'd seen train avatars many times, but never something moving along the road like this. He'd heard stories of the marvellous machines back in Rajthana, but he'd never known whether to believe in them. Whatever the case, it looked as though the Rajthanans were bringing in their most powerful devices now.

The rebels didn't stand a chance.

A Rajthanan officer riding nearby stopped his horse for a moment, closed his eyes and made a small gesture with his hand.

The avatar shuddered and groaned, then began to creep forward again.

None of the onlookers seemed to have noticed the man, but Jack knew he must be a siddha – a 'perfected one'. Only a siddha could command an avatar like that.

The siddhas were yogins who, after long years of practice, had developed one or more of the miraculous powers. It was the siddhas who created and controlled the avatars, studied the yantras and learnt to smelt sattva. But they guarded their secrets closely – few Europeans, or even Rajthanans, knew much about them.

Jack, however, knew more than most. After all, he was, in a sense, a siddha himself.

The avatar grumbled past, the scent of coal and sattva wafting about it, the chains along its sides snapping tight as it hauled a covered wagon. Soon it disappeared into the grainy murk up the road, the wagon trundling behind.

A bank of grey cloud rolled across the sky. Raindrops began to spatter the ground, the cart, Jack's head. Jack stood and leant against the mound of cabbages as the cart bumped along the road. Ahead, through the thickening drifts of rain, he saw the wall of the Goyanor estate. The red towers at the top of the house peeked out above the dark-green trees surrounding the property.

The cart pulled up at the gate and he jumped to the ground. His tunic was wet and heavy, and the wound in his chest ached. All he could think about was crawling into bed.

He banged on the gate.

The slot opened and Edwin's face appeared. 'Who's there?'

'It's me – Jack.'

'Well, now. Could be an intruder. How can I be sure?'

'Open the gate, you bloody idiot.'

Edwin swung the gate open and stood there in a long cloak,

his hair drenched and coiling into his eyes. He smiled cheekily. 'Afternoon, Master Casey.'

Jack sighed and smiled back. Edwin wasn't a bad lad. He would come right in the end.

And suddenly Jack found himself hoping for the best for the boy, hoping for his safety in a future that seemed to be darkening every day.

2

Jack sat cross-legged in his small room, staring straight ahead. A couple of sticks of incense burnt in a holder on the floor, the smoke filling the room and making his head swim. Morning light slipped under the door and through cracks in the walls, but otherwise the room was in fuzzy darkness.

He took a deep breath. His thoughts were racing today.

'Your mind is like a rippling pool.'

Basic yoga training. He remembered sitting with the other men on the parade ground as the drill sergeant took them through the meditation.

'Sit down, men. Cross your legs. Back straight. Hands on knees. Focus on the standard.'

The regimental standard – three red lions running in a circle on a blue back ground – was always strung up before them during yoga practice.

'Focus on the standard, men. Don't let anything else into your head.

'Now close your eyes. Keep them shut. Anyone opening their eyes will be on the end of my boot.

'Keep the standard in your mind. Keep every detail of it there. Don't let your thoughts jump.

'Your mind is like a rippling pool. Still it.'

But today Jack found it hard to calm his thoughts. He tried to concentrate on the standard, but images and memories flickered in his head . . .

Elizabeth standing in the snow last Christmas, waving goodbye as he pulled away on the back of the cart . . .

Elizabeth, as a child, running towards him across a meadow, her long dark hair flowing behind her . . .

And then Katelin, his wife, on her deathbed, her face glistening with sweat as the fever took hold, her skin so pale he could see the blue veins clearly beneath. Her Celtic cross necklace rose and fell with her slight breathing. She reached out to him with skeletal arms and the feeling of her fingers on his cheek was like the chilling touch of death, as if she were already gone, calling to him from the spirit world . . .

He snapped his mind back to the standard.

He breathed slowly and felt his heart beating, beating, each beat telling him he was still alive.

Gradually, he tamed his mind. He bent all his thoughts towards the standard, suppressed anything else. He saw every detail of the three lions: the open mouths, bulging eyes, twitching tails, extended claws.

His spine tingled, warmth pulsed in his forehead and energy trickled over his scalp. Sattva prickled his nostrils. He was touching on the spirit realm now, the realm of heaven, of God . . .

A loud knock on the door snatched him out of the trance. He sat still for a second and composed himself.

Another knock.

He opened the door and saw Sarah standing there in a blue dress and a white bonnet. The rain had cleared during the night and the day was bright and warm. He squinted in the sudden glare.

'There you are,' Sarah said. 'The master wants you. There are some people – they've come to see you.'

'People?'

'Army, I think.'

Jack frowned. Why would anyone from the army visit him? He'd had nothing to do with the army for nine years.

He walked with Sarah to the opening in the wall bordering the servants' compound. Before he went through, she tugged his sleeve and looked at him with concern. 'What did the doctor say?'

'Nothing. I'm fine.'

She arched an eyebrow. 'You didn't go, did you?'

'Of course I did. Really. There's nothing wrong with me.'

She smiled. 'Thank God.' Then the smile slipped from her face and she looked away. 'I was worried about you.'

'Don't you worry.'

He considered patting her on the shoulder, but decided not to and instead stepped out into the garden, where a pair of peacocks strutted across the lawn.

Shri Goyanor was standing near the stone bridge, fidgeting. His spectacles flashed as they caught the light. 'There are some army officers here. They need to speak to you.'

Jack nodded and followed his employer into the formal garden. He heard birds chirping in the trees and smelt the steam of the drying earth. Water burbled from fountains and shivered across ponds.

'Look, Jack,' Shri Goyanor said. 'You're not in any kind of trouble, are you?'

'No, sir.'

Shri Goyanor nodded. 'Of course not. Good.'

They came to the gazebo – a circular, wooden structure with a thatched roof and trellis walls covered in jasmine vines. The jasmine leaves bobbed as bees flitted from flower to flower. Two Indian men sat cross-legged in the shade. Jack stopped and blinked in surprise.

One of them was Captain Jhala – commander of his old army company, and his guru.

Jhala stood and smiled.

Jack instinctively did a deep namaste, going down to his knees and prostrating himself for a moment, before getting back to his feet. You had to show proper respect to your guru. Jhala was the siddha who had given him the secret training.

Jhala put his hands together and bowed slightly. 'Namaste. It's a pleasure to see you again, Jack.'

Jhala had aged a great deal since the last time Jack had seen him. Although he would only be in his mid-fifties now, his face seemed to hang from his scalp, giving him a slightly morose appearance. His cheeks were jowly and he had large purplish bags under his eyes. What was visible of his hair – poking out from under his red and white turban – had gone silver, as had his eyebrows.

He'd always been a strong man, but he'd suffered from occasional bouts of a fever he'd caught in Rajthana when he was young. Jack recalled him being confined to bed with it on several occasions. Perhaps the illness had caused this premature ageing.

'Captain Jhala, I don't know what to—' Jack began.

Jhala smiled again and tapped his turban. Jack noticed the golden braids woven into the material.

'Forgive me, *Colonel* Jhala.'

'And this is Captain Sengar.' Jhala gestured to the other officer standing beside him.

'Namaste.' Sengar spoke with a strong Indian accent. He looked a little younger than Jack, perhaps mid-thirties. His thick moustache was waxed into curls at both ends, and his face was angular and handsome. His green turban indicated that he was an officer in a French regiment of the European Army. Like Jhala, the sun-clan insignia was embroidered on the left side of his tunic.

'He's a good boy,' Shri Goyanor said in Rajthani, wringing his hands as he stood next to Jack.

'Of course,' Jhala said. 'He's one of the finest army scouts I've ever met.'

Shri Goyanor's eyes widened. He glanced at Jack. 'Yes. We're very lucky to have him. I've always said that.' He switched to

English, seeming to forget Jack could largely understand Rajthani. 'Haven't I always said that, Jack? We're very lucky to have you.'

'Yes, sir,' Jack replied.

'Thank you for letting us speak to him,' Jhala said.

'No problem at all. Would you like chai? Sweets?'

'No, thank you,' Jhala said. 'We'll be fine.'

'Good. Excellent.'

'Shri Goyanor, would you mind if we spoke to Jack in private?'

'Oh. Of course not. No problem at all . . . well, then. Just send for me if you need anything else.'

Jack glanced back to watch Shri Goyanor make his way to the house. He could see many of the servants, including Sarah, standing about not even pretending to work, peering to make out what was going on in the gazebo.

Jhala and Sengar sat again.

'Sit down, Jack.' Jhala gestured to an ornate cushion-seat. 'Relax.'

Jack removed his boots and lowered himself tentatively. He'd never sat in the gazebo before. He smelt the warm fragrance of the jasmine and heard the hum of the bees. Greenish light found its way through the vine leaves and speckled the floor.

As his surprise wore off, Jack realised how pleased he was to see Jhala again. Jhala had been more than a commander and guru to him – he'd been a friend, if such a thing were possible between European and Indian. They'd served together for fourteen years, in France, Macedonia and Eastern Europe, as well as in England. They'd been through the fire of the Slav War and the gentler times of the quiet posting in Newcastle. You couldn't go through all that without a close bond developing.

'How many years is it?' Jhala asked.

'Nine.'

'Amazing. It goes so quickly, doesn't it?'

'Yes, sir.'

'The regiment's much the same. Chimney Pot's long gone, of course.'

Jack smiled. 'Chimney Pot' was the nickname the troops had given to old Colonel Hada, who'd puffed on a hookah so much he was constantly surrounded by clouds of smoke.

It said a lot about Jhala that he knew this nickname. It showed how close he'd been to the men, to the point where he could share their jokes. He'd always kept a certain distance, of course – an officer had to – but he'd been closer to his troops than any other officer Jack had ever met. Perhaps part of this was due to his expert knowledge of the English language and culture. Jhala had actually taken it upon himself to study the English people. In his spare time he would read books and monographs on the subject. He could speak English better than many natives, and his knowledge of English history was extensive. In fact, much of the English history that Jack knew he'd learnt from Jhala.

Jack still distinctly remembered Jhala telling him the English were a 'special race'.

'You have a proud heritage,' he'd said. 'Never forget that. Your knights were the only ones in Europe to expel the Mohammedans. You overthrew them, just as we did in India. We're alike, you see, the Rajthanans and the English. And both strong with sattva.'

Jhala shifted on his cushion-seat. There was a scraping sound nearby as one of the gardeners pushed a wheelbarrow along a gravel path.

'Where are you posted now?' Jack asked.

'Here, in Poole. You know the barracks?'

'Yes.' Jack had seen the sprawling military compound from the road many times. It lay a few miles to the north-east of the city. But of course he'd never actually visited it, having left the army so long ago.

'Been there for about a year now,' Jhala said. 'You should come by sometime. You'd be most welcome.'

'Thank you, sir. Can I ask something?'

'Of course.'

'How did you know I was here? I mean, working at this place?'

'It was just a stroke of luck. You remember you saw Sergeant Kershaw a few months ago?'

'Yes.' He remembered now. He'd bumped into David Kershaw, one of his old colleagues from the regiment, in Poole during the winter. They hadn't spoken much – Jack had been in a rush to complete an errand for Shri Goyanor. He hadn't even realised at the time that Kershaw and the regiment were now based in Poole.

'Well, Kershaw happened to mention it to me,' Jhala said. 'He told me you were working as a guard around here, so I looked you up in the register.'

All guards were required to register with the local sheriffs, who kept a logbook containing the names and addresses of everyone working in security in the area.

Jhala coughed a few times and Jack wondered whether he was suffering from the fever at the moment. Finally, Jhala cleared his throat and looked around at the gardens. 'It's very pleasant here.'

'Yes,' Jack replied.

'You like it, then?'

'Shri Goyanor's been good to me.'

'Of course. I'm sure he has. But still, you must miss the old days sometimes.'

'Sometimes.'

'Ever think about coming back?'

'No. I mean, I made my decision. I think it was for the best.'

Jhala looked up at the roof of the gazebo, as if there would be some sort of inspiration up there. 'Never did quite understand why you left, Jack. If you'd stayed on you'd be ten years off getting your pension now.'

It was true. If he'd stayed on he would be closer to receiving the all-important, much-admired army pension, a smallholding where a man could live out the rest of his days in peace, if not actual luxury. It was what all soldiers dreamt about, after they'd served for a few years.

'You're right, sir, but I had that accident.'

'The injury wasn't bad. The doctor said you could stay on.'

'Yes, sir. But . . . things changed.'

Jack's fingers tensed around the corner of the cushion beneath him. The accident had been the result of karma and he'd vowed not to go back to the army after what he'd done. But he'd never spoken to anyone about this, apart from Katelin.

'Well, I suppose we all have to make our choices in life,' Jhala said. 'But what would you say if I told you I could arrange for you to get your pension after all? Immediately.'

Jack's heart quickened. Could it be possible? 'Sir, I would be most grateful.'

'Have to say, you've earned it. You were one of the best. I've got a lot to thank you for. All those times tracking the Slavs in the mountains. Never would have done it without you.'

'Thank you, sir.'

'There is a catch, though. We need you to do something for us. A small mission.'

Jack paused. 'I don't want to cause offence, but I can't join up again. Those days are over for me.'

'You won't need to join up. We just need your tracking skills.'

'I've heard all about your talent,' said Sengar, who had been quietly observing the discussion so far. 'I'm most anxious to see you at work.'

By 'talent' Jack assumed Sengar meant his power, his ability not only to track a quarry using the usual signs – footprints, broken twigs, grasses parted, droplets of blood – but also to follow the trail a person or animal left in sattva, a trail that was invisible to most, but impossible to erase.

The Rajthanan siddhas had all sorts of powers, but none of them could do what Jack could do. He was a so-called 'native siddha', one who had a natural, often unique, ability. He wasn't a siddha in the proper sense – it took years of study and practice to achieve that – but he had an innate skill, bred into him through being born amongst the strong streams of sattva that criss-crossed England.

'I know your injury is a problem,' Jhala said. 'But you'd only have to use your power briefly. I've known other men with the same condition who've done that.'

But Jhala didn't know the wound had spread. For all Jack knew, using his power now might kill him. One more reason to refuse.

'Sir, Captain Sengar,' Jack said. 'I appreciate your offer, but I can't accept. I have my life here now. I can't help you. I'm very sorry.'

Sengar sucked on his teeth and looked across at Jhala.

Jhala leant back against his seat's bolster, folded his hands in his lap and stared straight at Jack. He sighed. 'I'm sorry too. It's this damn mutiny. Nasty business.'

'Yes, sir.'

'Don't know what's come over those English regiments. They've killed women and children – did you know that?'

'I heard something about it.'

'Never thought I'd see it. It's a pity for all of us to be living in these days.'

'Colonel Jhala, with respect,' Sengar said in Rajthani. 'We're wasting valuable time here. He has to—'

'He can understand you, Sengar.' Jhala glanced at Jack. 'Isn't that right?'

'Yes. I understand some. Picked it up in the army.'

Sengar breathed in sharply, nostrils flaring. He spoke to Jack with his voice clipped. 'Very well, then. You might as well hear it straight – you *have* to help us. You don't have a choice.'

Jack felt a ripple of nerves.

'Calm down, Captain Sengar.' Jhala raised his hand and patted, as if dampening an invisible flame. He leant forward, studied the mat before him, then looked up at Jack. His skin appeared too heavy for his face to support. His eyes were large and watery. 'Jack, there's a bit more to it than we've told you so far.'

Jack sat back a little. What would the other servants be thinking? He could imagine them gossiping furiously about why their head guard was talking to army officers for such a long time.

'William Merton,' Jhala continued. 'I'm sure you remember him.'

Of course Jack remembered him – he'd been Jack's best friend in the army, probably the best friend Jack had ever had. No one who met William could forget him. He was a giant man, with a giant laugh and a big heart. Larger than life.

'Quite a soldier, wasn't he?' Jhala said. 'Quite a man.'

'Yes.'

'Do you remember the time he wrestled me?'

Jack smiled – he remembered it well. They had all been mad about Malla wrestling at the time and William had been one of the best. Jack himself had tried wrestling his friend a few times and had been quickly beaten.

The Indian officers were also obsessed with Malla, but they almost never wrestled with their men – it wasn't the done thing. Jhala, however, broke all the rules and happily took part in his men's contests. And he always won as he was something of a Malla guru.

At any rate, William had been going around bragging that he would be European Champion if the competition were opened up to natives. Jhala, hearing about this, put down a challenge and there was a mighty fight between them a few days later. Jack could still remember the bellowing of the men as they sat watching in the training tent.

The thing was, after many bruising rounds, William pinned Jhala for the count. There was a shocked silence. No one knew how to react to a native beating an officer. But Jhala stood, raised William's arm, and pronounced him the winner. He did it so quickly and graciously that it seemed the most natural thing in the world and everyone cheered and stamped their feet. Jhala actually grew in stature, despite being beaten.

'Brave man, wrestling an officer like that,' Jhala said. 'That's what makes it all the harder.' He looked down, lost for words for a moment, then looked up at the bright sky, squinting a little. 'You see, Merton's mutinied. He's gone over.'

Jack sat up straighter. He hadn't seen William since leaving the army. They'd written a few letters but had lost touch. What could have driven his friend to become a rebel? What madness?

'Hard to believe, isn't it?' Jhala said.

'It is.'

'After all that time. He'd made it to sergeant major too.'

'I can't understand it.' Sergeant major was the highest rank a European could reach.

'He wasn't with our regiment any more. He'd gone to the 8th a few years back. One of those reshuffles, you know how it is. I'd like to think that if he was still serving with me . . . well, who knows? Who knows anything any more?'

They all went silent. Jack felt uncomfortably hot in the gazebo. The smell of jasmine was suffocating.

'Anyway, you may have heard of the "Ghost",' Jhala said. 'That's what they're calling Merton now. He's leading a group of bandits up in North Dorsetshire.'

'I've heard about it. But I didn't know . . .'

'No, not many people know his real identity. The locals are superstitious. They call him all sorts of names. The thing is, he's causing us quite a bit of difficulty. By all accounts he only has a small band of followers – mostly mutineers – but they've proved a menace, hitting the sattva links, train lines, that sort of thing. We've sent in troops, tried hunting him down with trackers and dogs, but he's always managed to slip away. You remember what he's like – his power.'

Jack nodded. William was a native siddha too, another of Jhala's protégés. His power enabled him to conceal his tracks, making him almost impossible to follow.

'Well, we've tried everything,' Jhala said. 'And we still can't get him. That is, of course, where you come in.'

'I see . . . I'm shocked about what's happened with Merton. But still, I can't hunt down an old friend. You understand, he saved my life.'

Jhala gazed out at the gardens. 'Yes. Mine too, if you remember. But that's not the point. We all know that in the army you obey orders, no matter what. It's what you sign up to. To mutiny is the greatest dishonour.'

'Yes. You're right. It's just . . . sir, as I said before I can't go back into the army. Perhaps there's another tracker . . .'

'I'm afraid not – not with your skill. You're the best in England, without a doubt.'

'This is ridiculous,' Sengar snapped at Jhala. 'We're wasting time, sir.'

'Captain Sengar,' Jhala said without turning, 'you will hold your tongue.'

Sengar glared back for a second and then looked away. 'Sorry, sir.'

Jhala stared at Jack. He appeared tired, as if the whole mutiny had been his fault. 'There is one further . . . factor in all this.' He took a deep breath. 'Your daughter, Elizabeth Casey.'

'Elizabeth?' Jack sat forward.

'Yes, I'm sorry to tell you she's gone over to the rebels as well. She's been helping them – spying, giving them supplies—'

'No, sir. Elizabeth would never do that.'

'I'm afraid it's true. She was caught red-handed. There's no doubt.'

Jack's hand trembled. His heart raced. Elizabeth? A rebel? 'Where is she?'

'We're holding her in the barracks. We've got a few of them.'

'Can I see her?'

'Of course. We'll take you there . . . in a few minutes. First, you need to understand your situation. Jack, I really had hoped it wouldn't come to this, but Elizabeth is due to be hanged.'

Jack felt dizzy. The sound of the bees, the smell of the jasmine, the heat all swirled around him.

'It must be a dreadful shock, I know,' Jhala said. 'But I can make sure Elizabeth is spared – just so long as you help us. Do you understand?'

What was happening? Was Jhala using Elizabeth as a pawn in some game? 'I understand, sir. Can I see my daughter now?'

They arrived at the barracks in a two-horse, four-wheeled carriage covered in intricate gold designs. Jhala stared out at the plains, resting his chin on one hand, while Sengar sucked on his teeth, which made his moustache curl and uncurl like a cat stretching.

Jack sat in silence, feeling lost in a maze. He glanced at Jhala, but his old commander cleared his throat and looked away. Jack had always thought of Jhala as someone he could trust, but now he didn't know what to think.

An icy breeze crossed his skin. Elizabeth was due to be executed.

A stone wall surrounded the main complex of the barracks. Outside the wall to the north stretched the usual vast shanty town of wooden shacks, tents and dusty marquees that housed the European troops, along with the numerous camp followers who worked as bearers, servants, orderlies and cooks.

The carriage drew up at the main gate, which was open but guarded. To the side stood a row of flagstaffs, one of which flew the standard of Jack's old regiment – the 2nd (Maharaja's Own) Native English Infantry. Jack looked up at the blue flag with the three red lions chasing each other in a circle. He'd meditated in front of that flag so many times. He'd believed in it.

Inside the walls lay a series of long wattle-and-daub buildings with thatched roofs. The buildings were solid but typically plain and functional. Jack had often wondered why the Rajthanans didn't build grander structures for their armies, given how much they seemed to love pomp and ceremony. Rajthanan soldiers in turquoise tunics and turbans strode about or stood guard.

Jack, Jhala and Sengar climbed out of the carriage and walked across the flattened, dusty ground until they came to a stone building with a single arched entrance. They went up the steps and into a small foyer. It was dim inside, lit only by a few lanterns. Three guards slouched against the walls but snapped to attention when Colonel Jhala appeared.

Jhala spoke to one of the guards, then turned to Jack. 'You can see your daughter for a few minutes.'

The guard unlocked an iron door, which groaned open, and led Jack down a gloomy corridor. To either side stood cells with bars that stretched from floor to ceiling. Men and women – all European – sat hunched on mats. Dirt streaked their faces and their clothes were tattered, as if they'd been living in the wilderness for weeks. As perhaps they had. They watched as Jack and the guard went past, some listless, some puzzled, some defiant. Most of them were silent, but a few whispered amongst themselves.

The guard stopped near the end of the corridor and pointed through the bars. Jack looked into the cell. He couldn't see clearly at first as the only light came from a tiny window high up in the wall. Then he saw her.

She recognised him at the same time, gasped, ran up to the bars and grabbed hold of his arms. She looked thin, much thinner than when he'd last seen her, and her long dark hair was matted and greasy. She wore a torn and dirty dress and her hands were discoloured with ground-in filth. She looked like a vagrant.

'Father . . .' She kneaded his arms and cried dirty tears.

'Elizabeth. What . . . what happened?'

'I'm sorry. I didn't mean for you—'

'Why?' He put his hand through the bars and brushed the hair away from her face.

'I know you won't understand, Father. We have to be free.'

'We *are* free.'

'Not in the way we could be.' She started sobbing, looking at the ground, her shoulders shuddering.

Jack realised he was crying as well. It felt as though his life up until this moment had been mere theatre and now all the props and costumes had been put away. 'Elizabeth, you stay strong. I'm going to get you out of here. I promise.'

She looked up, her face red, her expression flickering between disbelief and hope. 'How?'

'I'll get you out.'

'Time,' the guard said.

Jack clung to his daughter's hands.

The guard put his hand on Jack's shoulder. 'Come on.'

Jack stroked the side of Elizabeth's face and then let himself be led away. He looked back only once at the small, forlorn figure in the cell. She was just a child. How could they hang a child?

Two guards took Jack past the parade ground and over to a bungalow with a veranda across the front. A storm of thoughts whirled in Jack's head and something cold shifted in his stomach. Even now he found it hard to believe Elizabeth was a rebel. But she hadn't denied it.

He paused at the bottom of the steps. How could he convince Jhala to free Elizabeth?

He shut his eyes for a moment, breathed deeply and walked up to a sparse office. Jhala sat behind a desk and Sengar sat nearby in a wicker chair.

'Have a seat.' Jhala gestured to a chair.

Jack sat down stiffly. Jhala was his friend – surely he would help. A hundred memories from his army days tumbled through his head. He and Jhala had fought alongside each other many times. There had been a bond between them. That wasn't something that could easily be broken.

Jhala gave a deep sigh. 'I didn't want this, Jack. You need to understand that. It's the mutiny – it's changed everything.'

'Sir.' Jack's voice cracked. 'Elizabeth made a mistake, but she's sorry. She won't do anything like that again. I give you my word.'

Jhala held up his hand. 'I understand you're worried about her.'

'She's just fifteen, sir.'

'I *will* free her, but first you need to help me.'

Jack paused. He wanted to beg or shout or plead for Elizabeth, but he held himself back. 'You want me to track Merton.'

'Yes. I was hoping you would do it of your own accord. Merton's dishonoured the regiment, all of us.'

Jack looked down. That was true. But how could Jhala expect him to hunt down his friend?

Jhala shifted in his seat. 'I know this isn't easy. But think of your daughter.'

Jack pictured Elizabeth in the cell and a flame of anger leapt in his chest. 'How did you know she was my daughter?' he said softly.

'When she arrived here she was screaming about her father who used to be in the army. When I saw her surname I talked to her and realised.'

'Look, you have to do your duty,' Sengar said.

Jack glared at Sengar. 'Doesn't look as though I have much choice.'

Jhala sighed again, opened the top drawer of his desk, took out an envelope and held it up. 'This is a pardon for your daughter, signed by the Raja of Poole. It was difficult to get, I can tell you. I had to call in quite a few favours. Now, I know you can find Merton. All I need is for you to lead us to him, and then,' waving the envelope, 'your daughter will be free. I give you my word.'

Jack looked at the yellow envelope. How could he agree to this? 'I'll try.'

Jhala and Sengar exchanged glances.

'You'll have to do better than trying,' Sengar said. 'The pardon states that your daughter will only be freed if you give us Merton. If we don't catch Merton and bring him back here, dead or alive, the pardon is forfeit. Do you understand?'

Jack nodded slowly.

'I'll be travelling with you, with a squadron of cavalry. You will have four weeks to find Merton, otherwise . . .' Sengar looked over at Jhala.

'Yes, that's right.' Jhala cleared his throat. 'We couldn't give you an indefinite amount of time. Four weeks should be plenty. But after that, the pardon expires and your daughter goes to the gallows. I'm very sorry.'

Jack shoved a spare tunic into a satchel and battered it to the bottom with his fist. He whirled round. What else did he need to pack? He couldn't think straight.

Someone knocked at the door of his hut.

Christ. What now? He felt like hitting something.

He threw the door open and it smacked against the wall. Sarah squeaked and jumped back.

Jack glared at her, as though she were an enemy soldier, then managed to calm down. He ran his fingers through his hair. 'Sorry.'

It was dark outside, the only light coming from a few of the other servants' huts. Crickets chirped in the distance.

Sarah stepped forward again and stood on tiptoes, looking past him and seeing the half-packed satchel on his sleeping mat. 'So it's true. You're leaving.'

'Bloody hell. News travels fast around here.'

'Where you going?'

'It's not important.'

She rolled her eyes. 'I'm not going to follow you.'

'I'm helping the army with something.'

'What?'

He thought quickly. 'Training new scouts.'

'Is this to do with the mutiny?'

'Something like that.'

She moved closer. 'You'll come back, won't you?'

'I'll try to.'

'And then maybe—'

'You're better off without me. Really.'

Her eyes glistened. 'I'm worried, Jack. What's going on with this mutiny? What's going to happen?'

At that moment he wanted to take her in his arms and comfort her. But he knew that wasn't a good idea. 'Nothing's going to happen. It's all going to be over soon.'

A tear crawled down her cheek and she wiped it away with her sleeve.

He hadn't meant to hurt her, but there wasn't much he could do about it now.

'You take care, then,' she said quickly and slipped away into the darkness before he could reply.

He closed the door and now his whole body was leaden. He didn't feel like hitting anything any more, just sleeping.

He reached under his tunic and drew out Katelin's Celtic cross necklace. Katelin had always worn this – apparently it was an heirloom from the Welsh side of her family. On her deathbed she'd pressed it into his palm with fierce, desperate strength. He'd been wearing it ever since.

He gazed at the ringed cross. Katelin's faith had been simple and strong, but for a long time he'd been confused when it came to religion. He believed in God, Christ and the Madonna – of course they were all true – but Jhala had told him they were incarnations or forms of the great powers of the spirit realm.

Sometimes when Jhala spoke about these powers, they seemed more like forces than beings. Sometimes Jack wondered whether Jhala and the siddhas believed in gods of any sort at all.

'Katelin,' he said. 'Wherever you are, I'm letting you know I'm going to get our little girl back.'

He then kissed the cross and put it back under his tunic.

3

When Jack thought of Elizabeth in the cell, smudged tears on her face, hair matted, clothing torn, behind the bars and stone walls and guards . . . when he thought of her, his stomach knotted and his throat felt as though it were in the grip of an invisible hand.

He grasped some water from the stream and splashed it on his face. His eyes burnt with tiredness. He'd hardly slept during the night; whenever he'd closed his eyes he'd seen Elizabeth. Even now that it was morning, he knew that if he shut his eyelids she would be there.

He drank some water, but his throat stayed dry.

Jhala.

He'd trusted his old guru, followed him, believed in him. But now Jhala was using Elizabeth as a weapon.

Was Jhala being forced into it? Commanded?

No, that didn't make sense. Only Jhala himself could have come up with the plan to hunt William. Only he knew enough about Jack to think of it. No one was pressuring him.

When had Jhala hatched the plan? Was it when Elizabeth was first brought to the barracks? Or was it even before then? Had Jhala been wondering how to coerce Jack when Elizabeth had fallen right into his lap?

Jack realised he'd clenched his hand as he held it in the stream. He released his grip.

Back in the old days Jhala had always talked about dharma,

which defined your role and duty in life. But where was the dharma in forcing a man to hunt down his friend?

Jack heard a footstep on the path behind him. Then another. Someone was coming up the slope, stepping lightly but not making a great effort to be silent. He tensed instinctively. Was it one of his party? He felt the cold metal of a knife beneath his tunic, stuck into his hose. He lifted his hand from the water but didn't yet reach for the blade.

Glancing downstream, he saw the French cavalrymen watering the horses. Had one of them left the group to shadow him? There should be fifty of them, but he had no time to count.

Then he caught a whiff of soap and perfumed oil. A Rajthanan. You could always tell because of their excessive cleanliness. He studied the sound of the footsteps. Boots crunching on grass and dry earth. A large stride – a tall man. Weight about eleven stone. Walking quickly and confidently. Close now.

'You want something, Captain Sengar?' Jack said without turning, still hunched beside the stream.

The footsteps stopped.

'Get up.' Sengar spoke in Arabic, the common language of the army.

Jack stayed where he was. 'Just filling my water skin.' He took the skin out from the folds of his tunic, then heard a ring as a scimitar was unsheathed.

'Get up now,' Sengar said.

Jack returned the skin. He thought about the knife, stood slowly and turned.

Sengar was a few feet away with his scimitar drawn. He sucked on his teeth and his moustache roiled on his top lip. 'Let's get something straight. I won't put up with any insubordination. You understand?'

Jack stared straight back, without blinking or looking away even for a second. 'I understand . . . *sir*.' He said the last word as though he were spitting it. He'd been speaking that way to Sengar all morning, since they'd left Poole. It felt strange talking to an officer like that, but the thought of Elizabeth in the cell was burning in his skull and he couldn't have stopped himself even if he'd wanted to.

'No. I don't think you do understand. Let me explain. As far as I'm concerned you are a piece of shit. The only reason I'm not having you flogged is because I need you at the moment to find Merton.'

'Flogged? What for?'

Sengar's face went red. 'For any bloody reason I want. You think you're a clever bastard, don't you? But you're just a pink European. No better than an animal.'

Jack said nothing.

'Don't think you can cross me, Casey. You want to see your daughter alive?'

Jack's face flushed. He balled his hands into fists. 'Yes.'

'Then you'd better listen carefully. From now on you do exactly as I say. If you don't, I will make absolutely certain your little slut of a daughter hangs. Do you understand?'

Jack ground his teeth. He imagined dodging under the scimitar, getting out the knife and going at Sengar. He wanted to do it, the desire was white hot. 'Yes, sir. I understand.'

'Good.' Sengar whipped the scimitar back into the scabbard. 'You have five more minutes' break, then be back at the horses.'

The Captain strode away and Jack pictured getting out the knife and throwing it into his back. He exhaled sharply and tried to calm down.

His head spun. He'd never felt this way towards an officer.

Most Rajthanans were fair, but there were always a few like Sengar who were harsh. The ones straight from Rajthana who didn't understand Europe were often the worst. But Jack had always coped with this type without reacting. Now, however, whenever Sengar spoke to him all he wanted to do was shove his fist in the Captain's face.

Below him, the ground sloped down to the road, with the green and yellow fields of Dorsetshire beyond. They were two hours out of Poole, having left early that morning. Jack had said goodbye to the other servants as first light came across the sky. Everyone lined up at the back of the house and the men shook his hand and the women kissed him on the cheek. Edwin gave him a broad grin and promised to look after the grounds while he was away. The only one who didn't come to see him off was Sarah.

He retied his ponytail and walked back to the horses. A few of the French scowled at him as he approached. They were heavily built men with straggly beards and heads shaved to iron grains of stubble. One of them, who'd been introduced to Jack earlier as Sergeant Lefevre, said in Arabic, 'Captain give you a good thrashing, *Ros Porc*?'

The other Frenchmen sniggered. *Ros Porc* was a term of abuse for the English, referring to the fact that they ate pig meat.

Jack was in no mood to back down before a Mohammedan. 'At least we English kept the true faith.'

'You kept a filthy, infidel faith.' Lefevre spat at the ground. 'Why follow that pig you call a Pope?'

'Because we didn't give in like you cowards.'

Jack had experienced this game of taunt and counter-taunt many times in the army. The French had been Christian once, but they'd abandoned it during the five centuries they'd been ruled by the Moors. It was only in the British Isles that the true faith, the faith of old Europe, had been kept alive.

Lefevre stepped closer. He was at least half a foot taller than Jack and wide at the shoulders. 'You call me a coward? I'll enjoy showing you otherwise.' He switched to halting English. 'I like kill Englishmen.' He gave a throaty gargle that must have been a laugh, and the other cavalrymen chuckled along with him.

Jack found his thoughts going to the hidden knife again. The fifty Frenchmen carried pistols and scimitars, and carbines were strapped to their saddles as well. Jack hadn't been issued with a firearm and Sengar had told him he wouldn't be getting one.

He stayed calm, shook his head and walked around Lefevre towards his horse. Why get into a fight he couldn't win? How would that help his daughter?

'You see,' Lefevre said after him. 'You English – cowards, all of you.'

'Right, men.' Sengar marched across the slope with a young lieutenant named Kansal. He stepped up on to a rock and surveyed his gathered troops, while Kansal stood to the side on the lower ground. The Lieutenant had a youthful face with bushy, owlish eyebrows, and Jack noted that he had no clan marking on his tunic – no sun, moon or fire insignia that showed he was from a military jati. His family must have purchased his commission at great expense.

'Over there in those hills are lands controlled by the Earl of Dorsetshire.' Sengar gestured towards the Dorsetshire Downs rippling in the distance. 'The rebels have been hiding there. The Earl said he'd weed them out, but so far he's done nothing, so we're going to have to do it for him. Now, the Earl's supposedly been loyal since the start of the mutiny, but we need to go carefully. Things could change at any time. Keep your wits about you.'

'Yes, Gaulmika,' the cavalrymen responded in unison, using the Rajthani word for 'captain', as was the custom in French regiments.

Jack glanced at the downlands. The Earldom of Dorsetshire was one of the so-called 'native states' that dotted England. It was supposedly an independent country, but the Earl ruled there only by the grace of the Rajthanans.

And somewhere within those hills was William. Jack felt a tremor of foreboding. William, his old friend, now a rebel . . .

They rode down the slope and then along the road. Sengar and Kansal went at the head of the party, followed by Sengar's batman – a large, baby-faced Rajthanan. Jack rode alone a few feet behind, and to the rear came the fifty cavalrymen, their gaze an uncomfortable presence on his back.

The day turned muggy as the sun rose higher behind a skin of cloud. At first they saw carts, which moved to the side of the road to let them pass. But as they approached the downs, the road emptied and the cultivated fields gave way to grassland. The hills ahead were hazy and covered in jade grasses and thickets of trees, and the numerous slopes folded in on each other, protective arms about a secret.

'What's that?' Kansal pointed to a thick column of smoke rising about a mile away to the west.

Sengar frowned, called a halt and peered through a spyglass. 'Can't see. It's coming from behind a hill. Nothing to do with us, anyway. We'll carry on. We have to get to Pentridge Castle before night.'

They rode on for a few minutes, and then an Englishman burst out into the road, waving his arms. 'Sirs! Help!'

Sengar jerked to a halt and drew a pistol. 'Get out of the way.'

'Don't shoot, sir.' The man backed to the side of the road. 'We need help. Please.' He flung himself to the ground, his head bent in supplication. He wore the starched, white uniform of a servant from a major household, but it was marred by streaks of dirt.

Sengar's moustache elongated. 'What happened?'

'The train from Barford, sir.' The man raised his head. 'We were attacked. They blew a hole in the engine.'

'Attacked? Who?'

'Don't know, sir. Some reckon it was the Ghost.'

Sengar glanced around the nearby hills, as if the Ghost could be up there watching them at that moment. His horse moved skittishly beneath him.

Jack's throat went dry. His wound pinched and a fine line of pain wormed its way across his chest. His injury was worsening – the last thing he needed now.

'We're all stuck out here in the middle of nowhere,' the man said. 'The train's injured. It won't move. My master sent me to get help.'

'Very well,' Sengar said. 'We'll take a look.'

They left the road and cut across the gentle curves of the countryside. The servant rode behind one of the cavalrymen and pointed towards the column of black smoke. 'There. That's it.'

They found the train standing motionless on the tracks. The carriages were decorated with wood panelling and brass plaques of Rajthanan gods and goddesses. The engine lay at the far end, hidden by a cloud of smoke and steam. The passengers had all disembarked and now stood in knots about their luggage.

'Glory to Shiva!' a woman cried in Rajthani. 'We're saved! Help!'

Sengar sawed at his reins to turn his horse. A tight circle of around twenty Rajthanans huddled in the middle of the crowd. Their trunks and cases lay at their feet and they eyed the Europeans milling around them. Four European servants in shining white stood guard just outside the circle, although they appeared unarmed.

'They want to rob us,' shrieked the woman, one of the Rajthanans. 'Help us.'

Jack was sceptical. The Europeans didn't look as though they were about to attack; for the most part they were ignoring the Rajthanans, although a few did seem to be watching out of curiosity as much as anything.

Sengar paused for a second, then shouted in English, 'All of you, get back.'

A few of the Europeans began shuffling away, but most just looked up in confusion. Some even moved closer to the Rajthanans, unsure where they were supposed to be moving to.

Sengar drew his pistol and fired in the air. The loud crack made the whole crowd jolt like a whipped horse. A few European women whimpered and covered their ears.

'Get away from those Rajthanans,' Sengar shouted. 'Hurry up.'

The Europeans moved away from the train, pushing and shoving and dragging their sacks and wooden crates. Soon there was a clear space around the besieged Rajthanans.

'Oh, Captain, thank you.' The woman wore a yellow sari laced with golden thread, as well as a quilted jacket, which she hugged close to her. 'I don't know what would have happened if you hadn't come. They're murderers and thieves, all of them.'

Sengar smiled, clearly enjoying himself. 'No problem at all, my lady. It's a pleasure to be of service.' He dismounted and namasted the Rajthanans. 'Now, tell me what happened.'

'A band of ruffians,' the woman said. 'Pink ruffians.'

'Yes, about twenty of them,' a tall Rajthanan man said. 'They came out of the hills on horseback and threw some sort of bomb at the engine. There was a huge explosion. The train carried on for a few more miles after that, thankfully. I don't know what would have happened if we'd had to stop right there.'

'What did they look like, these men?' Sengar asked.

'Just filthy Europeans,' the woman said. 'Peasants.'

'I didn't get a good look at them,' the man said. 'But yes, just peasants, that's all. There was one man with them, though . . . a tall brute with a shaved head. He seemed to be their leader. It looked as though he was shouting at them and ordering them about at any rate.'

Sengar shot a look at Jack, who was still sitting astride his mare.

Jack tried to read Sengar's expression. Was he supposed to recognise William from that description?

But Sengar said nothing and looked back at the Rajthanans. 'Do you know where the driver is?'

'Somewhere up there, I think.' The Rajthanan man pointed towards the smouldering engine.

'Right,' Sengar replied. 'Wait here a moment.'

Sengar ordered two cavalrymen to remain as guards, then mounted his horse and led the party towards the head of the train. Hundreds of European passengers had spread out along the tracks. Some were wealthy merchants or officials in fur-trimmed cloaks and feathered caps, but most were poorer and would have been crowded into third class with standing room only. People were beginning to give up on the train ever starting again and were drifting away towards the road, dragging heavy sacks and boxes along with them.

Jack caught a waft of sattva and felt a familiar ripple across his skin. The railway line, as was common, followed a strong stream – it meant the avatars could run faster and with less coal.

The smell grew stronger as the dark shape of the engine appeared ahead in the smoke and steam. Two figures stood nearby, indistinct in the haze.

Sengar paused and called out, 'Where's the driver?'

One of the figures waved his arm in a broad stroke. 'Over here.'

Sengar glanced back, then snorted and shook his head.

When Jack looked over his shoulder he saw that the French were several feet behind, muttering and dithering. Sergeant Lefevre peered nervously into the steam and scowled when he noticed Jack watching him. No doubt he believed sattva and avatars were the work of Shaitan.

'You stay here,' Sengar said to the French. 'Kansal, Casey, come with me.'

Sengar, Kansal and Jack dismounted, left their horses with the cavalrymen and walked into the sooty mist. The black, lobster-like train avatar loomed over them, hissing and steaming within the casing of the engine carriage. Its claws, stalks and feelers drooped towards the ground and the only sign of movement was the slight, irregular back and forward motion of a piston on its side.

The driver wore a blue tunic, smeared grey with coal dust and oil, and a partially unravelled turban. He had the dark-olive skin of a Gypsy or half-caste – the only two groups who would work for the railway service. His eyes were red-rimmed and watery. 'It's terrible, sirs, terrible.'

His colleague, also in railway-service uniform, nodded.

'She won't move, can't move.' The driver dabbed at his eyes with his sleeve. 'Reckon she won't live much longer.'

'Where's the damage?' Sengar asked.

The driver nodded and took them around to the other side of the avatar.

'Big engine,' Kansal said over the sound of the steam. 'Never seen one that size.'

'They grow large in England,' Sengar replied. 'Strong sattva.'

Jack had often heard this said about England. His homeland apparently had some of the strongest streams of sattva in the world – stronger than the rest of Europe, or even India.

As they crossed the tracks, the avatar gave a deep growl that Jack felt through the soles of his boots. Its legs scratched at the ground and it bucked, lifting the front of the engine carriage up a few feet.

Jack and the others flinched, but the driver raised his hands before the beast and called out, 'Down. Down.'

The creature groaned, then settled back on to the tracks with a crunch. Although the driver was clearly no siddha, he obviously knew the creature well enough to control it.

'She's hurt,' the driver explained. 'Never done that before.'

Once they reached the other side of the train, the driver stopped and pointed. 'Look what they done to her. Poor beauty.'

A large hole had been wrenched in the side of the avatar, leaving a mess of twisted and half-melted metal. A black substance, thick as honey, oozed out of the wound, as well as rising streams of smoke. The heat of the engine pressed against Jack's face. The smell of sattva overpowered him and made his eyes water.

'Was it the Ghost?' Sengar asked

'I wouldn't know,' the driver said. 'No one knows what he looks like.'

'Who else could it have been?'

'Well, now that you say it, no one else, I wouldn't think.'

Sengar's moustache tightened, then unfurled. He turned to

Jack. 'Could you pick up the trail from where the train was hit?'

Jack blinked. He went to reply, then stopped himself. Now that it came to it, he realised just how much he didn't want to do it, didn't want to betray his old friend.

'Well, can't you speak?' Sengar said.

Jack tensed. In his mind he was getting out the knife and running at Sengar. 'Yes.' His voice was thick. 'I could track them from there.'

'Good.' Sengar fixed his eyes on Jack for a moment. Then he turned back to the driver. 'How far away were you when you were attacked?'

'About ten miles,' the driver replied. 'My beauty managed to keep going all the way to here, bless her, getting slower and slower.'

'Ten miles – that's in the Earl's lands.'

'That's right, sir. The line crosses the border for a distance.'

Sengar looked at Kansal. 'Ten miles isn't far.'

'We could follow the tracks there now,' Kansal said.

'But there's still the damn protocol. We should have an audience with the Earl first.'

'Is it necessary, sir?'

'Things could get difficult if we don't at least go through the motions. These pathetic little lords can make a fuss. No, we'll go to Pentridge first. It's in the same direction as the train line anyway. We'll pick up the trail tomorrow.' Sengar smirked, his moustache coiling even higher than usual. 'Looks as though the Ghost has given us quite a gift. A fresh trail. We'll have him in no time.'

4

They rode between the hills at a steady trot, dust rising from the horses' hooves. As before, Jack was behind Sengar and Kansal, with the French bringing up the rear.

They'd crossed into the Earl's lands three hours earlier and since that time the narrow, winding, poorly maintained road had hampered their pace. Added to this, they'd lost an hour at the train arranging for carts to be sent from Fern Down to rescue the stranded Rajthanans. Now the late afternoon shadows were pooling in the valleys and gullies and they still hadn't reached the Earl's castle.

Jack gazed at the rolling countryside – the scene in the native fiefdom was quite different from the Rajthanan-controlled lands to the south. The farms were mostly smallholdings with ramshackle huts and barns. The few hedgerows were unkempt and wild. There were patches of dense forest and heaths that seemed never to have been cultivated. He often saw small shrines on the hilltops, their simple stone crosses dark against the white cloud.

This landscape was familiar, yet also strangely unfamiliar. It was twenty years since he'd last visited a native state. He'd been born in Shropshire, but since his parents had died he'd hardly been back. The years had created a distance.

The people lived a simple life here, working the land and following the old feudal laws, a life that had changed little during the hundred years of Rajthanan rule. Or the two hundred years of the Moorish Caliphate, for that matter. And it struck him now in a way it never had before: this way of life hadn't changed for century after century, going all the way back to the time of the ancient Normans, and even before . . .

Rounding a corner, they approached a village that clung to a slope. The cottages were crumbling and the walls of the tiny stone church were cracked, worn and swarming with vines.

Villagers in tattered clothes appeared on the side of the road. They were thin – far too thin – and many had hollow eyes and grey skin. Women hugged babies, old men watched with quivering lips, younger men stared with eyes that glinted with defiance.

'Food,' some shouted as Jack clattered past.

Jack shivered and tried to ignore them. He'd heard the crops had been blighted in many states, and the mutiny had only made things worse.

A small boy darted out into the road, his hands outstretched, his face dirty and his feet bare. 'Please, sir,' he shouted.

Jack yanked at the reins, swerved to avoid the lad, then spurred his horse on. He wanted to get away from these people and their cries.

Soon he was out of the crowd, the village disappearing around the corner of the road.

Throughout the afternoon they passed further hamlets where thin and ragged people shuffled out to beg for food. In one village a baby wailed so loudly Jack could hear its cry on the wind even after he'd left it far behind.

It was dusk when Pentridge Castle came into view, its stone walls and towers rising from the summit of a squat, dome-shaped hill. As they rode up the path, Jack could see that in many places the battlements were crumbling and the ageing spires were riddled with holes. The moat appeared to have long been empty of water and was now little more than a ditch overgrown with grass. The drawbridge was down, but the portcullis was closed.

Sengar called up to the guard tower, 'I am Captain Rajesh

Sengar of the Maharaja's European Army. I request an immediate audience with the Earl of Dorsetshire.'

At first there was no sign that the tower was even occupied, but then a guard with long, lank hair bent out of a window and peered down. 'It's late. You'll need to come back tomorrow.'

'Open the gate. I demand to see the Earl immediately.'

'The Earl isn't . . . available.'

Sengar's moustache rolled across his top lip. 'You will open this gate or I will return with a larger force and raze this castle to the ground.'

The guard rubbed his eyes. 'I understand, sir. Wait a moment.'

The guard disappeared and left them waiting for at least ten minutes. Sengar muttered to Kansal in Rajthani – Jack could just make out various curses and expletives.

Finally the portcullis rattled up and the guard stood before them, bowing and saying, 'Namaste.' Stable hands admitted them into a courtyard and took their horses.

The guard escorted Sengar, Kansal, Jack and five cavalrymen down corridors lit by infrequent lanterns and sputtering torches. Faded, moth-eaten tapestries lined the walls. Statues of knights and heroes from antiquity flickered in gloomy alcoves.

The audience chamber was better lit and had pale walls leading up to a distant ceiling. The Earl sat on a carved wooden throne at the far end of the room. To either side of him stood guards in old chain mail and courtiers in long robes embroidered with gold. The Earl himself was a short man, almost too small for his chair, with a large fleshy head and red cheeks. He wore bits of what appeared to be ancient plate armour – a breastplate, greaves and a single gauntlet – but the pieces were ill-fitting and the steel discoloured. He slumped to one side and perspired heavily. Above his head hung a banner displaying the family crest: two leopards about a shield.

Sengar and Kansal walked across the room, the sound of their boots echoing.

'Namaste, Lord Dorsetshire,' Sengar said. 'I have been sent here by order of the Raja of Poole and the Maharaja's Army in Europe.'

'Greetings, Captain.' The Earl's speech was slurred and he moved his hand listlessly, as if tossing something aside. He appeared to be drunk.

'I request leave to pass through your lands in search of a band of renegades led by the man known as the Ghost. We believe these rebels are hiding in the hills under your jurisdiction. You are also requested to afford me all possible assistance in bringing the Ghost to justice.'

The Earl gave a guttural laugh. 'Good luck to you, my friend. The army have sent in hundreds of men over the past few months. They haven't caught him yet.'

Sengar's eyebrow twitched. 'I assure you, I mean to succeed. And you would do well to remember it is your responsibility to deal with bandits within your own borders. Some might say you have been more than remiss in failing to capture these rebels.'

The Earl stopped smiling and chewed air. 'It's not a simple matter. Of course, I've tried to deal with them, but my lands are large and I have few men—'

'There was an attack on the Barford train today.'

'Yes, we heard about it.'

'I need a guide to take us to the place tomorrow.'

'You can certainly have a guide. All of my men are at your disposal. But I'm sad to say you can't expect much. Half of them are traitors anyway.' The Earl glowered at his own guards and courtiers, who shifted uncomfortably. 'I can't trust anyone any more.'

'You will naturally be held responsible for the actions of your own men.'

The Earl took out a handkerchief and mopped his brow. 'I will do all I can. But be careful, Captain. The train was attacked out in the wild lands. As well as the rebels there are all kinds of bandits and devils up there.'

'Thank you for your concern.' This with a smear of sarcasm. 'Just organise the guide and give us lodgings tonight. We'll have this Ghost captured or killed in a matter of days.'

Jack paused as he left the stables. It was night and the stars and moon were shut out by the cloud, but he could still make out the walls of the castle's inner bailey and the two guards leaning beside the portcullis. Off to his left, the stable hands and some of the other castle servants sat about a fire. They were laughing and joking, but they all fell silent as he wandered across to them.

'Greetings,' he said. 'Can I get some water?'

He'd been given a corner of the stables to sleep in, but thirst had distracted him when he'd tried to meditate.

The servants stared at him, their faces glossy and wavering in the firelight. They wore no uniform and their clothing was little better than that of the peasants scraping at the dry earth outside the castle walls. Most were munching on pieces of burnt chicken.

'Get him some water,' grunted the master groom, who Jack had met earlier.

One of the servants carried over a full wooden bucket.

Jack bent to refill his skin, then noticed, out of the corner of his eye, a dark shape in the corner of the bailey – a blackened iron post about ten feet high and surrounded by a mound of ash and charred wood. He felt a chill. He knew what it meant.

The master groom noticed where Jack was looking. 'Witch burning. Caught one two days ago. Evil bitch.' He tossed a chicken bone into the fire and sucked his fingers. 'Had a lot of problems with them lately. Been cursing the crops, they have.'

'We burnt her good and proper.' Another man grinned toothlessly. 'Should have heard her squeal for mercy. Well, she's where she should be now, feeling the fires of hell licking at her.'

A few of the men chuckled while others crossed themselves.

Jack plunged the skin into the bucket. He hadn't heard talk of witch burning for years. The Rajthanans had stamped it out in the lands under their rule, but here in the native states it lingered on like a disease. Jack despaired of his countrymen for a moment. These men were mired in superstition and they clung to wicked traditions. There were no witches – just old women.

'You eaten?' the master groom asked.

Jack lifted the skin out of the water and slipped in the stopper. He hadn't eaten, and now that it was mentioned he felt hungry.

'You're welcome to join us, stranger.' The master groom held out a chicken drumstick.

Jack knew he should eat – he needed all his strength for tomorrow – but he was reluctant to spend any time with these . . . natives. Then the sweet, smoky scent of the chicken hit his nostrils and he found himself sitting down.

The chicken tasted good, despite being stringy and overcooked, and grease ran over his hands as he ate.

'You're with those army men, aren't you?' one of the servants said.

'That's right,' Jack replied through mouthfuls of chicken.

'Looking for the Ghost?' the same servant asked.

Jack looked up from his food. The circle of men all had their gleaming eyes on him. 'Something like that.'

'Don't think you'll have much luck. No one's caught him yet.'

Jack continued eating but could feel the knife beneath his tunic. He didn't like the tone of the servant's voice.

'We were a bit surprised when we saw you come in with those soldiers,' the servant continued. 'Some reckoned you must be a half-caste or some such. But I reckoned you must be a Mohammedan.'

Jack looked up. 'Any man who says I'm a Mohammedan has got a fight on his hands.'

'Hey, hey,' the master groom said. 'There'll be no arguments here. And you watch your mouth, John Carter.'

'I apologise to you, stranger.' The servant, John, grinned. 'I meant no offence. Just curious.'

'Who I am is no concern of yours.' Jack finished his chicken and threw the bone into the flames.

'Who do you think you are?' a young man, no more than sixteen, blurted out. 'Coming here and talking all fancy. The Ghost is a great man. And Sir Gawain and the King—'

'Shut your mouth, you idiot.' The master groom stood quickly. 'All of you shut up.' He glared at them and they all looked down, including the young man. 'Now, we should be showing some hospitality to this fellow, no matter who he is or where he's from.'

'It's all right.' Jack stood and wiped his hands on his tunic. 'I'm going to rest now anyway.'

'Aye,' the master groom said. 'I think we should all be doing that.'

As Jack rearranged his things and flattened out his sleeping mat back in the stables, the master groom walked over carrying a lantern that cast the furrows on his brow even deeper.

'Pardon me, sir,' he said. 'I want to apologise for before.'

'No need.' Jack continued straightening the sleeping mat.

'The boy . . . what he said. He doesn't mean it. Doesn't know what he's saying.'

Jack stood and offered a weak smile. What was this about? 'It's all right.'

The master groom fiddled with the lantern. 'You won't . . . you won't mention it to your masters, will you?'

'The Rajthanans?'

'Yes, them.'

So that was it. 'No. I won't mention anything.'

'Ah, you're a real gentleman, you are, sir.'

The master groom shuffled away and Jack massaged his face

with his hand. Why should he mention anything to the Rajthanans? What did he care if some idiots wanted to bleat on about the mutiny?

And then it struck him – Elizabeth and William supported the mutiny. What could have led them down that foolish path?

William must have changed. Changed a lot.

But Elizabeth? She'd been the same as ever when he'd last seen her at Christmas. There'd been nothing to make him think she was about to throw her lot in with the rebels.

Something must have happened. Someone must have led her astray. A man, perhaps. His stomach knotted. That was it, she'd fallen for some rebel and now she was caught and in twenty-seven days she'd be hanged.

His heart galloped. He had to slow it; he was no use to his daughter dead.

He sat, crossed his legs and took several deep breaths. He could hear the stable hands preparing their own beds and some were already snoring in the darkness. For a moment he wondered how safe he was. Any of the servants could attack him in the night, but he doubted any of them would try it. They seemed afraid of the Rajthanans, and none of them looked like hardened fighters. All the same, he took out the knife and slid it under the sleeping mat, within easy reach should he need it in a hurry.

He circled his shoulders to loosen them and twisted his neck to either side. To find William he was going to have to use his power. Would he still be able to do that after all this time? Was he too out of practice? And what would happen if he could? The army doctor who'd examined him after the accident had told him to avoid using his power – it was too dangerous. Now that the wound had spread to his heart, surely it would be even more risky. Would it kill him?

Better to find out now.

He swept the straw away from the ground in front of him, then, with a stick, scratched a circular design into the compacted earth, first the outer rim, then a point in the centre, then a series of triangles and lines within the circle.

When he'd finished, he blew away the disturbed dust and stared at the image for a moment. The marks only depicted the main outline – the full design was much more complex. Would he be able to remember all the details?

He shut his eyes and concentrated on the design. The circle and the main outlines appeared to him, glowing white on a black background. He moved his mind's eye around and forced each tiny flourish, curlicue and shape to blink into view. Soon the circle was full of twisting, interconnected lines, triangles and smaller circles.

Good.

It was the native siddha yantra, the yantra that gave him his power.

He remembered Jhala showing him the design for the first time as they sat in the training tent. Jhala had handed him a piece of cloth with the image embroidered on it and said, 'You know what this is?'

Jack shook his head. He was twenty-one at the time and Jhala, who was in his late thirties, seemed ancient to him.

'It's a yantra,' Jhala said. 'Meditating on it will connect you to the spirit realm, which we call purusha and you call heaven. If you meditate properly a power will channel through to you.

'All the powers come from the yantras. But to use a power you must first learn its yantra. That means memorising every detail of the design, every single line and marking. You must be able to hold the entire image still and perfect in your mind, without any other thought intruding. Only then will you be able to use the power.'

At first Jack had thought this wouldn't be so difficult. But the more he stared at the yantra, the more he realised how complex it was. There were many minute details that he hadn't even noticed at first.

Almost every day for three months he met Jhala in the tent and tried to memorise the design. When he asked whether he could take the cloth to study it in the evenings, Jhala plucked it away, saying, 'The yantras are secret. The oath you gave when we began this training must be upheld. You cannot remove the design from this tent.'

Jack began by copying the image on to sheets of paper, then moved on to drawing it entirely from memory. Finally, he tried to hold the design still in his mind. This proved the most difficult task by far. Not only did he have to recall the whole yantra, he had to keep it the sole focus of his thoughts. The moment he thought of anything else or concentrated on just a piece of the design, the meditation was broken.

Jack grew frustrated and even Jhala at times seemed to think the task might be beyond him.

Jhala sighed once and said, 'You are doing as well as you can, Casey. This is a difficult task for Europeans.'

But Jack persisted. Jhala had spotted his special sensitivity to sattva and taken on the task of teaching him. He didn't want to let his guru down, particularly when Colonel Hada had been reluctant to agree to the training in the first place. Hada was a traditionalist who disapproved of native siddhas. Jhala, however, was one of those who argued that natives should be trained to the extent of their abilities.

Jack didn't want to let himself down either. He was one of the few Europeans who would ever receive this training, and he meant to make the most of it.

Finally, one day in the middle of winter with rain pelting down the outside of the tent, the image became whole and focused in his mind and it suddenly blinded him with light.

Jhala beamed as Jack opened his eyes. 'You are now a siddha,' he said. 'And also my disciple.'

Jack felt a surge of pride and bowed low before his master . . .

But now he found himself flinching at the memory, as if at a raw wound. He tried to sweep thoughts of his old guru aside – they were only distracting him.

He had to focus on the present, on the task at hand.

He'd been able to recall the yantra, but would he be able to use it?

He scratched out the yantra he'd carved in the ground, shut his eyes and straightened his back into the correct posture for meditation. Unfortunately, he wasn't in a strong stream. He would have to make do with whatever he found about him.

'Your mind is like a rippling pool.'

The drill sergeant, Jhala, all the yogins repeated this phrase. And it was true. The mind danced and jumped and wouldn't settle. You could only tame it through yoga.

The horses about him muttered and shifted. The wind picked up and the timber building creaked.

He relaxed his muscles and his hearbeat slowed . . . beat after beat . . .

A stillness settled over him like snow.

He brought the yantra to his mind and it glowed white on a black background. He tried to hold it still, but his mind's eye latched on to the upper-left quarter. Each time he pulled his mind's eye back, his focus clicked back to the upper left.

After a frustrating few minutes, he finally got the yantra in place. But then a memory of Elizabeth as a child appeared in his head. She was running across a meadow towards him, sunlight washing over her pale skin and her dark hair floating behind her.

He wrenched his thoughts back to the yantra, but now further memories flooded his mind . . .

Katelin on her deathbed, blonde hair lank and her weak hand reaching up to him . . .

Jhala in the gazebo, telling him Elizabeth was due to be executed . . .

Then the boom of artillery and a flash like sheet lightning. A grey, sodden plain, pocked with shell craters and churned mud and soldiers who lay screaming as they died. The Battle of Ragusa – the Slav War. It had never left him.

Boom.

He was running across that plain with the rest of his battalion. William was beside him and Captain Jhala was up ahead with his scimitar raised and glinting in the early morning light. Ahead of them rose an immense earth wall, more than twenty feet high. Their objective was to get over it before the Slavs could butcher them all.

The wall erupted with gunfire – bright gobbets of flame and bulbs of smoke and a rumble that reverberated across the countryside. Round shot whistled and grape shrieked. A sergeant beside Jack jolted as his chest exploded in a mist of red. A private's head was knocked straight off by a ball.

Jack's breath shortened and his lungs burnt. He had to keep running. The air was so thick with hissing shot he was amazed he hadn't been hit. He heard someone roaring and then realised it was himself.

Boom.

He was falling into the ditch at the base of the wall. Slavs fired down with muskets and the bullets shredded the mud like hail. A writhing mass of the wounded and dying lay at the bottom. He fell amongst the bodies, hearing bellows and screams and shouts. For a moment he was smothered and suffocated by other men tumbling in after him, but then he pulled himself free.

He caught a glimpse of the ladder men, already in the ditch and raising their ladders against the wall. He struggled to his feet, standing on hands and arms and legs, many still moving. Powder smoke stung his eyes and musket balls whined in his ears. He grasped the nearest ladder and joined the swarm of men rushing up the rungs, wondering now where the hell William had got to.

Boom.

He was on the wall and jabbing with his knife-musket at a Slav.

The blade slid through cloth and skin and his opponent glared at him with blood bubbling in his mouth.

Boom.

He was on the ground on the far side of the wall. A Slav had kicked him in the head and the world now rang and whirled about him as if he were clutching a maypole. Jhala lay beside him, wounded in the shoulder by a musket ball, his breath shivery.

As Jack tried to sit up, he sensed someone standing nearby. A Slav pointed a musket at him and smiled with yellow teeth. Jack had no weapon – he'd lost his musket when he'd fallen. Jhala was unable to move, although still alive. The battle continued, but in this one spot everything seemed calm. The Slav's finger rested on the trigger. The musket was fully cocked. Jack shut his eyes. Soon, it would come soon. Now . . .

A tearing shout. He opened his eyes. William burst through the powder smoke and smacked into the Slav. Time moved forward again. The two men fell and tussled. William had a dagger out in a second, jabbed, missed, jabbed again and caught the Slav in the stomach. The Slav released his grip and his face contorted. William shifted his grip on the dagger, then plunged it into the man's chest. The Slav fell forward and flapped about like a caught fish.

William stood over Jack, grinning as he wiped his dagger on his tunic.

Jhala moved, moaned softly. 'Well done, Private Merton. Well done.'

Boom . . .

Jack flung his eyes open. The dark stables swirled about him. He could hardly breathe, pain stabbed his chest and his heart was beating so frantically he was sure it would stop at any moment.

He rasped down some air, but his heart still thrashed within his ribs. He took a few deep breaths. And finally his heartbeat eased.

He sighed and rolled on to his back, lying in the musky

darkness, panting heavily. The pain in his chest subsided to a dull ache and he wiped the sweat from his forehead with his shaking arm.

He hadn't been able to hold the yantra still in his mind, but he'd got close for a split second, and that had been enough to make his wound blossom.

That was a bad sign.

He took a deep, ragged breath. It was going to be difficult to use his power. And if he couldn't do that, he couldn't track William.

And Elizabeth would die.

5

'How much further?' Sengar was sitting on his horse and scouring the hills and forests rolling away in all directions.

They'd been riding since sunrise along a goat track that meandered unevenly across the downs. Now it was mid-morning, clear and hot, and they still hadn't reached the railway line.

'Not far now, sir.' The guide, a hunched man with wide eyes and long oily hair, was riding an old mule that could manage little more than a trot.

Sengar sucked on his teeth and examined his pocket watch. 'You said that an hour ago.' He was converting to European time.

'Yes, sir. This way.'

The guide nudged his mule forward. Sengar, clenching his reins until his knuckles whitened, followed, with his batman and Kansal just behind.

Jack rode ahead of the cavalrymen and he could hear Sergeant Lefevre muttering in one of the French dialects, none of which he'd ever been able to understand.

The countryside had become progressively wilder the further they'd travelled from Pentridge. Jack had seen few signs of habitation and the forests swelled unchecked over the slopes. Deer watched from within the trees and the open ground was clotted with gorse.

His thoughts whirled. He tried to convince himself that when the time came he would find a way to use his power, but he knew it would be difficult. He'd slept badly again, but he hardly noticed the tiredness as a wiry alertness had overtaken him.

After half an hour, they skidded and slipped down an escarpment thick with trees and finally came out at the train line. The tracks glinted and slid away between the heavily wooded slopes of a gully. Trees had been felled to clear the way, but that must have been several years ago as branches were starting to reach out towards the tracks again. Clumps of grass bubbled between the wooden sleepers.

'Up that way.' The guide pointed north-west along the line.

'Where exactly?' Sengar asked. 'Show us.'

The guide nodded and led them along the tracks.

Trees swarmed down both sides of the gully: birches, elms, oaks, all bedecked with vines. Jack heard the hum of bees and the liquid tinkle of birds. He tried to adjust to tracker-thinking. He had to both expand and sharpen his focus, reading the movement of leaves, the sudden burst of silence from the birds, the faint scents that tinted the air. The world thrummed with signs and markings and portents and he had to be alert to them all.

Faintly, he smelt sattva. The train line, as usual, followed a strong stream.

The guide stopped at a point where a cutting formed a wall of earth, brambles and tree roots to the right of the tracks. He pointed at the train line without saying anything.

Jack rode forward until he was beside Sengar. The tracks were undamaged, but streaks of soot, coal and fragments of metal radiated out in a wide circle across the bottom of the gully.

The sun beat down and Jack felt sweat trickle beneath his tunic. Could he bring himself to track William? Would he even be *able* to do it?

'Well?' Sengar asked.

Jack ignored the Captain and climbed off his horse. He crouched and studied the ground. The black marks from the explosion were far darker and thicker to the left side of the tracks – the bomb had clearly been thrown from that direction.

He trod lightly away from the line, but at first saw nothing. It was the worst time to be tracking – the sun was high overhead and the shadows were short, making any prints difficult to spot. But finally, as he scanned the surroundings, he noticed an indentation in the grass around ten feet away. He approached this slowly, as if it were a venomous snake – he didn't want to disturb any other signs that could be near to it. As he came closer he made out the half-moon curve of a horse's hoof print.

'Sir,' the guide said behind him. 'If you don't mind, I should be getting back to Pentridge.'

'You'll go nowhere,' Sengar said. 'Even once we find the trail we'll still need a guide.'

The guide was silent for a moment. 'I'd like to help, but I was told only to lead you to this place. I need to get back.'

'You'll stay where you are.'

The guide's mule spluttered. Jack stood and looked back. The guide licked his lips, his gaze shifting from Sengar to the cavalrymen, who stared back, cold and impassive.

'Carry on, Casey,' Sengar said.

Jack went to continue but stopped as the guide began fumbling about in his tunic. It took Jack a second to realise what was happening. The guide tore out a pistol and, with his eyes bulging, fired at Sengar. The weapon gave an echoing crackle – it sounded almost too loud for a pistol – and a glob of smoke emerged. The guide's hand was flung back: the firearm seemed to have kicked harder than he'd expected.

Sengar's horse reared up on its hind legs and gave a high-pitched squeal. The Captain gripped the reins and tried to control the animal, but so far as Jack could see he hadn't been hit.

The cavalrymen wrenched out their pistols as the guide lined up another shot. The guide pulled the trigger and the hammer clicked down—

Nothing happened. The pistol must have fired off all its rounds at once.

Lefevre roared and the cavalrymen spattered a volley at the guide. The guide jerked as he was hit and the mule screamed, rolled its eyes and fell with its legs twitching, bright wounds along its side.

The guide lay trapped under the mule, injured but not yet dead, straining to free himself with hands streaked with blood.

'Hold your fire,' Sengar shouted as the French prepared to shoot again. He'd regained control of his horse, but his eyes simmered and his moustache was stretched thinly.

The cavalrymen lowered their weapons. But a second later Jack heard the pop of a musket and a chime near to him as a bullet hit a rail. More pops followed and a patter of bullets through leaves. The ground puckered and rattled as the missiles struck.

They'd been ambushed.

The Frenchmen shouted and their horses danced beneath them. Smoke puffed from the trees covering the left side of the gully, but the undergrowth was too thick for Jack to see the attackers. Bullets whispered past him – evil sprites. He leapt over the tracks and fell against the wall of the cutting, between two tree roots, but this provided little protection.

Damn Sengar for not giving him a weapon.

The French fired blindly up the slope. Lefevre's top lip curled into a snarl. Kansal tried to aim at something with his pistol. In a matter of seconds, five cavalrymen had thudded to the ground.

Bullets sizzled into the earth wall near Jack's head. He ducked down as far as he could. A tree root next to him was slashed open with a crack. His heart raced and his chest felt heavy.

He caught a powerful waft of sattva. Why could he smell sattva so strongly?

Sengar sat still on his horse, mouthing words silently, eyes closed. Suddenly the light in the gully went dim, as though cloud had passed before the sun. But when Jack looked up, the sun was still bright. Wind coursed through the trees, shaking branches and rippling leaves. The smell of sattva grew stronger. The French were unnerved and slowed the pace of their firing – perhaps even they could smell sattva now.

Sengar took on a strange glow. Only it wasn't a glow, but a sharpening of his appearance, as if he were coming into focus through a spyglass. He opened his eyes – they were diamond-bright. He held his right hand before him in a fist and the air just beyond it crinkled as in a mirage. The wind stopped. For a moment there was a sharp silence in the gully and everything seemed still. Then the wavering air formed into a twenty-foot globe and throbbed into orange flame. The fireball roared and boiled and the heat scoured Jack's face. The cavalrymen's horses reared and whinnied.

Sattva-fire. Jack was sure.

Sengar bellowed something, opened his hand and the flaming ball flew straight at the slope, slashed through the trees and exploded with a peal that flung Jack back against the cutting. Branches, clods of earth, soot and sparks shot upwards. Trees cracked open and shrivelled with flame. Black smoke billowed and swayed and soon hid most of the slope.

Jack blinked dust from his eyes. The explosion had been as powerful as ten shells going off at once. Only a siddha could do something like that.

'It must be the rebels. After them!' Sengar leapt from his horse, drew his scimitar and charged into the smoke, his green turban bobbing for a second, then vanishing.

The French gave a joint cry of 'Allah is great!', jumped to the ground and raced after the Captain, leaving behind a couple of men to guard the horses. Kansal followed, struggling to draw his scimitar, which seemed to have caught on something.

Jack lurched up and stumbled across to the other side of the gully. His heart pulsed in his ears. He couldn't see much through the smoke, but he could hear shouts and the crackle of muskets. He started up the tree-shrouded slope – he didn't know why. Did he want to see if William was there? Did he think there was something he could do to save his friend?

The smoke coiled thick within the forest and he couldn't see more than a few feet before him. He had to cling to branches and bushes as he clambered up the steep incline. He slipped at one point and slid down a short distance on his knees before he got up and carried on. His chest was taut and the smoke was bitter in his throat. He could hear his own breathing, loud and ragged.

He passed the edge of the smouldering crater left by the explosion. Trees lay dashed to the ground, their charred limbs stretching up like the masts of a shipwreck. Flames crackled and slithered about the perimeter.

His wound quivered. He remembered the sattva-fire striking him in the chest and he hesitated for a second. Was he afraid?

Then he heard shouting and shooting further up the scarp, and he took a breath and pressed on. A memory wasn't going to stop him.

A bullet smacked into a tree trunk next to him, ripping a hole in the bark. He dived behind some brambles and waited for a moment, listening. Nothing. Shocks of pain coursed across his chest. Darkness welled before his eyes and he fought to stop himself from passing out.

Damn his injury.

He coughed violently, wiped the dribble away from his mouth. He had to pull himself together.

After a few minutes he climbed to his feet and peered over the brambles. The smoke had cleared a little and he could see the shifting lace of the undergrowth spread out across the forest floor. He waited for a minute more, and when nothing happened he stood up straight.

There was a crunch nearby, a step on fallen leaves. He froze.

Barely thirty feet away stood a man with a musket pointed straight at him. His heart juddered. The man wasn't a Frenchman or a Rajthanan – no uniform.

Jack prepared to jump for cover. But then – like a punch in the chest – he recognised the figure.

It was William. A little older, of course, and with his head shaved, but unmistakeable.

William's face creased as he stared along the musket's sights. Then he frowned and lowered the weapon. Puzzlement snaked across his forehead. He went to call out something, but was interrupted by a couple of pistol shots that sent bullets whistling through the woods to the left. He slid behind a tree.

More pistol shots. Jack saw two Frenchmen leaping over shrubbery as they ran across the slope towards him.

William stepped back further, looked at Jack, frowned again, then slipped into a patch of dense bushes and vines. In a second he'd vanished.

'Where'd he go?' one of the Frenchmen shouted.

'That way.' Jack pointed up the slope in a different direction from the one William had taken – he didn't know why. It was instinctive. He couldn't help but try to protect his friend, even as he was betraying him.

As the French charged off in the wrong direction, Jack scrambled over to where William had disappeared. He spotted a set of broken twigs. Just beyond them was a footprint in the damp ground and then the obvious sign of brambles pushed aside. He started along the trail. Maybe if he could talk to William and explain, then . . .

Then what?

The firing stopped and the quiet was strange after the sound of the battle. Birds started chirping again high in the trees. He jogged along, keeping an eye out for signs and trying to make as little sound as possible. He could have called out to his friend, but then that would have alerted the French.

William's trail was clear – he'd been moving quickly, with no time to cover his tracks. Jack recognised the telltale inward turn of his friend's right foot. The smoke had largely faded now and Jack scanned the trees ahead. But he saw nothing, not even a branch left swinging.

He remembered all those times he'd tracked enemies while he was in the army. But back then William had been beside him, encouraging him on, and Jhala had been there too, and the other men from the company, and they'd been on the side of dharma, and their enemies had been on the side of chaos and ruin, and they'd all been part of the most powerful army in the world.

He came out of the trees and found himself blinking in the sunshine – the light had returned to normal after the strange darkness that had come across the gully. Above him rose a grassy slope, at the top of which stood Sengar, Kansal and half of the French. They were all looking down the far side of the hill.

'Up here, Casey,' Sengar shouted.

Jack hesitated for a second. He could see William's footprints leading straight up the slope. Had his friend been captured by Sengar? His heart drummed.

He clambered up the incline, pain weighing on his chest and black welts expanding before his eyes. He was rasping fiercely by the time he reached the summit. Lefevre looked at him with an eyebrow raised and a trace of a smile on his lips, seemingly pleased to note Jack's weakness.

'Down there.' Sengar pointed to the steep, barren slope on the far side of the hill.

A group of men were scrambling down the last stretch of the slope and jumping on to horses that had been picketed at the bottom. William was amongst them, his shaven head rising well above those of his comrades.

'Can you see Merton?' Sengar asked.

Jack tried to regain his breath. He couldn't bring himself to speak. He wouldn't betray William. 'Yes, he's with them,' he said hoarsely.

Sengar slammed his scimitar back into its scabbard. 'Right. We'll soon have the bastard. I'll teach him to take on the Maharaja's Army.' He turned to his men. 'To the horses – quickly. And check for survivors as you go.'

Jack was the last back down to the rail line. He'd gone as quickly as he could, but he was still fighting for air and there was a constant throb in the centre of his chest.

'No rebel survivors,' Kansal reported to Sengar. 'The wounded all shot themselves before they could be captured.'

Sengar's eyes narrowed and he gripped the pommel of his scimitar. 'No matter. We'll track them. It's up to you now, Casey.'

Jack glared back at the Captain. The top button of Sengar's tunic had come undone during the fray, revealing a purple thread that hung from his left shoulder and across his chest – the mark of a siddha. Just as Jack had suspected, the Captain had been given the secret training.

The rebels wouldn't stand a chance against Sengar. No European, let alone an Englishman, had ever trained to become a true siddha.

There was a groan nearby. The guide was still alive and trapped beneath his fallen mule. He was frail from blood loss, but he still fought to pull himself free.

Sengar sucked on his teeth, strode over to the guide and stood with his legs apart and arms folded. 'Where will the rebels go?'

'I-I don't know what you mean,' the guide said.

Sengar frowned and drew a dagger. He crouched with his knee on the guide's chest and raised the dagger to the man's throat. 'The rebels must have a camp. Where is it?'

'I had nothing to do with—'

'I've no time to waste.' Sengar pressed his knee harder into the guide's chest.

The guide grimaced from his wounds, then stared back at Sengar and spat. Sengar shifted his grip on the dagger and stabbed the guide hard in the mouth. The guide jolted and his eyes widened. Sengar stabbed again, smashing at the man's teeth and then driving into the back of his throat. Then he hammered at the man's eyes, pounding in a mad fury. Blood splashed his hands and tunic. The guide's face was mangled and shattered, but somehow he was still alive, his chest rising and falling. Sengar stabbed over and over again at the man's throat until it was a bloody, open mass. Finally, the guide lay still.

Sengar stood. There was a splatter of blood on one of his cheeks. His eyes blazed.

Jack stared at the blood-soaked corpse. There'd been no need for the Captain to kill the man that way. He could have just shot him in the head. Any other officer would have. Jhala would have.

'How many have we lost?' Sengar barked at Kansal.

'Five dead and seven wounded, sir.'

Sengar looked over to where five French bodies had been laid side by side on the grass. Nearby, the seven wounded men sat propped against the cutting. Some had relatively minor wounds, having been shot in the leg or arm. But others had been hit in the torso and were pale and almost unconscious. Sengar stood over them and surveyed their wounds. He commanded those who were least injured to help the others on to horses. They were to ride back to Pentridge as best they could to seek treatment. No one could be spared to go with them.

'You others, follow me,' Sengar shouted to the remainder of his troops. 'We'll pick up the trail on the other side of the hill.'

They charged along the train tracks and within fifteen minutes reached the end of the gully. The forest thinned to a few twisted trees and it was easy to follow the base of the hill around to the point where the rebels had mounted their horses.

Sengar halted the party with his hand and looked at Jack. 'Get on with it, Casey.'

Jack nudged his mare forward. The pain in his chest had faded and he was breathing relatively easily again.

He dismounted and studied the ground. The trail was clear and simple – thankfully there was no need for him to use his power. He saw the sliding boot prints of the rebels as they came down the slope, the stamped cups left by the hooves of the waiting horses, the churned earth where the animals had raced away down the valley.

He noted the hoof prints, each one unique. You could tell a lot about a horse just from its prints: size, speed, age, health, which legs it favoured, the weight it was carrying. He took a moment to memorise the most distinctive markings: the horseshoe that was worn steeply on the left side; the shoe with the missing nail; the deep prints of the animal carrying a heavy load.

But he took longer than he needed. Even when he was sure he would be able to follow the tracks, whatever the terrain, he still delayed. He knew he should get back on his horse, get on with it, but the reluctance dragged at him. He thought for a second about refusing to track William – he would have liked to have seen the look on Sengar's face when he said it. But, of course, he couldn't do that.

Finally, he climbed back on his horse and led the group off along the trail, with Sengar riding beside him.

The ground flattened into a wide, open valley and they spurred into a gallop, the horses' hooves pummelling the soft earth.

Jack kept an eye on the rebels' tracks, looking out for fresh signs, the places where stones had been scattered or grasses parted. Sometimes he had to slow down, and at one point he stopped completely and dismounted to examine the terrain more carefully.

Sengar clenched and unclenched his reins as he waited. He snapped open his spyglass and gazed at the hills.

The trail took them west across open ground, then north between a row of hills, then west again through a rocky ravine and over a saddle. William appeared to be weaving across the downs in an attempt to lose them, plunging ever deeper into the area known as Cranborne Chase.

Jack wished there was some way he could get a message to his friend, to explain himself. But it was pointless to wish for something like that.

After about two hours they came to a shallow river surrounded by willows. Before them lay a well-used ford and the tracks of numerous animals and people criss-crossed the nearby bank.

Jack leapt from his horse, crouched and searched the beaten soil. Amidst the other tracks, he could see the fresh marks of the rebels' horses leading straight into the ford.

He stepped into the water; it was shallow, no higher than his knees. He walked across to the far bank, where he found dozens of trails again, but no sign of the rebels. He frowned and gazed along the bank, looking for any sign of the horses leaving the river. But there was nothing.

He walked back to the middle of the river. Sengar scowled at him, while Kansal and the others watched intently.

He knew the rebels must have travelled either upstream or downstream, but it was impossible to tell which way. He looked down, but the water was murky and the river bed stony. Any mark the horses might have made would have been washed away within seconds. He would either have to conduct a long search over both banks, or—

'What is it?' Sengar called.

'Nothing,' Jack replied. 'Just making sure of something.'

'Hurry up.'

Jack closed his eyes. This was it. He would have to use his power. There was no other way.

The water was cold and swift, making it difficult to stand still.

'Your mind is like a rippling pool.'

He thought of the yantra and it glowed white before him.

He breathed deeply and concentrated on the air passing in and out of his nostrils. His heartbeat slowed, the centre of his forehead trembled, and then he noticed a trace of sattva.

He reached out to his surroundings with his mind. He was deep enough into the meditation now to sense he was in a medium stream. Good. He would have preferred a strong stream, but this was better than nothing.

Jhala had said to him, 'To use a power you need three things: sattva, a yantra and your mind. Sattva is the fuel, the yantra provides the instructions and your mind is the engine. The more sattva available, the easier it will be for you to use your power.'

The yantra glimmered and wavered. But each time he brought it into focus, his mind's eye zoomed in on the bottom right. He kept forcing his mind back to the full design. And finally he managed to hold the yantra steady. Now he just had to keep it there a little longer—

Then his mind snapped back to the bottom right.

He gasped and opened his eyes. His heart was racing, his breathing was shallow and his wound pulsed. How could he do this? He couldn't even hold the yantra still.

'What are you waiting for?' Sengar called out from the bank.

Jack tried to ignore the Captain. He splashed some water on his face, then wiped it off with his sleeve.

Now. He had to do it now.

He closed his eyes again and focused on the yantra. But it kept sliding away. His mind wouldn't rest.

Elizabeth flickered in his thoughts. He saw her in the cell, lank hair over her face, tears on her cheeks. And the question of why she had ever joined the mutiny kept pounding in his brain.

Was it because of a man she'd fallen for? Now that he thought about it, this seemed unlikely. When had Elizabeth ever done anything just because someone else told her to? Even as a child he'd called her 'wilful'.

A wilful child who'd run away one night. He remembered this now . . .

He'd been sleeping in his cottage and something had made him sit up and stare into the dark. He panted. Something was wrong. But he couldn't see or hear anything untoward. Katelin was shifting and sighing on the straw mattress beside him and he could see the vague bundle of his five-year-old daughter in the corner. There was nothing to worry about; he should get back to sleep.

The wind tugged at the shutters and crackled in the thatching.

Something about his sleeping daughter didn't look right. He slipped across to the corner of the bedroom.

He stood dead still and the floor seemed to drop.

Elizabeth wasn't there. The bundle he'd seen was just her bunched blanket.

'Elizabeth!' he shouted.

'What is it?' Katelin was already standing.

'She's not here.'

They were both outside in seconds, both calling out, although the wind ripped the words straight out of their throats.

'You get help in the village,' Jack shouted. 'I'll head to the forest.'

'I'll come with you.' Katelin clung to his arm and her long blonde hair swam around her face.

'No. We have to spread out. She could be anywhere.'

He pulled himself away and ran across the field towards the dark line of the trees. He glanced back once and saw Katelin's pale form flitting along the road. The village was only a few hundred yards away and she would soon be there. Old Jones and the others would help her look for Elizabeth.

Halfway to the woods he realised it was pointless just charging around. He had no idea which direction Elizabeth had taken, or even when she'd left the cottage. He would have to track her, and the best way to do that at night would be to use his power.

He called her name one last time, hoping—

And then there it was, a faint cry that found its way through the whirling wind.

He called out again, and the tiny voice responded.

He ran in the direction of the voice, shouting her name over and over again, his throat cracking at the effort. He stumbled into the trees and battered his way through branches and leaves as if fighting off an enemy. He tripped on a tree root, fell, got up, fought on.

Her voice guided him through the speckled dark.

And finally he found her, huddled in a hollow, dirt on her face and scratches on her hands.

He scrambled down to her, took her in his arms. 'What happened?'

'I'm sorry I ran away.'

He searched her face. 'Ran away? Why?'

'I was looking for the Grail.'

'The Grail?'

'Like Sir Galahad.'

He half laughed, half choked at her reply. And he lifted her up and carried her out of the hollow and back through the moaning, uneasy trees.

And now, finally, these thoughts were slipping away and the night that Elizabeth disappeared was fading . . .

The yantra shimmered and he locked his thoughts on it.

He reached out again for the sattva about him, drawing it in, using it to feed his meditation. The scent of sattva grew stronger. A good sign. He was smelting, extracting sattva from his surroundings and processing it with his mind.

A tingle built in his spine. He became more aware of the slurping water, the hush of the wind, the faint heat of the sun.

The spirit realm was close now. God was close.

The yantra froze in his mind. He held it there . . . and then the design burst into blinding light. Spirit and matter, purusha and prakriti, touched.

Fire rushed up his spine and crackled over his scalp. A grand, vaulted cathedral sprang open in his mind.

He was in the centre of a vast and intricate lattice . . . interconnected.

6

Jack lifted his eyelids. Everything was sharp and distinct. He could see every coil of water in great detail, every shaking leaf on every tree, every flying insect embroidering the air. At the same time it all seemed unreal, as if viewed from a great distance. He sensed the sharp pain in his chest and the pulse of the sattva-fire, but this was distant too. His body was not his own.

He stared beneath the surface of the river and spotted a misty, silver ribbon twisting in the water. He noticed another thread nearby, then another. He stood up straight and glanced around. Patches of gleaming mist were dotted under the water, along both riverbanks, across the ground beyond, everywhere.

Trails in sattva. The marks all living things left as they passed through the streams.

He'd done it.

But for how long? The pain in his chest was worsening, and although it seemed far away he could tell it was growing fierce. He had to move quickly.

He scanned the river and searched through the myriad trails of people and animals. The shining skeins were thick in the ford, but more sparse elsewhere. Soon he saw them – the bright, fresh tracks of more than fifty horses going upstream.

He looked over at Sengar. 'This way.'

The party rode into the river, Sengar's batman leading Jack's mare. Jack strode through the water at their head, following the phosphorescent trail. By focusing his attention on the glowing strands, he forced all the other trails from his vision. The trees thickened on either bank and the river narrowed. Branches from both sides almost met overhead, forming a green-tinged tunnel. The smell of dank moss merged with the constant sweet scent of sattva.

After fifteen minutes, the trail forked. Most of the horses had veered over to the left bank – the same bank from which the rebels had entered the river – but around five had gone to the right. Jack paused. To the left he could see the silver glinting on the bank and disappearing into the trees. But there were no hoof prints, no broken twigs, no scratches in tree trunks, nothing to otherwise suggest the rebels had passed that way. He'd seen this before – the trail had been hidden using a power. And one of the few people who possessed this power was William. It was a skill that, like Jack's ability, could not even be learnt by the siddhas.

Jack glanced at the right bank and saw clear hoof prints leaving the river and passing over a muddy beach.

Sengar followed Jack's gaze. 'This way?'

'Wait,' Jack said.

He pushed his way through the water and stepped, legs dripping, on to the beach. He studied the tracks of the five horses. The sattva trail wormed and shifted just above ground level and led off into the brush. But there was something strange about the hoof prints. He bent and stuck his finger into the ground – the mud was soft and his finger slid in easily. He looked again at the hoof prints. The impressions weren't nearly as deep as he would have expected. The horses hadn't been carrying riders.

He stepped back into the water. It was an old trick, sending a few riderless horses in one direction as a decoy while the main party went the opposite way. But why? William knew all about Jack's power: the regiment had relied on it often to pursue its enemies. So why would William use his power to hide the tracks when he knew Jack could see the sattva trail anyway?

The answer came to him with the same heightened clarity with which he viewed his surroundings. William was giving him a chance. Jack could easily tell the others that the trail led to the right. No one would doubt him. He could then follow the roaming horses and eventually claim to have lost the trail altogether.

But it was more than just a chance – it was also a test. If Jack led the soldiers along the false trail, then William would know that Jack was still a friend, perhaps held captive by the Rajthanans. But if Jack followed the real trail then William would know that his old friend, for whatever reason, had become an enemy.

'What's the problem?' Sengar snapped. 'Let's get after them.'

Jack looked up at the Captain sitting astride his horse, moustache rolling. It would be so easy, almost a pleasure, to lead Sengar along the false trail. He was breathing heavily now. William had given him a way out – he had to take it.

But then he thought of Elizabeth in the cell and the pardon sitting in the top drawer of Jhala's desk. He couldn't abandon his daughter.

'This way.' He walked over to the left bank and the true trail.

'There's nothing that way, sir,' Kansal said to Sengar in Rajthani.

'He knows what he's doing,' Sengar replied. 'He'd better, at any rate.'

Jack followed the quicksilver trail out of the water and through the undergrowth. The ribbons danced and rippled a few feet above the ground. He climbed back on to his horse and picked his way between the trees.

They passed out of the medium stream and Jack sensed the sattva thin to a weak residue. He had to scratch about with his mind to find something to smelt, and the effort took its toll. From far away, he noticed he was shivering and the breath was being squeezed from his lungs. His legs and arms grew heavy and he slumped in the saddle. How long could he keep going?

After around ten minutes he saw hoof prints once again, and other signs that the rebels had passed that way – snapped twigs and a torn spiderweb. The area concealed by William's power had come to an end. He exhaled and let himself slip out of the trance. Immediately, pain thumped him in the chest and he leant forward and gasped for breath.

'What's the problem now?' Sengar asked.

Jack gulped down air and the pain eased. Finally he was able to say, 'Nothing.'

Sengar's moustache stiffened, but he didn't reply.

Jack took a swig of water, forced himself to sit upright and tried to ignore the stabbing sensation in his chest. He shook the reins and the horse eased into a trot. His surroundings were now dull and blurry; the shining trail had disappeared, but the tracks in the material world were easy enough to follow.

They came out of the woods and on to a stretch of flat ground. The trail led to a steep slope and they zigzagged up, the horses slipping and sliding in places, whinnying in complaint. After half an hour they reached the summit, by which time Jack was exhausted again.

The sun weighed on the exposed hill. He paused for a moment, drank some more water, blinked and shook his head to clear his thoughts.

'Which way now?' Sengar asked.

'Hold on,' Jack said.

He circled about the hilltop on his mare and studied the ground, finding a confused mosaic of hoof prints, all in varying states of dryness. Some marks were light-coloured and brittle, at least two hours old. Others were darker and more moist, clearly more recent.

He found the point where the churned earth of the tracks led down the far side of the hill towards a forested plateau. The rebels had left only one hour earlier, at the most.

He looked back the way they'd come. He had a clear view of the trees with the glinting river twisting between them. He could make out the ford and the plains beyond. Slowly he pieced together the rebels' movements – it all made sense. William had led his men down to the river, set up the decoy, and then taken them up the hill. From the summit he must have waited for an hour to see whether Jack would follow the true trail.

A chill crawled across Jack's skin. William, probably using a spyglass, would have been able to watch him as he deliberated over which path to take out of the river. William had seen him follow the true trail.

So that was it. He and William were on opposite sides of the mutiny now.

And Elizabeth was on William's side.

He called over to Sengar and pointed towards the forest below. 'They went this way. They're only an hour ahead of us.'

Sengar searched Jack's face. 'Good work.'

They thundered down the slope and into the trees. It was dim beneath the canopy and the late afternoon sun slanted through at an angle, like light underwater. The rebels had followed a path that was clear of undergrowth and the way was easy, despite the uneven ground.

For three hours they kept up the pace. The trail wound through the forest, across two brooks, and up and down slopes. Eventually the trees petered out and the tracks climbed higher into the hills. At times they could see the corrugated countryside stretched out below, washed in the amber glow of the summer evening.

Jack's injury came and went. Sometimes he recovered and the pain subsided completely. But then it would get worse and he would almost pass out. He tried to hide it from Sengar and the others, although he was sure they were starting to notice. At least he hadn't needed to use his power again.

Sunset burnt the sky red and gold. The air turned a hazy pink. They paused on a hilltop and watched as shadows fingered the downs. Fireflies appeared in fairy curtains.

The trail now became more difficult to follow. Jack carried a lantern and had to slow the pace to a walk. He bent as low as he could in the saddle to light the ground and he often had to dismount and study the earth for several minutes. He could tell that the rebels had also had to slow their pace – the distance between the hoof prints had lessened markedly.

'We'll follow them through the night if we have to,' Sengar said. 'We can't let them get the advantage now.'

Jack's limbs ached and the tightness in his chest grew. He shut his eyes for a moment, but snapped them open when sleep leapt at him. Sengar was right, they couldn't let William get ahead.

The gloom thickened. They travelled across valleys and scarps largely devoid of trees. The hills and rocks were indistinct in the dark and picked out only by moon-frost.

At one point Jack lost the trail completely. He climbed off his horse and hunched over the ground, enclosed in the globe of the lantern light. His eyes felt full of grit. He searched, but found no markings in the grass and dust. Eyes intent on the ground, he crept ahead a few yards, but still found nothing.

The rebels seemed to have vanished.

Perhaps William had used his power again? But that was unlikely. Why pause to use it when Jack could still follow him?

But then, where were the tracks?

Jack walked to his horse. 'We'll have to go back a while.'

Sengar stared at him. 'Why?'

'Lost the trail. But I'll find it again.'

Sengar sucked on his teeth but said nothing.

They retraced their steps. Jack peered at the ground, but the markings of his own party had crushed and scattered those of the rebels and now it was impossible to tell the two trails apart. After he'd gone a quarter of a mile, he stopped his horse. Sengar and the others drew up behind him. He gazed at the scalloped prints in the earth. He should have been able to see the rebels' trail by now – he could remember riding past this point with the tracks clear before him.

He dismounted, but moved too quickly and almost fainted as

his feet hit the ground. He leant against the rump of the horse and the animal stomped nervously. Steadying himself, he raised the lantern and searched the chaotic tracks more closely.

Sengar rode up beside him. 'Why's it taking so long?'

'I'll find it.'

'Perhaps a rest stop—' Kansal began.

'Out of the question,' Sengar said.

Jack sat down and crossed his legs. There was nothing else for it – he would have to use his power again. He shut his eyes and tried to focus his mind, but the pain beat in his chest and the air creaked in his lungs. He wanted to sleep – he felt as though he could sleep for ever – but he fought off the feeling.

He reached out to his surroundings and found he was in a medium stream. He called up the yantra and tried to repress any other thoughts. He repeatedly thought he was going to pass out, but each time he pulled himself back before the darkness closed over him entirely.

Finally, after more than ten minutes, he felt the familiar sensation of the world branching and interlocking. He vibrated and slipped outside himself. Energy shot up his spine, and then he was in.

He smelted sattva to keep himself in the trance and the sweet scent radiated out from him. But his body shuddered with tiredness, and even though he observed this from a distance he knew he couldn't remain in this state for long.

At least he could see the sattva trails now – they fanned out in the dark like foam on the sea. He focused on the ground directly ahead, which made the markings further away vanish. The fresh tracks of his own party coursed before him, although the silver cords were faint and translucent – even sattva trails were hard to see at night. He gazed at the shifting tendrils, trying to make out the rebels' tracks beneath those of his own group. But he couldn't see anything.

He noticed himself sigh. His body seemed to be fading. And

he watched all of this from far away, something that had happened a long time ago to someone else . . .

'Casey,' Sengar barked.

Where was he? What had happened?

He felt as though he'd just woken from sleep. But he knew he hadn't been asleep because he could still see the sattva trail and the trance would have been broken the moment he drifted off. His consciousness itself seemed to have blinked out, while the rest of him had stayed sitting still. He shook his head. Nothing like that had happened to him before. He wasn't even sure how long he'd been out for.

Sengar glared down from his horse. 'What's wrong?'

'Nothing,' Jack replied. 'Just looking at the tracks.'

'He went as pale as a corpse,' Kansal whispered to Sengar.

'He's fine. Tell the others to take a break. We'll move out in half an hour.'

Sengar dismounted and stood looking down at Jack, lips pressed together tightly. 'Jhala told me you were the best. You've got thirty minutes.'

Sengar strode off to speak to his men, who now stood talking quietly and looking warily into the darkness. Sentries took up places in a wide circle, watching with lanterns raised beside them.

Jack examined the glowing tracks. His own party's trail was still visible, but now that he was no longer under such great pressure he could make out the slightly older rebels' tracks, a fainter, thinner set of wavering lines. For a few minutes he studied the markings, until he was sure he would be able to follow them.

He stood. 'We can carry on.'

'Break's over,' Sengar shouted. 'Quickly now.'

They all climbed back on to their horses and turned to head forward again. Jack put out his lantern – the light was distracting him from the sattva trail. He gazed at the luminous tracks and tried to keep his mind still.

His body shook, pain cracked his chest and his breath was short and wheezy. He sensed all of this and knew he couldn't last much longer, but he pressed on regardless.

A few minutes later he saw the dull silver veering off to the right between a pair of boulders. He looked at Sengar and pointed along the trail. 'They went this way.'

They followed the tracks into a wide valley where sparse, wind-swept trees bent in prayer to the moon. The trail glimmered as it arced away across the valley floor.

He was aware that his breathing had become shallow and intermittent. He sagged in the saddle. He tried frantically to pull in more sattva, but he'd passed into an area where there was almost none.

Suddenly, he flicked out of the trance. His chest felt as though it had been pierced by a spear. A dark cloud moved across his eyes and he slipped off his horse. He felt himself falling, falling for a long time without hitting the ground. He heard Sengar and Kansal shouting . . .

Cold water slapped him in the face. He sat upright with a start, gasping and blinking the water out of his eyes. Sengar and Kansal crouched in front of him, faces ghoulish in the lantern light. It was still night and he could see the gloomy valley and the hills ranged behind the officers. Lefevre stood nearby with an upturned canteen in his hand and a smirk on his lips.

'Can you hear us?' Kansal asked.

Jack nodded. He felt slightly better. His chest was no longer constricted and he could breathe more easily.

'Can you stand?' Sengar asked.

Jack tried to get up, but he was still weak and dizzy. He had to lean against a tree in order to raise himself.

'He can't go on,' Kansal said. 'He looks terrible.'

'He'll do exactly what I tell him to, Lieutenant,' Sengar said. 'As will you.'

'Of course, sir.'

Sengar stood with his face close to Jack's, moustache rolling on his top lip.

Jack stared back.

'We'll make camp here,' Sengar said finally, turning away. 'We start again at first light.'

'What the hell's wrong with you?' Sengar's moustache was taut.

Jack was sitting a few feet away from the campfire and the main group, eating vegetable stew from a mess tin. He put his spoon down and looked up. 'Nothing.'

'Nothing? Thought you were dead.'

Jack took another mouthful of stew and chewed it slowly.

'Your injury, is it?' Sengar said. 'Jhala said it wouldn't be a problem.'

'I'm all right.'

'Well, I don't care what's wrong with you, so long as you stay alive long enough to find Merton.'

'I'll find him.'

'Good. Just remember what's at stake.'

As if he could forget.

Sengar walked back to the fire, spoke to his batman, then strode off into the brush. He sat cross-legged a few yards away from the fire, put his hands on his knees and closed his eyes. He seemed to glow faintly as he meditated. No doubt he was 'replenishing' – true siddhas, unlike native siddhas, had to replace their mind's store of sattva after using a power.

Jack wondered what other powers Sengar had, apart from sattva-fire. It would be useful to know. But he wasn't even sure what kinds of powers existed. Jhala had never told him the extent of the powers and because siddhas were so rare in Europe he'd only occasionally seen them in action. He'd seen military siddhas use sattva-fire on the battlefield. And he'd seen siddhas commanding avatars. That was all. He'd heard all kinds of rumours about what the siddhas were capable of, but he didn't know how much of this was true.

After meditating, Sengar was served a meal specially prepared by his batman. Kansal didn't eat with the Captain, which confirmed he was from an inferior jati, but once Sengar had finished, Kansal strolled over and Jack listened to the two officers speak in Rajthani. The cavalrymen had laid out sleeping mats and had already started resting. The horses had been picketed beneath a row of trees and sentries stood further away.

'Bloody country.' Sengar picked with a stick at something in the sole of his boot. 'Freezing cold and damp. Full of filthy barbarians. France is no better.'

'It's not Rajthana,' Kansal said.

'Shouldn't even be here.'

'Sir?'

'Family's high up in the sun clan. I never should have been sent here. Soon as this damn mutiny's over I'm putting in for a transfer back home.'

Kansal was silent and stared at the fading embers of the fire.

'I'll get a commendation, so long as we get Merton,' Sengar said. 'I'll make sure you get a mention too.'

'Thank you, sir.'

Sengar put the stick down and wiped his boot on the grass. 'Just so long as I can get the hell out of here. I'm not going to rot in this place.'

Jack rolled on to his side and pulled a blanket over him. He'd often heard the Rajthanans talk about returning 'home' to their country far across the sea in India. Even those who'd been born in Europe, like Jhala, seemed to dream about it.

'Rajthana – a beautiful country,' Jhala had often said. 'The deserts, the cities, the peepul trees.'

Jack shut his eyes. Why did his thoughts keep turning to Jhala? He tried to blot out the memories, but they swept uncontrollably around him.

For a moment he recalled the time he'd gone to Jhala for money. The landlord was threatening to evict him and his family from their smallholding. He'd tried everything to raise the rent and had borrowed as much as he could from family and friends. But he was still short.

Away with the regiment, he received a desperate letter from Katelin saying they had only a month to find the money. With no other option, he went to Jhala. It wasn't uncommon for native soldiers to turn to their officers for loans, but Jack had always been too proud for that. Now he stood in front of Jhala, trying to find a way to ask, yet unable to bring himself to do it.

'You need money,' Jhala said.

Jack was startled. 'How did you know?'

'Word gets around.' Jhala smiled. 'William told me.'

Jack lifted his chin and stared straight ahead. 'Sir, I don't like to beg, but could you help?'

'How much?'

'Ten pounds.'

Jhala glanced at the ceiling, swilled the idea around in his mouth, then grinned. 'No problem.'

'Sir.' Jack sank to his knees and namasted deeply.

'Get up. There's no need for that. You'll pay me back when you can.'

'I don't know how to thank you.'

'Get up, Casey.'

Now, Jack's throat tightened as he remembered this. Jhala was capable of great kindness. And yet he was threatening to kill Elizabeth. It was as though Jhala had completely changed, as though he'd been killed and replaced by an impostor.

Jack's wound nipped with each breath, his chest felt bruised and every joint in his body ached. He turned on to his back and opened his eyes for a moment, staring up at the lost stars wheeling far above.

Everything had been turned upside down.

7

'Wake up, Casey,' Sengar said.

Jack prised apart eyelids clogged with rheum. Sengar stood over him, prodding him in the chest with his boot. He ached all over and was stiff from the slight chill.

'We leave in half an hour,' Sengar said. 'Eat something.'

Jack sat up as Sengar walked away. The sky had clouded overnight and now a fine drizzle veiled the countryside. Grey sunrise filtered through the cloud.

The French had laid out mats in rows and were reciting their prayers, standing, sitting and prostrating themselves in unison. Jack cleared his throat and spat on the ground next to him.

He ate a few dry biscuits, drank some water and tied his hair back in a ponytail. He felt better than he had the night before and was even optimistic for a moment, until he remembered the task before him.

He stamped his feet to shake off his sleepiness and warm himself up, then walked to the edge of the camp. He found the rebels' tracks again; they were clear in the soft soil, leading away into the mist, a cord connecting him to William.

Kansal came up beside him, moisture beading his turban. 'Feeling better now?'

Jack nodded, still looking into the distance.

'What was wrong?'

'Don't know.'

'Chest pains? Short of breath?'

Where was this going? 'Something like that.'

Kansal looked down and nudged a clod of earth around with his boot. 'Sounds like heart trouble. My father has it.'

'Sorry to hear that.'

'He's all right. Recovering.'

Jack continued to stare straight ahead.

'Jatamansi,' Kansal said.

Jack frowned. 'Sorry, sir?'

Kansal grinned, seemingly pleased to have got Jack's attention. 'Jatamansi – it's medicine, for the heart. It's what my father takes.'

'Right. I'll look for it in Poole.'

'You do that.'

Kansal stood there for a while longer, clicking his tongue and seeming to search for something else to say. 'Well, best be getting ready.' He glanced at Jack as he left.

Jack gave him a nod and forced a smile. 'Thank you, sir.' It had been a kind gesture.

Jatamansi. He would try it – if he lived that long.

They rode through the shrouds of drizzle, the hills phantoms all about them. The trail was easy to follow and Jack spurred his horse into a gallop, trying to make up for lost time.

The rebels appeared to have ridden through the night – there was no sign that they had stopped to make camp. Their pace must have quickened as day broke because their horses' hoof prints became more widely spaced.

Around mid-morning, the tracks led down a wooded slope and out on to the edge of a swift river. The water was brown and high, swelling over the banks and smothering the nearby meadows.

The rebels' hoof prints followed the river south.

Sengar paused to study a map. 'The Stour River. There's a bridge to the south – the rebels may have crossed it.'

The river widened as they rode on, the water swilling far across the fields on the opposite bank. Black cloud flooded the sky from the north and the air chilled. A speck of rain struck Jack in the face, followed by another. Soon the drops came beating down. An earthy smell rose from the ground as it moistened.

Damn.

The rebels' tracks began to melt into the mud. Rain was the curse of the tracker, destroying markings and covering signs. If it rained hard enough for long enough he would be left with only the sattva trail to follow.

The cavalrymen pulled on overcoats, but Jack had no wet-weather gear and his clothes were soon drenched.

Just as he began to think he'd lost the tracks completely, he noticed something jutting into the river ahead. Staring through the slanting downpour, he made out the remains of a wooden bridge. The central section of the bridge had vanished, leaving only shattered poles and planks. Pieces of wood continued to break free and slip downstream.

A flock of sheep milled about on the bank. An old shepherd stood with them, speaking to a man dressed like a peasant but wearing a surcoat displaying the coat of arms of the Earl of Dorsetshire – Jack recognised the crest of the two leopards from Pentridge Castle.

The shepherd and the Earl's man were both sodden and speckled with mud. They namasted when they noticed the approaching cavalrymen.

Sengar squinted at the smashed bridge. 'What happened?'

'The Ghost,' the Earl's man said. 'Hit us this morning. Blew it to pieces, sir.'

The sheep bleated. They were scrawny beasts and many looked as though they wouldn't last more than a few days.

'You were guarding the bridge?' Sengar asked.

'Yes, sir. With another.'

'Where's he, then?'

'Took off.'

Sengar sucked on his teeth and his moustache wriggled. 'So, the Ghost and his men are on the other side?'

'That's right. Crossed over and then blew it.'

Sengar looked at the water – it was far too wide and deep to cross. 'Where's the next bridge?'

'Well, now. The river's flooded. The fords will be washed out. Your best bet is the stone bridge downstream.'

'How far is it?'

'Quite a distance, I'm afraid – eight miles.'

'Rough road that one too,' the shepherd said.

Sengar jerked out his scimitar and pointed it at the shepherd's chest. The man gulped and stepped back two paces.

'You will not speak to me unless I speak to you first,' Sengar said.

'I-I'm sorry,' the shephered replied. 'I meant no harm.'

'He meant no harm,' the guard agreed.

Sengar jammed his scimitar back into the scabbard, glared at the guard, then looked back at his men. 'We ride to the next bridge. Quickly now.'

They raced along a rough road that cut into the hillside high enough to avoid the floodwater. Rain lashed Jack in the face and he felt each drop strike through his damp, clinging hose.

He brooded. William and the rebels were now well ahead of them and he wondered how long it would take to catch up. William was a wily adversary; it seemed more and more doubtful that they would be able to capture him.

He shot a look at Sengar, who was riding at his side. The Captain's features were so still they seemed locked in place and his eyes were almost unblinking as they stared at the road ahead. Sengar would never give up the chase, Jack was sure of that. And neither, for that matter, would he. It seemed that he and Sengar were united in this at least.

After around twenty minutes they drew up at a fork in the road. One path twisted away into the hills while the other dipped to follow the river. A simple shrine, little more than a pile of rocks topped by a white stone cross, stood nearby.

Sengar crackled open the map and he and Kansal hunched over it, trying to protect it from the rain.

Sengar pointed at the path leading uphill. 'That road takes the long way around. We can save time by sticking to the riverbank.'

And so they charged down to the foot of the hill and then along the floor of a valley. Steep, forested scarps stood solemnly to either side.

The river continued to rise and soon spilt over the road. The horses had to slow to a walk as they splashed through the deepening pools.

'Ground's getting tricky, sir,' Kansal said.

Sengar's moustache tightened. He led the party off the road and along the grass to the left.

But soon waves slopped across the grass as well. As the water rose, the current grew stronger and the horses struggled through whorls and eddies. One of the creatures skidded and fell to the side, trapping its leg between two rocks. The rider tumbled off unharmed, splashing into the river. But the horse was now stuck and its leg was twisted at such an angle it could only be broken. The animal squealed and trembled, its eyes rolling white with pain.

'Put it down,' Sengar said.

One of the French shot the animal in the head. The sound of the pistol rolled across the hills like distant thunder.

'We'll go on foot,' Sengar said.

They all dismounted and led their steeds through the churning flood. The current dragged at Jack's legs and he slipped at times on the muddy ground. The hiss of the rain merged with the rushing of the water.

Ahead, the river expanded across the entire floor of the valley.

'Looks deep,' Kansal said. 'Should we head back to the road?'

'No.' Sengar clenched his jaw. 'That hill over there.' He pointed to a slope directly ahead where the valley curved to the west. It was largely free of trees. 'We'll go over that.'

They waded over to the hill. The scarp was too steep to ride up, so they continued on foot, hauling the horses along with them. They scrambled over rocks and rises, getting covered in mud.

Jack felt pressure on his chest and the air was thin in his lungs. But he was becoming accustomed to the discomfort. You could get used to anything – he'd learnt that long ago in the army during twenty-four-hour marches on half rations.

The way became even steeper and more broken and he had to pull his horse to keep it moving. Rows of gorse and brambles blocked the way and cut into his skin as he pushed through.

Kansal stopped. Seeing how tired Jack looked, he motioned to Lefevre. 'Sergeant, take his horse.'

Lefevre walked across the slope. With the rain drooling over his shaven head and his skin grey in the dim light, he looked like some golem formed from the mud. His beard, thick with grease and dirt, had forked into two rough prongs.

'Out of the way, *Ros Porc*.' He grasped the reins of Jack's mare.

Jack stared back, still holding the reins for a moment before he let go. He didn't like showing this weakness before the Mohammedan. But at the same time he was exhausted and pleased not to have to drag his horse any longer.

They struggled on until a chalk cliff appeared ahead like a ghostly wall in the whirling rain. As they came closer they could see it would be impossible to climb.

'What now, sir?' Kansal asked.

Sengar sucked on his teeth as he squinted up. 'We'll go around it.'

The Captain led them to the right, following the bottom of the cliff. Jack slipped at one point, but managed to regain his footing. Sengar, noticing this, ordered a five-minute break. They all huddled beneath an overhang that provided a small degree of cover. Jack leant against the rock with his head bowed, strands of his hair falling over his face and dripping on to his neck. The wind moaned through the fissures in the stone.

They continued following the cliff face until it lowered and then disappeared. Sengar led them on uphill and a few minutes later they reached the summit.

They all stopped dead still.

Below them, on the far side of the hill, the valley opened into a plain at least a mile across . . . all of it covered in floodwater. Scattered trees rose from the murk and a few knolls poked up. But otherwise the ground was totally submerged.

To the east tumbled wooded hills that would be difficult to cross. To the west lay the river. And straight ahead stretched the flooded plain.

'We can't get through that, sir,' Kansal said.

'I'm aware of that, Lieutenant,' Sengar replied.

And so they headed back downhill in the direction of the road they'd left hours earlier. Jack stumbled along, his legs so tired they shook and refused to obey him. The wound in his chest throbbed. The men around him were all silent. No doubt they would be thinking, like him, of how far ahead the rebels would now be.

Jack felt a trace of grim satisfaction. William had outwitted Sengar. Half a day ahead and with his tracks being washed into the river, William might well get away. But now Jack's stomach coiled and he felt light-headed. He couldn't let William escape. He had to find the trail again. A new resolve spread through him, as though he'd breathed in a djinn. Up until now there had been that vague thought – maybe he could let William get away and still find some other way to save Elizabeth. But there was no other way, and he'd been a fool to entertain this idea – even for a second, even hidden in the back of his mind. He would root the idea out now, destroy it and set his mind firmly on what he had to do.

Sengar's horse skidded to its knees and then clambered quickly back up again. The Captain thrashed the animal over and over again with his riding crop, letting out small hissing sounds. When he stopped, he glared at Kansal and the cavalrymen – even they appeared shocked at their captain's actions. Cavalrymen didn't hit their horses. And siddhas usually showed more restraint.

'Get on with it.' Sengar flicked his riding crop, spraying water. 'Keep going.'

They staggered downhill for another hour, then forced their way through the ever-rising flood. Finally, they reached the road, the crude shrine glowing white and marking the point at which they'd set off.

Now they followed the road to the south-east, giving a wide berth to the countryside they'd just tried to cross. Sengar ordered them into a gallop when the ground was even enough.

Jack's chest ached so constantly he almost didn't notice any more.

By late afternoon the path arced back to the west and they splashed across ground marshy from the flooding. They reached the stone bridge, which was high and wide enough to span the swollen river. A hamlet huddled on the far side, its lights winking in the gloom.

Sengar led the way across the bridge, the horses' hooves clattering on the flagstones, and then followed the road back upstream. They passed farmers and shepherds herding their sickly livestock.

The rain eased back to a velvet drizzle. The light faded and night spread ink behind the clouds. Jack shivered in his damp clothes as the temperature dropped.

The road weaved through the dark hills and eventually coiled to the east. Just before ten o'clock the Stour River appeared before them. Water still smothered the bottom of the valley, but the river was more sluggish than before. There was a smudge of moonlight and Jack could just make out the black ruins of the bridge on the far riverbank. On the near side, a few feet upstream, a short stretch of smashed jetty stood just clear of the water.

'Five-minute break,' Sengar said. 'Casey, pick up the trail again.'

Jack climbed down. He felt faint, and black globes circled him. He longed for sleep, but he knew he had to find the trail soon. The longer he delayed, the harder it would be to find it.

He lit a lantern and searched the ground around the jetty. The soil was a sodden pool of mud and he couldn't make out any trail at all. He worked his way carefully up the road, but all he could see were the recent tracks of his own party. And, of course, the rebels might not even have taken the road. It was more probable they'd struck out across the countryside. But how would he find the start of the trail at night, with most of the markings washed away?

He looked at the boiling, grey and black sky. A netting of moisture fell over his face, a chill crawled up his spine and his head and throat began to throb; he was coming down with something.

He looked back at the cavalrymen, who stood next to their horses and talked quietly or chewed paan. Sengar stood to one side, hands on hips. Although Jack couldn't make out the Captain's face, he could tell Sengar was watching him closely.

He would have to use his power again. He'd noticed a sattva stream as they'd ridden up the road, and now he walked back, searching for it again. Finally, he passed through an invisible barrier and his skin tingled. He sniffed. It was a strong stream, strong enough for him to sense without even meditating.

He sat under a tree with a canopy wide enough to protect him from the rain, then he shut his eyes. What would happen if he used his power now? Would he survive?

He concentrated on the yantra. Twice he began to fall asleep, but he woke up again straight away.

Although he tried for fifteen minutes, he wasn't able to prod his mind into the trance. He panted and wiped his running nose on his sleeve. His throat was thick and a tremor built up from his abdomen. The tiredness was knotted deep within his muscles, as though it were a part of him, and always had been.

He was about to give up, when the yantra suddenly went still and he slipped into the trance, almost without meaning to. Distantly, he sensed the pain tear like lightning through his chest. He closed his eyes and sat still. Would this be the end?

No. Although the pain pierced his chest, he hadn't used his power for more than a day and he'd recovered some of his strength. For the moment he was alive.

He stood and gazed around him. The ground was speckled with the dull glow of dozens of trails, some fresh, some days or even weeks old. He saw the floating flecks left by sheep or goats; the larger, coarser streams of horses; the globular tendrils of human beings.

He put out the lantern and walked, hunched, along the side of the road. He searched the long grass and clumps of heather and gorse, and it wasn't long before he saw the ghostly tracks of around fifty horses leading north into the darkness.

'Over here,' he called to the others, retrieved his horse and led the way up the valley.

He wasn't sure how long he would be able to stay in the trance – he was weak and fading quickly. Sengar and Kansal glanced at him from time to time and he tried to sit up straight in the saddle.

The valley widened and the trail turned to the north-west, leaving the river behind.

Blink.

What had happened?

He shook his head. His consciousness had blacked out, as it had the day before. He seemed to have vanished for a moment, while his body still rode ahead like an automaton.

'I have to stop,' he said.

He couldn't risk continuing now as he could pass out at any moment.

Sengar sucked on his teeth and his eyes flashed, but he nodded his assent. 'We'll sleep for three hours only, then press on.'

They didn't bother to make camp or light a fire. After eating a few biscuits, Jack collapsed on his sleeping mat and pulled a damp blanket over himself. The drizzle still feathered his face, but he fell asleep so quickly he didn't even have a chance to notice it.

He woke to the sound of the Frenchmen packing their things and preparing to leave. It was still dark and the cloud hid the moon. But the rain had stopped and the air smelt fresh and the wet earth sweet. A line of pain crossed his chest, his skin crawled hot and cold, and his eyes and nose oozed mucous.

He sat up and saw Sengar drinking from a canteen by holding it above his mouth and pouring the water through the air to purify it. Kansal brushed his teeth and spat out the black paste. The Rajthanans maintained their rituals of cleanliness even when camping out in the wilds. They were a puzzling people, but the way they stuck to their habits was impressive.

Jack clambered to his feet and soon had his things packed away on his horse. Sengar rode over to him and motioned with his head for him to continue.

Jack massaged his forehead and studied the ground ahead of him. There would still be no ordinary tracks to follow – the rain would have destroyed them all – so he would have to use his power again. He hesitated. His chest smarted with each breath and he felt as though he were floating as he walked along. Was he strong enough to continue?

He drew out Katelin's necklace for a moment, kissed it. Maybe Katelin would help him, or God. Had he been a good enough Christian for God to help him?

Wearily, he sat and closed his eyes. He tried to will the trance to come on, but in doing that he only distracted himself. Meditation was not about trying, it was about not trying.

'The will cannot help you,' Jhala had told him. 'It will only hinder your progress. You have to let go of the will, otherwise you will never break through the illusion of this world.'

The illusion of the material world was a favourite topic of Jhala's. He'd once told Jack, 'Your soul dwells in the spirit realm and always has done. But your mind reflects your soul, and so your soul comes to be confused. It imagines it is part of the material world. But once you break through this illusion you will see that you are, have always been, free.'

A bolt of pain shot through Jack's chest. His eyes sprang open. His ears were ringing and what was visible of the gloomy surroundings seemed to reel slowly about him. He shook his head and the world stopped turning. The pain in his chest subsided to a steady ache.

Damn it. He was right out of the meditation now.

He tried again, calming himself, trying to let go and give himself over to whatever was offered to him. He put himself in the hands of God, or karma, or the forces of the spirit realm, or whatever was in charge of this world.

And it worked. The yantra steadied and he jumped into the trance, which instantly blotted out his pain and tiredness. He opened his eyes and saw hundreds of patches of dull silver dotting the ground ahead. The bright trail of the rebels' horses stood out clearly, and he focused solely on this, making the other trails flicker and then disappear.

He climbed on to his horse and they rode out. But he sensed his strength draining away within minutes. Soon it was as though he hadn't slept at all. His eyes watered and he had to rub them to keep them clear enough to see the trail.

Blink.

He'd snapped unconscious again. He slumped forward in the saddle with his face just above the horse's mane. The animal jerked nervously and let out a small whinny.

'Casey.' Sengar rode up beside him. 'Pull yourself together.'

'I'm fine.'

'Merton's miles away now. What are you playing at?'

'Nothing.'

'Just remember—'

Jack nudged his horse forward so that he wouldn't have to listen to the Captain. For a moment his only thought was that he'd like to see Sengar dead one day.

The valley opened on to a plain and the trail continued to the north-west.

He rode on for a few more minutes until he felt himself slipping away again. The ground dragged at him like a magnetic force and he grasped at the sattva around him with his mind, as if that could prevent him from falling. But it was no good – he couldn't hold on.

He released his mental focus and was immediately flung out of the trance. The air seared the inside of his throat as he gulped it down. But at least he stayed on the horse and continued riding forward without Sengar noticing that anything had happened.

He calmed himself, and his heart rate and breathing eased. His whole body hurt when he coughed and sneezed.

The sattva trail had now vanished, but the countryside was relatively flat and the rebels had followed a straight path across it. Could he assume that William had continued in the same direction? It was hard to know. He had no idea where William was headed. But his friend was no longer weaving across the downs – he probably thought he'd thrown his pursuers at the river. So Jack decided to keep on straight and hope for the best. He had little choice as he had no strength for further meditation.

A cup of first light appeared across the hills and picked out the copses, rocks and clumps of grass. Jack glanced at Sengar, who stared straight ahead, features silvered.

The sun had risen by the time they reached the edge of the plain and again entered the hills. The cloud thinned to a blotchy splatter and a warm wind dried out most of Jack's clothing. He felt stronger now and was breathing almost normally. When he sensed the quiver of a powerful sattva stream, he decided to try his power again.

'Wait a moment,' he called over to Sengar. 'I need to check the trail.'

They all stopped and Sengar paced about on his horse while Jack meditated. Jack prayed he hadn't made a mistake in assuming which direction William had travelled in. If the rebels had veered off, he would miss the trail and then he would have to retrace his steps and start all over again.

The stream was one of the strongest he'd been in for years. He began smelting almost the moment he shut his eyes and the sattva flowed into him without him needing to reach for it. He entered the trance quickly, with none of the previous struggle.

He opened his eyes and looked around. He saw sattva trails everywhere, but not those of the rebels. His heart sped. William must have changed direction after all. Jack had lost the tracks and wasted the whole morning.

But then he saw a glint, like a fragment of glass reflecting the sun, on a rise off to the right. He squinted and noticed another glint near to the first. Then a third. Could it be?

He climbed back on to his mare. 'Follow me.'

They clattered over the undulating ground and Jack saw the dots of light brighten and lengthen until they blazed beneath the morning sun. Relief flooded through him; he could see the distinctive sattva marks of the almost fifty horses.

But as he turned to follow the trail up towards a saddle, the pain blossomed in his chest and his lungs felt thin as parchment. He observed all this distantly, like some fascinating storm seen far out at sea, but he knew he was in trouble. He couldn't stay in the trance for much longer – it was taking too much of a toll.

He peered at the saddle rising above him. A single pointed rock jutted above the skyline, and just to the side of it he could make out the silver of the trail. At least if he kept on towards the rock he would be on the right track.

He let himself skip out of the meditation and the pain tore through his chest. For a second he was sure he would die. He shut his eyes. Was this it?

But then the pain subsided, like waves retreating across the shore, and he fought to regain his breath.

He broke into a fit of coughing and had to stop and drink some water.

'What the hell's wrong now?' Sengar asked.

'Nothing.'

'Merton's getting away. Is that your plan?'

'No.'

'Then bloody get on with it.'

Jack led the way up the slope, the warmth of the sun revitalising him a little. As the heat intensified, the ground breathed dampness.

Half an hour later, as they arrived at the pointed rock, he told Sengar they would have to stop again.

'Why?' Sengar asked.

'The trail. I need to check it.'

'Why do you keep losing it?'

'It's difficult. The rain . . .' He didn't even have the energy to say more.

Sengar went silent and scanned the surroundings with his glass, gripping it so tightly his knuckles whitened.

Jack sat and meditated in the shade of the rock. The horses' hooves crunched behind him as the cavalrymen paced in circles and he could hear Lefevre grumbling to his comrades in French.

'He's not well,' Kansal said to Sengar in Rajthani. His voice was lowered, but Jack could still easily hear him. 'Heart, I reckon. Maybe we have to think of something else.'

'Something else?' Sengar said. 'You going to track Merton yourself?'

'No, sir. I just thought—'

'Casey has to find Merton. He has no choice.'

Jack wondered for a moment whether Kansal knew about Elizabeth and the impending execution. It didn't sound as though he did. Jhala and Sengar had probably kept it quiet – it was their own private arrangement with Jack.

He tried to forget all these concerns, all these ripples across his mind. He felt the air passing in and out of his nostrils, then brought up the image of the yantra. Everything around him went quiet and his skin tingled and shimmered. The spot in the centre of his forehead throbbed.

Sleep opened below him. Not even sleep, but a chasm of darkness that would be more like a coma. He was tempted to let go and fall into it. It would be so easy. His limbs felt heavy and were pulling him down and down. Sengar, Kansal, the French, the trail, William, even England were slipping away from him and it was all so calm. If he let go now it would be over. Bliss. Perhaps this was what Jhala had always meant when he talked about defeating the illusion of existence.

But Jack fought off these thoughts, as if sweeping aside cobwebs. It wasn't yet time to let go.

He pulled himself back from the darkness. He could hear the horses again and Sengar and Kansal talking and the wind buffeting his ears . . .

The yantra went perfectly still.

Energy crackled up his spine and his mind unfolded into that vast and sacred space.

He lifted his eyelids and the trail dazzled him immediately – he was sitting right on top of it. The ribbons twisted and tangled down the slope on the far side of the saddle and flowed across a plateau.

A shudder passed through his torso. Then another – stronger this time. His hands shook and his teeth chattered. He tried to stop it, but his body wouldn't obey him any longer. The muffled, distant pain ripened in his chest and he knew the moment he left the trance it would be severe.

Blink.

He lost consciousness for a moment. He swallowed and gasped air.

Blink.

It happened again. He seemed to be vanishing completely, slipping over to the spirit realm. He struggled to draw in more sattva.

Blink.

He couldn't hold on for much longer. He would have to leave the trance. He quickly surveyed the plateau and memorised the path the rebels had taken. He could see the trail disappearing into a patch of trees in the distance.

Blink.

He jumped out of the trance and fell forward, limp and unable even to put up his arms to protect himself. His head thumped on the ground.

He heard voices. Arms lifted him back up again.

'Casey. Casey!' Sengar's voice.

He opened his eyes and everything looked watery and unstable, but he blinked until the Captain's face came into focus. 'I'm all right. I can get up.'

To prove the point, he dragged himself to his feet and stood swaying with his head whirling in the clouds. He staggered towards his horse and the ground rolled and bucked beneath him. He fell against the mare, the animal snorting, then grasped the saddle, got one foot in the stirrup and heaved himself up.

'Perhaps a break, sir,' Kansal said.

'No,' Sengar replied. 'Men, back on your horses.'

Jack clung to the reins and nudged his horse down the slope. The day seemed overly bright now and everything he looked at hurt his eyes. The wound in his chest pulsed.

They reached the bottom of the incline and then set off across the plateau. He looked up repeatedly to check the position of the yew trees where the trail had disappeared; if he could just keep on towards those trees then at least he would be going in the right direction. But what then? He couldn't go into the trance again. There was no strength left in him. None at all.

He reached the line of yews and came out on the edge of a shallow basin, where he paused, his breathing slow and harsh.

Which way would William have gone next? He studied the ground. The basin was about a mile wide – William would probably have headed straight across, rather than wasting time going around the side.

But riding down the short slope, his horse skidding in the mud, he started to doubt his reasoning. Maybe William had taken a different route? Maybe he'd gone to the left or right, rather than straight ahead?

Jack had failed – he was sure of it now. He would have to rest for at least a day before he was strong enough to try his power, and by then William would be long gone. He saw Elizabeth in the cell, hair in tangled clumps, greasy tears on her cheeks. He was failing his daughter.

He stopped for a moment at the bottom of the incline and noticed a rocky outcrop jutting from the edge of the slope off to the right. It would be a good place to make camp – the best place he'd seen for miles. It made him think . . .

No, what was he thinking? He was getting confused.

But then he considered it further. William and the rebels would have believed they were no longer being followed. Perhaps they would risk stopping.

It was a remote hope, he knew, but he had to try. He led the way over to the overhang.

'Where are you going now?' Sengar snapped.

'Just need to take a look at something.'

'You'd better not be wasting our time, Casey.'

They arrived at the shelf, which was large enough to form a

shallow cave with the shadow thick beneath it. Jack dismounted and his feet almost gave way. He wheezed, clung to the side of the saddle, steadied himself, then walked towards the overhang. Sengar climbed down and followed him.

They had to stoop to enter the cave and it took a moment for Jack's eyes to adjust. In front of him were the remains of a campfire, surrounded by boot prints. Off to the left, just outside the overhang, were the thicker indentations left by a group of horses. He crossed to the hoof prints, bent slowly and studied the markings. His sight was blurry at first and he had to blink several times before he could see clearly. He saw the horseshoe worn on the left side, the shoe with the missing nail, even a set of boot prints with the right foot turning slightly inward.

He almost fainted as the relief rushed over him.

He stood with difficulty and turned to Sengar. The Captain was staring at him with his moustache a crisp line.

'It's them.' Jack's voice was cracked. 'They made camp here last night, then left this morning, after the rain. Tracks are fresh. They're about half a day ahead of us.'

Sengar smiled, his moustache parting. 'Must've thought they'd thrown us. Otherwise they never would have stopped. Well done, Casey.'

They pressed on into the afternoon, spurred by the discovery of the campsite. Jack could hear the French laughing and joking behind him, no doubt anticipating getting their hands on the infamous Ghost. Jack felt a ripple in his stomach. William didn't deserve to be killed by French Mohammedans.

The trail was easy to follow – the prints were deep in the damp ground and the rebels had made no effort to conceal their tracks. As the day wore on, he recovered a little. The ache in his chest remained and every muscle in his body was tired, but he was getting stronger now that he no longer needed to enter the trance.

Afternoon faded to evening and the hills turned gold and then grey. As the light dimmed, he held a lantern to light the way, but his eyes were raw and the prints became too difficult to make out. There was no point continuing. He would only lose the trail in the dark and he couldn't use his power until he'd revived further.

'Can't go on,' he said eventually.

'Very well, we'll stop here,' Sengar said. 'Let's just hope the rebels have also made camp tonight.'

Jack sat near to the fire, wrapped in a blanket. He shivered and sneezed, but at least the pain in his chest had gone and he could breathe more freely. He watched the sparks from the fire rise into the night, souls floating to heaven.

Kansal walked over to him. 'You need to eat.'

'I've eaten a little.'

'I should be practise my English.' Kansal spoke broken English, with a heavy accent.

'It's all right, sir. There's no need.'

Kansal smiled and switched back to Arabic. 'You're probably right. My English is still terrible. French dialects aren't much better.'

Rajthanan officers were required to learn only Arabic, but some made an effort over time to learn the native languages of their men.

Kansal reminded Jack of the subalterns who'd been sent to the regiment from time to time. Those young men, fresh from Rajthana, had often been enthusiastic, but usually had no experience whatsoever. As sergeant it had been Jack's job to teach them the ways of the army, and in particular the customs of the English soldiers.

Kansal squatted next to Jack. 'It's quite a skill you have – the tracking, I mean. How do you do it?'

'Born with it.'

'A native siddha – heard about it, but never thought I'd meet one.'

'Well, there you go, then.'

'So, you could track from when you were a child?'

Jack sighed. He wasn't a sergeant now and didn't need to teach anyone. 'I could track in the ordinary way when I was young. My father taught me. Sattva tracking I learnt in the army.'

He remembered well the day when, after six months of Jhala's training, he'd finally been able to smelt sattva and hold the yantra still at the same time. The glowing trails had bloomed over the ground before him, and he'd immediately understood what they were and how to use them. That was the strange thing about the powers – once you got a yantra right, you automatically understood how to use the power. The information flowed into you as if you'd always known it.

Apparently it was typical for a native siddha's power to match his skills. Jack was a tracker, therefore he had a sattva-tracking power. William had been a poacher, therefore he could use his power to cover his tracks.

'Yes, I heard you were in the army,' Kansal said. 'Sergeant, wasn't it?'

Jack looked at the ground and sneezed a couple of times.

'Well, I should let you rest.' Kansal stood. 'Early start tomorrow.'

Jack thought for a moment, then grasped a clump of grass and handed it to Kansal.

Kansal's face slackened with surprise. 'That's very kind. You know?'

Jack nodded. He'd learnt the traditional Rajthanan gesture from Jhala. Apparently, centuries ago, Mohammedan sultans had ruled northern India. The ancestors of the Rajthanans had been forced to hide from the sultans' armies, sometimes having nothing to eat but grass. Rajthanans, when camping, remembered those dark times by placing grass under their pillows and their scimitars beside them, should they need to move again in a hurry.

Kansal namasted solemnly and took the grass.

Jack watched him walk back to the fire. He was a good lad. In another time Jack could have been his sergeant. But they weren't living in another time, and there was no point in thinking about things like that.

He gazed at the flames. Four days had passed since Jhala had given him his mission. But that still left three and a half weeks to find William. If he could just keep going, just keep following the trail – that was all he needed to do.

8

Captain Sengar sat on his horse and studied the terrain through his spyglass. His moustache rose and fell gently. It was a clear day, with little hint of the previous rains. Thick forest, sizzling with insects, smothered the hills to either side.

Jack sneezed. He felt cold, despite the warm day, and his bones ached. But at least the ride that morning had been easy and the tracks had been simple to follow, without him even needing to use his power. A crack of pain crossed his chest from time to time, but it was less severe than the day before.

Sengar stopped and adjusted the glass, his gaze fixed on one point in the distance. He gave an oily smile, handed the glass to Kansal and pointed into the hills. 'Smoke.'

Jack looked to where Sengar had indicated, and even without a glass he could make out two grey cords rising from the trees several miles away.

'You sure it's them?' Kansal asked.

'There's no one else out here,' Sengar said.

It was true – they'd been riding through wilderness without seeing a single other person. And the tracks had been sparse, mainly animals. But on the other hand it could be woodsmen, or bandits.

They trotted ahead into the speckled darkness beneath the trees. The trail led along a track overgrown with brambles, and the trees were close together and shaggy with vines. The sound of birds and insects was loud enough for them to hear over the tread of the horses and the jangle of their kit.

After an hour they came to a clearing on the summit of a low mound. The smoke was much nearer now, straight ahead and only two miles away.

'Back into the trees,' Sengar said, and they rode quickly across the open space.

They went more slowly now and everyone was alert, glancing into the depths of the forest. The intricate mesh of green shadow and tree trunks prevented them from seeing much further than ten feet. Jack, still at the head of the party, was mindful of the last time they'd encountered William and he cursed Sengar for not giving him a weapon. What was he supposed to do if they were attacked again? At least he still had the knife – he could feel the cold metal against his skin.

Something rustled in the greenery off to the left. He stopped his horse and peered into the lattice of branches. He heard the sound again – it was coming from around thirty feet away.

The cavalrymen drew their pistols and cocked the hammers.

'Wait for my command.' Sengar held up his hand and gazed into the gloom.

The rustle grew louder and began moving towards them, slowly at first, then picking up speed. Jack's hand crept towards the knife. The cavalrymen pointed their pistols into the woods and squinted. Twigs cracked and leaves shuffled. Whatever was making the sound was large and running now. It was only a few feet away.

And then he saw the squat form of a boar tearing through the undergrowth. The creature burst out of the trees, shot across the path and disappeared into the woods on the other side, giving a squeal as it went.

Several of the cavalrymen chuckled.

'Your dinner, *Ros Porc*,' Lefevre called up to Jack.

'Silence!' Sengar looked at Jack. 'Carry on, Casey.'

They continued along the path and after fifteen minutes the trees thinned and opened into a glade, where a stream slithered across stones. On the far side of the clearing, the smoke rose in two grey lines that evaporated in the fierce blue of the sky. Jack sniffed and smelt the faint trace of the burning wood.

Sengar turned to his men. 'We'll scout ahead. Lieutenant Kansal, take three men to the left. Fire twice if you're spotted. Casey, Lefevre, you come with me. The rest of you, wait here. If you hear shots, ride straight at them – where that smoke's rising from.'

Sengar led Jack, Lefevre and another cavalryman into the forest, skirting the glade and crossing the stream where it wriggled back into the trees. The ground sloped upward and the undergrowth thickened.

They dismounted, tethered the horses and then Sengar took them uphill. They crept, bent double. Jack's old training came back to him and he trod silently. The lumbering cavalrymen were noisy by comparison and he became concerned the enemy would hear them. He searched the woods for any subtle movement, any twinge of a branch or quiver of a leaf, that could indicate there was someone watching. But he saw nothing.

The climb was steep. Soon he was panting, his chest sodden with pain. He stopped, leant against a tree and tried to get his breath back. The others continued up the slope and he had to scramble to catch up with them.

He came out of the trees and on to a ledge of exposed rock at the top of the hill. Sengar and the cavalrymen were already lying down and peering over the edge.

Below was a cliff face at the base of which, half concealed by trees, stood two men. Both had scimitars at their sides, and two muskets leant against a stump nearby. The men appeared relaxed and were talking idly to each other.

Sengar raised the glass for a better view, then whispered, 'It's them. I recognise the one with the short hair from the ambush.'

Jack stared. He couldn't make out the men's faces, but he could see that one man's hair was closely cropped, while the other's was long and hung over his eyes. The long-haired man had his arm in what appeared to be a sling.

The short-haired man looked up the hill, to the right, and began gesturing excitedly to his comrade. The long-haired man stood up straight and grasped his musket with his good arm.

Sengar frowned and glanced behind him. 'Damn it.'

Jack turned and looked up too. Trees covered the entire slope and near the top, amongst the dark green, a sharp light blinked on and off. He recognised it straight away – a heliograph.

They'd been seen.

The two men below ran off into the woods. Sengar drew his pistol and fired twice into the air, the sound ringing in Jack's ears.

'Back to the horses,' Sengar said and charged down the slope, with Lefevre loping after him.

Jack followed as quickly as he could, sliding and skidding and grasping at branches to stop himself from falling. His breath caught in his throat. By the time he got to the horses the others had already mounted and Sengar was glowering at him.

Jack jumped on to his mare and they rode off towards the smoke, which was still visible between the trees. The main bulk of their party would already be ahead of them and Jack listened for the sounds of a fight, but heard nothing.

They broke into the open ground and charged across the stream, the wet stones crashing like smashed glass. Back amongst the trees, they slowed as they wound their way along the path.

Minutes later they burst into a clearing containing around ten army tents and a larger marquee. A fire, which had burnt down to the embers, stood in the centre. A smaller fire with a black pot hanging over it lay near the perimeter. The French had dismounted and were searching the tents.

Kansal rode over. 'There's no one. Must have just got away. Left most of their kit behind.'

'Casey, which way?' Sengar shouted.

Jack rode around the edge of the clearing, dodging the guy ropes of the tents. He tried to stay calm as he searched for tracks, but his chest felt crushed. Everywhere he saw the signs of a hasty departure – the sandy soil had been kicked around by men and horses in a hurry. On the far side of the camp he found the point where the horses had been picketed. The animals' hoof prints and dung were thick. A fresh trail led around the edge of the glade and then struck off down a path.

He took a deep breath, his heart quickening, and called to the others.

They charged down the path in single file, Jack at their head and Sengar immediately behind. The track appeared to be little used and branches scratched at them as they raced past. It was hot and close beneath the canopy.

Jack glanced repeatedly at the ground to check that the trail was still there; the markings were fresh and easy to make out. He couldn't hear the rebels – or see them through the dense forest – but they would be no more than ten minutes ahead. It seemed impossible now for William to escape. It was over.

But after fifteen minutes, the path widened and then forked, one route going west and the other east. Jack drew his horse to an abrupt halt and glanced at the ground. The main group of rebels had gone east.

But a single horse had gone west.

'Which way?' Sengar shouted. 'Hurry up, damn you.'

'Wait a moment.' Jack jumped from his saddle and inspected the ground. The single horse had undoubtedly carried a rider, but who? Was it William? He couldn't tell from the tracks. The markings of the horseshoes were all different, but he didn't know which animal belonged to his friend.

Cunning. William still had a few surprises left.

Jack would have to use his power – there was no other way – and even with that it was going to be difficult.

He sat on the ground and crossed his legs.

'We're wasting time, Casey,' Sengar said.

But Jack ignored him, closed his eyes and began to meditate.

Sengar paced up and down on his horse and muttered curses to Kansal in Rajthani.

Jack focused all his attention on the yantra. He hadn't used his power for a day and he felt stronger than the last time he'd meditated. All the same, he found he was in only a medium stream and he struggled to enter the trance.

The yantra flickered and bounced in the pool of his mind. He saw Elizabeth as a child again and although he tried to shake off the memory, it kept returning . . .

She was sitting next to him on the riverbank near their cottage. The autumn sky was swollen with cloud and the river was sluggish and grey. In the distance, a hawk dipped and hovered above the fields.

He was telling her, yet again, the story of the quest for the Holy Grail, but then he noticed a tear well in her eye. It wasn't hard to know what she was thinking.

'You missing her?' he asked.

Elizabeth nodded, her bottom lip jutting out. Katelin's death had been hard on her – she was only seven.

Jack drew her to him, hugged her, felt her small head press into his side. 'You had enough of the story?'

'No,' she said with a ring of determination.

'All right. I'll carry on, then.'

She'd always been fascinated by the old stories of King Arthur and the Knights of the Round Table. He'd been telling them to her for years, just as parents had been telling their children in England and Wales for centuries. But the search for the Holy Grail was the part that enthralled her the most.

Once again he told her how the country had been in the clutches of black magic, how King Arthur's knights set out in search of the Grail in order to free the land, how only three knights – Bors, Perceval and Galahad – were sufficiently pure in heart to find the Grail castle, how Galahad – the purest of the three – touched the Grail and so released the land from enchantment, how Galahad was later taken up to heaven, and how Bors alone returned to Camelot to tell the tale to King Arthur.

'I'll find the Grail one day,' Elizabeth said.

'Will you, now? So long as you don't run off again.'

'No, but I will find it.'

Jack glanced at her and the steel in her gaze surprised him for a moment . . .

Then the memory dissolved and Jack found himself in the trance, almost without realising it at first. He was surprised at how easily it had come. When he opened his eyes, the forest crystallised into sharp focus and the bright, fresh tracks wove before him like luminous smoke.

He concentrated on the trail of the single rider first, staring at the shining threads until blue spots floated before his eyes. He saw the long strands left by the horse mingling with the pearl-necklace bundles of the rider. Were they the markings left by William? To be sure he would need to know William's exact size and weight and the actions he was performing as he swept past. But Jack had only seen William briefly at the train line and his friend had obviously changed in the past nine years. Despite staring at the trail for more than a minute he couldn't tell for certain whether it was William's.

He had only one option left – imagining himself into his quarry's mind. Every tracker needed this skill, but it could be amplified by the trance, although it was still prone to error.

Jhala had said to him, 'This type of enhancement is more to do with the imagination than yoga, but your power can assist you. Be wary, though. It is unreliable and not to be trusted.'

He breathed slowly. His trance deepened and the surroundings now faded to a translucent white. He drew in more sattva and the sweet smell grew stronger. Far away, pain unfolded in his chest and his lungs felt bruised. He shivered. He couldn't hold on for much longer.

He tried to imagine he was William, tried to think like his

friend. They'd been close for fourteen years, shared a tent on campaign, fought together, tracked the enemy in the mountains, drank together, ate together. Jack had known everything about William, but had his friend changed? Did he think differently now? William had joined the mutiny – William, the loyal soldier. He must have changed a good deal to betray the army like that.

Jack tried to clear his mind of doubts. He had to believe he was William.

He imagined himself at the rebel camp, hearing that the enemy were riding towards them. He shouted to his men to mount their horses. He led them through the forest and then to the fork in the path.

And then what did he do?

He stopped and looked back. The enemy were near, but invisible through the trees. He made a decision. He knew they couldn't win in a fight. They couldn't defeat the siddha officer and they couldn't escape from Jack, who would track them wherever they went. But he was also sure it was him they wanted – he was the rebel commander, the Ghost. He would sacrifice himself. He would ride off on his own to draw the enemy after him and leave his men to continue the fight without him.

And so he rode to the west and his men to the east. That was what had happened. Jack was sure.

Jack slipped out of the trance and the pain thumped him in the chest. He gasped for breath so loudly Kansal and two of the cavalrymen jumped to the ground and rushed to his side. Still sitting cross-legged, he slumped forward and coughed up strings of spit. One of the cavalrymen handed him a canteen and he swallowed a mouthful of warm water. He felt a little stronger now and managed to stand.

He turned to face Sengar. The Captain's moustache was tight and his eyes were tiny glints in the dim light.

'He went this way.' Jack gestured towards the path heading west. 'Alone.'

Sengar grinned slowly. 'We've got him.'

They spurred their horses down the path. The way widened enough for them to ride two abreast and Sengar rode alongside Jack. The trail was still fresh – William was only around twenty minutes ahead of them.

At each tread of his horse, Jack felt a jab in his chest. It would be typical of William to sacrifice himself; he'd always had a strong sense of dharma and loyalty to his company. That was why he'd been such a popular sergeant and why the men had followed him without question, even when they distrusted the Rajthanan officers above him.

The path climbed and arced about a hill so that eventually they were travelling north. They burst out of the trees and into the open. Ahead, the path cut across a grass-covered slope. Below them the scarp fell away into a valley, while above it was dotted with scrub and rocks all the way to the summit. William's trail continued along the path.

They galloped forward, following the curve of the hillside. Forest appeared ahead in the distance. William must have already made it into the cover of the trees.

A blast ruptured the hill. A wall of air smashed into Jack from behind and threw him forward, his mare slipping away from under him. For a long moment he was flying, then the grass rushed up at him and he landed on his side with a crunch.

He couldn't breathe. Pain welled on one side, in his ribs. He smelt sattva and his ears whined from the explosion.

He gasped for air, took some in. He swallowed and breathed again, then sat up, flinching at the pain.

Looking around, he felt he'd been plunged into a dream. The previously empty hillside was now engulfed by dust and a fine golden powder that shimmered in the sunlight. Dimly, he could make out men and horses lying in the grass, some moving, some still. He heard shouts and screams.

What the hell had caused the explosion?

Brittle musket fire started. Up the slope, figures moved like phantoms in the dust, crouching and darting behind rocks and scrub.

Another ambush.

Dabs of flame erupted at each shot and bullets peppered the slope. He was completely exposed as he lay in the grass, and he looked around quickly for cover. Thirty feet above him was a line of rocks. Although they were only waist height, they were his best hope at that moment. He went to crawl towards them, but pain streaked along his side as he moved. He looked down and felt along his tunic, finding no tear in the material or signs of blood. At least he hadn't been hit, so far as he could tell. He might have broken something, though.

A bullet hushed past his cheek. He would have to get up to those rocks as quickly as he could.

He started to crawl again and the pain lanced his side. Gritting his teeth, he pressed on. His breath came in jagged clumps, and tremors crossed his chest.

As he drew closer to the rocks he could see that the surviving cavalrymen were now huddled there in a row, firing blindly up the slope. Grey smoke squirted from their pistols.

He hauled himself up and sat leaning against a low boulder. The French were spread out to his left, but in the haze he couldn't tell how many they were. They emptied their firearms in rapid succession and then fiddled about with powder flasks, percussion caps and ramrods. They used the new multi-chambered pistols, which could fire six shots without reloading, as well as carbines.

The glittering dust from the explosion was drifting away, but was being replaced by clouds of powder smoke. Bullets rattled and screamed on the rocks. Jack's chest felt pressed by a heavy weight.

The nearest Frenchman peered over a boulder to fire and then jerked as a shot smacked into his head. He staggered back, grasping at the side of his face, slipped on a clump of grass and rolled downhill a few feet. His body came to a halt and lay still, half hidden by the wreaths of smoke.

The Frenchman's pistol lay where it had fallen, less than five feet away from Jack. It gleamed softly and the intricate engravings along the barrel seemed to shift in the grainy light.

Jack turned, the pain shooting through his side. Finally he could get something to defend himself with. He began to drag himself along the line of rocks.

A hand clamped down on his shoulder. He jumped slightly, looked behind him and saw Lefevre with a greedy smile on his lips. The Sergeant's cheeks were flushed and alive with red filigree. He shook his head. 'You leave that to me, *Ros Porc*.'

Jack's hand crept towards the concealed knife. Lefevre was unarmed and seemed to have lost even his scimitar in the explosion. Jack was breathing hard. He wanted that pistol and he wouldn't mind having a try at Lefevre either. But he was also weak and he wasn't sure he could win in a fight – the Frenchman could easily take the knife and use it against him.

The Sergeant grunted, and Jack let him push past and crawl towards the pistol.

Lefevre stopped when he reached a gap between the rocks – he would have to cross that gap to get at the firearm. He waited a few seconds, shifted on his haunches, then shot out across the open space. But he stopped suddenly halfway, bent double and slid to the ground. A red welt expanded across the middle of his chest. He put his hand to the wound, then lifted it and stared at the blood on his fingers.

Jack crawled along until he reached the edge of the gap. Lefevre was clawing at the earth, but didn't have the strength to drag himself out of the line of fire. He made gasping sounds and when he looked up blood filtered from his mouth, down his chin and into his beard. '*Ros Porc*.'

Jack glanced around. The closest Frenchmen were fifteen feet away at least and almost concealed by the smoke. Nobody had noticed Lefevre get hit – they were all too busy trying to survive themselves.

Lefevre's face seethed as he strained to raise himself further. His eyes locked on Jack. 'Pull me over there.' His voice was etched out of granite. 'Now.'

Jack clenched his hand into a fist. Why should he risk his life to help Lefevre? A bullet struck the side of the rock near his head, producing a puff of grit. Another two bullets were sucked up by the ground.

'*Ros Porc*.'

Then a shot hit the Sergeant in the throat, flinging out a spray of blood. A droplet landed on the back of Jack's hand. Lefevre slumped to the ground. His chest still moved faintly and with each breath a high-pitched wheeze came from somewhere. His fingers twitched.

Jack edged back from the opening. He could still see the pistol, but the bullets were hailing down and he couldn't risk trying to get across to it. He coughed and the pain in his side made him moan. Black spots spun before his eyes. He heard Lefevre groaning like a wounded bull and he even felt sorry for him . . . but only for a moment.

Then he caught a dark flicker of movement out of the corner of his eye. Something leapt over the boulders and slipped up to the path a few feet above. He raised himself until he could see through the gap in the rocks.

What on earth?

Sengar stood on the path, directly in the line of fire, with his scimitar raised in defiance. He held his left hand before him and jerked it in a circular motion. The rebel muskets spat bullets down the slope, but a crackling netting rushed out from Sengar's outstretched palm and spun about him like strings of fireflies. The bullets sparkled and vanished as they battered the netting, and Sengar remained unharmed.

Now the Captain balled his hand into a fist, muttered some

words, then opened his hand again and raised his palm. Bullets continued to snarl into the netting. The air shivered and wrinkled and formed into a giant globe. With a rumble, the ball burst into flame, rolled and writhed for a moment, then shot up the slope. It tore through the powder smoke and hit the ground with a shattering roar that jolted Jack in the chest. A blast of sattva-tinted wind hit him in the face. Ash and earth and smoke jetted into the sky.

The Frenchmen gave a cheer. 'Allah is great!'

The musket fire eased. Jack thought he could make out shouts from the rebels above, but when he looked up all he could see was the thick black smoke from the explosion.

Sengar, still surrounded by his glittering mantle, shut his eyes and mouthed a few more words. There was a shrill whistle further up the slope, then a white flash. A droplet of gold fire arced downhill, picking up speed as it descended. Sengar opened his eyes, frowned, appeared confused. He waved his hand quickly in a circle, but it was too late. The droplet slapped into the ground about ten feet from him. The earth burst open and disgorged a fountain of dust and stone. Jack was flung back against the rock and everything went black for a moment.

He opened his eyes, spat dust from his mouth. He had no idea what had caused the explosion, but the smell of sattva was thick on the hill. He glanced at Lefevre, who now lay silent and still, coated in a patina of dust.

Musket fire clattered against the rocks, just as hot as before. He looked up again through the opening and was astonished to see Sengar still standing on the path, apparently unharmed. The netting sizzled and encircled the Captain as he held his clenched fist to his forehead, eyes closed in concentration.

A golden glow appeared uphill and began rushing down.

What the hell was that?

Within seconds a bearded Indian man in an orange tunic and turban burst through the smoke, an aura of gold blazing around him. He ran quickly, unbelievably quickly, his feet skimming the uneven ground. He held up his hand, palm open, and droplets of fire sped out towards Sengar.

The Captain opened his eyes wide and his jaw dropped. He waved his hand in front of him and the netting sped faster. The droplets sparked as they hit the strands. He seemed to fight desperately to maintain his defence, dropping the scimitar and working with both hands to keep the weaving strings moving. The fire droplets thickened and crackled about him. The Indian man plummeted down. More droplets. Then an explosion that lit up the hill. For a second everything was bright and stark and frozen.

The pulse hit Jack in the chest. He stopped breathing, gasped for air. Blackness. He slid down, the ground embracing him gently.

9

Jack was aware of his pain, that was all – a sharp pain on one side of his ribs and a deeper, more general ache in his chest. But he was alive. He took a few breaths to confirm this. Yes, he was definitely alive and his heart was still beating.

He opened his eyes. William stood over him, scowling and pointing a musket straight at his chest. Jack studied his friend's face, noting the newer scars and dents cast over the old.

William's hand trembled as it rested against the trigger. For the first time in a long while Jack said a Hail Mary in his head.

Then William broke into a grin, his crooked teeth coming out of hiding. He lowered the musket. 'Jack Casey. Well, well.'

Jack coughed and found himself smiling despite everything.

William crouched down. Jack was sitting against a rock. He was still on the grass-covered slope, but the battle was over and the dust and smoke had cleared. He heard birds chirping in the distance and smelt wild flowers. Behind William, the rebels were busily packing their horses.

'He's awake, then.' The man with the long hair and his arm in a sling appeared beside William and leered at Jack. His two front teeth were missing. 'Shall I finish him off, then, sir?'

William shook his head. 'I'll talk to him.'

The long-haired man squinted at Jack for a moment, then looked back at William. He nodded slowly and walked off to join the others.

'Don't mind Harold,' William said. 'Just a keen young lad.'

Jack thought about the knife, but could no longer feel it stuck in his hose. He tried to sit up straight, but the pain was sharp in his side and he grimaced.

'Easy there.' William grinned. 'Getting a bit old for this, aren't you?'

Jack snorted. 'Could say the same about you.'

William chuckled and rubbed his shaven head with his large hand. 'Thought we'd lost you. You were out cold. If it wasn't for Kanvar there, you'd be dead.' He nodded towards the Indian man in the orange tunic, who stood aside from the others, gazing out at the green folds of the countryside.

Now Jack remembered – the man was a siddha and had attacked Sengar. Many questions formed in his head. 'A Rajthanan? You have a Rajthanan helping you?'

'He's not a Rajthanan. He's a Sikh.'

Jack had heard of the Sikhs, but had never met one. He'd been told they had their own country, separate from Rajthana, and had fought wars against the Rajthanans in the past. But he'd never fully believed that Indians would ever fight against each other.

'The Sikhs are our allies now, since the crusade started,' William said. 'They'd like to see us give the Rajthanans a kicking. They've sent siddhas to help. Kanvar's just joined us. Bit of extra firepower.' William grinned. 'Bet you lot didn't see that coming.'

'No.' Jack couldn't stop himself marvelling at William's cunning and audacity. 'You led us here, into the ambush. You knew we'd never guess you had a siddha.'

'That's right. I was sure you'd follow my trail. I see you haven't lost any of your talents.'

Jack smiled ruefully. 'Was that the plan all along? Since the first day.'

'No, it wasn't quite like that. Didn't know what we were dealing with at first. Didn't know *you* were with them for one thing. Thought we'd lost you at the Stour River, but I always have a backup plan – you know that. Gave us a bit of a shock when you showed up at the camp, but we put the plan into action straight away.'

Jack looked across the slope. There was no sign of the fight, except for two craters that had obliterated a section of the path. 'What about the others? The French?'

'All dead. No prisoners, you know how it is.'

'The officers too?'

William nodded.

'There was a young lieutenant—'

'He fought bravely.'

Jack paused. 'Good. He was a good officer. Would have made a good captain one day.'

William made the sign of the cross. 'May he rest in peace, in that case.'

'So . . . why keep *me* alive?'

William raised his eyebrows, then laughed. 'Jack, I would never . . . Look, you must've had your reasons for helping them.'

William hadn't changed. He was still as generous and loyal as he was tough. Jack felt a coil of sickness in his stomach when he thought how he'd hunted him. 'Yes, there is a reason.'

William eyed him closely. 'What?'

Should he tell William? Was there any point in lying now? 'They've got my daughter, Elizabeth. They say she's a rebel. She's due to be executed.'

'I see. And if you helped them, they would free her?'

Jack nodded. A blanket of shame settled over him.

William looked out over the hill, the sun bright across his craggy features. 'You were in a tough spot. I understand.'

'I don't expect you to—'

William held up his hand. 'There's no need to talk about it any more.'

They both fell silent.

Jack could see that the rebels had almost finished their packing.

'We're off to London,' William said. 'The war's changing. The Rajthanans have built up an army at Christchurch. They're marching on London. It'll be the decisive battle.'

Jack nodded, slowly absorbing this information. London – the stronghold of the rebel leader, Sir Gawain, and also of old King John III, who had somehow become caught up in the mutiny.

'When we're finished at London I'll bring a force to Poole,' William said. 'We'll get your daughter out.'

Jack's voice caught in his throat. 'They execute her in three and a half weeks.'

'It's three days' ride to London. Less than a week's forced march to Poole. We'll do it.'

Was William serious? Was he mad? 'You can't win. The Rajthanans are too strong.'

William's smile evaporated. 'We can win. We can definitely win. The Rajthanans don't have the will to fight in this country.'

Jack shook his head. 'They'll never give up the sattva.'

'You remember Ragusa?'

Jack hesitated. 'Of course.'

'Didn't look like we'd win there, did it? Outnumbered, outgunned. But we had spirit. It was us that won – the English.'

'With Rajthanan guns.'

'With our own blood. You were there. You saw it.'

'It's different. We had discipline. We had the Rajthanans running things.'

'And we still have discipline. Look at these men.' William motioned towards the rebels on the slope. 'They will fight to the death, each and every one of them. And there's thousands like them all over this country.'

'It's not enough. The Rajthanans have war avatars, better guns—'

William drew a dagger and glared at Jack. 'I tell you, we'll win.'

Jack stared back for several long seconds.

Then William's expression melted. 'Look what they've made us do. Two old friends. Fighting.'

Jack looked at the ground. 'It's not right.'

'You could join us.'

A dark thought crossed Jack's mind. If he joined the rebels he might get a chance to . . . to what? Kill William and take his body back to Poole?

William seemed to be considering this possibility as well. 'No. They've got you by the balls. I can see that.'

Jack nodded and sighed. He couldn't bring himself to deny it, and William would never trust him now anyway.

William called over to Kanvar. The Sikh moved suddenly, a statue come to life. He bounded across the slope like a mountain cat and squatted beside William. He was a young man, perhaps in his mid-twenties, with a thin face, black beard and wide, pale eyes.

'Will he be all right now?' William asked.

Kanvar leant forward, put his ear to Jack's chest, listened for a few seconds, then sat back again. He felt along Jack's side with his hand until Jack flinched from the pain, then he closed his eyes and hummed tunelessly for a few minutes. Jack noticed the scent of sattva building.

The Sikh was obviously a medical siddha. Jack had never been treated by one of those before. They were usually reserved for officers, if they were available at all, while the men were treated by ordinary doctors.

Kanvar jerked back slightly, opened his eyes and frowned. He stared at Jack's chest, as though he could see right through the tunic, even the skin.

'Sattva-fire?' William asked. He knew about Jack's accident – he'd been there when it happened.

'Very severe.' Kanvar met Jack's eyes. His voice was soft, with a thick accent. 'It is in your heart.'

'I know,' Jack said.

Kanvar shut his eyes again, hummed a little longer, then opened his eyes again and shook his head. 'Strange.'

'What?' Jack asked.

'I'm not sure . . . haven't seen this . . . have to think.' Kanvar muttered to himself in an Indian language, as if William and Jack had disappeared.

'We haven't got all day,' William said.

Kanvar looked up in surprise, as if he'd been interrupted while meditating. 'Oh. Yes.' He leapt up, strode to his horse and returned with a small brown vial, which he handed to Jack. 'This is jatamansi. Take one drop whenever you get an attack. You also have a broken rib. You need to be careful over the next week. You must let it heal.'

Jack took the bottle, examined it for a moment, then put it in his pocket. He was getting better medical advice these days than he'd ever had before.

Kanvar gave Jack a final stare with his pallid eyes, then left abruptly and walked across to his horse.

'Strange one, that.' William cocked his thumb at Kanvar. 'Useful, though.' He put his hand on Jack's shoulder. 'I'm going to have to leave you here. I'm sorry about your daughter. If there's anything I can do for her, I'll do it. I promise.'

Jack saw Elizabeth in the cell for a moment and he swallowed hard. 'William, why?'

'Why what?'

'The mutiny. You were a good soldier.'

William snorted. 'A good soldier. Yes, I did as my masters told me. And where did it get me?'

'You took the oath.'

'You still believe in that?'

Jack recalled sitting cross-legged before the regimental standard, staring at the three red lions running in a circle, repeating his oath of loyalty to the army.

His heart beat faster. Jhala had betrayed him. He'd followed his commander without question all those years, but that seemed to have counted for nothing once the mutiny started.

He didn't know what he believed in any more.

'I know in your heart you're with us.' William dug his hand

into the dry soil, raised it and let the grains run out between his fingers. 'This is our land. The land of our ancestors. The Rajthanans have taken it from us and we have to get it back.'

Jack watched the dust spirit away on the wind. William's goal was a dream that would never happen, but still, the slight tremble in his voice made Jack pause. William had always known how to inspire the men, encourage them when they were broken with tiredness and the task before them seemed hopeless. He was a good sergeant major.

The dust vanished and the breeze tugged at Jack's hair. He thought of Elizabeth again and it felt as though the ground were slowly sliding out from under him. William was leaving for London, and with him went Elizabeth's last chance.

'Well, you take care of yourself,' William said.

Jack couldn't speak. He was failing Elizabeth. He tried to move, but the pain in his side was too severe.

'You'll probably want this.' William took out Jack's knife, spun it in his fingers and dropped it, tip first, into the soil, where it quivered, catching the light. He then handed over a few dry rations wrapped in a cloth. 'You're going to have to walk back to Poole.' He motioned to the path running into the forest. 'That's the quick way back to the camp. Keep going straight. Ignore the turn-off. I'm sure you can find your way.'

William stood and turned to leave, then changed his mind. 'I'll look for you when all this is over. We'll have an ale or two.'

Jack nodded. He couldn't think of anything except Elizabeth. But as he watched William walk away, he realised it might be the last time he ever saw his friend. He wanted to call out something, but there was nothing to say.

The rebels filed past and William glanced down once, before leading his men away into the forest.

Harold looked down as well, shaking the hair out of his eyes and giving Jack a toothy sneer. 'Traitor.'

Soon they were gone.

Jack shivered. When he sneezed, a shock of pain crossed his chest. He leant against the rock, the sun on his face and the wind hushing the grass. For a moment the fight that had just taken place, the mutiny, London all seemed like a strange dream. But the thought of Elizabeth brought him back to reality.

He retrieved the knife from where it stood like a tiny burial cross, then climbed, wincing, to his feet. He found he could walk – he didn't feel as bad as he'd expected – but every time he turned his torso, even only slightly, his fractured rib lanced him.

He went up to the path and looked out across the endless, rolling green of England. The sky was deep blue with a range of white cloud far off to the north. The land of his ancestors. William had spoken well, as always, but it was just words. Empty words. William and the other rebel commanders were leading England towards a disaster. Thousands would die. Elizabeth would die.

He walked stiffly along the path in the direction William had taken. After a couple of minutes he stopped again. Bodies lay scattered a few feet down the slope. The French were on their backs, some with their mouths open and brows twisted, statues of pain, while others appeared to be sleeping peacefully. Lefevre looked calm, despite the jagged holes in his neck and chest.

Kansal and Sengar lay beside each other. Kansal had a dark-red wound in his stomach and his youthful face was pale. Sengar had no obvious injuries, and it was unnerving to see him lying there with his eyes open, as though he were still alive.

Jack tried to summon some satisfaction at seeing Sengar dead, but he felt nothing. What had Sengar said? *I'm not going to rot in this place.* It seemed, after all, that he would.

Jack crossed himself and walked on. He didn't know what he was doing or where he was going. Everything was pointless now that he'd lost his chance of saving Elizabeth.

He entered the cool forest and staggered downhill, tripping on tree roots. A stream bubbled beside the track and he stopped to drink. The water was icy, fresh and he drank for a long time. When he went to fill the water skin, he found he'd lost it at some point.

He stumbled on. After twenty minutes a path split off from the main track and headed east, the rebels' trail turning down this new route.

He paused. He could either walk straight along the main track, going back to the camp, and from there begin the long hike to Poole, or . . .

Was there really a choice? How could he even think of following the rebels? They were on horseback and riding as fast as they could to London, through wild and largely uninhabited countryside. He would never catch up with them. And even if he did, what was he going to do? Fight all of them single-handed? Capture William?

And yet, Jhala had said the pardon would only apply if William were brought back, dead or alive. If Jack went to Poole now, Elizabeth would be hanged. There would be nothing he could do about it.

On the other hand, if he followed the rebels, there was still hope, although the most remote hope imaginable. Maybe, somehow, he would be able to bring William back himself. It was madness and the task seemed impossible, but he couldn't give up on Elizabeth. He would rather die than give up.

He amazed himself as he turned to follow the rebels. But he also knew that it was his only choice, even though he was certain he would fail.

He walked all day without leaving the forest. He followed the horse tracks, as he'd been doing for days. The markings were emblazoned in his mind and even when he closed his eyes he could still see them.

The fever thickened within him, waves of hot and cold crossed his skin, and his broken rib sent lines of fire along his side. But at least the pain in his chest had receded to a vague heaviness.

As daylight faded, he tried to continue, using his power to follow the phosphorescent sattva trail. But he was too weak to stay in the trance for more than a few minutes. Finally, he slept in a hollow at the base of an ancient oak tree. In his dreams he walked on, following the trail through a dark and endless landscape.

He woke late, the sun already high in the sky. He was hot, far too hot. The fever made everything unreal and confusing, and for a moment he couldn't remember where he was or what he was doing.

He trudged on. The tracks were still easy to follow – the rebels had stuck to the path as it wound between the hills. The land levelled out and he guessed he'd travelled so far east that he'd reached Salisbury Plain. The trees thinned and he could see the sun clearly between the branches.

Late in the afternoon, cloud spread across the sky and then it started to rain. Drenched, shaking from the fever, he staggered on.

As night approached, he spotted large forms brooding behind the trees. He stopped, swaying, and made out the high walls of a building. He couldn't imagine what kind of structure would be out in the forest, but he needed shelter, so he left the track and pushed his way through the branches and brambles.

An ancient, crumbling wall, several storeys high, loomed before him. It was made of pale stone and covered in vines, but in places he could make out the remains of blue, geometric mosaics. Above rose an ethereal dome, also half buried by vines, and four broken minarets. The building was a mosque, a remnant of the old Caliphate, which had been predominant in the south-east of the country.

He walked until he found a hole in the wall, pushed aside a screen of vines and entered what must once have been a grand chamber. The area was enclosed on three sides by walls covered in arches and niches. The fourth side was open to the forest, the wall having fallen long ago. The rain outside descended in a glowing curtain. He smelt moss and undergrowth. Birds flew about inside the dome, roosting amongst the intricate series of ledges.

He sat in a corner and leant against the wall, shuddering. His face felt swollen from the heat of the fever, his side ached constantly and his lungs were compressed.

A metallic flash lit up the inside of the building, followed by a solemn crack of thunder. The rain came down harder, a crushed roar. Water drooled down from a gap in the wall opposite and smashed on the floor, the droplets forming a fine mist that wafted through the chamber.

The ruined building spun slowly in front of him. Sheet lightning flickered repeatedly, sending the elaborate stonework rearing up before him like a divine vision. He slipped in and out of his dreams so often that eventually he couldn't tell whether he was asleep or awake. He seemed to float in a half-lit world. Sweat snaked over his body and he trembled like a whipped animal as he coughed.

He could smell sattva. Strange. He wasn't meditating and he wasn't in a strong stream.

He drifted outside himself, as if in the trance. But it wasn't the trance and he couldn't see the glowing trails. At the same time, the smell of sattva grew stronger and his eyes and nose watered. His mind seemed to both spiral inward and expand out to engulf his surroundings. It was as though he were being enchanted by a strange mingling of sattva, the fever and his own dreams.

He was flying. The stars, the sun and the moon swirled within him. The world spun endlessly below: oceans, continents, mountains, forests, rivers, deserts, fields of ice.

He was outside time and could somehow see the grand procession of history, with its wars and empires and dynasties and kingdoms. From this great height it all played out in a moment. Cities rose from the dust and then crumbled back to the earth. Battles raged on torrid plains and were then smothered by green fields. Kings and queens ruled for a day, before they were sealed within tombs. Empires crawled across the world, then rotted away from within. All of it over in a fraction of a second.

He saw a succession of English rulers marching in a long line that stretched back into the darkness. There were the Romans, the men and women of that ancient empire that had once engulfed Europe, followed by the 'savage' kings of old England, then the Normans. The line was broken with the arrival of the Moors, then there followed caliphs in white robes and loose turbans, with closely cropped beards and ornate sabres. Then he saw King Edward V, with his simple crown, who had cast the Moors out of England and restored the royal line. And then came the monarchs of the last 200 years, through the blood-stained era of independence and then the peace of Rajthanan rule. And finally, the ageing King John III appeared, sitting on the throne in London, brooding over whether or not he would survive the coming onslaught of the Rajthanans.

Thunder burst straight overhead and the sound vibrated throughout the cavity of the mosque. He sat up with a jerk and opened his eyes. His heart thudded and his face throbbed with heat. The visions had disappeared and all he could see were the indistinct building and the silver traces of the rain outside the fallen wall.

He swallowed, wiped the sweat from his face and walked over to where the rainwater guttered down through the hole. He put his head into the cold liquid and let it run through his hair and over his face, then cupped his hands and drank several times.

He staggered back to the other side of the chamber and sat down again. The wind whined and blew icy kisses through the gaps in the stone. He closed his eyes and tried to rest, but he was afraid he wouldn't survive the night. The miasma of fever floated around him. He wondered whether he would ever wake up if he fell asleep, but even as he was considering this he had already drifted off.

He woke with the image of Elizabeth as a child receding like morning mist. The rain had stopped and strands of sunlight stretched from tiny perforations in the walls and dome. The visions of the night before had gone and he wondered at what he'd seen. He wasn't sure if he'd dreamt it all, hallucinated from the fever, or genuinely been able to see into the past through the power of sattva. No matter. It was the *present* that was troubling him.

Dazed and shivering, he left the mosque and walked back through the trees. When he reached the path, he stopped and darkness threatened to envelope him for a moment before he fought it off. There was no sign of the rebels' tracks – they had all been washed away by the rain. He thought about using his power, but he was sure he would be too weak. Instead, he just set off along the path, assuming the rebels must have done the same.

Late in the morning, the way splintered into three separate trails. He searched the ground, but couldn't see any indication of which way the rebels had gone. He sat down and tried to enter the trance, but he was too weak and the pool of his mind was turbulent.

He tried for half an hour but nothing happened. He lay on his back and let sleep engulf him.

He woke up, and could tell by the sun it was late afternoon. He was still at the fork in the path, and wild with thirst. He stood and chose the left-hand trail at random.

He woke up again, at night, lying next to a pool in a clearing in the forest. He couldn't remember how he'd got there and he couldn't see any sign of the trail in the dark. His body pulsed with heat and the ground seemed to circle beneath him. Could he survive another night?

He remembered Katelin lying on her deathbed, wilting with sweat, hair plastered to her scalp, skin so pale it shone in the candlelight. He must look like that himself now.

What about the jatamansi? He reached into his pocket and found the bottle still there. It was worth a try.

He was too weak to sit up, so he lay back and poured a drop into his mouth. It tasted slightly sweet and smelt of rosewater.

Nothing happened.

He waited a few more minutes and still nothing happened, although his chest did tingle slightly. The jatamansi was clearly useless – although that could be because it was a treatment for the heart rather than fever.

He shivered.

Then he had another idea. He knew he wasn't thinking straight, that the idea was crazy, but what did he have to lose?

He would try the yantra he'd stolen.

He was supposed to know only the native siddha yantra – that was all Jhala had taught him. He'd asked to learn more, but Jhala had said Europeans weren't mentally capable. Then one evening, about a year after he'd finished his siddha training, he'd been given a chance.

He'd stopped by Jhala's office and been puzzled to find the door ajar, but no light inside.

He pushed the door open, blinked in the gloom. 'Captain Jhala?'

Something rustled in a corner of the room, and when he investigated he found Jhala lying on a mat with cushions scattered about him. Jhala rasped and edged his head around to look up at Jack.

'Sir?' Jack crouched.

'Fever,' Jhala managed to say, his voice hoarse. He grasped Jack's hand and his skin was ice cold.

Jack knew about Jhala's occasional bouts of illness, but he'd never seen his commander so incapacitated. He immediately ran to the hospital and brought back a pair of orderlies and a doctor. They lifted Jhala on to a stretcher and rushed him away. Jack was about to follow when he noticed what looked like a small mat poking out from under one of the cushions. Something about the intricate design embroidered on the cloth intrigued him.

He glanced back at the open door. There was no one about, so he pulled out the cloth and held it up to the moonlight. He saw a complex, circular design.

A yantra. He was certain.

It was broadly similar to the native siddha yantra, although the minor details were quite different.

He looked at the door again. There was still no one in sight.

All yantras were supposed to be kept secret. If he were caught taking the cloth, he was sure he'd be flogged. Furthermore, what would Jhala think of him? Jhala had argued with Colonel Hada for Jack to receive the siddha training. How could Jack betray his guru's trust?

But he wanted to try the yantra. One power didn't seem enough, and here was his chance. It wasn't like him to disobey orders, but he was young and reckless then.

He eased the door closed, hunted around the office and found a large sheet of paper, a pen and a pot of ink. By moonlight, he drew the yantra as carefully and accurately as he could. Every detail had to be perfect. Any deviation from the design would make the yantra useless.

He listened for footsteps, certain someone would come soon. But no one did.

He felt a twinge of guilt. Shouldn't he be checking on Jhala rather than sneaking around? He would stop by the hospital as soon as he'd finished.

After half an hour he held up the paper and the piece of cloth, looking between the two. The copy was good enough.

He placed the cloth back under the cushion and slipped out of the door. No one had seen him.

Jhala recovered within two days, and Jack spent months learning the design in his spare time. He wondered what power the yantra would give him. Most yantras granted a single power – the native siddha yantra was unusual in that it provided different powers to different people.

In the end he was disappointed. Although he managed to hold the yantra still in his mind, and it glowed white to confirm he'd got it right, he didn't develop any power. He guessed what Jhala had said was true – Europeans couldn't learn the higher powers.

Over the years, he tried the yantra from time to time, but it never worked . . .

And, of course, there was no point in trying the yantra again now. Why would it suddenly start working?

But he found himself focusing on it all the same. He wasn't strong enough to sit upright, so he just lay there, doing his best to calm his mind. He shut his eyes and tried to ignore the fever roaring within him.

He recalled all the details of the yantra easily enough and eventually it blazed brilliant white in his head.

And then . . . nothing.

Just as he'd expected. The meditation had been a pointless waste of energy.

He gazed up at the sky, but his sight blurred and the stars gummed together and the earth whirled beneath him.

Sunlight warmed his face and he forced open his heavy eyelids. He was still alive.

Everything was bright, painful to look at. He was still lying beside the pond and the water was fiery from the sun. He rolled on to his back, ignoring the pain from his broken rib.

He smelt a trace of woodsmoke. He sat up slowly and looked around, his eyes adjusting to the light now. He couldn't see any sign of the track, but a finger of blue smoke rose above the trees, perhaps a mile away.

He walked around the clearing and managed to find his own tracks leading back into the forest. He considered following them to the path, but he knew he couldn't continue for much longer. The fever was too severe. And he would need more food soon – the dry rations were almost finished.

He started off in the opposite direction, towards the rising smoke. The ground was flat and the trees far apart. After a few minutes the pain in his side worsened, darkness swirled around him and the ground rushed up.

He opened his eyes and found he was lying on the forest floor. He picked himself up and leant against a tree. He coughed and sneezed, pain crippling him. He somehow staggered on, stopping each time he felt faint and resting until he gained the strength to continue.

He didn't know how long it took him to walk the short distance to the smoke. It seemed like hours. Eventually, the trees parted and he came out on to an open plain that stretched for as far as he could see in all directions. He felt giddy with the sense of space after the confines of the woods.

A village of white-walled cottages stood less than half a mile away. Nearer to him was a single house, set apart from the others, with smoke rising from a hole in its roof – the smoke he'd been following.

He walked unsteadily towards the cottage, the ground seeming to bounce about in front of him. Outside the building, a woman was bent over with a hoe, tending a small vegetable plot.

As Jack came closer, the woman looked up, narrowed her eyes and pointed the hoe at him as if it were a spear. 'You keep away.

I've got my husband indoors and I'll call for him if you come any closer.'

'I need food.'

'You be on your way.'

'Please.' He took a few steps forward.

The woman shook, her eyes bright with fear. 'Keep away. One step closer and I'll—'

Everything spun in front of him. The woman, the cottage and the vegetable plot raced up to the left of his vision. He heard the woman shriek as he fainted and fell forward.

PART TWO
THE CRUSADE

10

Jack heard a grunting sound near to him. Snuffling. Squeals. The sound of pigs.

He opened his eyes. It was dark, but not pitch black. He was lying on his side on a bed of straw. In front of him was a wall of wooden slats, and through the gaps he could smell the stink of the pigs.

He rolled on to his back, eyes adjusting to the light. Above him stretched rafters and a thatched roof, and about him were rough wattle-and-daub walls with shuttered windows. He was in a peasant hut – a single room with an adjoining pigsty. He was instantly reminded of his parents' cottage, of being a child.

An open door let in grey light from outside and a fire glowed in the centre of the room, the smoke rising through a hole in the roof. The smell of the smoke was everywhere and the thatching was black with soot.

He tried to sit up, but his arms were too weak to even support him.

'You be careful there.' A woman stood in the doorway – the woman he'd startled when he first appeared out of the forest. 'You need to rest.'

She came bustling over to him; she was thin and might have seemed frail if it weren't for her gleaming eyes and firmly set jaw. Her black hair was pulled back in a ponytail and she looked about Jack's age – late thirties.

'Where?' he said. 'Why?'

'Lie back down.' She knelt beside him.

'What am I doing here?'

'Lie down, you fool.'

He made a sound halfway between a laugh and cough and eased himself back. 'How long have I been here?'

'Two days.'

'Two days!'

He tried to sit up again. William and the rebels would be well ahead of him. He had to get back to the trail.

But he couldn't even raise himself into a sitting position.

'Lie down,' the woman said. 'You're going nowhere at the moment.'

He lay back with a sigh and stared up at the dark beams and the indistinct roof. The thought of Elizabeth cloyed his throat. Two days. That meant it was . . . nine days since he'd left Poole. Eighteen days until Elizabeth was executed. He tried to keep his eyes open, but they were painfully dry and he had to close them.

'That's right,' the woman said. 'Rest.'

He drifted in and out of sleep for he didn't know how long. He was aware sometimes of other people in the room, but didn't open his eyes to look at them. He was too weak to move. Sometimes it was light, sometimes dark. Sometimes everything was silent and black and at those times he briefly wondered if he were dead.

Memories of Elizabeth . . .

He saw her again as a child running across a meadow towards him, her dark hair flowing behind her in the wind . . .

Elizabeth sitting beside him as he told her the story of King Arthur. And her asking for him to retell it again and again . . .

Elizabeth running away to find the Grail. And him racing through the night looking for her and hearing her voice on the wind and finding her in the forest . . .

Then walking with her down a country road last year, the sky heavy with cloud. She'd just turned fifteen and he'd come back to the village to see her. They'd visited Katelin's grave and left two bunches of wild flowers.

'I've been thinking,' Elizabeth said. 'I'm definitely going into service.'

'We've already talked about it,' Jack said. 'The answer's no.'

'I'll be fine. I've been offered a job, in Dorsetshire.'

Jack stopped. So Elizabeth had gone against his wishes. 'Listen, you're too young.'

'I can't stay at the Jones's for ever.'

After Katelin died, Arnold and May Jones had taken in Elizabeth, as she couldn't stay with Jack at the Goyanor estate.

'Elizabeth, you'll do as I say,' he said.

She hung her head, then looked up again, took his arm. A dry breeze braided her hair. 'I'm not a child any more.'

Jack had been away for a year and it was true, she looked more grown up now. But underneath that outer appearance wasn't she still the same girl who'd run off to find the Grail?

'I know what you think,' she said. 'But I'm not like I used to be. I'll prove it.'

He searched her face. She seemed serious and thoughtful, different from the headstrong child he'd always known. 'Maybe.'

She smiled. 'Thank you.'

'I said maybe.'

'I'll prove I can look after myself.'

He smiled and shook his head. But he was beginning to believe Elizabeth really had changed. Perhaps this new Elizabeth could manage on her own. Perhaps he had to let her try.

He put his hand on her shoulder for a moment as they walked on. And they were silent as they made their way back to the village, as the light slowly bled out of the sky.

When he woke, the woman was squatting beside the fire, stirring a blackened pot. The door was open and he could see it was light outside. He heard chickens clucking, but the pigs were restful, only grunting occasionally.

'How are you today?' The woman glanced at him, tucking a stray lock of hair behind her ear.

Jack thought about the question. He found he was strong enough to sit up. He felt well, alert. The pain of his broken rib had gone and the fever had lifted. 'Good . . . hungry.'

She gave a small laugh. 'I've got some pottage on the boil here. It'll be ready in a minute.'

'What's your name?'

'Anne . . . Anne Carrick.'

'I'm Jack. Thank you. For everything.'

'Well, what's the world come to when we don't help those in need. You were in a terrible state when you showed up here.'

Jack recalled arriving at the cottage and seeing Anne standing outside with her hoe. 'Where's your husband?'

'Husband?'

'When I got here you said you'd call him.'

'Oh, I only said that to scare you off.' She turned back to the pot. 'He died a long time ago.'

'Sorry to hear that.'

'Life goes on.'

Jack thought of Katelin. 'It does.'

He watched her stir the pot for a moment. The sleeves of her dress were frayed, the elbows patched and one shoulder had a tear in it. It would be hard for her without a husband. With his army salary, Jack had always ensured Katelin had new clothes when she needed them, and the cottage they'd rented was far larger and better built than Anne's hut, with several separate rooms.

Anne soon came over with a steaming bowl of barley, peas and beans. He inhaled the scent of the bland soup laced with onion and bacon fat.

She sat on a stool and watched him eat. Within minutes he'd finished and wiped the bowl clean with his finger.

'You must be feeling better,' she said with an amused smile.

He half smiled back. The food glowed in his stomach, but with his hunger satisfied he again thought about William. 'So I've been here two days.'

'Three. You slept another day.'

He felt a quiver of anxiety. William had estimated it would take three days to get to London by horse. If that were true, the rebels would be there already. 'I need to go.'

'You need to rest.' She put her hand on his chest and looked at him for a little too long, then seemed to get embarrassed and removed her hand. 'Anyway, you can't leave without meeting my son. He'll be back soon.'

Jack braced himself to stand, but paused when he heard the scrape of a boot outside and the chickens cackling as they scurried out of the way. A figure appeared, silhouetted in the doorway.

Anne stood. 'He's woken up.'

The figure stepped into the room. It was a man in his early twenties, with long sandy hair and bright eyes. His features were smooth, with a trace of youthful fat. He wore a European Army uniform – dark-blue tunic, brass buttons, light-grey trousers – but had a patch with a red cross on a white background sewn on to the left side of his chest: a St George's cross. No soldier would normally deface his uniform in this way – the punishment was a minimum of thirty lashes. It had to be the mark of a rebel.

Jack would have to be careful what he said.

'This is my son, Charles,' Anne said.

'Pleased to meet you.' Charles smiled as he walked across to shake Jack's hand.

'Jack Casey.' He sat up straighter, with his back against the wall. 'Pleased to meet you too.'

Charles sat on a stool and his mother brought him a bowl of pottage, which he slurped slowly as he spoke. 'Just got in the other day. Bit surprised my mother's taken in a lodger.'

'I'll be gone by nightfall,' Jack said. 'I'm much better.'

'You wait until you're completely well.' Anne was tidying the pots and bowls on a set of shelves.

Charles grinned and winked at Jack. 'Think she's taken a shine to you.'

Anne slapped him across the top of the head and he laughed as he raised a hand to fend her off.

'Seriously, though,' Charles said, 'you stay here as long as you like. You're welcome.'

As Anne stepped outside, Charles pulled his stool closer and said more quietly, 'Pleased there's someone here to look after her, to be honest. She's on her own. I'm leaving again in a couple of days.'

'I'd like to stay, but I can't.'

'That's a pity.' Charles drew back. 'Where you headed?'

Jack paused, thinking quickly. 'London.'

'London? Well, that's where I'm . . .' Charles looked at Jack more closely. 'You're going there to fight?'

Jack cleared his throat. 'Yes.' An idea was forming in his mind. 'How are you getting there?'

'Mule cart.'

'I'll come with you.'

Charles shook his head. 'You'll never get better in time.'

'I'm better now. I'm fine.'

A grin slipped across Charles's face. 'You've been out for days and now you're fine?'

'Yes. Listen, I used to be in the army—'

'Is that right?' Charles leant forward. 'Which regiment?'

'The 2nd Native Infantry.'

'By St Mary. I'm with the 12th. So you've switched sides as well, then?'

'You could say that. I left the army nine years ago.'

'Injured?'

'No . . . just had to leave.'

Charles put his spoon down. 'Nine years ago. You must've seen a few battles.'

'A few.'

'What campaigns were you in?'

'Poland, Dalmatia, Ragusa—'

'You were at Ragusa?' Charles's face lit up.

'What're you two gabbling about?' Anne came back into the hut with a large pot between her arms.

'You didn't tell me we had a war hero here,' Charles said. 'Jack was at Ragusa.'

Anne put the pot down in a corner of the room and stood with her hands on her hips. 'There aren't any heroes in war. Just dead people.'

'Mother, please.' Charles turned back to Jack. 'Don't mind her.'

'That's right,' Anne said. 'What do I know?' Anne looked at Jack and pointed to her son. 'His father was in the army. Died fighting in Macedonia.'

'And he got a commendation for it,' Charles reminded her. 'His captain came to this village, this very hut, to give it to us. I remember it.'

Anne retrieved something from a shelf, blew dust off it and held it up; it was a circular metal brooch embossed with three lions. Jack recognised it straight away – a Special Commendation, a great honour.

'That's all we got.' Anne's jaw was locked and her eyes misty. 'Thirteen years' service and that's all we've got left of him.'

'Mother, it's all right.' Charles stood and put his arm on her shoulder. 'Come on. Let's put that away.'

She sighed and placed the medal back on the shelf. She wiped her eyes on the edge of her sleeve and turned back to Jack. 'I'm sorry. It's just hard to see your men going off like that.'

'I know.' Jack remembered all those times he'd said goodbye to Katelin.

'Anyway,' Anne said, 'I'm going down to the village. You stay where you are, Jack. You're in no fit state to go anywhere.'

'I'll keep an eye on him,' Charles said to her.

She put on a bonnet and stepped outside. She looked at Jack as if about to say something, but then changed her mind and walked off.

Charles opened one of the window shutters and stood looking out. From where Jack was sitting all he could see was the white cloud covering the sky.

'You know, I'm back here rounding up men for the crusade,' Charles said. 'We need as many as we can get. They say the Rajthanans have a huge army.'

'How big?'

'Don't know. I heard forty thousand. There're lots of rumours.'

'It'll be tough. They'll fight hard.'

'Of course.' Charles seemed to brood on this until his face brightened. 'But we'll fight harder. The Grail will help us.'

'The Grail?'

'Haven't you heard? Everyone's saying it. The Grail's coming back.'

'Yes . . . of course.' That rumour hadn't made it to Poole. Did the rebels really believe this? The Grail was just a legend, a superstition. 'Let me come with you. I'm going to London anyway – you don't want to make me walk.'

Charles grinned and pointed out of the window. 'You see the village over there?'

Jack stood and hobbled unsteadily to the window. Half a mile away was the cluster of cottages, dominated by a stone church.

'There's an alehouse down there,' Charles said. 'Tomorrow, at midday, I'm speaking to everyone there. Trying to get them to join the fight. If you can walk down on your own and drink a pint of ale, I'll take you to London.'

Jack drank ale from an earthenware mug. He was sitting on a bench in a corner of the alehouse, elbow on a trestle table. All around him were men from the village in their dusty clothes and drooping cloth hats. They drank and talked loudly, some puffing on the hookahs that gurgled and smouldered on each table. Soft tobacco smoke floated through the room.

The building was a simple longhouse with numerous windows letting in the watery midday light. Chickens and dogs ranged about the earth floor and the high thatched roof harboured sparrows and starlings that watched the proceedings with their glossy eyes. Like all the buildings in the village, the alehouse was in need of repair. Even Jack's tiny hut at the Goyanor house was in a better state.

Charles stood in his army uniform on a raised platform at one end of the hall. He fidgeted and appeared uncertain whether to begin. The St George's cross on his chest shone faintly in the haze.

'Gentlemen,' he called out, but no one paid him the slightest attention. 'Gentlemen!' he called louder, and now the talking subsided and the men looked up from their mugs. Soon it was completely silent, save for the clucking of the chickens and the bubble of the hookahs.

'Thank you all for coming.' Charles's voice wavered and he looked at his feet for a moment before continuing. 'You all know me. I grew up here. Most of you have known me all my life. You also probably know why I'm here. You don't need me to tell you there's a war on. Now, I'm not much good at giving speeches. But what I've got to say is important.

'The heathens have taken our lands. Their black magic is everywhere. Long ago King Arthur's knights freed this country with the power of the Grail. King Edward and his knights found the Grail again and fought off the Caliph. The Grail's coming back and now we have to fight again.

'The heathens will march on London any day now. They want to sack the city and murder our King. They'll burn our churches.

They'll kill our women and children. The King has called on every able-bodied man in England to go to London to defend the city. I leave tomorrow. Who'll come with me?'

The room was silent.

Jack thought Charles's claims were somewhat overstated – the Rajthanans wouldn't destroy London or murder the innocent. They would simply put down the mutiny as quickly and efficiently as they could.

After a few seconds, a middle-aged man with curly hair stood and rested his hands on his round belly. His cheeks were tinged red and he smiled broadly as if he were proud of something he'd just accomplished. 'This isn't our fight. This is Wiltshire – an independent state. The Earl has not in any way supported these rebels.'

A few of the men muttered their agreement into their mugs.

Charles met the gaze of the middle-aged man. 'Bailiff Warburton. Glad you could come.'

The crowd laughed. The Bailiff, as Jack knew, would be the representative of the local lord.

'True, Wiltshire is independent,' Charles continued. 'But only at the whim of the Maharaja. It is a part of England. We're English. While the Rajthanans are here we'll never be free.'

A murmur rippled around the room.

'England,' the Bailiff said. 'There is no England. It's an idea from the past. There's been no England since the Rajthanans got here a hundred years ago.'

'Then it's high time we reclaimed our country,' Charles said. 'Gentlemen, this is an opportunity that may not come again. Ever. If we don't fight now, we never will.'

'A lot of our young men have gone already,' said an old man with only a single tooth in his sunken mouth. 'Three of my sons are in London now. Do you want me to send my youngest as well? Do you want me to go there myself with my walking stick?'

Glancing around the room, Jack noted that there were indeed few men under the age of thirty in the alehouse.

'Of course not, George,' Charles replied. 'We can all only do what we're able to. But we have to realise this is our chance now. Our one chance. We have to give everything we can.'

He turned to a group of lads, all no more than sixteen years old, who sat together at one of the tables. 'How about it? Who'll come with me?'

The young men looked at the ground nervously and smiled at some secret joke between themselves.

'You stay where you are, Henry,' called out an older man with wild hair that was speckled with straw and burrs. 'I'll not have my son running off with no rebels.'

Henry stared harder at the ground and went bright red. The crowd sniggered at the exchange.

'Saleem.' Charles turned to a young man who sat on his own near the front. 'What about you?'

'You even taking Mohammedans now,' someone called out, to loud laughter around the room.

Jack peered over the heads of his neighbours and could see that the young man indeed wore a Mohammedan skullcap. It was common enough to find a few Mohammedan families in the villages the further you travelled into the south-east.

'Of course we'll take Mohammedans,' Charles said. 'You're still an Englishman, aren't you, Saleem?'

Saleem mumbled something that was impossible to hear.

'What was that?' Charles put his hand to his ear. He seemed to be enjoying himself now, buoyed by the laughter from the crowd.

Saleem mumbled more loudly, but was still inaudible.

'He says he's a proud Englishman, happy to serve the Christian King of his country,' Charles reported.

The crowd roared with laughter at this. Jack knew it was unlikely a Mohammedan would ever say such a thing. The Mohammedans might be born in England, but their allegiance was to their religious leaders in far-off countries.

'So, gentlemen,' Charles called out above the now raucous gathering. Men shouted at each other across the room, the banter lively, but good-natured.

'Gentlemen!' Charles tried again, and his audience quietened enough for him to be heard. 'As you may know, a friend has been staying with my mother over the past few days. He's an ex-soldier, a veteran of Ragusa . . . Stand up, Jack.'

Everyone in the room turned in their seats to look at Jack.

Jack shook his head at Charles. This wasn't what he'd expected.

'Come on, Jack,' Charles said.

There didn't seem to be any way out of it. Reluctantly, he stood up and the crowd stared at him – the proud war hero.

'Jack's changed sides and he's coming with me to fight,' Charles said. 'He's an inspiration to all of us.'

A few men clapped and many talked amongst themselves. Jack nodded his acknowledgement to the crowd and sat back down quickly. It was awkward. He didn't want to be an impostor, but what else could he do?

The man next to him patted him on the back. 'Wondered who you were, stranger. Have another ale.'

'I leave tomorrow,' Charles said. 'From the marketplace, at sunrise. There's room in my cart for six more men. I hope to see some of you there.'

'Buy me an ale and I'll be there,' one man shouted.

'Buy me six and I'll bring six men with me,' shouted another.

The crowd laughed and talked excitedly, calling for more ale and more tobacco, the alehouse owner and her daughters running about as quickly as they could to serve everyone.

'You spoke well,' Jack said as he walked back with Charles after the meeting, still limping from his injuries.

Charles grinned. 'Did my best. We'll see if anyone comes.'

Jack looked across at Charles. It was such a waste – a young man like that, going off to fight in a war that could never be won. He wanted to talk him out of it. But Charles was his only way of getting to London, and he doubted the lad would listen to him anyway.

'When did you join the . . . crusade?' Jack asked.

'A couple of months ago. Missed the first lot of fighting. I'll make up for that when we get to London, though.'

'Why'd you join?'

'What do you mean?'

'What convinced you? You know, how did you finally decide?'

Charles shrugged. 'Same as everyone else, I guess. The lads in the regiment were talking about it for weeks. After London and Westminster fell, the talk got louder and some of the men even started answering back to the officers. There was a secret meeting one night, just outside the barracks. I went there with all the other lads and a rebel leader came and spoke to us. He made us all see how we've been treated like slaves in our own country. What he said, the way he said it, you just knew he was right. He's famous now, that man. You might have heard of him. They call him the Ghost—'

Jack tripped on a stone and almost fell. Charles rushed to his side and supported him.

'I'm all right,' Jack said.

'You need to watch yourself.'

'Just tripped, that's all . . . so you know the Ghost?'

'No. Only saw him speak the one time.' Charles frowned. 'You look pale. You sure you're strong enough to go to London?'

'I'm fine.' Jack pulled away.

Charles smiled and shook his head. 'You're really an inspiration, you are. Wish there were more like you around.'

Charles turned and continued to walk back to the cottage. Jack felt tired. The light seemed greyer now, wintry. He didn't want to deceive Charles, but he had no choice. For a moment, he wished the mutiny could be over and everything could go back to the way it had been. He recalled Jhala's sagging face as he'd said in the gazebo that it was a pity for all of them to live in these days.

Jhala was right.

Perhaps it would have been better to have been killed on that battlefield at Ragusa, rather than go through these dark times.

Jack stood in the empty marketplace. Dawn etched in the surroundings, the sleeping cottages, the sullen church, the fields beyond. The cart rested nearby. Anne patted the mule and glanced at the growing light on the horizon as if it were an enemy. Charles stood a short distance away, with a young woman who'd been introduced to Jack as Mary. The two youngsters held hands and Charles stroked Mary's long brown hair. They looked at each other intently and spoke in hushed voices.

A cock crowed in the distance.

Jack walked over to Anne, his boots crunching on the stony ground. 'Doesn't look like anyone's coming.'

'No.' Anne avoided looking at him and instead stared at the mule's neck.

'I'm sorry about Charles going. It wasn't my idea—'

'I know. He would've gone without you.'

'He's a good lad. He wants to fight for what he believes in.'

'And that's a good way to live, is it?' She looked up at him, her bottom lip trembling.

He gazed at his boots and coughed awkwardly.

'You look after him,' she said suddenly.

'I will. I promise.'

'If he doesn't come back . . . I don't . . . She stared across the grey fields, eyes crystal.

'I'll look after him.'

Charles walked over, holding Mary's hand. 'We'll wait a few more minutes. After that, we'd better go.'

Mary sniffled and tears streaked her cheeks. Charles massaged her hand as he held it.

Then there was a crunch, crunch as someone walked across the square. They all turned and saw a figure emerge from the shadows – Saleem, the Mohammedan. He was a young man, around sixteen, with ginger hair that coiled out from beneath his cap. The beard he was trying to grow was also ginger. With his sleepy eyes and wide smile he looked as though he were drunk, but this was impossible as it was forbidden by his religion. He wore a white tunic that was too big for him and the sleeves hung down, almost covering his hands.

He stopped in front of them. 'Greetings.'

'Saleem.' Charles blinked in surprise. 'You're coming with us?'

'Yes.' Saleem looked at the ground shyly, his smile broadening further.

'To London?' Charles asked.

Saleem nodded.

Charles gave Jack a questioning glance. Jack was uncertain what to say. Saleem looked harmless enough – he was no threat, even if he was a Mohammedan. On the other hand, he could be a liability. His youth and naivety might put them in danger. And beyond that Jack felt a tug in the pit of his stomach – did he really want to encourage any young man to go to London, perhaps to his death? But he couldn't say this. He had to pretend to believe.

'Can you shoot a musket?' he asked.

'Yes.' Saleem didn't meet Jack's gaze. 'Had an uncle in the army. He showed me.'

Jack dithered. He couldn't think of any obvious reason for rejecting Saleem. Resigned, he nodded his assent to Charles.

'All right,' Charles told Saleem. 'You can come with us.'

Saleem had a few possessions wrapped in a piece of cloth, which they threw into the cart, along with some provisions, utensils, blankets, an army-issue musket and an ancient-looking pistol. They hid the weapons beneath a sheet of canvas.

Jack and Saleem sat in the back as they pulled out, while Charles was in front, driving the mule ahead. Anne and Mary stood close together, waving, faces sombre. The two women faded into the semi-dark as the cart clattered away, the white cottages and fields to either side of them and the black forest behind. Soon they were no more than two pale blots, unreal, before they were gone completely.

11

Three soldiers stood in the distance, blocking the road through the vast plains. A chessboard of green and yellow fields rolled in all directions, dotted with villages, the church spires of which were like playing pieces: rooks, bishops, kings and queens.

'They're the Earl's men,' Charles said to Jack as the cart juddered over the uneven path. 'They won't give us any trouble.'

As the cart drew closer one of the soldiers held up his hand and Charles brought the mule to a halt. The man wore a surcoat with the crest of the Earl of Wiltshire – a blue and yellow shield with a knight's helmet above – emblazoned on the chest. He carried an ageing musket over his shoulder.

Charles jumped to the ground and smiled. 'Richard'.

The two men embraced, slapping each other on the back.

'Where you headed?' Richard asked.

'London.'

Richard breathed in sharply. 'Wouldn't do that. Big Rajthanan army on the move – they say it's headed there.'

'I know. We're going to defend the city.'

Richard smiled and shook his head. 'Always looking for trouble, aren't you?'

'You should come too. We need good men.'

'Can't do that. The Earl's forbidden us to take part, on pain of death.'

'Well, that's too bad.'

Richard went silent for a moment. He glanced at Jack and

Saleem sitting in the cart, using his hand to shield his eyes from the sun. 'You going through Hampshire?'

'That's the plan,' Charles said.

'Not a good idea. Been a lot of fighting there the last few days. The Rajthanans sent in an advance party.'

'But we have to get to London quickly.'

'Then go north-east to Oxford and south again after that. Only way you'll avoid the fighting.'

'Oxford? That's right out of our way. How long would it take us to get to London?'

Richard rubbed his chin. 'Bad roads that way. About four days by cart, I'd say.'

'Risky. The army might get there before us.'

Charles looked back at Jack, who climbed down from the cart and joined the two men. He gazed out over the plains: the scene was tranquil, expansive. Wars and fighting – it all seemed impossibly distant, something happening in another world.

'How many days to London if we go straight through Hampshire?' He'd never been to the south-east of England, never even been to London. It was strange to think that he'd travelled to so many foreign places and yet had little knowledge of his own country.

'You could make it in two or three days,' Richard replied.

'Two days is possible.' Charles said.

'And the army?' Jack asked. 'How long to march from Christchurch?'

'Four or five days – that's what my commander told me,' Charles said.

Jack nodded. 'Doesn't look like we have much choice.'

'Seems that way,' Charles said. 'Through Hampshire it is.'

'Then the best of luck to you.' Richard patted Charles on the shoulder.

Charles forced a smile but said nothing.

They travelled on across Salisbury Plain, the day bright and hot. They saw men and women at work in the fields, oxen with ploughs, sheep, goats, and endless farmland flowing to the horizon.

They constantly passed through strong sattva streams, Jack shivering each time. Salisbury seemed to have more than its fair share of sattva.

At midday Saleem, who'd been virtually silent the whole trip, said, 'Can we stop, please?'

'What for?' Charles asked.

'Prayers.'

Jack knew Mohammedans were required to perform five daily prayers – he'd seen this often in the army – but he knew this number could also be reduced when on campaign. 'You can just pray in the morning and evening. That's all that's needed when you're travelling.'

Saleem looked at the bottom of the cart, still with the usual slight smile on his face. 'That's not what my father says.'

Jack gritted his teeth. Mohammedans – they were always a problem. In the army the French, Andalusians, Neapolitans – all the Mohammedan troops – had always been impossible to get on with. 'Your father's not here now.'

Then Saleem's eyes widened and moistened and Jack regretted his harsh words. He sighed. 'All right, let's stop for lunch.'

Charles brought the cart to a halt. Saleem laid his mat on the side of the road and studiously did his prayers, standing, kneeling and prostrating himself in turn.

Jack and Charles munched on bread and ate an apple each. In the distance they saw a grass-covered mound topped by a circle of standing stones. Shadows collected at the base of the stones and rippled a short distance out across the grass.

'You see them all over the place around here,' Charles said.

'I heard.' Jack remembered Jhala explaining the theory that the circles had been built by the ancient Britons as a way of marking the sattva streams.

'It seems your ancestors may have known a little about sattva,' Jhala had said. 'At least, they knew it was strong in some places and weak in others and that the strongest strands are stretched into streams. They may have had superstitions about the streams or regarded them as sacred.'

That might be true, but the Britons had never developed this knowledge further. That was one of the differences between Europeans and Rajthanans. Europeans had lived with sattva all around them for millennia, but had never thought to do anything with it. It was only the Rajthanans who had discovered how to harness the secret power.

They continued through the afternoon and eventually dusk crawled across the countryside. They came to a stretch of grass beside a brook.

'Good place to camp,' Charles said.

'We should keep going,' Jack replied.

'Could be dangerous travelling at night. You get bandits around here sometimes.'

'We have to get to London in time.' Jack was well aware that if they didn't get to the city before the Rajthanans there would be little chance of him finding William. William could be killed or captured – in the chaos of battle anything could happen – but neither occurrence would ensure his friend was taken back to Poole. Jack would have to make sure that happened himself.

'We'll be there in a day and a half, well before the army,' Charles said. 'Besides, I fancy a drink.' He reached back and flung aside a piece of cloth, revealing a cask of ale.

Jack shook his head. He couldn't believe Charles had brought along such a lot of alcohol. He was reluctant to stop now – he would have happily travelled through the night – but he didn't want to risk an argument. It was Charles's mule cart, after all.

The campfire was dwindling, the embers shivering in the chill breeze. The sky burned with stars, the night hummed with the sound of frogs and crickets, and the plains were hidden in the dark.

The cask was half empty, most of it having been drunk by Charles. Jack had sipped down a couple of mugs to keep the lad company, but the ale tasted sour and he was in no mood to drink. All the same, the alcohol seemed to go to his head more quickly than he'd expected and he felt surrounded by a vague bubble of drunkenness.

'Saleem,' Charles said, voice slurred. 'Why don't you have a drink?'

Saleem, who'd sat quietly during most of the evening, stared at the fire and shook his head.

'Go on,' Charles said. 'Just one little drink. It'll do you good.'

Saleem resisted Charles's continued goading.

Eventually, Charles stood unsteadily and walked over with his mug. He crouched and pushed the mug into Saleem's chest. 'It'll make a man out of you.'

'All right,' Saleem said finally. 'Just a sip.'

Charles watched intently as Saleem put the mug to his nose and crinkled his face in disgust. 'Get on with it,' he said.

Gingerly, Saleem took a sip. He thought about the taste for a moment, then grimaced and spat it out into the fire. He coughed and wiped his mouth.

Charles roared with laughter, rolling back into the darkness, shaking.

'Don't know how you can drink that stuff.' Saleem wiped even his tongue on his sleeve as he tried to expunge the taste.

Charles sat up and patted Saleem hard on the back. 'We'll get you drinking yet.'

He staggered over to the cask, filled his mug from the tap, then sat back down against a tree and waved his mug in Jack's general direction, spilling some ale. 'A toast to you, old soldier.'

Jack raised his own mug in an effort to be sociable.

'So tell us about the old days, Jack,' Charles said. 'Tell us about the battles you were in.'

'Not much to tell,' Jack replied.

'What about Ragusa?'

Jack hesitated. For a moment he saw that barren plain, grey in the dawn, the bodies in the mud, the seething pit of the dying at the base of the wall. 'How many battles you been in?' he asked Charles.

Charles's head lolled to one side as he tried to focus. His eyes wandered about like drowsy flies. 'A few . . . the Scottish brigands.'

Jack knew all about the brigands on the Scottish border – he'd served there himself for three years. It was wild country – Scotland had never been conquered by the Rajthanans. But at the same time chasing bandits around the hills was hardly a battle. The bands of Scotsmen were small and usually went into hiding as soon as they were confronted. The entire time Jack had been posted there he'd hardly fired a shot.

He looked at Charles, the lad's youthful face swaying and ruddy in the firelight. He could see bravado there, but what was there to back it up? Nothing. The lad was inexperienced, had never even seen a proper fight.

And then there was Saleem, looking into the flames with a dreamy expression on his face. He was no more than a boy, with no idea what he was getting himself into.

Jack stood suddenly and the ale rushed to his head. The night air roared around him. 'Back in a moment.'

He stumbled into the darkness and urinated against a tree, the liquid rumbling as it hit the bark.

What was he doing? Why was he here, slightly drunk, on Salisbury Plain? Why was he still following William? He had no plan of any sort. Was he going to capture William? Kill him? And how would he do that and get out of the city before the Rajthanans arrived?

It was going to be hard enough just getting to London. He had to get past the Rajthanans in Hampshire, and his companions were two lads who had virtually no fighting experience. He glanced back at the camp and saw the two figures dark against the glow of the fire. They were just boys . . .

And he recalled Private Robert Salter, who'd also been just a boy – sixteen years old – when he'd joined Jack's regiment. Jack could still see the lad's pale face with a bowl of straight, black hair and a mouth continually pursed as if he were about to spit. The boy was useless. He was sullen, given to complaining and often out of time during musket drill. Jack wasn't sure if he could ever be turned into a proper soldier.

Jack was nearing thirty at the time and had reached the rank of sergeant. They were on campaign in Swedeland, their mission a simple matter of clearing some hills of bandits. The bandits were poor fighters, easy to track, and they often surrendered.

The regiment had set up camp in one of the larger valleys and forays were sent into the surrounding hills. Jack and his platoon, seconded to a unit under a captain named Roy, were charged with hunting a band of more than sixty bandits, who'd proven to be a more difficult quarry than the others. They tracked them for three days, winding all over the hills in the biting cold, Jack following the sattva trail.

Roy, a thin man with a quartz scar over one eye, became increasingly irritated at their failure to catch the Swedes. He ordered the men to keep marching through long days with little rest, and his commands were short, sharp and peppered with the constant threat of flogging.

On the third night they made camp with the wind moaning in the dark and the desolate hills laced with moonlight. As sergeant, Jack was in charge of assigning the sentries, but he was tired and frustrated from a fruitless day – Captain Roy had bellowed at him for half an hour for losing the trail on several occasions.

He stood in the camp, trying to remember who he'd assigned to sentry duty the night before. But he couldn't think straight.

'Anderson, Wills, Salter – you're on tonight,' he said to his men.

'Pardon me, sir—' Salter began.

'Just get on duty.' He waved away the Private. The boy had been annoying him for days. He was too slow and kept complaining of a sore foot. He literally jumped every time he heard a musket fired. He was a liability more than anything else.

The next morning Jack woke to the sound of Roy shouting. He got up and walked across the camp to where the Captain was berating Salter, with a group of the men gathered around. Roy was red in the face and spat as he raged, while Salter stood with his head bowed, terrified.

'This is the worst flouting of campaign rules I've seen for years,' Roy shouted. 'You're a disgrace, Salter. A complete disgrace.'

Roy turned as Jack arrived. 'Sergeant Casey, I found this man asleep on sentry duty this morning.'

Jack froze. This was a serious dereliction. On campaign it was punishable by death, which was why it happened so rarely. He glanced at Salter, who was visibly shaking.

'It was a mistake, sir,' Salter said. 'Must've only been for an hour. No more.'

'One hour, two hours – we could've all been shot in our sleep, you pink bastard,' Roy said. 'Sergeant, this man is under arrest. Bind his hands.'

Roy strode away across the camp.

Jack knew what was coming. He told the other men to leave and they skulked off, but stood around watching from a few yards away.

'What the hell did you think you were doing?' Jack hissed to Salter.

Salter was sweating despite the chill in the air. 'I was tired. I didn't mean to.'

'Tired? We're all bloody tired.'

'But it was my third night on duty. I haven't slept for three days.'

Jack's skin prickled. 'What?'

'I tried to tell you.'

'Christ. I forgot. I thought you were off the night before.'

'No.'

'Look, I have to tie your hands now. Don't worry, I'll talk to the Captain.'

Jack fetched a piece of rope from a nearby packhorse and tied Salter's hands behind his back. He then walked across the camp and met Roy striding in the opposite direction, his red and white turban bobbing up and down, pistol in his belt.

'Sir,' Jack said. 'There's been a mistake. Salter's been on duty three nights running.'

Roy's eyes narrowed. 'Why's he been on so many nights?'

Jack went silent. 'It was my fault, sir. Made a mistake.'

'A bloody stupid mistake.'

'Yes.'

'I'll be mentioning it to the Colonel.'

'Of course.'

'But it's still a dereliction of duty. Salter will have to be shot.'

'Sir, I thought that given the circumstances—'

'The rules are clear. Salter should've stayed awake regardless.'

'But sir—'

'Out of my way, Sergeant.'

Roy marched on and Jack followed, feeling sick.

Salter stood beside a boulder on the edge of the camp. His hair was slick with sweat and he blinked constantly. He looked like a dog who'd just been kicked by its master.

'Up there.' Roy pointed to the slope above them.

The three of them walked uphill, Salter stumbling a few times on the rocky ground, finding it difficult with his hands tied. He glanced at Jack, raw fear in his eyes. Jack looked away and cleared his throat.

They came to a group of pines and Roy led them into the trees until they were out of sight of the camp. The fallen needles were soft beneath their boots and the sharp scent of pine surrounded them.

Roy pointed at a tree. 'That one there.'

Jack took Salter over to the tree and tied him firmly to the trunk, facing outward. Roy stood a short distance away, watching, the pistol now in his hand.

'Thought you were going to talk to him,' Salter said.

'I did,' Jack said. 'I'm sorry.'

His mind was racing. He tried to think whether there was anything he could do. But Roy was in command and there was no way he could question the decision of an officer.

He stepped away and Roy walked over.

'Private Salter,' Roy said. 'You are guilty of dereliction of duty whilst on campaign, namely sleeping whilst assigned to a sentry post. I hereby sentence you to be shot until you are dead.'

Jack smelt piss. A dark stain spread down Salter's trousers from under his tunic.

Roy stepped to the side, lifted the pistol and held it near Salter's temple. Salter shivered fiercely and made small choking sounds. He squeezed his eyes shut and twisted his body slightly as though in some way he could avoid the bullet.

Roy fired. The sound echoed across the valley and birds flew squawking from the trees.

'Be more bloody careful next time, Sergeant.' Roy turned and marched back down to the camp . . .

Jack stared up at the night sky, at the stars reeling over Salisbury Plain. He hitched up his hose.

It was Salter's death that had made him leave the army. It was a strange thing – it was just the death of one young man. He'd seen so many die, young and old. He'd thought he was immune to it. But the death had haunted him. Even back from campaign he'd dreamt about that final moment in the forest. He'd spoken to Jhala, but the Captain had pointed out that Roy had followed the regulations to the letter.

And, of course, Jhala was right. Jack himself was to blame. He was the one who had made the error. And this weighed on him. He should have listened to what Salter was trying to tell him that night. He shouldn't have let tiredness get in the way of doing his job properly. If only there were some way he could correct the mistake.

Three months later, on a battlefield in Denmark, a stray sattva-fire ball struck him and he was laid up in hospital for a month. During that time he realised he'd been punished for Salter's death. Karma must have caused the accident. Or perhaps it was God. He wasn't sure. But he'd undoubtedly been punished.

Once he recovered, he tried to continue with his duties, but in secret he felt he no longer deserved his sergeant's cap-stripes. He didn't deserve to wear an army uniform at all.

Within months he'd handed in his resignation.

Jhala had tried to convince him to stay, saying 'There's no need for you to leave, Casey. You've recovered well enough to serve, even if you can't use your power as often as before. I don't tell many people this, but I was once badly injured myself. I got better, though, and I carried on. You should too.'

But the words weren't enough to change Jack's mind . . .

Now he wandered back to the campfire, where Charles and Saleem were discussing something, Charles's voice loud and Saleem's soft and barely audible.

Charles belched as Jack approached. 'We were just talking about . . . What were we talking about?'

Saleem shrugged.

'Oh, yes. How we're going to give the Rajthanans a thrashing.'

'Is that right?' Jack sat down. He tipped the remains of his ale into the fire where it hissed and bubbled.

'You'll meet my regiment in London,' Charles continued. 'The 12th. They'll all be there. Greatest bunch of lads. You'll meet them—'

'We should get some sleep,' Jack said.

'A few more pints,' Charles drawled.

'You've had enough. Get some sleep.'

Charles's head wobbled. He peered at Jack across the fire, puzzled. 'You're right. Sleep.'

And he slumped to the earth and lay there, blowing dust across the ground with his open mouth.

Charles let Jack drive the cart the next day, while he lay in the back, hand on his forehead, groaning each time they went over a bump. Jack admonished himself for letting Charles drink so much. He wouldn't make that mistake again. They had to get to London before the army and he couldn't let anything slow them down.

At around ten o'clock in the morning, hills appeared in the distance.

Charles sat up. 'Hampshire Downs. We're near the border of the Earl's lands.'

'You'd better get out of that tunic,' Jack said.

Charles frowned and looked at his dark-blue uniform. 'You think so?'

'If we come across Rajthanans you'll attract attention.'

Charles nodded, took off the tunic and replaced it with an old jerkin. He slid the tunic underneath the canvas, with the firearms.

'No,' Jack said. 'Better get rid of it. They could search the cart.'

Reluctantly, Charles held up the tunic, looked at it for a moment, as if inspecting it before going on parade, then rolled it into a tube and threw it out into a field.

A cloud of dust appeared across the road ahead. At first it was a tiny smear, but then it grew into a huge globe that obscured the hills. Jack held the reins tightly.

'What is it?' Charles asked.

'Don't know.' Jack stopped the cart and climbed down. He knelt on the pitted road, put his ear to the ground and listened intently to the vibrations in the earth. The immediate surroundings were deserted, but far off he could detect the tread of thousands of feet.

'The army?' Charles asked as Jack climbed back into the cart.

Jack shook his head. 'A lot of people, but they're not marching in time. Just ordinary walking.'

'Who are they, then?'

'Can't be sure. Give me that pistol.'

Charles took the pistol out from under the canvas. Jack examined the weapon. It was an ancient flintlock single-shooter, with a prowling lion etched along the side. Similar weapons were being phased out of the army when he'd first joined twenty-three years ago. He wondered whether it would even work. He checked the pan and the barrel – they were both clean. He then measured and poured powder into the muzzle, and rammed in a ball along with a greased patch of cloth. After priming the pan, he balanced the weapon carefully on the seat beside him, under a blanket.

'You'd better load that musket too,' he said.

Charles bit open a cartridge. He stood in the cart as they bounced along, jabbing with the ramrod and watching as the dust cloud spread before them.

The countryside changed. The farms thinned out, then vanished, leaving open, uncultivated grassland. No one worked the fields, no other travellers moved along the road.

Figures formed in the dust: peasants, thousands of them,

trudging along the road in a vast, broken column that snaked away into the distance. As they came closer Jack could see their ragged clothes and gaunt features. They dragged their feet as if carrying heavy weights. There were men and women, children, babies clinging to their mothers, all staring straight ahead.

The first groups barely acknowledged Jack and his companions. They walked, with their heads bowed, on one side of the road so that the mule cart could pass. Some had sacks with a few possessions on their backs, but many carried nothing at all. They were thin, the skin hanging from their faces, their arms feeble sticks. Soon they were all about the cart.

'Where are you going?' Jack called out.

A bearded man scowled at him. 'Away from here.'

'Why? What happened?'

'The Rajthanans.'

A man peered over the edge of the cart. 'Hey. They've got food in there.'

An excited murmur ran through the crowd. It was true, there was food in the cart, but only a small sack of barley and a few parsnips and carrots.

'Give us food,' an old woman cried out.

The peasants crowded about the cart, pushing and shoving each other. One man tried to climb on to the back, but Charles forced him down again. Another tried to reach over the side. Saleem yelped and hit him on the arm so that he drew back.

'Food,' called a multitude of voices.

They rocked the cart and reached up. They were like a stormy sea thrashing about a small boat.

Jack stood and fired the pistol in the air. The crack rolled across the plains and white smoke curdled around the flintlock. The crowd stopped and fell back a few paces.

Jack remained standing on the seat. He waved the pistol as he spoke, even though it was no longer loaded. 'We've only got a few rations. Not enough even for the three of us.'

'We've got nothing,' the bearded man said. 'The Rajthanans burnt everything.'

'We're going to fight the Rajthanans,' Charles shouted, standing quickly.

The bearded man laughed sourly. 'Then good luck to you. If you're going to Hampshire you'll be dead in a day. Take your food. Good riddance to you.'

The peasants turned away, frowning and muttering amongst themselves. They filed past the cart, seeming to have lost the will even to fight for food.

Jack shook the reins and the mule plodded forward. The refugees streamed past, flotsam and jetsam after a flood. Gradually, the crowd lessened, the last stragglers limped past, and then the fading dust was all that was left of them.

Jack, Charles and Saleem fell silent as the hills swelled to their left and the road curved slightly to the south-east. Cloud spread across the sky, the light changing and casting the scene gloomy and silvery.

A deserted guard post, little more than a wooden hut, appeared on the side of the road.

'The border of Wiltshire,' Charles said as the cart juddered past. 'We're in Hampshire now.'

Jack looked across the plains. Rajthanan territory. He stopped the cart for a moment and reloaded the pistol.

The grassland gave way to simple farms again, but there was no sign of life. The fields were empty and no smoke rose from the scattering of cottages.

A line of darkness stretched across the land ahead. The wind carried a trace of soot. The fields of barley rose and fell and the light gave everything a metallic sheen.

The dark stain expanded across the ground as the cart advanced. For as far as Jack could see the fields had been burnt, leaving only scorched plains and the clawed remains of trees. It was as though the landscape had withered beneath the harshest winter.

Jack glanced back at his companions. Saleem shivered, while Charles stared ahead, his long hair fluttering behind his head.

A cottage rose to the left, a burnt tree bent beside it – something hung from a branch, but Jack couldn't make out what it was. A dead horse lay beside the road and crows stood on it, pecking. The birds had flayed open the side of the carcass, revealing the white ribs and dark-red innards within.

The cart trundled past the cottage. The roof had been burnt away and black streaks marred the walls.

Saleem caught his breath as the front of the house came into view. A peasant woman lay still in the mud near the front door, her eyes wide open and her neck twisted at an unnatural angle. Two children lay nearby, a boy on his back and a girl on her side, curled up as if cuddling a toy. Their skin was grey and shiny and speckled with soil.

Crows gathered about the bodies, but fled, squawking throatily, as the cart came by. There was a hum in the background – flies.

And now Jack could see what was dangling in the tree. It was the body of a man, hanging from the neck and spinning slowly, like rotting fruit. The crows lined up on the branch and waited for the cart to leave before descending again. One of the man's eyes had already been picked clean and the exposed socket wept dried blood.

Charles clenched his jaw and tightened his fists. 'We'll avenge them.'

Jack made the sign of the cross.

Saleem whimpered. 'Why did the Rajthanans do this? They're only farmers.'

'To stop them helping the rebels,' Jack replied. It was standard practice. He'd torched huts himself in Dalmatia when the officers had suspected the locals of aiding the enemy. But he'd never seen women and children blatantly murdered like that. It wasn't the way of the army – not the army he'd joined at any rate. The officers might have overlooked looting or even raping, but slaughtering innocents wasn't tolerated.

The cart rattled on along the path and they left the bodies to the cackling birds.

More blackened fields ranged about them, more charred houses, more bodies. They saw corpses lying in ditches beside the road, slaughtered sheep, bodies burnt to soot and bones and grinning skulls. And everywhere the crows, with their harsh cries and glossy black feathers, hopping and flying, watching as the cart went past before returning to their feasts.

'Damn birds.' Charles threw a parsnip at a group of the creatures gathered about the body of a man. The birds fluttered away a short distance, but soon returned.

Jack felt his face darken. The destruction was too complete to be a tactic to cut off the rebels. It looked more like revenge. He remembered the stories of the massacre at Westminster – all of Rajthanan society had been outraged by the news. He'd been outraged himself. But now the Rajthanans seemed to be engaged in the same actions, breaking their own code of honour.

A shot rang out, a distant thunderclap. Crows flew into the sky.

Jack stopped the cart. He heard another crack, closer this time. He squinted up the road and saw that what had at first appeared to be a cottage was in fact an elephant, with a figure atop it, ambling across a field.

A puff of dust rose from the road. Four horsemen – Rajthanan cavalry in russet tunics and turbans – came galloping towards the cart.

Another shot.

Charles raised the musket.

'No.' Jack pushed the muzzle down. 'We'll have to run for it.'

They leapt from the cart and charged across the field to the left, Jack with the pistol and Charles with the musket and a satchel of ammunition. Their boots scattered ash. Dead sheep lay about, burnt so badly they were like skeletons dipped in tar. Saleem made tiny yelps as he ran along. Jack's heart flew and his chest pinched.

A row of stark trees appeared ahead. Two shots were fired and this time Jack heard the whistle of the bullets. Looking back, he saw the cavalrymen leave the road and race across the field, black clouds of soot rolling out from the horses' hooves.

He reached the trees, and found a short slope on the far side. A grey river ran along the bottom of the slope, and beyond this lay further charred fields.

A bullet swished past.

He led the way down the slope and stood on the bank. The river was more than 150 feet wide, with no crossing in sight. He stared into the water, but it was too murky to gauge the depth.

He strode in, the cold enveloping him, and within a few paces the water was up to his chest. He looked back at Charles and Saleem. 'Quick.'

The three of them began to swim. Charles held the ammunition satchel out of the water, but there was no way to keep the firearms dry.

Halfway across, pain suddenly split Jack's chest. He gasped for air and lagged behind the others.

Damn his injury.

Charles slowed and looked over his shoulder.

'Keep going,' Jack said, but he was finding it difficult to swim. He floundered about in the cold water.

Charles paused, handed the satchel to Saleem, then swam back.

Jack spluttered. 'I said to keep going.'

Charles didn't reply and instead put his shoulder under Jack's arm and began to swim along on his side. Jack helped as best he could by kicking and flailing with one arm.

Shots slapped the water as they neared the bank. Charles and Saleem hauled Jack out on to the grass. He tried to stand, but his legs buckled and he slipped to the ground. He rasped and choked and the world circled dizzily about him. Distantly, he could hear the clatter of pistols and carbines.

'We've got to run,' Charles shouted.

Jack looked up and saw the lad's worried features through what seemed like wavering gauze. He swallowed and tried to stand again. This time Charles and Saleem were at his side and held him firmly when he almost slid down again.

A bullet lisped in his ear, and this was enough to spur him forward. He jogged with Charles and Saleem to either side, their arms locked about his back.

A three-foot-high earth embankment stretched a few yards away. They climbed over this and as they stumbled to the other side the breath was squeezed completely from his lungs. He slipped, a dead weight that not even his two companions could support, and rolled on to the ground, back against the embankment and just below the line of fire. He tried to breathe. Nothing. He tried again and this time air wheezed down his throat and the curtains of darkness began to recede.

He wiped the water and sweat from his forehead, his arm shaking slightly. When he glanced at Charles and Saleem he was taken aback by their expressions – they were both staring at him with their brows creased and jaws slack.

'I'm not dead yet,' he said.

Charles gave a small laugh and shook his head. 'You all right now, though?'

'Of course.'

Carbines spattered and bullets shrilled past.

Jack turned and raised his head gingerly over the top of the ridge, blinking away the water running into his eyes from his damp hair. The Rajthanans were pacing up and down on their horses on the far bank, seeming to consider whether or not to cross. When they saw him they fired another volley and he ducked back down again.

'We have to get out of here,' he said. 'Can't wait for that lot to find a way across.'

'Can you run?' Charles asked.

'I'll be all right.' He reached into his pocket, took out the vial of jatamansi and unscrewed the lid.

'What's that?' Charles asked.

'Medicine.'

He took a sip. Would it work?

At first nothing happened, but then, after a few seconds, his chest began to hum with warmth. The constriction and his breathing eased a little – he was sure he wasn't imagining it.

He shouldn't have doubted the jatamansi. Indian medicine was the best in the world.

A minute later he felt strong enough to stand again. He limped as they ran across the field, but he was still able to keep up the pace. The Rajthanans fired a couple of times but soon gave up.

After fifteen minutes they left the charred fields behind and crossed grassland untouched by the devastation. The ground inclined slightly towards the hills. Jack looked back from time to time, but no one was following them.

They slowed to a jog. The low hills buckled around them and the sky above was slate.

'Up there.' Jack pointed to the woods covering the summit of one of the hills.

They ran up the slope, but then slowed to a walk when Jack lost his breath. They reached the trees, stood beneath the canopy and looked down the way they'd come. Jack could see the drab river cutting across the black and grey fields, and beyond that the pale line of the road. Traces of dust revealed riders moving along the road in both directions.

'We have to keep moving,' he said.

They followed the line of the forest, across the summit, down into a valley and then over further hills. Jack kept an eye on the land below and saw riders on the road occasionally, but no sign of anyone coming across the fields.

He was tired and stumbled over tree roots and rocks.

'We should rest,' Charles said.

'No,' Jack replied quickly. But then he saw the look of concern on his companions' faces. 'All right. Until nightfall, then we carry on.'

They rested in a gully, hidden amongst the rocks and trees. They took off their damp tunics and draped them over stones to dry. Saleem gave a yelp as he laid out his clothing – he lifted the hem of his tunic to show a perfectly round bullet hole in the material.

Jack grinned. 'You were lucky.'

Saleem's eyes were wide and his face pure white. He licked his lips and put the hem down again.

Jack examined their weapons and supplies. When he opened the ammunition satchel he found that Charles and Saleem had kept the bag of powder dry, but there was only a handful of cartridges, percussion caps and pistol balls. The musket and the pistol had both received a good soaking in the river, and he carefully took them apart with the musket tool and tried to clean the pieces as best he could with a cloth.

Charles assisted and Jack noted that the boy was quick at reassembling the musket. Jack nodded with approval when Charles screwed the lock into place and held the weapon up with one hand.

They slept into the evening, taking turns to keep watch. Jack tried to rest, but his mind spun ceaselessly.

'Remember, in the army we are here to uphold dharma,' Jhala had said to him many times. 'Dharma defines the rightful order of things. The Empire has brought dharma to Europe. We are upholding the rightful kingdom, Rama's kingdom.'

But Jack kept seeing those bodies lying in the burnt fields below. Was this dharma? Was this Rama's kingdom?

He'd thought he knew the Rajthanans. Some were kind, some were harsh. But, at a basic level, they were an honourable people. Now he wasn't so sure.

When it was dark they set off again and picked their way up the side of the gully. Cloud smothered the moon and there was little light beneath the trees. An owl hooted.

Jack paused at the top of the scarp to get his breath back.

A man's voice in the dark said, 'Greetings, friend.'

Jack jumped and Saleem gasped. Charles had the musket off his shoulder in a second and released the knife-catch, the blade clacking out.

'We're friends,' the man said. 'Don't shoot.'

Jack narrowed his eyes. It was difficult to see in the dark. He made out a rocky ridge, and beneath it about thirty hooded figures, some sitting, some standing.

'Who are you?' He took a few steps towards them, his hand resting on the pistol in his belt. Charles and Saleem came up behind him.

'Just travellers, like you.' The man stood, his face hidden by his cowl.

'They're lepers,' Saleem hissed. He pointed at the castanets that were tied to the man's bleached wrist – all lepers were required to carry these when they travelled.

'We are,' the man said. 'You'd best keep your distance.'

Saleem and Charles backed away.

Jack looked around the forest. 'You live here?'

'No. We left our colony when the Rajthanans came. So far they've left us alone but we're not taking any chances. We're headed for Wiltshire.'

Jack nodded. 'Good luck to you.'

'Which way are you going?' the man asked.

'To London.'

'You're going east? The quickest way is through the Thames basin. But don't go that way. Go to the north instead, towards Oxford.'

'We can't make a detour. We have to get to London quickly.'

The man's cloak rustled as he moved. 'Something bad happened at the mills. I heard rumours. The rebels destroyed the place months ago and now the air's poisoned with sattva.'

'We'll have to take our chances.'

'Then God keep you.' The leper raised his white hand, the castanets rattling like bones.

'God keep you too,' Jack said.

He turned. Charles and Saleem were staring at him and shifting nervously. Silently, he led them away through the forest, still heading towards London and the Thames basin.

'What did he mean – poisoned with sattva?' Saleem asked as they walked.

'Don't know,' Jack replied gruffly.

'Shouldn't we go another way?' Saleem tripped on a stone, but regained his footing.

Jack stopped suddenly and turned. Saleem was starting to irritate him. 'The Thames basin is the quickest way. Right, Charles?

'Yes.' Charles's voice was slightly cracked.

'Then that's the way we'll have to go. You're both free to go home if you want to.'

'I'm carrying on,' Charles said without hesitation.

Saleem paused. 'So am I. I'm going to do my bit.'

Jack's muscles felt heavy. He didn't even have the strength to be irritated any more. When he looked at Charles and Saleem he could see that, despite everything, they were determined to get to London. He couldn't think of anything to say to discourage them, unless he was going to reveal that he wasn't a supporter of the mutiny at all, that he was . . . a traitor? That was what Harold had called him. But that was right, wasn't it? That was what he truly was.

He paused, then nodded at Charles and Saleem without speaking, turned and led the way along the track again. He could hear his companions' footsteps behind him, the steady strides of Charles and the smaller steps of Saleem. He wasn't going to shake off those two in a hurry, he could see that.

For the moment, they were his men, his tiny platoon.

12

Jack, Charles and Saleem crouched behind the undergrowth and looked down from the hills to the Thames basin. The plain appeared to smoulder beneath the first trace of yellow dawn. Obscure buildings spread out across the east in a tangled, steaming line: thin towers, smoking chimneys, walls, slanted roofs. They formed a tumbling barrier, blocking the way to London. Half-submerged fires glowed here and there, and Jack smelt coal smoke and the faint, sweet scent of sattva.

'Are those the mills?' Saleem whispered.

Jack nodded. He'd seen mills before in Europe, although never on such a large scale.

'Are they still working?' Saleem toyed with his wispy beard.

'They're abandoned,' Charles replied. 'That's what I was told. The Rajthanans were driven out by the crusade.'

Saleem bit his bottom lip. 'My father said there're demons inside them.'

'No,' Jack said. 'They're avatars – like machines.'

Below them, at the base of the slope, ran a north–south road. As they watched, a squadron of cavalry appeared and trotted past.

'Looks like the Rajthanans are pushing into this area,' Jack said. 'We'll have to wait until nightfall.'

He was anxious about the delay, but there was little choice. They'd spent more than a day getting across Hampshire. They'd kept to the hills and forests, travelling only at night and keeping an eye out for Rajthanan patrols. Three days had passed since they'd left the village and the army might now be close behind.

There were twelve days left before Elizabeth was executed.

'What about the poison?' Saleem asked.

'Sattva's not poisonous,' Jack replied. Not as far as he knew anyway.

They found a shallow cave, hidden by vines and bushes, and slept through the humid day. Jack took the first watch, then handed over to Charles in the early afternoon.

As he slept, Jack dreamt he was back at Ragusa, on the muddy plain, running. The guns flashed but everything was silent. Despite the chaos and destruction and bullets and shot, he heard nothing.

His battalion was far ahead of him – it was hard even to see them in the battle smoke. A few feet before him a body lay in the mud – Private Robert Salter, staring straight up, dead eyes reflecting the grey light. Jack stumbled and fell to his knees, then bullets pelted the ground around him and he got back up and ran on.

More bodies. Lying all around him. He had to dodge to avoid stepping on them.

He saw Sengar and Kansal, lying close together, their tunics and turbans stained with mud. He saw William – the older William. Then he saw a woman. It was Katelin, her long blonde hair splayed out as though she were floating underwater. Her face was drawn, as it had been in her last weeks, but she was still beautiful. The Celtic cross necklace hung to one side, against her shoulder. He felt sick. He stopped to look at her, but the bullets rained about him and he had to continue.

He tripped on a body and saw it was Charles, and nearby lay Saleem. He tried to shout, but couldn't make a sound.

He staggered on. One further body emerged from the fog. He slowed. Even before seeing the face he knew it was Elizabeth . . .

He woke with a start, sweating and gasping.

'Easy.' Charles crouched beside him. 'You all right?'

Jack nodded. He wiped the sweat from his forehead and looked around. It was growing dark, the light faint on the cave walls. 'We should go.'

They woke Saleem, who blinked and scratched himself. 'I'm hungry.'

'There's nothing to eat,' Jack replied. The day before they'd shot a couple of hares and cooked them over an open fire. But they couldn't waste time hunting now.

Jack loaded the pistol and Charles the musket, then they left the cave and looked down over the plain. The sky was darkening and merging with the charcoal landscape. The mills were indistinct crenellations and the fires were brighter now, livid red in the gloom.

They skidded down the slope, the smell of smoke and sattva growing stronger. At the bottom, the road ran along the top of an embankment. They scrambled up the side and paused, looking both ways. When they saw nothing in either direction, they crossed quickly and went down the other side.

They jogged across the plain. The ground was barren – coarse grass and rocks. Fragments of coal lay everywhere. There were no trees, nothing to give them cover. But at least it was a dark night and the moon was shut out by the smoke.

After a few minutes, Jack heard the distant clop of horses behind and to the north. He stopped and looked along the road. He couldn't see far in the thickening dark, but after staring for a moment he made out grey traces of dust. The sound grew louder, the horses drawing nearer.

'What is it?' Charles couldn't hear the sound yet.

'Patrol, I reckon,' Jack said.

He glanced around the flat and desolate plain. The first of the mills would take at least fifteen minutes to reach, even if they ran. But closer, standing alone, was a two-storey stone tower topped by a brass rod – a sattva link. It was the only place nearby he could see to hide.

They sprinted towards the tower, the brittle ground crunching like snow beneath their feet. Jack led them around the base of the octagonal structure until they were out of sight of the road. He panted and leant against the wall, sensing the quiver of a strong stream in the air. The smell of sattva coiled out of an arched entryway at the base of the building. He wondered for a moment whether there would be any guards inside, but he doubted it – normally they would be posted outside the entrance. And there would be no operators within either. Even though he'd never used the link himself, he could tell by the size and shape of the tower that it was a way station and not a terminus.

The jingle and clop of the horses grew louder. He edged around the wall and looked back. Ten horsemen cantered past along the road. He could just discern the red-brown of their uniforms – Rajthanan cavalry. They didn't slow their pace or even look in Jack's direction.

He slipped back around the tower and saw Saleem standing beside the entryway, staring up into the darkness.

'Keep away from it.' He didn't want Saleem to do anything stupid. For extra effect he added, 'There's one of your demons up there.'

Saleem stepped back quickly, his fingers fiddling with the bullet hole in his tunic as if it were an old wound.

Jack peered ahead to the jagged row of mills. The buildings were closer now, but still partially concealed by the dark and the blotches of smoke. Two red fires flickered like a pair of watchful eyes at the top of one of the nearer towers.

'Which way now?' Charles asked.

'Over there, I reckon.' Jack pointed to the open ground between two clusters of mills.

They struck out across the plain, with one silent gathering of mills to the right and another rising from the gloom to the left. The ground suddenly changed to gravel beneath their feet.

When he looked down, Jack could tell they'd come to a road – he saw the faint trace of the route snaking away across the flat land.

He stopped, listened carefully and heard more horses coming towards them. Squinting, he saw the wisps of dust from the hooves and the dark patches of the animals moving against the even darker background.

'Another patrol.' He looked around. The nearest mills weren't far – less than five minutes away if they ran. 'Follow me.'

They sprinted across the open ground. Jack hoped they hadn't been seen. It was dark, so they might be lucky, but on the other hand they would stand out clearly on that empty plain. The breath became tight in his lungs and the familiar pain wormed across his chest.

A ten-foot-high stone wall stretched around the mills for as far as he could see. An arched entrance lay less than fifty yards away to the right. He looked back and made out the horses cantering along the road. They were close enough now for him to see the red tunics of the riders.

With his throat burning and his legs aching, he finally reached the arch. Charles and Saleem drew up beside him. Cracks fanned across the wall and the parapet was shattered in places. Pillars stood to either side of the entrance, listing slightly to the right, and a statue of the elephant-headed god Ganesh squatted above, also tilted to the side.

Jack glanced back and his heart lurched when he saw the riders leave the road and strike out towards them.

'Think they've seen us.' He nodded towards the arch. 'In there.'

They ran through the opening and came out in a silent, cobbled street that was lit by the red gleam of the two floating fires. Crumbling stone buildings formed a hacked line against the night, and a wide crater lay across the middle of the street.

The sound of the horses grew louder. Jack led the way to a structure that was little more than a broken wall and a mound of rubble. They hid around the side of the collapsed masonry and peered back at the archway.

Jack heard a distant, regular thumping. It sounded as though some of the mills were still working – although that seemed unlikely, given that the place had been abandoned.

Five Rajthanan horsemen clopped through the arch and into the street. Their leader raised his hand to halt them and then scanned the surroundings. Pain jabbed Jack in the chest and he heard Saleem breathing hard behind him. He drew the pistol from his belt.

The riders spoke to each other for a minute, but Jack couldn't make out what they were saying. Finally, the leader ordered them back out of the entrance and Jack heard the horses trotting away.

'Have they gone?' Charles asked.

'Think so,' Jack replied. 'Wait here.'

He crept back down the street, keeping close to the walls and the thick shadows. When he reached the arch, he pressed himself beside it, then looked out. He could see the plain, with the hills they'd left behind in the distance, but nothing else. He stuck his head out further and spotted the horses disappearing in the direction of the road. It looked as though the Rajthanans had given up – perhaps they'd been unsure about what they'd seen, or decided that three people on foot were no danger and not worth pursuing.

Jack went back to Charles and Saleem. 'They've gone. For now, at any rate. We have to keep moving. They might be back at any time.'

They all glanced up the street. The ruined buildings melted towards the earth and the walls were pocked with holes. Sticky soot bled over the stonework. The ground was gored by shell craters and spent round shot lay scattered about like giant animal droppings.

'What happened here?' Saleem asked.

'There was a battle for the mills,' Charles said. 'But the Rajthanans were beaten.'

Jack remembered the news reports. About a month after London fell, the mutineers had marched on the Thames basin and routed the Rajthanans.

'Which way now?' Charles asked.

'We'll go through the mills.' Jack nodded up the street. 'It'll be slower, but it'll be easier to hide if we need to. There're too many patrols about.'

'Are the Rajthanans back here?' Saleem asked. 'I mean, here in the mills?'

'Looks deserted.' Although Jack could still hear the faint, monotonous pounding. 'Keep your eyes peeled, all the same.'

They sneaked forward, picking their way around the holes in the road and staying in the shadows as far as possible. The buildings were all the same – large rectangular blocks with no decoration, save for cupolas and spires that floated far above. Giant entryways and shattered walls opened on to gloomy interiors. Smaller roads led away to the left and right, but Jack ignored these and kept straight ahead.

The air was thick with coal smoke, and tiny tremors continually crossed Jack's skin. They'd passed into a sattva stream so wide it was more of a lake.

He noticed Saleem holding his arm up to his face and breathing through his sleeve.

'Poison,' Saleem said when he saw Jack looking at him.

'Sattva's not a vapour,' Jack said. 'You can't breathe it in. It's everywhere. In everything.'

Saleem's eyes widened as he looked at the invisible enemy all around him.

'Anyway,' Jack said. 'Sattva smells sweet. Can you smell anything sweet?'

'No,' Saleem replied.

'Then there's nothing to worry about.'

Jack could smell sattva, but he knew it was too weak for his companions to make out.

Most Europeans, if they thought about it at all, believed sattva was a gas or a type of wind. But Jhala had told Jack, 'Sattva is what you English call an element. It is a part of matter. But the purest part, the closest to the spirit realm.'

Saleem gingerly lowered his arm and breathed in the smoky air, but his eyes stayed wide and glassy.

They set off again and after a quarter of an hour they reached a point where a wide boulevard intersected the street. Jack waved Charles and Saleem into the shadows behind him and peered around the corner. Smashed trees, stripped of all their leaves and most of their branches, lined the boulevard. A battered structure, which must once have been a fountain or statue, cowered in the middle of the road. The streets were otherwise empty in all directions.

Saleem gave a short gasp. Jack shot back into the shadows and had his pistol out in a second. The lad was standing deeper in the gloom beside a broken wall, looking down at a pile of rubble.

'What is it?' Jack whispered.

Saleem just pointed and said nothing.

Jack and Charles walked over and soon saw the grey-white bones of three skeletons. The flesh had been completely picked clean, and rusted scimitars and muskets lay nearby. Jack couldn't tell whether they had been Rajthanans or mutineers, as both sides carried the same weapons.

Jack and Charles crossed themselves.

Then they heard a metallic scrape from somewhere behind them. It sounded like a hollow drum being dragged across the ground.

'What was that?' Saleem's breath shivered.

Jack gazed down the road, but everything was still and silent, save for the perpetual muffled rumble in the distance. He cocked the hammer of the pistol, while Charles slid the musket from his shoulder.

There was another scrape, this time longer and deeper, like a growl.

Jack spotted movement near the corner of a side street. Something large was clambering over a pile of collapsed stones. At first he thought it was an elephant, but then he saw feelers and stalks protruding from the front of the shape, and the dull reflection of red light on black iron. He couldn't believe what he was seeing.

'A demon.' Saleem said.

'No,' Jack said. 'It's a train avatar.'

'But there's no train,' Saleem said.

It was true – the beast was hauling itself along entirely independently of any carriages. Jack had never seen that before. There had to be a siddha somewhere nearby controlling the creature. He glanced up and around, trying to see whether there was anyone on the roofs above.

The avatar snorted and puffed, smoke streaming out from its sides, then it turned into the street and clawed itself towards them like some giant crustacean.

'Follow me.' Jack charged across the boulevard and into the shadows on the far side. His chest tensed and ached once again.

After they'd run for a few minutes, he looked back and saw that the avatar was still coming towards them, and was now increasing its speed. It jerked along at a pace almost as fast as they had been running. He frowned. He could still see no sign of any Rajthanans, but the avatar had to be receiving instructions from someone.

He scanned the surroundings, his mouth dry. There was a giant arched entrance nearby. Going in there would be risky, but at least they would be out of view and away from the avatar.

They slipped across the street and into the shadowy interior. As his eyes adjusted, Jack could see they were in a vast, empty chamber. Iron girders criss-crossed far above and the walls rose in thick stone pleats. Far away at the other end of the hall lay a further arch, out of which floated a pounding noise and the scent of coal and sattva.

Keeping to the edge of the wall, they made their way across the chamber and stole up to the second opening.

Both Charles and Saleem drew their breaths in sharply as they peered around the side. Before them was an even larger hall, dominated by a steel leviathan more than a hundred yards long. It looked something like a whale and something like a giant caterpillar, its body consisting of thousands of metal ribs, through which Jack could see the flicker of frantically knitting needles. At one end, a fanged maw chewed the air. There was a ring of metal slicing against metal and a chugging roar. On one side, like a wound, a hatch lay open, revealing a coal fire within. The red light from the flames was the only illumination in the chamber.

'What on earth—' Charles whispered.

'It's a mill avatar.' Jack had seen one before, in Paris. 'It makes things – cloth, steel, all kinds of things.' He remembered seeing the raw materials fed into the creature's mouth, with the finished substances excreted at the other end.

The Rajthanans prized these beasts above everything else. The creatures grew fat in the rich streams of sattva that crossed Europe – fatter even than the avatars back in Rajthana. The Rajthanans would do anything to protect the sattva supply that kept the things alive. Jack knew they would never give up England and its sattva.

'I thought the mills were abandoned,' Saleem said. 'Why's it still alive?'

'Don't know.' Jack gripped the pistol more tightly. The Rajthanans might have fired the creature up again – and if they had, they might still be somewhere nearby.

He heard a tortured screech and a wheeze of steam. Looking back, he saw two train avatars silhouetted in the archway to the street. Their feelers swayed as they checked the air and their inner fires glowed through the joins in their carapaces. For a moment he considered running past the beasts and back to the road. But the avatars could move fast – much faster than he'd thought possible. Would they attack? He'd never considered this possibility before. In fact, he'd scoffed at those who were afraid of the creatures. But the beasts had claws and mandibles and he wasn't sure now what they might be capable of.

'We're trapped,' Saleem said.

'We'll fight them.' Charles swung the musket from his shoulder.

'No.' Jack put his hand on Charles's arm. 'We'll find another way out.'

He led Charles and Saleem around the edge of the chamber containing the giant mill avatar. He stuck to the thickest shadows and peered through the hazy dark, wondering whether there were any Rajthanans nearby. The sound of the avatar was deafening – a ceaseless shrieking and roaring – so there was no chance of him hearing the approach of any enemies.

As they drew closer, the mill avatar became restive. It writhed within its harness of chains, which hung from the distant, invisible ceiling and suspended the beast five feet or so above the floor. It emitted a deep groan, like a fog horn, and tried to turn its mouth in their direction. Stalks and feelers at the top of its head quivered. The chains shook and rattled and the avatar bucked and strained in the harness, but was unable to break free.

Saleem whimpered and Charles's jaw was tight as he gazed at the monster.

'Keep going,' Jack shouted above the roar.

They went more quickly now and in less than five minutes reached the far end of the hall. There they found an arch that led into a passage lit only by a faint, silvery glow at the far end. Jack drew the pistol and led the way down the hall. The thump and bellow of the mill avatar still echoed about them, but gradually became more muffled. The air was hot and close and Jack felt sweat beading under his tunic.

At the end of the passage he paused, looked cautiously around the corner and saw a small, plain room with a pile of coal against one wall. The only other exit was an archway with angular sigils engraved across the top. The markings looked like the secret script of the siddhas. Although he couldn't read them, he recognised the shapes from papers on Jhala's desk.

He paused before the arch. Beyond lay a further passage, slightly better illuminated by the same silvery radiance. A strong scent of sattva hit him in the face and the hair shivered on the back of his neck. He'd never been this deep into a mill and he couldn't help recalling the rumours he'd heard from his countrymen: that the siddhas drank human blood; that the souls of Europeans were trapped inside the avatars; even that the siddhas were the Devil's apostles on earth. These wild claims were far from the truth – Jack knew enough about the siddhas to be sure of that – but at the same time he found himself reluctant to go further.

He heard a metal screech behind him, louder than the din of the mill. He glanced back down the hall they'd just travelled along, seeing the faint red glow of the mill avatar, but nothing else.

'Was that one of those things?' Saleem tugged at the ginger fluff on his chin.

Jack couldn't see any movement at the end of the passage, but all the same, the train avatars could be close. It was too risky now to go back and find another way out.

'Follow me.' He strode through the archway, passing beneath the jagged sigils.

They jogged down the passage, the pale light growing stronger. The walls were made of some form of black, gleaming stone that was moist when Jack's hand brushed against it.

The passage turned to the right and then opened up into a larger, cooler chamber. The room looked something like a workshop and something like a fishmonger's. Dangling from hooks about the walls were what appeared to be the limp parts of smaller avatars – metal fish heads, lobster claws, backbones and fine ribs. Flayed and decapitated creatures lay on benches with their innards spilling out and bleeding oil. The whole place was lit by a sickly glow, but Jack couldn't determine the source of the light.

'What is this place?' Charles hissed.

'Don't know,' Jack said, although clearly this was where avatars had once been built and repaired.

He crossed to the far side of the room and parted a curtain of hanging avatar pieces, the metal scraping and tinkling like cutlery. Beyond this was another workshop, even larger than the first, dotted with openings that led in all directions to further chambers. The place was a warren and it would be easy to get lost.

'Jack.'

Jack turned and saw Charles pointing through the screen of dangling metal. Saleem was still standing at the entrance to the first room, licking his lips and staring at the grotesques hovering around him.

'Hurry up.' Jack was growing concerned at Saleem's nervousness. There was no telling what the lad might do if he got a fright.

Saleem took a step into the room. A harsh screech, like the cry of some giant bird, resounded up the passage behind him. He jumped and rushed over to Jack and Charles.

'Stay close,' Jack said. 'And pull yourself together.'

Saleem glanced up, eyes wide, and nodded as he bit his bottom lip.

Jack pressed on, keeping straight and dodging the benches that blocked their way. The train avatars could still be following them and he wanted to get as far ahead of the creatures as he could. At the same time, there might be further enemies within the workshops themselves and he kept a close eye on the surroundings, watching for any quick movement that might indicate the presence of something hostile.

They went through chamber after chamber, arch after arch. By travelling in a straight line Jack hoped he wouldn't get lost. He was increasingly surprised by the size of the place and started to wonder how long it would take to find a way out.

He heard another metal screech off to the left. He stopped and peered through the receding arches and suspended avatar parts.

He saw nothing, no movement of any sort. But then there was a further screech, slow this time, like a creature in agony.

'This way.' He ducked through an arch to his right and ran, smashing through the jangling metal screens.

After they'd charged along for about two minutes, he paused to catch his breath. With Saleem and Charles panting beside him, he gazed back through the swaying curtains. He saw no sign of anything behind them.

Saleem gasped, tripped and fell against a bench, sending pieces of metal clattering to the floor.

Jack grasped the pistol, spun round. His heart was in his throat.

Saleem was on the floor and scrambling back to his feet. In front of him, hidden in a recess, stood a train avatar. Jack pointed the pistol and almost pulled the trigger, but then noticed that the creature was completely still, its claws and stalks drooping and the fire within it dead.

He lowered the pistol. 'It's all right. It's not active.'

Saleem stood, knocking over further bits of metal, and edged back from the lifeless beast.

Jack went to turn away, then froze. One of the creature's feelers had flicked upright. Flame roared alight in its abdomen, the glow escaping between the cracks in the carapace. It raised its claw, gave a harsh squeal and lunged at Saleem.

Saleem stumbled back, slipped, almost fell, turned and sprinted across the room. Charles wrenched the musket off his shoulder and aimed. Jack fired and the pistol flashed and kicked. The ball tinged against the beast's iron cladding, but seemed to cause no damage.

The creature jolted to a stop. Chains held it in place, and although it struggled against them it couldn't break free. It roared, grumbled and snapped its outstretched claws.

'You all right?' Jack called over to Saleem.

Saleem nodded, eyes shining.

The avatar paused for a moment, then tried to lunge again.

One of the chains was wrenched from the wall and spilt across the ground, but the others held firm.

'This way.' Jack charged out of the room. He didn't stop to see if Charles and Saleem were following, but he could hear their boots clacking on the stone floor.

He ran through a wide arch that was bordered by more sigils, and then came to a halt so suddenly that Charles smacked into him from behind. They were in an octagonal chamber that was far larger than the previous workshops. Blackened pipes veined the walls, twisting up towards a distant ceiling. Pallid light trailed down like cold liquid, only faintly illuminating the room. In the centre rose a monolithic statue of a man sitting cross-legged, his chest bare and his long hair tied in a topknot. His eyes were closed and there was an ambiguous trace of a smile on his lips. A beaded necklace wound about his neck, and his hands, with index fingers and thumbs pinched, rested on his bent knees.

Jack reeled from the overpowering smell of sattva – it grated in his throat and lungs so that he felt he was drowning in honey.

'I can smell something sweet.' Saleem shoved his hand over his nose and mouth. 'Poison.'

'You'll be all right,' Jack replied. 'Let's find a way out.'

He shivered. It was cold in the room, but more than that he recognised the statue – Sarvesh Brahmarishi, the first siddha. He'd heard all about the Brahmarishi during his training in yoga. Jhala had explained that it was Sarvesh who had first discovered how to smelt sattva more than 800 years ago, and had gone on to form the order of the siddhas. The descendants of that order had fought alongside a prince named Jaidev Chauhan 200 years later to defeat the Mohammedan invaders and found Rajthana.

'What on God's earth is this?' Charles was standing to the side of the statue.

Jack walked over and saw a raised circular dais, on top of which stood a mass of pipes, tubes and wires, all covered in soot. Metal prongs rose like claws around the edges of the machinery and in the centre was an iron surface, engraved with what appeared to be a siddha in a robe and turban. The siddha held aloft an amorphous lump that looked something like a foetus.

'It's nothing.' Jack didn't want to alarm the others, particularly Saleem. But from the engraving it looked as though the device were something to do with binding avatars to the material world.

At any rate, the room gave him an unholy feeling, as if some violent crime had taken place there and still hung in the air like a wronged spirit.

He cleared his throat. 'Come on. We can't stand around here.'

They found an arch in the far wall, and Jack felt a weight lifting as they left the chamber.

They were in another workshop, with the same layout of arches leading to further workshops for as far as he could see in the dim, silvery light.

Which way now?

He picked a direction at random and set off, moving quickly, but no longer running. He tried to tread as quietly as he could. He gazed ahead through the disappearing arches and saw no sign of the avatars, but also no sign of a way out.

Once they were well away from the statue chamber, he paused to reload the pistol, and then they sneaked forward for another ten minutes or more. The sound of the mill avatar had now faded to a hushed thumping. A cool breeze touched his right cheek. He sniffed and detected a hint of distant trees and grass beneath the stronger notes of coal and sattva – the smell of the night air. There had to be an exit nearby.

He went to the right now, following the scent. Twice he lost the smell and had to retrace his steps until he picked it up again. Finally, he found an archway that took them out into another giant hall with ribbed girders arcing far above. A harness hung from the gloomy ceiling but there was no mill avatar within the chains. The only light filtered in from outside through a colossal arch in one wall.

'Thank the Lord,' Charles said. 'That place was unholy.'

'Praise to Allah,' Saleem said.

'We're not out of here yet,' Jack said. 'Keep your voices down.'

They crept about the side of the chamber and came to the arch. Jack peered outside and saw an empty square, dotted with spent round shot, cracked paving stones and shell holes. Vague white lines were scattered about – skeletons, hundreds of them. They lay scratching at the ground, grasping for weapons that had been removed long ago, the remains of their clothing now tattered fragments that lifted at each call of the wind.

There was no sign of any living creature – or avatar.

Saleem's breathing was short and loud.

'Let's go,' Jack said. Their best hope was to get out of the mill town completely, get back to the open ground. There might be patrols about, but it was better than dealing with the avatars—

A metal shriek.

Jack's heart jerked. The gigantic form of a mill avatar, free of its harness, rolled into the street. It raised itself up, the stalks near the top of its head rippling, its maw a scintillating vortex. It gave a bubbling growl, then undulated towards them on its metal ribs.

Charles shouted and fired the musket. There was a flash and a puff of smoke, but it had no effect at all on the creature. Jack couldn't tell whether the bullet had even hit its intended target.

'Forget it,' Jack shouted.

He turned and saw no one behind him. Saleem had vanished.

Damn. Where had the lad gone?

Then he saw, in the distance at the far end of the street, a speck of a figure in white disappearing through an archway. Beyond, he could just see the suggestion of the open plains.

'This way.' Jack sprinted towards Saleem. The lad was a fool, but at least he'd run in the right direction.

The avatar came after them, its ridged body grinding against the cobblestones and its teeth whirring and ringing. But it was slow – no faster than a man jogging – and within minutes they'd left it behind.

Smarting at the pain in his chest, Jack arrived at the arch. The open ground stretched for as far as he could see to his right, blurring into the smoke-laced murk. Ahead and to the left lay further mill towns, brooding behind their walls.

But there was no sign of Saleem. Where the hell had the lad gone? The idiot shouldn't have run off like that. He might have been afraid, but that was no excuse.

'Saleem! Saleem!' Charles shouted.

Jack looked down and noticed Saleem's boot prints leading off across the open ground. They were the only tracks he could see. 'Over here.'

They ran from the mills as the avatar came lumbering up the street. Jack heard a smack, the impact rippling through the earth. When he looked over his shoulder, he saw that the creature had run into the wall, cracking it in several places. Its mouth shimmered behind the archway, then it reared above the wall, roaring as it swept its feelers through the air. It gave a series of guttural cries that resonated across the plain, but didn't pursue them.

Jack's breath was short and black pools were expanding before him. He stopped, bent double, and took a swig of jatamansi.

'I'm all right,' he said between gasps when Charles came over to him.

'That thing's gone, at least.' Charles nodded behind them.

Jack looked back and saw that the creature had indeed slithered away up the street. The jatamansi spread a subtle warmth across his chest and he found he could breathe more easily. He stood up straight, grimacing at the continuing jabs of pain, and scanned the dark landscape. There was still no sign of Saleem. Where could the boy have gone? He couldn't have run fast enough to be out of sight already.

Again Jack's eyes fell upon Saleem's tracks in the sandy soil. They would be easy to follow, despite the dim light – there were few other markings and the prints were only minutes old. And yet, Jack didn't want to waste time tracking the boy. Why should he care what happened to Saleem? The idiot had run off on his own. Jack had to get to London and he couldn't let anyone slow him down.

But it would be hard to leave Saleem behind. The lad was only sixteen and somehow Jack felt responsible for him, even though there was no reason for it.

Damn it.

'He went this way,' Jack said. 'I can see the tracks.'

Charles glanced at the ground and frowned. 'Where?'

'Just follow me.'

Jack led the way across the plain, keeping an eye both on Saleem's trail and the empty landscape in case another patrol appeared.

'Saleem!' Charles shouted.

'Quiet,' Jack said. 'There might be Rajthanans about.'

After they'd jogged for ten minutes, Saleem's tracks suddenly stopped. Jack frowned and crouched to study the ground. A ten-foot-wide circle of soil had been disturbed, wiping out the trail. It looked as though the earth had been churned with a hoe and then flattened again.

'What is it?' Charles asked.

'Don't know.'

Jack walked across the circle to see if the tracks continued on the other side. A few steps in he smelt a powerful waft of sattva. He stopped. What could have caused that?

'I'm sinking,' Charles shouted.

At that moment Jack noticed the ground around his own feet was crumbling away from under him. 'Get back.'

But it was too late. The ground slipped away and down, funnelling into a rapidly widening hole. Jack grasped at the side of the newly formed crater, but the soil was loose and there was nothing to hold on to. Both he and Charles were sliding down, helpless.

The ground at the base of the crater seemed to boil. Metal feelers rose through the earth.

What the hell . . . ?

Jack clawed futilely at the earth. He found himself shouting involuntarily. For a second he saw mandibles and a steel limb of some sort beneath him, then something grabbed his leg and dragged him with immense force through a thin layer of soil.

13

Jack hit the floor of a tunnel – hard. He passed out.

The next thing he knew he was hurtling along at great speed. It was completely dark, but he could sense earth walls racing past him. He was being held by the leg and dragged along on his back. He could hear Charles shouting nearby in the darkness.

He passed out again.

He came round as he rolled down a slope, bumping against metal and wooden objects. A terrible stench, like rotting vegetables, hit his nostrils.

He landed on something soft, but the impact still jolted him badly. His head felt like broken glass and an ache oozed across his chest.

It was pitch black all around him.

He heard gasps nearby and then voices – Charles and Saleem's.

'Jack, are you there?' Charles called out.

Jack tried to reply, but his breathing was so intermittent he couldn't raise his voice beyond a wheeze. He tried to force his lungs open. Darkness spread over him – he was going to faint again. He felt along his side for the jatamansi bottle. It was still in his pocket, thank God. He pulled the stopper off and took a sip.

'Jack!' Charles called again.

Jack's chest eased and the air filtered back into his lungs. 'Over here.'

He heard movement, the clattering of metal and the slurp of

mud. A match fizzed alight and Charles appeared, holding the flame in front of him, his face heavy in the dim light. Saleem stood nearby, his features ashen.

Jack sat up and felt beneath him; he'd landed on a pile of damp straw. He could see little of the surroundings, other than a few mounds of rubbish and the steep earth slope he'd just rolled down. The smell of rot and filth made his stomach clench. 'Where are we?'

Charles and Saleem pushed their way towards him through the sludge.

'Don't know,' Charles said. 'Can't see anything.'

'What happened?'

The match went out and Charles muttered and struck another. As the light flickered brighter, Charles glanced up the slope, which disappeared into the darkness. 'There was some sort of creature. Don't know what it was.'

'Another demon.' Saleem looked around as if the beast would pounce on them at any moment.

Jack stared up into the gloom and listened carefully. He heard nothing. Whatever the creature was, it seemed to have left them for the moment. He glanced at Saleem, whose face was glistening and pale.

Jack gestured to the lad. 'Come over here.'

Saleem, forehead creased with worry, dragged himself up the mound of straw and squatted beside Jack.

Jack grabbed Saleem's tunic at the neck, twisted the material and yanked him closer. 'You bloody idiot. You could've got us all killed.'

Saleem yelped and tried to pull away.

'I should have left you behind.' Jack bunched his hand into a fist. He was going to hit the lad – he could feel it. The fool had put all his plans at risk, put Elizabeth at risk.

'I didn't mean it,' Saleem wailed.

'Hey, look what I've found.' Charles proudly held a brass lantern aloft. Then the match went out and darkness enveloped them again.

Jack felt Saleem try to pull away, but he held the lad firm.

A few seconds later, Charles struck another match and the lantern glowed into life. Sallow light pushed back the darkness. All around them stood piles of refuse and detritus: mangled iron and steel, festering cabbages, sawdust, hay, coal. Rough earth walls rose steeply on all sides. And when Jack looked up he could see no light above, no glimpse of the sky. They appeared to be in a pit somewhere deep underground.

'We have to get out of here,' Charles said.

'You'll never get out,' a man's voice in the dark rasped and then groaned.

Jack let go of Saleem, who slipped back and clambered away. Jack grasped for the pistol, but found it was gone. It must have slipped out of his belt as he'd been dragged along. He saw that Charles had also lost the musket, although the ammunition satchel was still over his shoulder.

'Who are you?' Jack called out.

The man groaned again, but didn't reply.

Jack struggled to his feet, pain cutting into his chest.

Charles raised the lantern and trudged through the filth in the direction of the voice. Soon the light revealed a Rajthanan cavalryman lying against one of the walls. His turban had come off and his short hair was stuck to his scalp with sweat and grease. He grimaced, as if in pain. Then Jack noticed that both of his legs had been severed at the thigh, leaving two stumps dark with blood. He appeared unarmed – not that he was in a fit state to use a weapon anyway.

'What happened?' Jack asked.

The cavalryman made a sound as though he were straining to lift something. He spoke with difficulty. 'That thing. Took my legs off.'

'What is it . . . an avatar?' Jack asked.

'How should I know? Some kind of avatar, yes.'

'Not a train engine?' Even as Jack asked, he knew it wasn't. He'd seen parts of the creature momentarily and it had been larger than a train avatar, with insect-like legs and a swollen abdomen.

'No. You'll see for yourself, soon. It'll be back. It'll kill us all. Ate my friend – I watched him die.'

Jack paused. 'What's going on here? There're avatars all over the place. Who's controlling them?'

The cavalryman gave a choking laugh. 'No one's controlling them. They're running wild.'

'How?'

'No idea. They've been left alone for months. After the rebels came. Must have gone mad somehow.'

'We'll have to climb out,' Charles said.

They all looked up the almost vertical earth walls. Charles clambered to the top of the tallest mound of refuse, sinking into the mire up to his knees. He tried to climb the slope, but the soil crumbled away beneath his hands and he managed to get up only a few feet before sliding back down again.

Jack eyed the other walls; they were all equally steep. 'There's no way.'

'Maybe we can build a ladder out of this stuff.' Charles kicked a heap of metal fragments.

Jack doubted it. Few of the pieces of metal or wood were large or solid enough, and there was nothing with which to bind the pieces together.

Saleem gasped and stepped back, almost tripping. He was standing in a far corner of the pit that was barely lit by the lantern.

'What now?' Jack muttered.

Saleem stared at the ground before him, chewing his bottom lip.

Jack eased himself down from the straw and, with Charles, clambered across to the other side of the pit. A putrid reek made his throat tighten. Near Saleem stood a pile of what at first looked like black slime. But as Jack stared, he noticed lines of white beneath the sludge. Bones – ribs, legs, arms, skulls, some human, some not.

Charles crossed himself.

'What're we going to do?' Saleem whispered.

A deep gurgling came from above. They all looked up. The back of Jack's neck crawled and Saleem gave a soft whimper.

At first they could see nothing but complete darkness. Then there was a movement, a gleaming line that shifted then vanished, followed by another. Gradually the outline of a huge metal creature, somewhere between a spider and an ant, became visible. It climbed slowly down the side of the pit, its segmented legs glinting in the lantern light. Its head was covered in quivering stalks and its mouth was a mesh of constantly moving mandibles.

'Find something to fight it off,' Jack said.

They scrambled over the bottom of the pit, looking for weapons. Jack noticed his hands shaking as he fumbled through scraps of metal, mouldering vegetation and slag. He stopped for a second, tried to pull himself together. He took another sip of jatamansi.

He found a steel pole, which he held in the middle like a double-ended staff. Charles picked up a rusted scimitar, while Saleem produced a piece of varnished wood, which he raised like a cudgel.

They backed over to the side of the pit and surrounded the Rajthanan.

'Kill me.' The cavalryman was grey and slick with sweat. 'There's no hope.'

'You'll be all right,' Jack said. 'We won't leave you here.'

The creature crept to the bottom of the pit, the scent of sattva and coal strong now. It raised its head and examined the surroundings with its feelers. Its abdomen was constructed of metal ribs, but over these had been welded an odd conglomeration of objects – old kettles, barbed wire, cartwheels, pots. The collection hung like shaggy fur and rattled as the creature moved. An inner fire glimmered through the joins in its armour. Jack had never seen an avatar like it.

The beast advanced tentatively, feeling ahead with one of its legs. Jack's heart hammered and his breathing slackened. Perhaps the creature could be scared off, like an animal? He shouted and struck the protruding leg with the pole. The creature drew back, growled and sat on its haunches as though about to pounce.

Jack shouted again and waved one of his arms, still holding the pole with the other. The beast took another step back. It was working. He'd managed to confuse and frighten the creature.

But then it sprang forward, maw agitated.

Jack jabbed with the pole, but the beast moved aside with great agility and ran towards Saleem. The lad cried out and swung the club wildly. The creature flicked its leg and sent him flying against the wall, then pounced on the prone Rajthanan.

Charles shouted and ran at the creature's flank. The scimitar rang as it hit the huge abdomen.

Without turning its head, the beast shot out a limb and knocked Charles off his feet. The scimitar slipped from his hand. He leapt up again and grasped the blade. He was about to attack again, when Jack grabbed him from behind, shouting, 'Leave him. There's nothing we can do.'

Charles panted, stared at Jack, went to say something, but then stopped.

The beast towered over the Rajthanan, who cried out and waved his arms. A pointed proboscis extended from the creature's mouth. The Rajthanan tried to knock it away, but it shot forward and speared him in the chest. He screamed and struggled, grasping at the proboscis. The beast gave a slurping sound and blood oozed across the Rajthanan's chest. The monster appeared to be sucking.

The cavalryman shut his eyes and groaned in agony. He sobbed and pleaded, saying words in Rajthani that Jack couldn't understand.

Jack looked away. No one deserved to die like that, but there was nothing he could do to prevent it.

It seemed to go on for a long time. Saleem, on the other side of the pit, put his hands over his ears to block out the sound.

Finally, the Rajthanan went limp. The creature gave a regular gurgle, like a purr, then opened its mouth wide and engulfed the dead man's head. Bone and sinew cracked. Gore and blood ran out. The creature's maw worked and crunched, as though eating a carrot.

Jack breathed heavily. Pain seared his chest and he took another sip of jatamansi.

'What now?' Charles asked.

'If it comes near us, we fight.' Jack gripped the pole with both hands.

After more than ten minutes, the creature had completely devoured the Rajthanan. It slunk away to the other side of the pit and, with a burbling sound, regurgitated bones covered in red mucous on to the pile. The stench was sickening. Saleem put his hand over his mouth and then vomited quietly.

The beast now moved into the centre of the pit and scratched around in the refuse. It found a tin plate, still clean enough to wink in the lantern light, picked it up, spun it around, then placed it against the underside of its abdomen. There was a series of sparks and a wisp of smoke, and then the plate was welded to the creature's body.

It looked up again, turning first to Saleem and then to Jack and Charles. They all stood poised. But the creature merely grumbled and then moved to the side of the pit. It scuttled up the wall and soon vanished.

Charles breathed a sigh of relief.

Saleem sank to his knees, pressed himself back against the wall and tried to curl up as small as he could. He stared across at Jack and Charles with wounded, watery eyes.

Jack ignored Saleem – it was the boy's fault they were in this mess in the first place. He deserved to suffer a bit.

Charles shouted up into the darkness. 'Help! Anyone!'

Silence.

'We're too far underground,' Jack said. 'No one will hear us.'

'But that thing will be back,' Charles replied. 'You heard that cavalryman.'

Charles was right, and for a moment the hopelessness of the situation gnawed at Jack. But he had to overcome the feeling. Had to – for Elizabeth's sake.

He glanced at the ammunition satchel still on Charles's shoulder. 'That powder still dry?'

'Guess so.' Charles opened the bag. The small bag of powder, the paper cartridges and the bullets were all dry.

'Good.' Jack looked around the pit, thinking quickly. 'We need something to make a bomb. Some sort of container.'

'How about this?' Charles picked up an empty glass water bottle.

'Perfect.'

Jack and Charles crouched, dropped a few bullets into the bottle and carefully tipped in the grey-black powder. They then bit open the cartridges and poured in the powder from these as well. By the end the bottle was two-thirds full.

'We need a fuse.' Jack looked around and his eyes settled on the lantern. 'That'll do it.'

He tore a strip from his tunic and wound it into a fuse. He then dipped this into the lantern's oil reservoir until it was dripping. He rested the water bottle on a flat sheet of iron and laid out the fuse beside it.

'We have to do as much damage as we can with that.' He motioned to the bottle. 'I'm going to get it down that thing's mouth. It'll blow up inside.'

'Down it's mouth?' Charles said. 'Won't be easy.'

'I'll need to get in close. Just before it strikes.'

'I'll do it,' Saleem said suddenly. 'If it eats me I'll hold on to the bottle. It'll blow up in the thing's face.'

Jack looked up. Saleem was standing now, clenching and unclenching his fists. His face was chiselled and in the dim light it even looked as though he'd lost weight – in a matter of a few hours, the baby fat in his cheeks seemed to have disappeared.

'You think that'll make up for everything?' Jack asked.

Saleem's bottom lip trembled and he bit down to still it. 'No. But I made a mistake. I want to fix it.'

Jack snorted. 'It's all right. I'll do it.'

'But I want to. I won't let you down.'

Jack searched Saleem's face for a second. Despite his obvious fear, the boy wanted to fight. Jack couldn't deny it was an act of courage. But all the same, he knew he had to be the one who threw the bottle – he couldn't trust either Charles or Saleem. There was only one chance now and he had to be sure they made the most of it.

'No, I'll do it.' His voice was softer now.

Saleem's mouth drooped and he looked at his feet.

'But we'll still need your help,' Charles said to Saleem. 'Isn't that right, Jack?'

Jack looked away and nodded. He could have said something to console the lad, but held back. He didn't want to let him off the hook that easily.

'You see,' Charles said. 'Jack agrees. We're all in it together. We'll fight this thing and get out of here.'

Jack and Charles sat cross-legged, facing each other, on a mat they'd made out of a piece of sacking.

'Back straighter,' Jack said, and Charles adjusted his posture. 'Keep your palms open, face down. That's better.'

Jack led Charles into a battle meditation, going deeper and

deeper, layer by layer. He'd been surprised at Charles's poor technique – standards were obviously slipping in the army – but the lad was learning quickly.

When they finished the meditation, they did a series of yoga exercises. The spirit realm drew close. The terrible reek, the pit, the refuse and the bones were all distant and they hardly noticed them. They were also distant from themselves, coolly observing this world of pain and illusion.

Then Charles took out his beads and silently worked his way through the rosary. Saleem said his own prayers.

Jack crossed his legs again and was going to meditate on the regimental standard, but then stopped. He couldn't bring himself to picture the three lions. Instead he said a few Hail Marys under his breath, repeating the words in the traditional Latin.

Finally, they put out the lantern to conserve oil and sat in the dark, each with his own thoughts. Saleem and Charles slept, but Jack stayed awake, staring into the blackness.

His mind formed phantoms in the dark. He sensed shifts in the air and felt invisible presences come close and recede. Once he lit a match and stared about him to reassure himself there was nothing there.

Would the bomb work? He'd tried to sound confident in front of Charles and Saleem, but he wasn't sure.

If he'd learnt more yantras, had more powers, then he might have been better placed to fight the avatar. But he would have to make do with what he had.

What about the yantra he'd taken from Jhala's office? Should he try it again now? After all these years would it finally work and give him some power he could use against the avatar?

Of course it wouldn't work.

But all the same, he shut his eyes and focused on it, bringing to mind every detail. It wavered on a black background and soon locked into place, shining a dazzling white.

But, as always, nothing happened.

He breathed out, slumped a little. The wound in his chest throbbed and his head swam.

Jhala was right, Europeans couldn't learn the higher powers. The native siddha yantra was the only yantra they could use.

And yet, was this true? Hadn't Jhala himself once said something that offered a different explanation for Jack's inability to use the stolen yantra?

Jack hadn't often thought about Jhala's words that night, about a decade ago, but they had always been there at the back of his mind. Hadn't he, in fact, been trying not to think about them? Hadn't he shrugged them off whenever they'd popped into his head?

The regiment had been on campaign in Denmark and about to march into Swedeland – this was shortly before Salter's death. Jack had been meditating beside the campfire after the other men had gone to bed. Jhala had appeared and sat across from him. They spoke a little about yantras and siddhas, and Jack soon realised that Jhala had been drinking opium.

Finally, Jack said, 'Sir, can I ask something?'

'Of course.' Jhala's voice was slurred.

'You're a siddha but I've never seen you use a power.'

Jhala frowned, picked up a stick and used it to poke the embers of the fire. He was silent for a moment. 'You're right. My powers are limited. I only have a few and none of them are military. I used a power too soon, you see. That stopped me.'

'Stopped you?'

'It's the law of karma. Every action creates a reaction.' As if to demonstrate his point, he jabbed the stick into the fire and sparks flew up in response. 'Using a power is a drastic action – it entangles spirit and matter – and that means there's a drastic reaction. The reaction is that you cannot develop any further powers. You stop progressing. You can study yantras, memorise them, call them to mind, but you can never use the associated power. You're blocked. Your learning is over.'

There was an edge of bitterness to Jhala's voice. He snapped the stick and threw it into the flames.

'Sorry to hear that, sir.'

Jhala looked up. 'Oh, it doesn't matter. Old news. I had to use a power to save my life. No way out of it.' He smiled. 'Obviously I wasn't meant to be a great siddha – a mahasiddha. Of course, if I was a mahasiddha I wouldn't be using any powers anyway.'

Jack was lost now. 'Why, sir?'

'The law of karma, as I said. A mahasiddha won't use a power, because that would mean he couldn't learn any more. He withholds his powers, you see, in the hope that he can develop as far as he can. If you see a siddha use a power, then you can be almost certain he's not a mahasiddha.'

Now, Jack stared into the stinking darkness of the pit.

The law of karma. Once you use a power you can't learn any other powers. You're blocked. Couldn't that be why the stolen yantra never worked?

When Jack had developed his sattva-tracking power, Jhala had told him to use it immediately. Jhala hadn't said anything about the law of karma. Shouldn't he have told Jack about it? Couldn't Jack have learnt more if he'd been given the chance?

It was hard to believe, but could Jhala have held Jack back intentionally? Had Jhala made Jack into what he himself was – a blocked siddha with only limited powers?

Jack's fingers found a piece of metal and gripped it tightly. Thunder clouds gathered in his chest.

Had Jhala tricked him?

Jack heard a sound. He'd been sitting in complete silence for a long time – hours. He shook Charles and Saleem awake and lit the lantern. They looked up to where the glow of the lamp trailed off into darkness.

Silence.

Just as Jack thought he'd made a mistake, the sound came again – a slow, steely ring, as though a knife were being sharpened. Up the slope they saw a flicker of movement. Then another. Legs became visible, then the distended thorax, then the head swarming with feelers.

The creature gurgled, as though water were bubbling in a well. The flotsam and jetsam attached to its body tinkled as it crept to the bottom of the pit. It stood facing them and swivelled its head from side to side. Charles had the steel pole now, while Saleem held a rusting spade.

Jack's heart poked at his ribs and the pit began to circle slowly about him. He swallowed some jatamansi and sensed a tingling spread out from his breastbone. He bent down, stuck the fuse in the bottle and lit it. The flame leapt and crept slowly along the cloth. This was it – his last chance. If he couldn't kill the avatar, then Elizabeth would die. He swallowed but his mouth remained painfully parched.

The creature took a step forward, a trace of coal smoke puffing from its side.

Jack took a deep breath and advanced, knees bent. He moved the flaming bottle about and saw the creature's head follow the light.

'Come on,' he cried.

But the beast scuttled to the side, towards Charles.

'Get back.' Jack moved quickly to block the creature's path, bottle raised.

Charles edged behind Jack.

The creature gave a metallic growl and steam escaped with a hiss. It sat back on its haunches, then, without warning, leapt through the air over their heads. It arced through the darkness, jangling and clanking, and landed, with a grating squeal, on the wall above Saleem. It scurried down. Saleem tried to run, but he was up to his knees in mud. The creature was almost upon him.

Charles shouted and charged. The pole slammed into the beast's head and a stalk broke off. The creature clicked and gurgled and turned to face its assailant. Jack grasped Saleem and dragged him out of the mud. Saleem scrambled away and Jack almost fell over, but managed to hold on to the bottle.

The creature kicked the pole and sent it flying to the other side of the pit. It roared and jabbed at Charles with its mouth. Charles fell back, crying out.

'Hey!' Jack ran in front of the creature, waving the bottle.

The creature bellowed and opened its mouth wider. Jack was so close he could see the kaleidoscope of blades and mandibles, smell the blast of coal, sattva and rot.

Now. He should throw the bottle now. But he waited. That mouth was wide open, but it was too far away for him to be certain of getting the bottle down it.

Let the beast come closer . . .

His hand was slippery with sweat and his heart was bashing in his chest and he'd actually stopped breathing, not because of his illness, but because he was concentrating so hard on what he had to do.

The avatar leant forward and prepared to strike. The pointed proboscis extended from its mouth. Jack glanced at the bottle. The fuse had burnt down almost to the lip. He paused, then threw. The bottle glinted as it sailed through the air. It hit the side of the creature's mouth, but bounced off and landed in the mud a few feet away. The fuse glimmered, then went out.

Jack felt sick.

He ran towards the bottle, but one of the creature's legs shot out and tripped him up so that he fell on his back. For a second he saw the proboscis fly towards him. He cried out and rolled to the side. The proboscis splashed into the mud and the creature gave a contorted howl.

His breath was like fire in his throat and blackness threatened from the corners of his vision. He tried to stand, slipped back to his knees, struggled up again and dived, getting his hand on the bottle. He looked up to see the creature raising its head again, mouth flickering.

He looked back at Charles, who stood grasping the pole once more, eyes wide.

'Matches,' Jack shouted.

Charles threw him the box, but it went wide and landed two feet away. The proboscis shot out again, like a jet of water – Jack ducked and felt the wind of its passing in his hair. The proboscis smashed into a pile of metal, scattering fragments.

Jack jumped to his left and grasped the matchbox. Hands shaking, he reversed the fuse and scraped a match against his boot. It didn't light.

Something smacked him hard in the back and he fell forward, the breath knocked out of him and his chest screaming with pain. He flipped over and saw the creature towering over him. It slammed its leg into his breast and the rounded piece of metal at the end pinned him to the ground. He couldn't breathe. He grasped the metal leg and tried to move it aside, but it was locked in place. He wriggled and kicked but couldn't free himself. Coiling darkness crept across his vision and he shook his head to keep himself from slipping into unconsciousness.

Both Charles and Saleem shouted and rushed forward. Charles rammed the pole into the side of the beast, while Saleem smacked with the spade against the leg holding Jack.

Weak, Jack scraped a match against an iron sheet. The match snapped. Cursing, he got out another.

The beast knocked Charles against the far wall. It kicked the spade out of Saleem's hands, then brushed the lad aside.

Jack frantically scraped the second match. It wouldn't light. He was choking on the pain and was faintly aware that he must have bitten his lip as he could taste blood in his mouth.

The creature turned its head to him, roaring. The pointed proboscis edged out a short distance. This was it. He only had a few seconds left. If he couldn't light the fuse now . . .

The match fizzed, then flickered. He looked at it as though he'd struck gold. He shoved it against the remnant of the fuse, which caught, the flame swelling against the bottle's lip.

The creature opened its mouth wide and the stench of rotting flesh boiled out. Jack struggled to take a breath and rally the last of his strength. He lifted the bottle, tensed his arm, then threw. The bottle twisted and rolled in the air, the fuse glimmering. It hit one side of the creature's mouth, bounced, hit the other side, rolled for a moment and then funnelled into the dark maw.

Nothing happened.

It hadn't worked.

He was about to die.

There was a sudden boom and the creature jolted. Then another boom, inside the metal casing. One side of the beast's thorax split open and shards of steel flew out. Steam screamed as it shot from several places.

The creature rolled on its side, squealing. Jack could see the cogs and brass pipes inside the wound, with the red fire in the centre. Steam and coal smoke filled the pit and made it difficult to see.

The leg that was pinioning him fell away and Jack was able to stand. He coughed and rasped down air. Charles cheered and slapped him on the back. Saleem also climbed to his feet, unharmed.

They watched as the creature writhed and shrieked, water bubbling fiercely inside it. The fire dimmed to faint embers and the steam cleared. But the avatar still moved, although slowly. It dragged itself over to the wall, only four of its legs still working. It began climbing the wall, pulling itself a few feet and then stopping, before pulling itself a few feet further.

Jack gulped down some jatamansi. 'Follow me.' He ran underneath the hanging monster and grasped the end of its thorax.

'What?' Charles said.

'We'll never get out of here otherwise,' Jack said. 'Hurry up . . . and bring that lantern.'

Charles and Saleem took hold of the metal ribbing. As the beast raised itself, they put their feet against the slope to support themselves. They sweated and strained, but managed to keep their grip. Despite the jatamansi, Jack's chest ached and he had to fight to stop himself blacking out. Charles fixed the lantern to a gap between the ribs so that they had light the whole way up.

The creature groaned as it hauled itself over the edge of the pit. In the yellowish light, Jack could see they were in a round chamber dug out of the earth.

'Quick.' He let go and pain shot through his body as his feet hit the ground. The creature looked severely damaged, but he was worried it might be able to repair itself.

Raising the lantern, he looked about the chamber and spotted a tunnel leading away to one side. They ran down this, tripping at times in the soft earth.

Jack listened for any sign that the creature was following them, but he heard nothing. For a moment he wondered whether there were more of the beasts, but he tried to put the thought out of his mind.

They came to an intersection, and kept going straight on until they found another intersection. Jack had no idea which direction to go in, but decided to keep straight ahead so that at least they wouldn't lose their way.

After fifteen minutes, cool air from a side tunnel touched his cheek. He looked up the passage and saw faint grey light in the distance. 'This way.'

They went on for another ten minutes, the air becoming clearer and the light growing. The tunnel sloped gradually uphill.

Finally, they came out at the bottom of a shallow crater. Dawn had cast the cloudy sky silver.

They scrambled out of the crater and stood for a moment looking back at the dark hole.

Charles made the sign of the cross.

'Praise to Allah,' Saleem whispered.

Jack felt something running on to his chin. When he dabbed it with his sleeve, he saw it was blood. He touched his lip – it was swollen and painful where it had been split.

He looked around. They were back on the plain they'd left hours earlier, the open ground grey and dreamlike in the growing light. More than a mile away he could see the dark form of the mill town, with the two red eyes of fire floating above.

'Let's get out of here.'

14

Jack woke when he heard the clomp of marching boots. He jolted up and for a moment didn't know where he was. Then, as he looked around, he remembered. He was in a shallow hollow surrounded by trees and bushes. They'd taken shelter there a few hours before dawn. After escaping from the pit, they'd run for several miles and then hidden for the rest of the day. During the night they'd stolen across the Thames basin, finally leaving the mill district behind.

It was Saleem's watch, but the boy was curled up asleep with a slight smile on his face.

The bloody fool. He'd put them in danger again – just like that Private Salter.

Jack held himself back from shouting to wake the lad – he couldn't risk it with the sound of the marching growing louder. He crept to the edge of the hollow and looked through a mesh of gorse bushes. Below him was a short slope and, beyond that, a road that was little more than a cart track. Thirty men were marching down the path. Although they were too far away for him to see clearly, it looked as though they were wearing European Army uniform.

'What is it?' Saleem whispered. He'd woken up and stood staring at Jack, sleep still clogging the edges of his eyes. He was toying with his beard and from the grey look on his face he seemed well aware he'd done something wrong.

'You idiot,' Jack hissed. He jabbed his finger at Saleem. 'You've bloody done it again. You'd be shot in the army for that.'

Saleem backed away. 'I'm sorry.'

'Sorry's not good enough.' Jack took a few steps forward. 'I've a good mind to thrash you—'

'Hey,' Charles said. While Jack had been berating Saleem, he'd woken up and had slipped over to the edge of the hollow. 'They're crusaders. Look.' He pointed through the bushes and down the slope.

Jack walked across and squinted in the mid-morning sunlight. The marching men were now close enough for him to see the patches on their chests bearing the cross of St George.

Charles went to stand, but Jack yanked him down again. 'Could be a trick.'

'There's no trick.' Charles pulled himself free and pushed through the bushes. He waved his hands and shouted. The soldiers stopped and in a fluid, unified movement whipped their muskets from their shoulders and formed two rows, the first row kneeling, pointing their weapons straight up at Charles. The crosses gleamed on their chests.

'Wait.' Charles held his hands above his head. 'We're friends. We're going to London.'

A man in his forties, with a moustache and goatee, lowered his weapon slightly. 'Who are you?'

'Private Charles Carrick, 12th Native Infantry.'

'Who's your sergeant major?'

'Peter Turnbull.'

The man broke into a grin and lowered his firearm completely. 'One of Peter's lads. Well, well. Used to serve with him myself a few years back. Namaste, Private.'

Charles put his hands together and bowed slightly. 'Namaste.'

The soldiers slung their firearms back on their shoulders.

Charles turned back to the bushes. 'You can come out.'

Saleem shot Jack a questioning look, but Jack just grabbed the boy by the scruff of the neck and thrust him through the gorse. Saleem cried out and stumbled down the slope. Then Jack himself climbed out and limped wearily down towards the soldiers.

As Jack, Charles and Saleem approached, the man with the goatee presented himself. 'Sergeant Howell Kendrick, 9th Native Infantry.'

Jack was surprised to hear a Welsh lilt to Kendrick's voice. Were the Welsh joining the mutiny now? It made some sort of sense – Wales, like England, was ruled by the Rajthanans. Of course, the Irish would stay out of the fight – why should they get involved when Rajthana had never occupied their lands? And as for the Scots, they were nothing but primitive tribes, on no one's side but their own.

'This is Saleem al-Rashid,' Charles said. 'And Sergeant Jack Casey, 2nd Native Infantry.'

Kendrick's face brightened and he gave Jack a deep bow. 'A pleasure to meet a fellow native officer.'

'Left the army quite a while ago,' Jack mumbled.

'He was at Ragusa,' Charles said. 'And he's led us from Wiltshire, across the mills.'

Kendrick's eyebrows gathered. 'You came through the mills? We heard it was too dangerous – poisoned after the fighting.'

Charles opened his mouth, but seemed unsure what to say and looked to Jack.

'There's *something* wrong with the place, that's for sure,' Jack said quietly.

'Well, you made it at any rate,' Kendrick said. 'All the land from here to London is under the control of King John and his general, Sir Gawain.'

As Jack had heard, the area had been taken early on in the mutiny and held by the rebels since then.

'We're falling back to London,' Kendrick said. 'You can come with us.' He looked them up and down. 'Are you fit enough to march?'

It was only now that Jack noticed how dishevelled he and his companions were. Their clothes were torn and filthy, their hair matted and faces haggard. They looked like vagrants.

'Of course we can march,' Charles replied.

Kendrick beamed and slapped Charles on the shoulder. 'Good lad.'

As Jack, Charles and Saleem fell into line at the back of the platoon, the men grinned and wished them well. One offered them a drink from his canteen, which they gratefully accepted.

They trudged through the increasing heat of the morning. The countryside quivered in the sunlight – green fields, hedgerows, stands of trees. The smoke and dismal plains of the Thames basin were now far behind them.

Jack noted that the soldiers didn't march in proper formation, or step in time. Their uniforms were flecked with dust, with threads unravelling in places and buttons missing. They would have been flogged in the army for this lapse. No discipline. At least, not enough. How could these men hope to take on the Rajthanans?

But at least he was getting closer to London. He saw Elizabeth in the cell and calculated that there were ten days left. He felt a flush of nerves. Just ten days.

Saleem was subdued and hardly spoke during the march. He appeared exhausted and often stumbled. Charles, on the other hand, seemed to have more life in him than ever and spoke to his new comrades enthusiastically whenever they stopped to rest.

Towards midday, a village bordered by willows appeared ahead beside the banks of a shallow river. It was little more than a collection of huts, although there was a larger stone house to one side and a small church.

As the platoon marched closer, villagers walked across from the fields and stood to either side of the road. The peasants cheered, clapped and whooped. Some shook pitchforks and hoes at the sky. Women in dirty bonnets held out tankards of water and pieces of fruit for the passing troops.

'Long live King John!' many shouted. 'Long live Sir Gawain! God's will in England!'

A tall man strode out of the village and up the road. He wore a dusty brown tunic and, over this, the gold-coloured surcoat of a sheriff. The Rajthanans, or their English officials, normally appointed sheriffs, but it seemed this man was continuing in office despite now being in rebel-controlled lands.

'Greetings.' The sheriff held up one hand.

'Good day to you, brother.' Kendrick put his hands on his hips and cast his eyes about the crowd. 'And to all your people.'

'You're welcome in our village. We'd be honoured to have you spend the night here.'

'I thank you for that. But we're headed to London, as quickly as we can. The heathens are on the way.'

'We heard. But word is they're moving slowly. They're three days off at least.'

Kendrick scratched his head. 'Three days, you say? London's only half a day away.'

'Go on, Sergeant.' One of the soldiers took off his cloth hat and mopped the sweat from his forehead. 'We're all parched, we are, and me feet are ready to burst out of me boots.'

Kendrick smiled and rested his hands on the belt that stretched over his ample belly. 'Very well. We'll stay the night here. But we leave at first light.'

Jack was surprised at Kendrick's lax discipline. As sergeant, he should be the one deciding whether to make camp or continue marching. And he shouldn't tolerate griping from the men. All the same, a break would be welcome. Even though Jack wanted to get to London quickly, his eyes were scratchy from lack of sleep, his legs were sodden with tiredness and there was a twinge in his chest. He needed to rest and gather his strength.

Only God knew what awaited him in London.

Jack lifted the axe, glanced up at the midday sun for a second, then swung the blade in a wide arc until it battered into a block of wood. The wood split halfway through. He stuck his foot on the block, wrenched out the axe and blinked as sweat ran into his eyes. It was a hot day. He would have preferred to rest, but you couldn't laze around while others were making camp.

He went to lift the axe again, then stopped and put it back down. He squinted across the field, which lay on the outskirts of the village. Nearby, the men of the 9th Native Infantry were carrying buckets from a well, peeling parsnips and carrots, or cleaning their muskets. But further away stood a bare knoll, on top of which rose a single blackened post. A witch burning – here in lands that the Rajthanans had held for a hundred years. Was this what the rebels were fighting to bring back?

'Jack.'

Jack tore himself away from the sight of the post and saw Charles walking towards him.

'It's Saleem.' Charles nodded over Jack's shoulder.

Jack turned and saw the boy sitting alone under a tree on the edge of the field. 'What about him?'

'He's . . . well, he's not in the best of spirits.'

'That so.' The boy deserved to be dispirited.

'Thought maybe you could talk to him.'

'What about?'

'Don't know. Buck him up a bit.'

'Reckon he'll need to buck *himself* up.'

'I know he's made a few mistakes. But he wants to fight, and we need all the men we can get. Go on – to help the crusade.'

Jack glanced over at Saleem again. The lad looked small and lost sitting there.

'Just a few words,' Charles said. 'I know he'd appreciate it.'

Jack sighed. 'All right. Just a few words.' He was getting too soft these days.

He picked up the musket, which Kendrick had issued to him

earlier, and slung it over his shoulder. He felt strange carrying a firearm again and making camp with soldiers. He'd sworn never to go back to the army after Robert Salter, but now it was almost as though he'd joined up again. He was even wearing a pair of grey infantry trousers that one of the men had given him to replace his torn hose.

Saleem glanced up as Jack walked over, then looked down again quickly. His eyes were red and there were grey smudges down his cheeks. A musket lay in front of him, along with an oil bottle, a small brush, a rag, a Y-shaped musket tool and a tin kettle. The musket's wood and metal gleamed – the lad had cleaned them well – but the thin knife blade and its rod were lying unattached to the weapon.

'Looks like you've got a problem there.' Jack had seen this many times before. A musket was easy enough to take apart, but putting it back together was much more difficult. The knife blade especially caused confusion for new recruits.

Saleem stared at the musket as though it were a dead child.

Jack squatted down. The weapon was a new model, but similar to the last musket he'd had in the army, back when the percussion lock was only just being issued to Europeans. He screwed the rod back into the end of the blade, then picked up the musket tool and unscrewed the lock and the knife plate.

'Here.' He pointed to the spring and the latches of the knife mechanism. 'You've got to lift those latches and get the knife in there first.' He wriggled the rod and blade into place, then took them out again. 'You try.'

Saleem took the blade and tried to get it into place, without any success.

'Lift the end latch with your finger,' Jack said.

Saleem curled his little finger against the largest latch and the blade popped into place easily.

'Good. Now put it back together again.'

Saleem reattached the knife plate and the lock without any

difficulty. His dreamy, distant smile crept across his face when he'd finished – Jack hadn't seen that smile since they'd arrived at the mills.

'Well done,' Jack said. 'Now check the knife mechanism's working.'

Saleem stood, picked up the knife-musket and looked uncertainly down the barrel.

'Stop. Your knife catch isn't locked. Never do that without locking the knife. If the catch slips out it'll have your face off.' Jack had seen more than one young man get a knife in the head by mishandling a musket.

Saleem reversed the musket quickly, locked the catch and then lifted the weapon, holding it at waist height as if against an enemy. He then unlocked the catch and pressed it forward. The knife shot out beneath the end of the barrel with a loud clack and he jumped a little at the sound.

'Good. Now relock the knife.'

Saleem pulled the catch back to retract the blade.

Jack nodded. The lad had done well. He'd cleaned the musket and reassembled it, which was harder than it looked.

Jack took the musket from Saleem, weighed it in his hand and gazed at the shining, richly engraved metal. 'You want to be a soldier, then?'

'I want to fight for England.' Saleem stared at the ground, cheeks reddening.

'Well, then. This musket will be your best friend. A fine weapon. Nalika the Rajthanans call it – that's the real name. But we Europeans call it a musket. French word, I think. Maybe Neapolitan . . . You know how to fire it?' Saleem had originally said he could handle a musket, but Jack was sure the lad had little real experience.

Saleem nodded.

Jack handed the musket back. 'All right, then. See if you can hit that tree over there.' He pointed to an ash tree about sixty yards away. A musket wasn't a weapon for a marksman, but it was still accurate at that distance.

Saleem bent and picked up his ammunition satchel. He put the musket butt-down on the ground, took out a cartridge and tentatively bit it open. He stared at the grey powder inside the paper.

'Quickly,' Jack said. 'Before it blows away.'

Saleem poured the powder, then jammed in the other end of the cartridge, which contained the spherical lead bullet. He slid the ramrod out from its loops beneath the barrel and thrust the bullet down to the base of the musket. After returning the ramrod, he lifted the weapon and cocked the hammer.

'No, no,' Jack said. 'You haven't got a cap in there, have you?'

Saleem's cheeks went red again and he fumbled in his ammunition satchel for a percussion cap. His hand shook as he lifted out one of the tiny copper cups. He tried to press the cap into the nipple, but his hand shook so much it almost slipped out of his fingers.

'Easy now, for God's sake,' Jack said.

Saleem swallowed and got himself under control. He got the cap in place, then lifted the musket again and lined up the sights. Finally, he pulled the trigger. The musket burst and sulphur-scented smoke puffed from the barrel. Saleem jerked back as the butt slammed into his shoulder. A duck quacked and flew away above the trees.

Jack took a step to the right so that he could see around the smoke. He shook his head. 'No. Missed it. Try again.'

Saleem reloaded. He did it more quickly and deftly this time – a good sign. He was learning already. Of course, it would be best to take him through the full drill so that he would be able to fire in time with his fellow soldiers, but that would have to wait.

Saleem raised the musket again and this time took at least twenty seconds to line up a shot. When he fired, he stood firm and absorbed the kick of the weapon without flinching.

Jack looked around the smoke. There was a yellow wound in the centre of the tree trunk. Well, well. Saleem had got lucky. 'Good shot.'

As the smoke cleared and revealed the tree, a broad grin slipped over Saleem's face.

'All right,' Jack said. 'You've done well, but don't get cocky. You've got a long way to go yet.' But he found himself grinning back at Saleem. The lad was trying – he might be a fool, but he was trying. Maybe he could be turned into a soldier after all.

Five fires roared in the darkness. The villagers had come out to the field that evening to offer a feast to the men of the 9th Native Infantry. Now the soldiers and peasants sat together, tinged yellow, laughing, talking and warming their hands before the flames. Casks of ale had been opened and boars hung on spits over the fires, the juices sizzling and falling into the embers, producing a rich, smoky scent. Garlands of flowers and lanterns had been hung from the branches of the trees, and minstrels played lutes, pipes and drums. Women from the village danced with the soldiers.

Jack sipped a mug of ale slowly – he had no intention of overdoing it. Charles, on the other hand, was drinking furiously and already seemed to be best friends with everyone. Saleem sat huddled to one side with his knees drawn up and his head resting in his arms.

The music stopped abruptly and several of the dancers voiced their disappointment, until a tall, bearded minstrel stepped out into an open space between the fires, clapped his hands and called out, 'Listen. Listen, all of you.'

The crowd quietened and gathered around.

'Listen. I'll tell you the story of King Edward and the Caliph.'

Everyone cheered and clapped.

The minstrel gestured theatrically at the dark sky, as if the story were about to be played out there. His whole body swayed and his red ankle-length robe swirled about him.

'It is two hundred years ago. For two centuries, the wicked Moors have ruled this country. Now the land is in the clutches of the latest Caliph and his black magic, known as dhikr.'

The minstrel hurled a handful of powder into the nearest fire, which rumbled and exhaled a cloud of sparks and scented smoke. The crowd gasped and murmured.

'Back then, all good Christians were beaten down and lived in fear of the Caliph's army. None dared speak out against the cruelty. Then the Caliph decreed that every person in England must become a Mohammedan. He planned to crush the Christian soul of the country.'

The minstrel raised his hand and clenched it into a fist.

'Some turned to the Pope in Dublin, but he had no power to help. People prayed and wept and hoped for a saviour. And God, in his kindness, sent Edward V, rightful descendant of the kings of England.

'Edward was a man beyond all others: tall, proud, fierce in battle. He told the people never to surrender to the Caliph's wickedness. He remembered the stories of King Arthur, and he summoned the bravest knights of the land and formed them into a company based on the brotherhood of the Round Table. Then he travelled the country, raising an army against the Caliph.

'But Edward also knew the Caliph's magic would be impossible to beat. The English needed a power to rival or better it. In the old stories, Arthur used the Grail to free the land from enchantment. So Edward assembled his knights and told them that once again they must search for the Grail.

'The knights set out, following in the footsteps of Arthur's men. They searched the land, but like Gawain, Lancelot, Hector and the others, they found nothing. The Grail is elusive. Only those pure in heart will ever reach it. The impure can search for as long as they like, but they will not see it, even if it stands right before their eyes.'

The minstrel cast his eye about the onlookers, as if judging who amongst them was suitably pure. He pursed his lips and nodded slowly.

'Just like Arthur's knights, Edward's men began to abandon the search. In the end, only one, Sir Oswin, continued, accompanied by his squire.

'In the meantime, the Caliph learnt of Edward's army, and marched his forces north to meet it. The two armies clashed near the River Humber and Edward's men were trounced and driven back. The Caliph's troops pursued the English, who were forced to make a stand at Garrowby Hill.

'Edward's men were weary. The enemy outnumbered them three to one. Many gave up hope. But Edward rallied them, told them to fight on. He promised them that one day God's will shall return to England.'

The minstrel thrust a stick into the sky, as if it were a sword. Then he lowered it and gazed at his audience. Everyone was silent. The only sound was the crackling of the fires.

'The Caliph marched his army up the hill. There were thousands of men, amongst them fakirs with the power of dhikr. Edward's men shook with fear but they stood firm. They would not betray their country.

'At the same time, far away, Oswin and his squire finally discovered the castle that housed the Grail. They entered the gate, the first to do so since Bors, Perceval and Galahad had come there centuries before. They found the Grail shining in a grand hall. The squire cowered from the blinding light, but Oswin – who, like Galahad, was completely pure of heart – strode forward and placed his hand upon the Grail. At his touch, the power flowed out across the country.'

The minstrel waved his arm, rippling his fingers.

'The power flooded through King Edward's men. With renewed strength, they charged the Caliph's army and smote it down.'

The minstrel swung the stick, the swish audible.

'The Mohammedans fled and Edward marched to London and there took his rightful place upon the throne. But everyone asked: "Where is the knight who found the Grail? Where is the man who released the power?"

'Soon, Oswin's squire arrived in London. He was weary, broken and barely able to walk. He explained how he and Oswin had found the Grail and how Oswin had touched it. Oswin had then been taken up to heaven by a host of angels, leaving the squire to make the long journey back alone.'

The minstrel smiled.

'The Caliph fled across the sea to France and was never seen in this country again. But King Edward was a kind ruler, and he pardoned those Englishmen who had fought with the Caliph – even those who had taken on the Caliph's religion.'

The minstrel nodded at Saleem, the lone Mohammedan, standing at the edge of the crowd. The onlookers all laughed and Saleem went bright red and looked at his feet.

'Down with the Mohammedans,' someone shouted.

'Now, now,' the minstrel said, still smiling. 'Let us keep King Edward's example . . . King Edward then ruled from that day forth, and his kingdom was fair and just – a true Christian kingdom. And Edward died an old man many years later, peacefully drifting off while asleep in bed.'

The minstrel held up his arms and gazed about him for a moment, then took a deep bow. The crowd burst into applause, and several men rushed forward to slap the minstrel on the back and offer him drinks. He took a mug of ale and raised it to the crowd, to yet more cheers.

Jack had heard the story many times before, in different forms. Every minstrel had a slightly different version. Much of it was true, of course, but much of it wasn't. Jhala had said that King

Edward really had defeated the Moors at Garrowby Hill, and the Moors really had possessed powers they called dhikr, although these came from a handful of yantras smuggled out of Rajthana.

But as for the Grail, that was just a myth. There were miraculous powers in the world, but they came from yoga, not some magical chalice.

'All right everyone,' Kendrick shouted as he strode into the open space. 'I've got a few things to say. Firstly, thank you to all you good people of Berkshire for your warm welcome.'

The crowd clapped and cheered.

'Secondly, a toast to the newest recruits to our regiment – Jack, Charles and Saleem.'

Everyone cheered again and stamped their feet.

Kendrick motioned at one of his men, who walked over with a bundle of clothing. 'Now. We can't have our new recruits going around looking like civilians.'

Everyone laughed at this.

'So, here are uniforms – gifts from our fallen comrades.' He unfurled one item. It was a blue European Army tunic with a St George's cross sewn on to the left side of the chest. Uniforms were expensive and were often retrieved from dead soldiers if they weren't badly damaged.

Charles went first. He bounded over, took the tunic and lifted it over his head. It was slightly too small for him, but not enough to hinder his movement.

'Jack . . . Saleem.' Charles gestured for the two of them to follow suit.

Saleem walked over and put on a tunic, which fitted him perfectly. He stood smiling and fidgeting as he looked at the ground.

Jack took the final tunic and thanked Kendrick.

'Put it on, Jack.' Charles was slurring.

Jack looked around. Everyone was watching him, flames in their eyes. There was no way out of it.

Slowly he removed his old brown tunic and put on the uniform. The fit wasn't bad and the tunic felt comfortable. The cloth had a distinctive smell that was intensely familiar. The weight of it was familiar too, and the feeling of it across his back and shoulders.

Charles cheered and the throng all joined in.

'Welcome to the 9th Native Infantry,' Kendrick said, to even more cheering.

Charles picked up his mug and held it unsteadily. 'And here's to giving the heathens a thrashing.'

The crowd roared with delight, stamped their feet hard and whooped into the darkness.

'The Grail will come again,' someone shouted.

The crowd cheered even louder. The Grail would come again and the crusade would throw the Rajthanans from England's shores, just as King Edward had cast out the Moors, just as Arthur had freed the land from enchantment.

Only Jack knew that would never happen. The Rajthanan army was marching across the countryside and would soon sweep them all away. Most of the soldiers about him would probably be dead within days.

He slipped over to one of the fires on the edge of the field, his thoughts like hovering crows. He wanted it all to be over. The mutiny. His pursuit of William. Pretending to be a rebel.

The people around him were fools. How could they put their faith in the Grail? They were going to get themselves killed because of a myth.

And then he recalled something he'd forgotten until now. Something Elizabeth had said to him when he'd visited her last Christmas. They'd been walking across the snow-covered fields near the house where she worked. He'd been struck by how much she seemed to have grown up within the space of six months, and he was proud of how she'd survived on her own.

They passed fences sagging with ice, and dark trees that cut the white sky. Then they plodded down to the small church where Elizabeth came for Sunday mass. The building stood beside a frozen pond and the snow lapped at knee height against the stone walls.

Inside, it was silent and empty. The air was even colder in there than outside, and their breaths were chalk dust about their mouths.

A handful of stools stood to the side of the room. Elizabeth grabbed one and sat down. 'I was thinking about the Grail the other day.'

Jack smiled. 'Remember when you ran off to find it?'

'Still looking for it.'

He shot her a look and she grinned back, then turned more serious. 'I'm glad you told me those stories. It's good to know about the past.'

'Well, it's not all true. You know that. They're just stories.'

'Maybe a story can be true even if it isn't real.'

'What do you mean?'

Her face was porcelain as she stared at the altar. Then she seemed to shake herself from a trance. 'Nothing. Just being silly.' She stood up. 'Let's go back.'

And she led him out into the glowing snow . . .

Now Jack stared into the flames. The minstrels started playing again.

Maybe a story can be true even if it isn't real.

It had been a strange thing for Elizabeth to say. Had she heard it from someone else? Had a rebel said it to her?

The Grail. King Arthur. King Edward casting out the Moors.

Was this what Elizabeth had been thinking about when she became a rebel?

Jack found Kendrick standing away from the fires and looking out over the moonlit sea of fields.

'Thanks again for helping us,' Jack said as he walked over.

Kendrick turned and stretched a smile across his face, but not quite quickly enough to hide the more serious expression that had preceded it. 'Not at all. We're all comrades. We all want the same thing.'

Jack stared out into the darkness. He smelt grass and earth cooled by the night. The minstrels and the crowd sang behind him, and frogs chirped in the distance.

He toyed with the rebel patch sewn on to his tunic. 'You been in London, then?'

'For a bit.'

'A lot of men there? To fight, I mean.'

'More coming in every day. Sir Gawain reckons we'll get a hundred thousand in the end.'

'You know Sir Gawain, then?'

'Met him. You see him around London. A great man.'

'Have you heard of the man they call the "Ghost"?' Jack tried to say it nonchalantly, as an aside.

'Of course. He's an inspiration to all of us. Fought the Rajthanans in Dorsetshire with just sixty men. Sixty!'

'So you've seen him, then? In London?'

'No. He wasn't around when I was there. But I heard he arrived a week ago. Why? Do you know him?'

'No.' Did he say that too quickly? 'Just heard about him, that's all.'

As they came over a rise, hot from marching through the muggy morning, London rose before them. They were approaching from the south-west, and from this angle the city looked at first like a single dark fortress. A vast stone wall swelled from the ground and climbed to battlements and bastion towers. Behind this, a spire floated above the trails of smoke and scratched at the cloudy sky.

Kendrick pointed to the spire. 'St Paul's.'

Jack nodded as he walked. He'd guessed as much – the cathedral was famous all over Europe. Four hundred years ago it had even been the seat of the Popes after the Moors took Rome. But, of course, the papacy had later moved to Dublin when the Moors invaded England.

Jack felt a knot of sickness in his stomach. London was close now and somewhere within those walls, he hoped, was William.

The day was overcast and the light like gelatine. To the left, across the fields, flowed the grey, sluggish Thames. A settlement squatted on the opposite bank, about a mile from the city walls. It was dominated by a white mosque that glimmered faintly as if with an inner fire. Icy minarets and a grand cloud-like dome topped the mosque. And about it were red and white Rajthanan buildings speckled with small cupolas and turrets. The town's reflection trembled in the water below.

'Westminster,' Kendrick said. 'The Rajthanans lived there until we kicked them out.'

Jack recalled the reports of the massacre. The rebels had stormed the town in the early days of the mutiny and slaughtered the Rajthanans – only a few had survived and escaped to the south-west. Apparently hundreds of women and children had been killed.

'And that's Westminster Mosque,' Saleem said quietly.

Kendrick nodded. 'Built by the old Moors.'

'Never thought I'd see it,' Saleem said. 'My father's not going to believe this.'

The road curved to the east and then turned again so that they were approaching the city directly from the south. On this side, the city had no wall and lay open before them, protected only by the river. A swarm of terraced buildings with sharply angled roofs tumbled over each other and down to the water's edge. Above these towered St Paul's and the steeples of numerous smaller churches. Away to the right, but still within the city walls, a fortress with a pale central tower stretched up from the riverbank.

'They call it the Tower of London,' Kendrick said. 'That's the White Tower in the middle, where the King lives.'

The road became clogged with people and animals: bullock and mule carts brimming with fruit and vegetables, men and women from the countryside on foot, and friars in black, white or grey robes. Drivers argued with each other as they tried to turn their vehicles or squeeze them through gaps. Buildings began to appear on either side of the road – at first small farmsteads and barns, but then larger houses, stone churches and roadside inns. Soon they were in a bustling township, surrounded by timber-framed, wattle-and-daub buildings that slanted haphazardly. Chickens ran across the street. Vendors shouted from their open-fronted shops. The smell of smoke and excrement swirled around them.

'This is Southwark.' Kendrick raised his voice over the din. 'We'll cross the river into London in a few minutes. We've been billeted on the north side of the city.'

The traffic slowed and they could only inch their way forward. Then the buildings opened out on to the riverbank. The city seethed and smoked on the far side, stretching for at least two miles in each direction.

The river was grey and choppy, and around 900 feet across. Dhows, rowing boats and old square-sailed cogs skimmed along. Both banks were jagged with wharves and quays where men worked to load and unload the docked vessels.

A single stone bridge spanned the water in a series of arches. Across the top, the sides were lined with buildings, as if the city had spilt out across the river, unable to be contained.

'London Bridge,' Kendrick said. 'It's the only way across. They say it's the biggest bridge in Europe.'

Charles appeared transfixed by the spectacle. 'Have you ever seen anything like it?'

Jack shook his head. The city was smaller than Paris and not as grand as the Rajthanans' settlements, but it was still one of the larger cities he'd been to, and the bridge was wider than anything he'd seen before. His countrymen had achieved much in the past without any help from the Moors or Rajthanans.

Crossing the bridge was like walking down a city street. The buildings crowded to either side and the river was only occasionally visible in between. Carts, people and animals jostled around them. Jack saw a bear standing on its hind legs with a chain around its neck.

About a third of the way across, a stone gateway arched over the road. It was topped by battlements from which flew two flags displaying the St George's cross. The drawbridge had been lowered to allow traffic in and out of the city. Guards in white surcoats watched passers-by, stopping some and questioning or searching them. On the guards' chests, Jack recognised the coat of arms of the City of London – a red cross on a white shield, with a sword in the top left corner.

For a moment he imagined he would be found out – a traitor trying to enter the city. But, of course, that was impossible. How could the guards tell what his real motives were when he proudly wore the uniform of a rebel?

One of the guardsmen welcomed Kendrick. 'A good omen yesterday. A crowd saw the Grail in the clouds above St Martin-le-Grand.'

Kendrick grinned. 'Then God is truly on our side.'

Jack was allowed to pass without any questioning. He walked with the others along the remainder of the bridge and into a maze of narrow streets. The buildings leant forward and in some places were joined across the road by wooden bridges. Jack noticed many European Army uniforms amongst the throng, and even spotted a few elephants being driven by army mahouts. The bells of a hundred churches were ringing Sext, the sound sailing above the cacophony of the streets.

After half an hour they reached their billet, a stone house four storeys high and the width of two ordinary terraced homes. A gate opened into an archway that led under the first floor and out to a cobbled courtyard, where men in army uniform stoked cooking fires, carried pots and skins of water, and cleaned muskets. Some sat about, talking and chewing paan.

A portly sergeant major with a red, gleaming face greeted Kendrick, then looked about distractedly.

'Three new recruits.' Kendrick gestured to Jack, Charles and Saleem.

'Good.' The sergeant major didn't even look at them. A soldier came over to ask him a question, but he waved the man away. 'Later, later.' He turned back to Kendrick. 'You'll have to sleep out here. Everything else is full.'

Ramshackle canvas awnings had been set up on three sides of the yard. Beneath these lay lines of sleeping mats and army rucksacks.

Kendrick nodded and turned. 'Men, make camp.'

They found a free space in a corner, dumped their things on the paving stones and began unpacking.

'I'm going to find out if the 12th are here yet,' Charles said and wandered off, asking after his regiment amongst the soldiers nearby.

Jack looked around at the busy men. They appeared organised, but it was strange to see not a single Rajthanan giving orders. This was an army that had lost all its officers. But he spent little time considering this. He was in London for one thing only.

He slipped away and went back to the sergeant major, who was still puffing as he directed operations.

'Sir,' Jack said. 'Sir.'

'What is it?' the sergeant major snapped.

'Have you heard of the Ghost? Is he in London?'

The sergeant major paused, his forehead shiny with sweat.

'Course I've heard of him. Can't tell you much more than that, though.'

'Do you know where he's staying?'

The sergeant major scowled. 'How the hell should I know? Get out of the way.'

Jack heard a shout behind him and he dodged aside as a man carrying an enormous iron pot full of water staggered past.

The sergeant major shouted at the men tending a fire nearby, seeming to have completely forgotten about Jack.

'You looking for the Ghost?' asked a soldier who'd overheard the conversation.

Jack nodded. 'That's right.'

'There's going to be a parade for him. He smashed a battalion of Rajthanans at Brighthelm.'

'Rajthanans?'

The soldier smiled. 'That's right. Not French or Andalusian. Actual Rajthanans.'

'That's . . . that's good news.' Jack felt his face tingle and realised he was grinning. Despite everything, he couldn't help but be amazed at his friend's achievement. Rajthanan forces were rightly considered far superior to European.

'He's a hero. Took a few thousand from the city and thumped the buggers at the coast.'

'Where's the parade?'

'Near the Tower. I'll take you tomorrow.'

Tomorrow? Jack's grin drained away. 'But he's in London at the moment?'

'Not yet. He's on his way back from Brighthelm. The news only came in this morning.'

'I see. Tomorrow, then.'

Another day lost and another day closer to Elizabeth's execution. But there was nothing he could do, other than wait for William to arrive. There were only nine days left now. Not much time, but there was still a chance. Tomorrow he would get close to William somehow.

And then?

Then he would have to act quickly if he were going to get his friend back to Poole.

15

'They're coming,' a soldier behind Jack said.

Jack leant against the stone rail and craned his neck for a better look. He was standing on a rooftop balcony with a group from the 9th Native Infantry, as well as Charles and Saleem.

Crowds swarmed along the street four storeys below and spilt out into the muddy square outside the Tower. At least half of the people were in army uniform, but the others were civilians – from peasants to wealthy merchants in colourful cloaks.

On the far side of the square, the Tower rose up in a series of ramparts from the moat to the pale keep in the centre. The White Tower quivered in the chalky light, as if formed from the mist of the Thames.

Jack strained to see up the wide thoroughfare. In the distance he made out movement, and then a man riding a white horse came down the middle of the street. Behind the rider marched a column of troops that snaked away into the maze of streets.

The crowd swirled and churned, then erupted into cheering.

Jack could see the rider clearly now – a muscular figure in an army uniform, his head shaven.

William.

Jack stepped back slightly from the rail, although there was little chance of his friend noticing him on the balcony. His heart quickened and his hand rested involuntarily against the knife that still lay hidden beneath his tunic.

Charles shouted down at the street, while Saleem smiled broadly, his eyes glazed.

As William crossed the square, people reached out to touch him, as if he were divine. Guards had to hold back the mob.

A raised wooden platform, guarded by a line of soldiers, stood in front of the Tower. William dismounted and climbed the steps to the top of the platform. His men stopped marching and stood watching with the rest of the crowd.

Horns blasted, the sound cutting through the roar, and the throng quietened.

Figures appeared from the Tower's fortified entrance, walked across the drawbridge and stepped up on to the platform. First came a group of men who looked like courtiers or noblemen in ceremonial robes, then a bishop wearing a mitre and carrying a hooked crozier, and then a band of Sikhs in orange tunics and turbans. Amongst them was Kanvar, the young siddha who'd given Jack the jatamansi in Dorsetshire.

Finally, a dark-haired soldier helped an old, hunched man up the steps. Jack couldn't see the men's faces from a distance, but he could make out the old man's pure-white beard and hair, and the simple crown glinting on his head.

There was a loud rustle as the whole crowd dropped to its knees.

'The King,' Charles said quietly.

'And that's Sir Gawain with him,' a soldier beside Jack said.

The King raised his hand and held it unsteadily above his head. He looked small and frail, and Jack remembered the rumours that the old man was senile and being manipulated by the rebels. Back in Poole, he'd assumed the King would never side with the mutineers unless he was out of his mind. There was too much to lose – the Rajthanans could end the royal line any time they wanted. And yet, although the old man looked weak, there was no reason to think he didn't know what he was doing.

And Jack felt something else. There was a stone in his throat and he had a sense of being humbled before greatness. This was the King, after all. His King.

King John now held out his hand to William, who had also gone down on one knee. William kissed the ring.

Sir Gawain helped the old man turn back to the crowd, and called out, 'The King wishes you all to arise.' His voice rang out clearly across the square.

Everyone stood, like a flock of birds taking off.

Sir Gawain then led the King to a chair that had been brought out from the Tower. The old man sat slowly and with great difficulty.

Turning back to the crowd, Sir Gawain held out his hand and gestured to William as if introducing an actor on stage. 'William Merton, the Ghost.'

The crowd gave a rumbling cheer and waved their fists. Charles bellowed until he was hoarse.

Jack gave a few half-hearted shouts – it would have looked strange if he hadn't joined in. He felt a flicker in his stomach when he considered what he had to do. He cheered more loudly, trying to drown out his racing thoughts.

After a few minutes, Sir Gawain raised his hand and the sound dampened.

'You've all heard about the great victory at Brighthelm. The Ghost has shown us what we can do when we join together to fight these invaders, these heathens who've taken our lands from us.

'Their main army is marching on the city, as you know. Within three days they'll be here. They want to take our city from us, and our King. They want to put us back in chains. But we will not let them.'

Sir Gawain gestured to the Sikhs who stood in two rows behind and to the side of him.

'These men have come from India to fight with us. They have sworn to destroy our mutual enemy. Once we win, we will embolden others to rise up, here in Europe and even in the New Colonies across the Atlantic. Everyone is watching us.

'Less than three days, my crusaders. It will be our chance to free ourselves from them for ever. We will not let them take our city. We will stand here, shoulder to shoulder, and we will defeat them.

'Do not lose heart. Victory is within our grasp. And years from now, free English men and women will look back and praise our bravery to the heavens.'

The crowd gave a wild cheer that punched the sky. Everyone was roaring, shrieking, embracing each other, some even weeping. Chants of 'God's will in England' surged and receded.

Charles slapped Jack on the back. 'We'll do it. We'll beat them.'

Jack nodded and gave a brief smile. They all believed, the people about him. They all truly believed they could defeat the Rajthanans.

But they were deluded.

He felt distant from them, as though he were in exile in his own country.

And he felt distant from Elizabeth. She stood on the other side of a divide he couldn't cross.

For a moment he wished the rebels really could win, that somehow they could find a way—

But he stopped himself. What was he thinking? The rebels could never win.

Was this what it had been like for Elizabeth – listening to some stirring words and then toppling over into the madness?

It could easily happen. But he wouldn't give in to it. He had to stay fixed on reality not dreams. He had to stay fixed on saving his daughter.

Jack slipped down a side street. It was dark, and in his black, hooded cloak he was hidden in the shadows. Ahead, the way opened on to a wider road, where he paused. It was close to midnight, but there was still a handful of people about. Lanterns hung from each building and light, laughter and singing spilt out from the open windows of a tavern.

He waited until the road was empty, then swept down it, keeping to the darkness, cowl low over his face. Two men stumbled out of the tavern, clinging to each other and talking loudly. Jack moved to the other side of the street and the men staggered on without even noticing him.

He took the next turn to the right, as he'd been told. It hadn't taken him long to find out where William was billeted – the whole city was alive with stories of the Ghost. The street ahead was narrower, with few lamps along it.

He'd gone only a few paces when he heard footsteps ahead. A figure carrying a lantern came round the corner. Jack turned into an alleyway, moving quickly, but not, he hoped, suspiciously quickly. He slid into the shadows.

The sound of the boots came closer. Jack wasn't sure whether he'd been seen. The figure with the lantern appeared at the end of the alley. It was a man in the uniform of the city guards – a nightwatchman.

Jack held his breath and pressed himself deeper into a doorway. There was no curfew, but anyone out late could attract attention.

The watchman stopped for a second, scratched his backside, spat, and then walked on.

Jack waited a few minutes and then went back to the street. No one. Silence, save for the sound of the tavern off to the left.

He pressed on down the street and soon the building he'd been looking for loomed on a corner. It was just as it had been described to him – a four-storey stone house with a gryphon carved in bas-relief above the double doors.

He shot past the entrance and into a gloomy alleyway that ran along the side of the building. Pausing in the shadow, he stared at the side of the doorway. There were no guards, but he had no doubt the doors would be locked – and even if they weren't, he couldn't just walk in. He would be recognised in no time.

He looked up the wall and saw windows in the storeys above, although there were none at ground level. He might be able to climb up, but the shutters were all closed and it would be hard to get them open from the outside.

Leaning back against the wall, he felt his heart thudding through his whole body. He shut his eyes for a second. What to do? He had to get into the building somehow. Elizabeth was depending on him.

For a moment he was running through the dark forest again, following his daughter's cries, unable to find her, slapping his way through branches, stumbling on the uneven ground . . .

He opened his eyes and tried to still his mind. He had to concentrate.

The sound of voices drifted from over a wall further down the alley. He peered into the shadows, but saw nothing other than the thin passage curving away out of sight. The voices became louder – two men talking.

He edged down the alleyway and stopped beside the wall. The voices were clear for a moment, but before he could catch what they were saying the men walked away, their boots scraping on stone.

He glanced around again. Seeing no one, he jumped up, getting his fingers over the top of the wall. Giving a slight grunt, he hauled himself to the top and hung there with his feet still dangling on the alley side.

Below him was a courtyard that backed on to the house where William was supposedly billeted. On this side of the building, every floor had windows, some with the shutters open and breathing soft light into the darkness. Two men were walking inside through a door.

He waited until the men had disappeared, then pulled himself up until he was sitting astride the wall. His chest was tight and painful. He paused, waiting until he got his breath back.

What should his next move be? He could easily get into the house – he only had to drop down to the courtyard and run through the half-open door. But what would he do then? It would be better to be cautious, scout out the building a little more first.

He lifted his leg, swung down to the ground and stumbled back into the shadows. After waiting a few seconds, he stole around the side of the yard and sneaked up to the wall of the house, pressing himself against the stone. Candlelight spilt out of the door. If anyone walked through that door now, they would be able to see him. He had to move fast.

He crept over to the nearest window. The shutters were open, but little light filtered out. He peered inside. The room was dark, lit only by lines of radiance around the edges of a closed door. After his eyes adjusted, he saw the chamber was empty, save for two rows of unoccupied sleeping mats and a few rucksacks.

He slipped past the window, came to the door, glanced through the opening and saw a hallway with stairs leading up at the far end. Three lit candles stood on a table about halfway along. The hall was empty, although he could hear voices nearby.

Scurrying past the door, he came up to the second window, which had one shutter open. Voices drifted from inside – several men talking. He strained to hear, making out snatches of a conversation about an army campaign in Macedonia. The men seemed to be reminiscing about past exploits.

He crouched and scuttled across to the other side of the window and the open shutter, careful to stay below the line of the windowsill. His breath shortened as he inched his head around the side of the window.

He needed only a second to take in the scene. Seven men in army uniform were sitting about a table. One of them was William, carving absently at the wooden tabletop with a knife.

Jack slipped back into the darkness. Pain jabbed him in the chest. William was so close to him – but what now? He fought to think clearly.

Once the night was out there would be just seven days before Elizabeth was executed. And he'd been told it would take two days to get to Poole from London on horseback – and even then only if he rode through the nights. Worse still, the Rajthanans were due in a few days' time and once they attacked everything would be out of his control.

Was he going to kill William? Capture him and hand him over to the Rajthanans?

Could he bring himself to do that?

He was in a worse position now than when he'd been hunting William in Dorsetshire. Back then at least he'd only had to *find* William – Sengar and the French would be doing the rest – but here in London it was all down to him.

He remembered all those times he and William had prepared to go into battle. He remembered standing in the trench at Ragusa, waiting in that terrible silence after the guns had stopped, waiting for the horns to sound the attack.

He should be fighting with William, not against him.

Maybe he could go to William and beg for his help?

No, there was no chance of that. William would never leave the city now with the Rajthanans approaching. Would he even want to help Jack after everything that had happened? And anyway, the English could never hope to raise an army large enough to march on Poole – the Rajthanans were too strong.

There was a creak and a scrape as the door opened. Jack lurched back from the window. A man stumbled out into the semi-dark.

Jack's mouth went dry. He eased himself into the corner where the house met the courtyard wall.

The man walked unsteadily away from the building, humming tunelessly to himself. He put his arms out before him, as if he were finding it difficult to balance. He seemed drunk.

He staggered in a diagonal away from the house, heading towards the wall where Jack was hiding. As the man drew closer,

Jack made out his features in the dim light. It was Harold – the long-haired man, one of William's rebels. The last time Jack had seen him he'd had his arm in a sling, but this was gone now.

Jack tried to stay as still as possible. Harold reached the wall, put out one hand and leant against the stone. Although Jack was hidden in the shadows, Harold would only have to turn his head to see him. Jack's hand tensed around the knife. What would Harold do if he saw him? In Dorsetshire he'd wanted to kill him.

There was a sound like rolling marbles and Jack realised Harold was urinating. Jack's hand eased slightly, but he still held the knife handle. A long time seemed to pass, but perhaps it was less than twenty seconds. Harold stood up straight again and looked back the way he'd come. But he didn't move. He just stood there, swaying, as if lost in thought. Jack willed Harold to move on. Why was he still standing there?

Finally, Harold belched and meandered back to the house. Soon he disappeared inside.

Jack breathed out. His heart was beating quickly and pain crackled in his chest. That had been too close. He would have to be more careful next time. If he was going to get William back to Poole, he needed to plan things carefully. And right now he could do nothing while William was sitting with his own men.

He stole around the edge of the courtyard and reached the wall opposite. Tonight he'd done as much as he could. Now he needed to think through what his next move should be.

He made his way back across London to his billet. A soldier guarding the gate admitted him with a nod and he went through the dark, arched passage and into the courtyard. The yard was silent. He could just make out the men sleeping beneath the canopies around the edges.

'Where've you been?'

He was startled by the voice in the darkness. To his left he saw a faint red glow. As his eyes adjusted, he saw the outline of a hookah with a man sitting cross-legged beside it.

'It's me,' came the voice, and this time he recognised it – Charles.

'What are you doing?' Jack walked over. He spoke quietly, not wanting to wake the others.

'Can't sleep.' Charles's voice sounded flat.

'Mind if I join you?'

Charles moved in the darkness, but didn't say anything.

Jack lifted a pipe and inhaled. The coals at the top of the hookah glowed brighter and Charles's face appeared for a moment – a red spirit – before vanishing again.

'You're out late,' Charles said.

'Met an old friend. From the army.'

'I found out about my regiment – the 12th.'

'They're here, then?'

Charles paused. 'No. Didn't make it.'

'What do you mean?'

'They were sent to south Hampshire after I left them. They were in the fighting. Rajthanans smashed them to pieces.'

'All of them?'

'Don't know. There were heavy losses. All the rest ran off. Who knows where they are now?'

'Ah . . .'

'End of the regiment. It's all gone. All the men, the officers, the standard. Finished.'

'That's evil news. I'm sorry.'

'Suppose that's war.'

'It is.'

There was nothing more to say.

They continued puffing into the night, the aromatic smoke swirling between them like silent words.

Jack glanced at Charles as they stood looking down from the city walls. Charles had been quiet all morning. The news about his regiment must have hit him hard. He was young. Probably the first time he'd had friends killed.

But Jack had his own worries. He'd agreed to come to the wall when Charles and Saleem had invited him, but he didn't plan on staying long. He had to get over to William's billet, had to find a way to get to his friend.

The wall stretched away from them in both directions, dipping and rising with the gentle curve of the land. Half a mile to the east lay the point where the dark stone changed to a lighter grey, the beginning of the so-called 'New Wall' built some 300 years ago by the Moors. The entire London wall had been extended, repaired and rebuilt many times and now the strength of the fortifications varied greatly. Jack had seen parts of the wall that looked ancient, the battlements worn and crumbling. But other sections were formidable, ten feet thick and at least fifty feet high.

At regular intervals, square, round and octagonal towers rose from the ramparts, and here and there guns had been set up, pointing out at the plains.

The four bastions that formed the fortress-like Moor Gate stood nearby. Looking down, Jack could see a column of people streaming out of the opening. They were mostly women, children and the elderly. The Rajthanans were two day's march away and Sir Gawain had advised all those who weren't going to fight to leave the city. Men waved goodbye to their wives, children and parents. People hugged, held hands, began to part, embraced again. A crowd had gathered on both sides of the road to watch the column amble away. People carried as much as they could on carts or on their backs – chairs, tables, wardrobes, rolled-up rugs, chickens, geese.

A quarter of a mile from the walls, the road split into a series of stone causeways that led across the marshes. A pair of villages lay in the distance, and beyond them heavily wooded hills. Away to the west, the city had expanded beyond the walls, and houses, cottages and churches trickled off into the fields.

There were shouts below. Five men had stopped a young man driving a cart. Even from up on the wall Jack could make out the cries.

'Coward! He's leaving the city!'

'Stay and fight!'

'Traitor!'

The man in the cart waved his arms about, as if shooing away flies. The crowd became agitated and more people gathered around. The man picked up what looked from a distance like a cudgel and the mob reacted quickly. The man was dragged from the cart and across the ground. Men swarmed around him like wild dogs, kicking and shouting.

Guards rushed out from the gate and forced back the crowd. The man clambered to his feet and limped over to the cart. The guards kept the mob at bay until he'd trundled away.

'Coward.' Charles spat on the walkway, then walked off and clattered down the steps.

'Charles.' Saleem went to follow.

But Jack held his arm. 'Leave him.'

They watched as Charles crossed the street on the inner side of the wall and disappeared into the bustling city.

'He told me about his regiment,' Saleem said.

Jack nodded. He looked back at the line of people leaving the gate. He thought of Charles's mother, of how he'd promised to protect her son.

'You sure this is your fight?' he asked Saleem abruptly. He surprised himself saying it.

'What do you mean?'

'You know. You're . . . not a Christian.'

Saleem looked at the ground and his eyes widened and moistened.

Jack cleared his throat. 'I just meant, you don't have to be here. No one expects you to.'

'I want to be here,' Saleem said quietly. 'I know what people say about me, but I'm going to prove them wrong.'

Jack clenched his fist. Saleem was irritating him again. The lad was a fool and knew nothing about what he was getting into. And yet, at the same time Jack's throat felt swollen and his face prickled. Saleem had spoken bravely – he was a true patriot.

Jack patted Saleem on the shoulder, his voice cracking slightly as he said, 'Good lad.'

Jack sat beside the window, slightly to the side and partially hidden by the open shutter. He was on the third floor and had a clear view across to the building where William was billeted.

He'd been watching all afternoon. He'd seen Harold come and go several times and other people had left regularly. But so far there'd been no sign of William.

One day had passed since he'd watched the crowds leaving from the Moor Gate. That meant there were just six days left. Four if he considered the ride back to Poole. And all he could do was watch and wait.

The thought of Elizabeth's execution boiled constantly in his stomach. From the moment he woke until sleep clutched him away, he was haunted by the image of his daughter locked in the cell. Even in his dreams, the threat hanging over his little girl tortured him.

He was in one of the many empty buildings left by those who'd fled the city. He'd come across the place by chance and now used it to spy on William. The rooms had largely been stripped bare, although the occupants must have packed in a hurry as they'd left behind several chairs, kitchen utensils, candles and a lantern.

Below, four men emerged from the double doors of William's

quarters. Jack sat forward and stared hard. One of them was William, another was Harold. The other two he didn't recognise.

Finally, a chance.

He ran down the stairs and unbolted the door to a covered walkway that ran along the side of a tavern. The tavern's wall consisted of little more than thin wooden slats, through which he could see men drinking and puffing on hookahs.

He slipped down the walkway. The door swung open behind him – the only way to keep it closed was to bolt it from the inside. He would have preferred to have locked it to stop anyone else using the building, but he didn't have the key.

He reached the main road and stood waiting. William and the others appeared from a side street, paused for a moment and then walked away in the direction of the Tower.

Jack ran across the road, darting out of the way of the carts that rattled in both directions. He saw William and his comrades disappearing into the busy crowd. His chest shivered and he took a sip of jatamansi.

He followed William at a wary distance. He tried to act nonchalantly, and stopped a few times to study the wares in the open-fronted shops. As far as he could tell, no one noticed him.

William was constantly interrupted by people who wanted to shake his hand and talk to him. At one point a mob of children gathered around him and shrieked with delight so loudly Jack could hear them even over the sounds of the city.

Jack followed as the group passed near to the Tower, continued to the stretch of wall to the north, and came to the heavily fortified Ald Gate. Guards stood to either side of the arch, watching the few people passing in and out. An elephant ambled past, dragging a gun on a carriage.

William and his comrades went up the steps to the parapet beside the gate. Jack slipped into a doorway near to the wall, took out a roll of paan and chewed the spicy mixture, attempting to look like an innocent bystander doing nothing in particular. From time to time he glanced up at the ramparts, trying to do it casually, as if checking the weather.

William walked along the wall. The battlements were now thick with guns and in the distance Jack could see that more were being winched up using wooden cranes and scaffolding. William seemed to be inspecting the artillery and stopped to speak to the men, who stood to attention beside their guns.

After twenty minutes, William came back down and the group went into a nearby house, along with a number of other soldiers from the ramparts.

Jack waited further up the street for at least an hour. Finally, William appeared, still with Harold and the others.

Damn.

Would William ever be on his own?

Jack shadowed the group as they worked their way through the streets and he soon realised they were travelling back to their billet.

Damn.

Should he try something before William went inside again? But what? William on his own was a formidable foe, but with Harold and the others at his side there was no chance.

Jack felt light-headed as he watched William go back into his billet and shut the double doors. He gripped the knife through his tunic and his eyes smarted a little at the thought of Elizabeth.

He ran back to the building beside the tavern, back up to the room on the third floor. There was no further movement from William's quarters.

He waited. A few people came and went, but William remained inside.

Jack stayed in the room until the early evening. Sunset painted the sky red.

The Rajthanan army was due tomorrow. He massaged his face. He wanted to do something. Perhaps this would be his last chance. But he was tired. He felt old.

Without planning to, he found himself whispering an Our Father. The Latin words had been lodged in his head since childhood, but he couldn't remember the last time he'd spoken them. It must have been years ago, with Elizabeth.

Finally, he conceded that there was nothing further he could do that night.

He went down the stairs, unbolted the door and went out into the walkway. He could see the lantern-lit interior of the tavern through the wooden boards. Light, voices and tobacco smoke dribbled out between the gaps.

A door rattled open a few feet up the walkway and the burly barman, wearing a stained tunic, rolled a barrel towards the street, the wood clattering against the stone. Jack had seen the man a few times, although they'd barely acknowledged each other.

'Mind,' the barman grumbled as Jack stepped back into the doorway to let him pass. The barman glanced up and grunted at Jack, but said nothing else, and soon disappeared into the street.

Jack went in the opposite direction and came out at a busy road. He crossed over to an alleyway and then came to an empty courtyard with a well in the centre. The well was boarded up, probably dry. He paused for a moment and leant against a wall, watching the light fade to grainy darkness. He felt too tired to go on, but there was nothing wrong with him – no chest pain, no shortness of breath. His heart was beating normally.

He swallowed, pulled himself together and walked on into the growing dark. He was determined to get a good night's sleep – he would need all his energy for when the Rajthanans arrived.

But for many hours he didn't sleep. He lay awake on his sleeping mat, listening to the snoring of the other soldiers, his mind flitting uncontrollably from memory to memory. He thought of

Elizabeth, as always, and William and Jhala and Katelin, the thoughts piling up feverishly, the living and the dead, the past, all merging into a chaotic present.

He didn't know why, but he kept recalling the time he was promoted to sergeant. He was standing in Jhala's office, while his guru sat at his desk, studying a piece of paper. It was summer and a bee had found its way into the room and buzzed against a window. Behind Jhala, the wall was lined with books, journals and folios. Jack was always amazed by how many books Jhala owned.

'I've won.' Jhala beamed and prodded the paper with his finger. 'Colonel Hada's agreed to the scout company.'

Jack knew that Jhala had been arguing with Hada for a year that the regiment should form a specialised scouting unit – with Jack and William, and their powers, at its heart. Hada had been dead against the idea and was still sceptical about the merits of native siddhas. Jack had even overheard Hada say to Jhala once, 'This idea that we can teach natives these things, it's foolish nonsense. It's like training performing monkeys.'

But Jhala now held up the paper. 'It's an order, signed by the Colonel. We can go ahead with it, Casey.'

Jack was struck by the way Jhala said 'we'. Jhala had been talking about the plan for months, but he'd never spoken in these terms before.

'It's down to you, Casey,' Jhala said. 'You and Merton. You've proved what native siddhas are capable of. Even the Colonel's had to come around to the idea.'

Jhala stood, walked over to the dusty window and gazed out with his hands behind his back. 'Casey, you've been my best disciple. I'm promoting you to sergeant.'

Jack felt suddenly taller. He squared his shoulders and raised his chin. 'Thank you, sir.'

The words didn't seem enough. He'd wanted this promotion for years. And he was stunned that Jhala had called him his 'best disciple'. Jhala had never said anything like that before.

Jhala pointed out of the window. 'Take a look.'

Jack walked across and stared out at the parade ground. Soldiers and followers strode in every direction. On the far side stood the flagpole, the standard of the regiment rippling in the breeze, the three red lions circling each other endlessly.

'I plan to make our new company the best in the regiment,' Jhala said. 'Then one day I'll lead this regiment and you'll be my sergeant major. And we'll make it the best damn regiment in the European Army.'

'Very good, sir.' Jack believed in Jhala completely at that moment. He had no doubt that together they would do it . . .

But now, as he rolled over on his sleeping mat, the memory stung him.

It was that day, more than any other, that had made him believe he had a bond with Jhala. His guru had called him his best disciple and promoted him to sergeant. He'd said they would rise through the ranks together.

But had there really been a bond?

Jhala was threatening to kill Elizabeth if Jack didn't give him William.

And hadn't Jhala blocked Jack from learning new powers? Hadn't he cheated Jack out of his chance to become a proper siddha?

It looked as though he had.

Jack shut his eyes. With a great effort, he forced the swirling thoughts from his head. These ripples across the pool of his mind weren't helping Elizabeth. They were just distracting him, making him weaker. On the battlefield, and in yoga, you had to focus your mind on one thing and forget everything else. And here he was, lying in the darkness letting his thoughts run totally out of control.

Without planning to, he found himself making a decision. He would forget Jhala. For weeks his thoughts had kept returning to his guru, but that was a waste of time and energy.

He would put Jhala out of his head now. Never think of him again.

It would be as if Jhala were dead.

He took a deep breath. He had to get some sleep.

16

A pillar of dust rose in the west. The crowd along the battlements shifted and spoke softly. Jack, Charles and Saleem glanced at each other, but said nothing. They were near the New Gate – on the west wall of the city – having found a spot after hearing that the Rajthanans were approaching. Sergeant Kendrick stood nearby, watching through a spyglass.

The scent of rot wafted up from the piles of refuse in the ditch running along the outside of the wall. Beyond the ditch, the narrow Fleet River flowed down a culvert and out into the Thames. Further off, large houses lined the road to Westminster. Westminster Mosque glimmered a mile away.

The dust cloud grew larger.

The musket on Jack's shoulder was a familiar weight. He'd marched hundreds of miles with a musket at his side.

'There,' someone shouted.

A murmur travelled along the wall. Faint, moving dots appeared in the base of the cloud. Jack borrowed the glass from Kendrick and the Rajthanan forces crystallised in the haze, marching in an immense column that coiled along the north bank of the river. The sound of kettledrums, low and cavernous, and of blaring horns floated over the city.

At the head of the column rode hundreds of cavalrymen – Rajthanans in russet and Europeans in blue, their lances glinting as they pointed at the sky. Behind these stomped thousands of foot soldiers – mostly French and Andalusian, judging by their officers' green and silver turbans. A forest of standards rose from amongst the men and flashed in the wind.

Elephants, with armour on their heads and blades on their tusks, lumbered behind the infantry, some carrying ornate covered howdahs on their backs.

Further back, still indistinct, came the horse artillery, followed by the heavy guns drawn on wheeled carriages by avatars that looked like beetles from this distance. To the rear came covered wagons, then the baggage train and finally the ramshackle line of the followers, so long it was impossible to see the end of it.

Dust enveloped the entire column, turning the men and animals into grainy apparitions.

Jack handed back the glass. He remembered all the times he'd marched with such an army, feeling the enormous power of it, thinking how their enemies must be shaking with fear. Looking at Charles and Saleem, he knew the two lads had no idea what the Rajthanans could unleash on them. As well as the guns, the Indians had war avatars – new, unimaginable devices were created all the time. What did the English have to combat these? Only a handful of Sikh siddhas.

'How many do you reckon?' Charles asked no one in particular.

'Forty thousand – no more,' Kendrick said quickly.

But Jack had marched with an army of forty thousand and he knew the one before them was much larger – maybe 60,000. It was larger than any army he'd ever seen.

'Well, we have a hundred thousand.' Charles said.

Jack had heard the figure of 100,000 bandied about often over the past few days. There might be that many men left in the city who were prepared to fight, but how many of them were trained soldiers? When Jack looked along the battlements he could see mostly men in army uniform. But when he looked back and down into the city, there was a mass in civilian clothing – standing in the streets, looking out from windows, clambering on the few flat rooftops – who carried ageing matchlocks, swords, axes and cross-bows. He even saw a few bearing scythes and pitchforks.

The army collected like a pool of water in the open ground to the north of Westminster, then spread out, one wave arcing to the north and the other to the south, occupying Westminster itself. Four riders appeared from the murk, one carrying a pole with a white flag. They stopped on the edge of a field just to the west of the Fleet River.

'They want a truce. They're afraid of us,' said someone along the line.

The men laughed but the sound seemed high-pitched and thin, whisked away by the wind within seconds.

Jack heard horses on the cobbles below. Looking back, he saw two cavalrymen crossing the street to the gate, one carrying a white flag. The portcullis squealed up and the gates grumbled open.

The two riders clattered over the Fleet Bridge and followed the narrow road along the far bank. Within minutes they were beyond the line of buildings and into the open ground. They halted beside the Rajthanans and the six men remained there talking for ten minutes.

'What's going on?' Charles asked.

'Negotiations,' Kendrick replied.

Less than two minutes later, the riders parted and the English came galloping back, rode into the city and dismounted in the square beyond the gate. The portcullis rattled down and the gates clanged shut.

'There'll be no truce,' shouted a soldier who came running up the steps to the battlements.

Suddenly everyone along the wall was talking. The news flickered down the line and soon a man was saying to Jack and the others, 'The Rajthanans said we have to lay down our arms and surrender completely. Sir Gawain's rejected that, of course.'

'So we'll fight.' Charles looked across the plains to the army already expanding to the north-east.

Barges appeared upstream and floated slowly down the turgid river. Some were pulled by teams of elephants that ambled along the bank, while a few had chimneys that belched smoke and were propelled by the avatar engines that churned within them.

The flotilla drew up at the Westminster quays, where the vessels were arranged in a line across the water and tied together. Wooden planks were laid over the decks to form a bridge-of-boats. Soon soldiers and followers were carrying huge sacks and crates across the bridge.

'They're surrounding the city,' Jack said softly. The musket seemed to drag at his shoulder now and the knife was as cold as a new wound beneath his clothing.

They were surrounding the city. How would he get William out now? His task, already difficult, had just become much harder.

Kendrick nodded. 'We'd better get back to our position. We need to make sure we're prepared.'

'They're well out of range.' The gunner shielded his eyes with his hand as he gazed across the plains to where the Rajthanan army was a sombre arc stretching west to east.

Kendrick stroked his goatee. The two men were standing beside a giant twenty-four-pounder gun on the battlements near to the Bishops Gate. The weapon's muzzle was moulded into the form of a serpent's head, with glaring eyes and grills of teeth.

Jack stood nearby, listening to the conversation as he watched the enemy make camp about a mile and a half away. As the day wore on, the army had fanned out in a huge oval and surrounded the city completely. Their shivering tents and standards were now visible in every direction.

Kendrick was inspecting his troops. The 9th had been assigned the area around the Bishops Gate, along with six batteries from the 2nd Native Heavy Artillery. The guns and mortars were dotted along the wall, most on wheeled field carriages but a few on block-shaped stands. Men stood to attention next to the weapons, pyramids of shot piled beside them.

A line of purple in the distance caught Jack's eye. He tapped Kendrick on the shoulder. 'Sir – siddhas.'

Kendrick lifted his glass and scanned the enemy. 'Hmm. Quite a few.' He handed the glass to Jack.

Off to the east, nearer to the Ald Gate, stood a collection of fifty purple tents and standards bearing the angular sigils of the siddhas. Jack had never seen a siddha encampment like it. He'd heard that in Rajthana the army had entire companies of siddhas, but in Europe you were lucky if you saw a single one on the battlefield.

A tent in the centre of the camp dwarfed the others. Standing three storeys high and hundreds of feet wide, it looked like a small palace. Windows, archways, pillars and cornices peppered its walls and it was topped by domes and spires flying brightly coloured flags. The walls and towers wavered in the breeze and here and there the canvas flapped open to reveal wooden scaffolding beneath.

Jack handed back the glass. 'That tent in the middle—'

'I saw it,' Kendrick said. 'Must be the Mahasiddha's.'

By now they'd heard who was leading the Rajthanan force – Mahasiddha Samarth Vadula, a siddha general known for his exploits in the New Colonies. Apparently the Mahasiddha had never lost a battle and his war avatars had decimated the Inca forces who'd opposed him.

'Have to keep an eye on that lot.' Jack nodded towards the siddha tents.

'Nothing the Sikhs can't handle, I'm sure,' Kendrick replied. But he said it quickly, his voice clipped, before walking off to continue inspecting his troops.

Jack would have to do something soon. There were only five days left.

He removed Katelin's necklace and gazed at the intricate markings knotted about the cross. More than three weeks ago he'd promised Katelin he would get Elizabeth back. So far, he'd got nowhere.

He was sitting in the empty room on the third floor, watching William's billet. He'd been there most of the afternoon and evening, and now the light had faded and the lanterns had been lit along the street. But there was no sign of William. He wasn't even sure if his friend was in the building.

He put the cross back around his neck.

The sound of voices rose from the tavern below. The men had been chanting patriotic songs earlier, but were now more subdued.

How long would it be before the Rajthanans attacked? He had no doubt they had the superior force, but perhaps they would wait, try to starve the city into submission. He knew how the generals would be thinking. They would want to weaken the enemy with an extended siege, but on the other hand they would be under pressure from their rajas to crush the mutiny as soon as possible.

Normally it would take days – even weeks – of bombardment to smash through a city's walls. But rumours were circulating that the Mahasiddha had magic that could create a breach in a matter of hours. Jack could believe it – he'd heard officers talk about powers like that when he was in the army, although he'd never seen them used himself. At any rate, everyone in London was convinced that once the Rajthanan guns began firing, the main assault would soon follow.

He thought about the pardon, imagined it lying in the top drawer of Jhala's desk, slowly ageing as the deadline approached. Elizabeth's freedom was so close, the Raja of Poole's signature already on the paper, and yet it was beyond his reach.

Damn Jhala.

He stood up and paced the floor, still glancing back at the building each time he passed the window. He picked up a loose piece of wood and hurled it against the wall, where it put a dent in the wattle and daub.

And William – how could he have been mad enough to join the doomed rebellion? Why couldn't he just have waited out the last years before his retirement?

Even Elizabeth was to blame. She'd gone and got herself into trouble, all for no reason. He should have been more strict with her when she was growing up, should have kept more of an eye on her since Katelin died, should have gone to see her more often. Maybe then he could have stopped all of this from happening.

He sat down again and tried to concentrate on watching the house. He rubbed his eyes. Every muscle in his body seemed tight.

The street below emptied and the voices from the tavern grew quieter.

He couldn't stop his mind jumping from memory to memory, and for some reason he recalled the time he and Elizabeth had come across a party of Rajthanans. They'd been walking home from the market when the people and carts in front of them had moved over to the side of the road. An elephant had appeared ahead. Some sort of dignitary sat hidden in the glittering howdah, while a cluster of Rajthanan guards and European servants marched along beside the beast.

Jack grasped Elizabeth's hand and pulled her out of the way.

'Where are we going?' Elizabeth was seven at the time and had hardly seen any Rajthanans before.

'Someone important needs to get past.'

'Who?'

'Just someone important.'

The way was now clear, except for an old man who stood leaning on a staff in the middle of the road.

'Hey, get out of the way,' someone in the crowd shouted.

Was the old man having trouble walking? Jack darted back into the road. 'Do you need help?'

The old man lifted his chin. 'I'm fine, thank you very much.'

'You have to move.'

'I'm fine where I am, young man.'

The boots of the Rajthanan guards crunched on the road.

Jack grabbed the old man's arm, but the old man shook him off. 'You leave me be.'

'Move! Now!' the leader of the guards shouted.

Jack backed away, unsure what else he could do. He stood beside Elizabeth and her small hand coiled into his.

The Rajthanan party came to a halt and the guards' leader strode up to the old man. 'Out of the way.'

The old man, still clinging to his staff, looked up at the guard. 'Now why should I do that? I can't walk too well. I reckon you should be getting out of *my* way.'

The guard's eyes narrowed. 'You will move immediately.'

The old man looked around him. 'Don't see why. Last I checked, this was my country. Don't see why an Englishman should move out of the way for anybody in his own country.'

The guard nodded slowly, then bunched his hand into a fist and pummelled the old man in the face.

A gasp rippled through the crowd. The old man crumpled backwards and his staff clattered to the road.

The guard walked over and kicked the old man in the stomach.

Elizabeth's hand tightened around Jack's fingers. 'Father—'

'Come with me.' He had to stop Elizabeth shouting something out, otherwise they might get into trouble themselves. He pulled her towards the back of the crowd. She tried to look over her shoulder at the road, but he turned her face away.

'Father, that man—'

'Keep going.'

'They were beating him—'

'Keep quiet.'

He dragged her into a field of carrots. They would have to walk across the countryside for a while and rejoin the road later.

He noticed that his face was hot and his heart was beating harder than usual. It was terrible to see an old man beaten like that, but the fool hadn't moved out of the way. What did he expect? You couldn't speak to your superiors like that and get away with it. You learnt that in the army from the first day you joined.

'Why were they hitting that man?' Elizabeth asked.

'It's just the way of things,' Jack said.

'But he was old.'

Jack stopped. 'Elizabeth, you're making me very angry now. You just be quiet and forget about it.'

He strode ahead and she stumbled on clods of earth as she tried to keep up. She said nothing for about five minutes and then burst into tears.

He bent down. He was feeling calmer now. 'What's wrong, little one?'

'My feet are tired.'

'All right, then. You can ride on my back.'

He turned, still squatting, and she clambered up and held on tight.

As he stood, he felt a trace of moisture from her tears on the back of his neck.

They'd never spoken about the incident again. He'd forgotten about it until now.

Maybe he should have done something to help the old man. But what? He couldn't fight against so many Rajthanans.

And what did it matter anyway? Why was he wasting time thinking about these things?

It was nearly midnight. He was tired and hungry. There was nothing more he could do now – sitting and staring at the darkened building wasn't achieving anything. If William were indoors he'd be unlikely to leave at this hour.

Feeling half in a dream, he lit the lantern left behind by the building's owners and carried it down the dark stairs. On the ground floor, he put out the lantern again, then unbolted the door and stepped out into the covered walkway. Light escaped between the boards that formed the thin wall adjoining the tavern. Inside he could see around ten men, some drinking and talking, some inebriated and sitting with their heads lolling and eyes closed.

Was Elizabeth going to die? For a moment he was sure she would. He'd been mad to think he could save her.

Should he give up and fight for his country instead?

Is that what Elizabeth would want him to do?

No, why was he even thinking like this? Elizabeth was going to live. He was going to rescue her.

Lost in thought, he walked down to the main street and left the walkway without even looking around first. He heard footsteps beside him. He glanced up and his heart leapt. Harold, William's long-haired comrade, was walking towards him along the side of the road. Their eyes met for a second. Harold frowned and mouthed something silently, revealing the gap where his two front teeth were missing.

Jack slipped back into the shadow of the walkway. Maybe Harold hadn't recognised him? He heard the footsteps quicken and he moved back a few paces.

Harold's silhouette appeared at the end of the walkway. 'Hey.' He sounded drunk. 'Is that you – what's-your-name?'

Jack stalled. He couldn't think what to do.

'It *is* you.' Harold stepped forward. 'The traitor. I see you there.'

Jack shot a look at the other end of the walkway. He could run, but then Harold would alert William. Anything could happen then. William might spread the word that he was a traitor, and then he would be a fugitive trapped in the city. He would never get close to William after that.

He made a split-second decision. He lunged forward, got a hand over Harold's mouth and held the knife to his throat. Harold was caught off guard and reacted slowly. Jack smelt the ale on his breath.

Harold struggled and gave a muffled cry, but Jack kept a hand firmly over his mouth.

Jack's heart roared in his ears. He saw the men in the tavern sitting mere feet away. If Harold managed to make a sound, they would hear it without a doubt.

'Stay still or I'll slit your throat,' Jack hissed.

But Harold continued struggling. He got his hands up to his face and tried to force Jack's hand away.

To Jack, the surroundings went sharp and clear. It was like the start of a battle, when the first shots were fired and you saw the first soldiers go down and suddenly everything was real and everything that had gone before, the waiting, was merely a dream. Jack's training took over, like dark metal poured into his veins.

'I tell you, I'll kill you,' he whispered.

Harold stopped moving and stood breathing heavily. Jack moved him down to the half-open door. The small foyer beyond was in darkness.

'Inside,' Jack said. But what then? Could he keep Harold bound and gagged in there?

Harold took a step up into the house, then tensed and swung himself round. Jack, surprised, slammed into the wall and his head hit the wooden door frame. A puff of darkness filled his eyes for a moment. His forehead throbbed and pain forked across his chest.

Harold slipped from his grasp and cried out, the sound like a gunshot in the quiet night. Jack threw himself forward with as much force as he could and slammed into Harold's chest, cutting his cry short.

Harold toppled back and the two of them rolled into the foyer. Jack sprang on top, got his hand over Harold's mouth again. Harold bit down and fire coursed through Jack's arm. Jack flailed with the knife and caught Harold in the side. Harold grunted and Jack felt moisture on his fingers.

He shifted his grasp and stabbed again, hitting Harold in the stomach. Harold wheezed and gasped, but then seemed to find new strength and fought back more ferociously. He punched upwards and struck Jack on the jaw. Jack's teeth snapped together and it felt as though needles had been fired into his gums.

Harold got his mouth free and attempted another cry. Jack pummelled down just in time. He smacked the back of Harold's head into the stone floor and there was a pop like a china bowl breaking. Harold went silent, stunned.

Jack lifted the knife.

Could he do it?

His hand seemed to hover above Harold for minutes.

He couldn't do it.

But he had to do it. Harold had seen him and would tell everyone he was a traitor.

Harold's eyes widened as he became aware of the blade above him. For a moment Jack stared back. Then he slashed down and across. The knife thudded heavily into Harold's throat, going in deep. Blood spurted everywhere. There was a gargling sound – Jack wasn't sure if it came from Harold's mouth or the wound in his neck.

Jack lifted the knife again. Harold's eyes gleamed – Jack couldn't stand it. He wanted them shut. He slashed again. Warm blood hit his face and he tasted salty drops in his mouth.

Harold lay still, his eyes staring at the ceiling, throat butchered. He wasn't breathing.

Jack threw the knife hard against the wall. He wanted to hit something but he held himself back.

Then he heard a voice outside and went cold. He turned. The door was still ajar and he could see strips of light from the tavern beyond.

'Anyone there?' came the voice again – the barman.

He tried to breathe but the air wouldn't come. With the room spinning, he dragged himself to the door and peered round the corner. Men still sat in the tavern, seemingly unaware of the fight.

But the door to the bar further down the walkway was open and two figures now stood outside it.

Jack slipped back inside. Had they seen him? He fumbled in his pocket for the jatamansi and took a swig.

'It's nothing,' one of the men said.

'I heard something, I tell you,' the barman responded.

Jack heard the scrape of boots as the men came down the walkway. He eased the door shut, and slowly and silently slipped the bolt across. He was in almost complete darkness, the only light coming from under the door.

The footsteps came closer.

'Hello?' the barman said. 'Anyone there?'

'It's empty. Let's go back.'

'Maybe you're right. Hold on.'

The door handle turned, the brass creaking slightly as it moved against the wood. Jack's heart pounded.

The barman on the other side pushed at the door. 'It's locked.'

'I told you, there's no one.'

'Looks that way.'

The men retreated and the sound of their footsteps faded.

Jack breathed out. He leant against the wall, then eased himself down to a sitting position. Black dots danced before him.

He took another sip of jatamansi and his heartbeat began to slow.

After a few minutes he crawled across to the body. Harold's eyes were locked open, two pieces of glass in the dim light. Jack kept seeing that final look of fear on Harold's face. He'd seen that look many times before – he'd lost count of how many men he'd killed – but this felt different. Was it because it had been so long since he'd been in a fight? He hadn't so much as raised his hand to someone for nine years. But it wasn't just that. Harold was an Englishman. Jack had never killed one of his own kind before.

He reached over and closed Harold's eyelids. He felt as though he'd crossed some dark threshold.

'God, have mercy on my soul.'

After an hour in the dark, his mind racing, Jack stood and opened the door slightly. The walkway was in complete darkness, the lights were off in the tavern and everyone had gone home. He saw no sign of life at either end of the walkway.

He rubbed his face with his hand. What to do? He could leave the body where it was, but he couldn't lock the door and it would swing open. The barman or someone else would soon notice the corpse.

He could move the body to another room, but the building was empty, with no hiding places. Anyone would be able to come in at any time and find it.

He realised that if he left the body anywhere in the building it would be too risky for him to come back. But he didn't want to give up his vantage point looking across to William's quarters. Furthermore, the barman had seen him several times and could point him out to the city guard if the body were discovered.

Then he remembered the boarded-up well in the nearby square. He could dump the body in it. No one would look there. And even if they did, there was nothing to draw attention to him, or his hiding place.

He closed the door and stood in the darkness. Was he thinking clearly? Was he panicking?

He sat cross-legged on the ground, breathed deeply and said a few Hail Marys. Slowly, things became clearer.

He knew what to do now. He had to hide the body. There were far too many risks involved in leaving it in the house. The well was the best place he knew – and it wasn't far.

He went through to the next room and lit the lantern. When he came back to the foyer he was shocked for a moment by the amount of blood everywhere. The white walls were splattered red and a sticky pool was spreading across the floor. Even worse, the front of his tunic was now stiff with hardening blood. He would have to clean the room, and himself. But first he would have to dispose of the body.

He extinguished the lantern and opened the door. The way was still clear.

He went back to the corpse. The face looked sunken, the skin beginning to hang off the bones. He'd often thought the soul didn't leave the body immediately. It lingered for a while, a silent presence, slowly ebbing away as the face and body collapsed inward.

For a moment he remembered holding Katelin after the fever had finally taken her, watching her transform from a person to a pallid statue with a likeness that was close to his wife, but not quite her.

He breathed in, then bent and pulled Harold up by the arms. He tried to get the body over his shoulder, but the weight was too great and he fell forward. The body rolled back on to the ground and the skull struck the stone with a crisp thud. Harold's eyes sprang open, as if he'd woken up.

Jack paused, then closed the eyelids again. He picked up Harold's legs and dragged the body, jolting it down the single step to the walkway. He waited a moment, then continued dragging the body in the direction of the well. Harold's clothes rustled and scraped on the ground. Jack tried to go as slowly as possible to reduce the noise. He was afraid the tavern door would open at any moment, but nothing happened.

He reached the end of the walkway, put the legs down and glanced around the corner. The road, busy during the day, was now empty. But lanterns floated above the doorways and the moment he stepped out of the walkway anyone passing by would be able to see him.

He hesitated for more than a minute. When no one came, he dragged the body across the street, the scraping echoing in the silence. He saw blood left behind on the cobbles, but it was faint amongst the dirt, straw and ordure. No one would notice.

He reached the shadowy alley on the far side. Then the corpse snagged. He tugged, but the body was stuck – the legs and abdomen in the alley, the rest still lying out in the road.

He pulled again. The body wouldn't move.

Christ.

He dropped the legs and bent down to investigate. He felt underneath the body and along the side, but couldn't find anything.

He heard footsteps up the road. A lantern bobbed in the distance, coming closer.

He searched frantically for the snag. What was it? Sweat erupted on his forehead.

The footsteps grew louder.

Then he found a pair of thick nails sticking out from a wooden door frame just beside the alley's entrance. They'd caught on Harold's tunic and dug into his skin.

He yanked the body away from the nails, then pulled it into the darkness of the alley. He slipped, lurched up again, pulled some more.

The footsteps quickened and he heard a man call out, 'Hey there.'

To his left he spotted an alcove, shallow but hidden in darkness. He rolled the body into this and it just fitted. But there was nowhere for him to hide himself.

'What's going on there?' The man appeared at the end of the alley and held up the lantern.

Jack saw a flash of red and white – the uniform of the city guard. He thought quickly. He knew his tunic was covered in blood and would give him away, so he ripped it off and threw it on top of the body. Naked to the waist, he slumped against the wall a few feet away from the alcove.

'What?' He slurred, trying to sound drunk.

The watchman stepped into the alley and raised the lantern higher. The light now illuminated Jack.

'What the Devil . . . ?' the watchman said.

Jack looked up. The watchman was in his fifties, with silver whiskers and a face marbled with red lines.

'Evening, good sir,' Jack lolled his head to one side. 'Sit down. Have a drink with me.' He watched the guard closely – he had no idea how well his acting was working.

The watchman frowned and narrowed his eyes. 'You're a mess. Is that blood on your hands?'

'It's nothing. I fell over.'

The watchman pursed his lips. He looked up the alley in the direction of the alcove. If he walked on a few feet he would be able to see the body.

'Come on, sir,' Jack said. 'A drink.'

The watchman returned his gaze to Jack. 'You're a disgrace. You're lucky I'm not going to lock you up. Get yourself home, and get some clothes on.'

'Yes, sir.'

Jack scrambled to his feet, pretending to be unsteady. The watchman looked him up and down, shook his head and went back to the road. Jack listened as the footsteps receded.

He went to the end of the alley and peered around. The lantern was already a speck disappearing into the darkness. He slipped back to the alcove, retrieved his tunic and started dragging the corpse down the alley. He went slowly and quietly, and it took him at least ten minutes to reach the end.

He looked out at the courtyard, washed with moonlight but otherwise unlit. The well stood like a large mushroom in the centre.

He left the body in the alley and sneaked across the yard. Boards had been placed across the top of the well, but only a few stones held them in place. He removed the boards and went back to the corpse. He listened, heard nothing.

He dragged the body across the courtyard, put his hands under the arms and lifted. He got the corpse over the lip of the well so that it hung there, as if Harold were peering down into the black depths. Then he tensed his arms and heaved. The corpse slipped over the edge and sailed down into the darkness. A crunch echoed up the shaft a few seconds later.

He looked around. No one had heard. No one had seen him.

He put the boards and stones back in place before returning to the alley. Then he ran quietly to the street, looked both ways, and slipped back to the empty house.

Inside, he bolted the door and lay down in one of the rooms. He was exhausted. He decided he could afford a few minutes' rest – he was through the worst of it now. He closed his eyes. He tried to stop himself falling asleep, but he was already gone.

He woke and sat up quickly. What time was it? Outside, it was still pitch black, with no sign yet of dawn.

He went back to the foyer and lit the lantern. The blood looked even worse than before – he couldn't believe so much could come from one body. He would have to clean it up before he returned to his billet.

He knew where there was a working well nearby – he'd seen it during the previous days. He stole through the night again, going down the main street and across to a market square, where the well stood to one side.

He lowered the bucket and the pulley squealed. Muttering to himself, he lowered more slowly to avoid making a sound. Once he'd raised the bucket, he cut it free from the rope, went back with the water and scrubbed at the walls and floor of the foyer with an old rag. The result wasn't perfect, but the worst had been removed.

He went back for more water and then cleaned his tunic, his

hands and his face. The St George's cross in particular was stained red and it took him a long time to get the blood out of it.

Tunic still damp, he crept back through the streets. Along the way he saw two nightwatchmen, but he avoided both by hiding down side streets.

A trace of light was softening the sky as he came to his billet. He paused. Up the road he could see the soldier guarding the gate to the house. He felt moisture trickle down his cheek. His heart quivered. It was blood. His hair was covered in gore and it was dripping down. He would be seen. Everyone would know that he'd killed an Englishman.

But when he touched his cheek and looked at his finger, it was only sweat.

'Where were you last night?' Charles asked.

Jack opened an eye. His vision was blurry, but he could make out Charles's sandy hair and oval face. He was puzzled for a moment, then remembered where he was – lying on his sleeping mat in the courtyard. He could hear the men around him rising and dressing.

The memory of the night before seeped into him, like poison.

He sat up, blinking and rubbing his face. 'Met up with my friend.'

'The one from army days?'

'Yes.'

'You must've been back late. I fell asleep.'

'Drank a bit too much.' He actually did feel as though he were hung-over. His throat was painfully dry and there was a metal ache behind his forehead.

Around him, soldiers were splashing water on their faces and shaving as best they could – they had no soap now that they'd left the service of the Rajthanans.

'Men, look sharp,' Kendrick shouted as he marched across the courtyard. 'We've got a visitor this morning – the Ghost.'

Jack's skin rippled. Had someone seen him with Harold?

Did William know?

'The Ghost? Coming here?' Charles was asking Kendrick.

'That's right.' Kendrick said. 'Come on, now. You can't go on parade like that.'

Charles had on only his undershirt and trousers. He turned to Jack, grinning for the first time since the news of his regiment's fate. 'Can you believe it? We'll get to meet him.'

Jack nodded and looked around quickly. The courtyard was busy with men. He couldn't slip out unnoticed.

The portly sergeant major, flanked by six corporals, marched in from the street and bellowed, 'He's here. On parade men. Now.'

The soldiers scurried into lines along one side of the yard, some hopping along with only one boot on or trying to get their tunics over their heads.

Jack tensed. The only way out was through the archway, but this was blocked by the sergeant major. The door to the main building was also across the courtyard and there was no chance of him getting there without being spotted.

He slunk back beneath the temporary awning. Men pushed past him. He reached the wall of the wooden building behind him and tried a door. It was locked.

Damn.

Then he noticed the door to the privy standing slightly ajar. He looked around to see if anyone had noticed him, then slipped inside.

The smell of excrement hit him immediately. He was in a tiny room with a wooden seat over a hole in the ground. Flies boiled over the seat. The only windows were thin slits high up in one wall.

He pulled the door until it was almost closed, leaving just a chink through which he could peer out at the yard.

William, with three henchmen behind him, marched through

the archway, spoke briefly to the sergeant major, then paced along the line of men.

Jack swallowed and his heartbeat quickened. William was searching for him.

He glanced around the privy again, as if an escape route would appear. But there was no way out.

William eyed the troops, his hands behind his back. When he got to the end of the line, he turned and surveyed the courtyard. Jack edged back slightly from the door and felt for the knife. This was it – the end. They would search the buildings and soon they would find him. He'd always known there was no hope. Once William had killed Sengar, he'd known there was no chance of saving Elizabeth.

'At ease, men,' William said.

Jack moved back to the door and looked out. William was standing in the middle of the yard, his back to the privy.

'It makes me proud to see you all here,' William said. 'Proud to see knights from across our country here to fight the heathens.'

Jack felt a rush of relief. Perhaps William wasn't looking for him after all.

'The battle may come at any time,' William continued. 'You need to be ready to defend the city. Make no mistake, we are facing a fierce enemy. If the Rajthanans are victorious they will spare none of us. We must fight them, or die. But I have faith in you all. It is we who will be victorious.'

'We won't let you down,' Charles shouted. Jack could see the lad standing next to Saleem in the second row from the front.

Suddenly all the other soldiers were shouting as well, proclaiming their loyalty, cheering, chanting, 'God's will in England!'

For Jack, the rest of that day was torture. He went back to the empty room and saw William return to his billet after doing a tour of the city. There were four days left now, meaning Jack had to get out of the city with William by the end of tomorrow. Otherwise, he would never get back to Poole in time.

He stood by the window and looked across at William's building, flexing his fingers around the knife. He was going to have to make one last, desperate attempt. He would charge into the building, fight off anyone who tried to stop him, and stab his friend. Then he would get the body out of the city somehow. He would try to slip through the Rajthanan blockade. And if he were caught, he would explain it all to the Rajthanan commanders, who would hopefully believe the story and help him . . .

Of course, it would never work.

Even if he could kill William, he would be killed soon after by William's men. Even if he could get William's body out of the city, he was unlikely to get past the Rajthanans. And even if the Rajthanans believed his story, would they really let him ride off to Poole with the corpse of the Ghost?

There was no hope. Elizabeth would die. All he could do was try something, even if it meant he would die as well. Better that than living with the knowledge that he'd failed his daughter.

But he procrastinated. All day he waited, thinking through various scenarios without acting.

In the end, in turmoil, he walked back through the evening to his billet. Tomorrow he would do it. He would wait until nightfall, then he would get into the building somehow and kill William. He would get the body out and try to escape from the city.

He would die trying.

At least he would have that.

17

A boom punctured the night. Jack sat up straight on his sleeping mat and grasped the musket beside him. Another boom rolled across the city, the ground beneath him trembling.

Artillery fire.

The men about him leapt from their blankets. They were bleary-eyed and confused, but realised instinctively that this was it – they were under attack.

Jack flung his tunic over his head. The assault had come too soon. How was he going to get William out of the city now?

'Move! Move!' Kendrick bellowed as he ran across the courtyard in his undershirt.

Charles appeared dumbstruck for a moment and stood rubbing his eyes as if it were all a dream. He glanced at Jack, who gave him an affirmative nod, as if to confirm it was real.

Saleem scurried from under his blanket and fumbled for his tunic. He crawled about on all fours, wailing, 'Where is it?'

Jack grabbed a lantern and cast the light about Saleem's sleeping mat. There was the tunic, neatly folded and clearly visible.

Saleem gave a nervous laugh.

'To the wall!' Kendrick shouted.

The courtyard became a jumble of men rushing for the exit, pushing and shoving as if the enemy were right behind them. A swell caught Jack and carried him through the arched passage beneath the house and out to the street. Charles and Saleem stumbled beside him.

Soldiers ran in every direction. Sergeants shouted contradictory orders. The blasts continued, increasing in frequency. The sky was still dark and smothered by grey continents of cloud, but distant, orange flashes lit up the roofs and gables. Patches of St Paul's spire appeared and disappeared, gleaming like lizard skin. Hundreds of church bells sounded the alarm.

The men of the 9th Native Infantry were running in the direction of the Bishops Gate, but Jack paused. He wasn't going to defend the wall, he was going to find William.

'What are you waiting for?' Charles asked.

Jack glanced at Charles and Saleem. They were both staring at him as if awaiting orders.

'You two go with the others,' Jack said. 'I'm going to join my friend. I'm going to fight with him.'

Charles frowned. 'But we've been assigned to the Bishops Gate.'

'I know. But I . . . I decided this with my friend the other day.'

'Then we'll come with you,' Saleem said.

Charles shot Saleem a look of surprise, but then seemed to think about it further. 'Yes. We'll fight with you. We've come this far together.'

Jack tightened his fists. The young idiots. Why couldn't they have stayed home in their village? Why had they been so stupid as to come to London? But he felt guilty. Hadn't he helped them get here? And more than that, he couldn't bring himself to let them down, couldn't break the pretence that the Rajthanans could be beaten, that London could be saved, that he was a proud patriot rather than a craven turncoat.

A strange howling split the sky. Looking up, they saw a bulb of blue flame arc above the roofs, rise into the turbulent cloud and then plummet down like a comet. The howling grew louder as the ball raced towards them.

Sattva-fire.

Saleem ducked, although there was no need. The fireball roared overhead and slammed into a building a street away. The cobbles jolted beneath their feet and Jack caught a whiff of sattva. Sparks and flames leapt into the night.

Saleem licked his lips.

Jack knew there was no time to lose. 'All right. You can come with me.'

They ran down the street towards the Ald Gate, the only place Jack could think to go. He'd seen William there often over the past few days and he assumed this was where he would find him now.

The roads were busy but not densely packed. Figures darted here and there – soldiers carrying muskets, city guards, peasants with ageing weapons. Those who weren't going to fight, but who'd been unwilling or unable to leave the city, watched from windows. Women and children, infants and old people stared out at the gathering chaos.

Fireballs sailed overhead, crying eerily. Fires sprang up throughout the city. In the distance, flashes of gunfire lit the sky like copper lightning.

As they turned down a street, a fireball moaned and throbbed above them, close enough for Jack to smell the sattva. It thumped into the front wall of a terraced house and spewed flame and lumps of daub across the street. A chunk of burning wood skittered along the ground towards them. Blue sattva-fire snarled and popped as it ran between the cobbles.

Jack skidded to a halt. His wound nipped.

The remains of the smashed house lay burning and sizzling before them. There was no way through.

City guards came running from a side street. They jabbed hooked poles into the buildings near to the fire, trying to pull them down before the flames spread. Pieces of wall came free like cake and the buildings tottered and leant forward.

Jack turned to Charles and Saleem. 'Go back.'

They retreated and followed a different route through the city.

As the wall drew closer, the churning of the guns grew louder. Steel dawn spread from one corner of the sky and Jack realised that up until now he hadn't even wondered what the time was. He heard Elizabeth's voice, lost on the wind. He tried to run faster, but his legs burnt and his breath was short and he couldn't will himself to go any faster.

He heard a whistle. A round shot, barely visible in the dark, plunged from the sky and smacked a hole in a wall ahead of him. Dust puffed out, but the wall stayed standing.

He charged through the dust, Charles and Saleem close behind. More whistles. A round shot lopped off a chimney. Another hissed through a thatched roof.

He turned a corner and came out suddenly into a square. The dark bulk of the Ald Gate and the wall rose before him. Guns flared along the ramparts, lighting up the battlements and tinging the clouds above orange. The forge-like pounding echoed up the streets. Figures flitted along the wall and soldiers ran about the square.

Someone shouted, 'Look out!'

A round shot hit the ground nearby with a metallic chime and bounced towards them at great speed.

'Move.' Jack wrenched Charles and Saleem back.

The ball hummed past and slammed into a fountain, where it hissed and steamed. Men rushed over to retrieve the shot – ammunition was precious and could be reused any number of times.

More balls swarmed over the wall, dark against the flickering sky. They battered through doors, crushed carts, plucked men off their feet.

A glinting shell swooped down and smashed through the roof of a nearby house. The building's top storey roared and burst into dust and splinters. A window shutter clattered across the flagstones.

'Where's your friend?' Charles shouted.

Jack looked along the ramparts. It was too dark to make anyone out. How was he supposed to find William in the dim light and confusion?

'We have to get up on the battlements,' Jack said. That was the last place he wanted to be, but it was the only place he imagined he would find William – in the thick of it, leading his men. He didn't know what he was going to do with Charles and Saleem. Eventually he would have to lose them – but how? The best thing for them to do would be to hide and then get out of the city as soon as they could, but he knew neither of them would agree to that.

They ran across the square to a stairway on the side of the wall. They scrambled up the steps behind a pair of gunners hauling a box of powder. Jack looked around constantly, but couldn't see William or any of the other rebels from Dorsetshire.

They reached the walkway along the top of the wall and stopped abruptly. All about them men laboured over the artillery, sweating as they sponged out the pieces, rammed home charges, lifted and loaded the heavy balls. Sergeants roared commands. The guns bucked and rocked, the serpent-head muzzles growling, flaming and belching white smoke. The sound slapped Jack in the chest. The intricate designs along the weapons' bodies blazed alive repeatedly, then darkened. Smoke, smelling of fireworks and rot, choked the ramparts and scratched at the back of his throat.

They looked over the parapet and Saleem drew in his breath sharply. Before them was an infernal scene. The plains below were dark, but peppered by thousands of fires. The enemy encampment glimmered more than a mile away. But closer, the blasts of artillery rippled in rows. The air between the wall and the plains was thick with wailing shot. Shells rose and fell like shooting stars.

Sattva-fire balls vaulted far above. But Jack noticed the Sikhs mounting a defence from atop the bastions of the Ald Gate. The men stood in groups, raising their hands to the sky, light dancing on their orange uniforms. Pink mist formed above each group, then condensed into red, flaming bolts that shot away from the wall. The bolts screamed into the dark, dipping and rising and weaving like flies. Each struck a fireball with a thump and a crack. Fireballs shattered into galaxies. Others roared and spun to the earth, smearing the ground with flame. Many were destroyed, but many more streaked on towards the city.

Charles stared up at the Sikhs. 'Black magic. At least they're on our side.'

Jack assumed Kanvar was up there somewhere, but he couldn't make out the young siddha from this distance.

'Take cover,' a gunner shouted.

Jack heard a sharp whine and pulled Charles and Saleem down below the parapet. They waited for what seemed a long time but in reality could only have been a second. The wall shuddered. The battlements a few feet away burst into dust and shards of rock. There was a deep reverberation like a gong underground. The nearest gun spun round, almost falling over the edge and down to the street, the muzzle smacked sideways as if made of butter. Men lay screaming and struggling, half buried by rubble. Part of the top section of the wall had been smashed, leaving a fissure ten feet deep across the walkway.

Men fought frantically to free their trapped comrades.

Jack, Charles and Saleem stood up. The fissure lay between them and the wounded men. Charles went to the edge, but Jack pulled him back. 'Leave it. We can't get across that.' The rubble at the bottom of the crack looked unstable. Trails of dust and small stones were trickling down to the street.

A tall man came striding along the walkway on the opposite side of the fissure. His shaven head was lit by the flashes of the guns and the scimitar at his side glowed. It was William, barking orders and waving for more men to come to help the wounded gunners.

Jack's heart thudded. This was it – his chance. But William was on the other side of the fissure and surrounded by men.

He stepped back behind Charles and Saleem, turned his face away.

'What's wrong?' Charles asked.

'Nothing,' he said. 'Let's get out of the way. Can't see my friend yet.'

He led them along the wall, past the teams of soldiers and thundering guns. He had to get far enough away to avoid William spotting him. At the same time, he couldn't go too far. He had to be ready to act the moment he saw William alone. But would he get a chance like that? Surely he should go down to the street and climb the wall further along, run at William, shoot him? No, that wouldn't work. The other men would turn on him for killing their leader. He wouldn't stand a chance.

A shell exploded nearby with a piercing shriek. The air in front of him split open with flame and smoke, and hot, sulphur-scented wind struck him in the face. Shards of metal and musket balls screamed in all directions. A large shell-fragment roared past so close he could feel the heat of it.

He slammed himself to the floor, below the line of fire. Charles and Saleem rattled down beside him.

'Are you all right?' he called to them.

'Yes,' they both replied.

'Keep your heads down, lads.' A corporal crouched against the ramparts nearby. Along from him sheltered an infantry platoon. 'That fire's getting bloody hot.'

'Aye.' Jack clambered over to the fire step at the base of the parapet. He looked back and saw William in the distance, towering over the other men.

'What now?' Charles shouted.

'We'll stop here,' Jack replied. There was nothing more he could do at that moment. An opportunity would have to come along eventually. Provided he could stay alive long enough.

'What about your friend?' Charles asked.

'Can't see him. Who knows?'

The corporal turned, peered gingerly over the top of the wall, then slipped back down again. 'They're bringing up the heavies. Just been softening us up with the light guns so far.'

As if to prove his point a deep rumble reverberated across the plains below. Seconds later, the wall shivered and groaned. About a hundred yards away, the top of the ramparts shattered, and dust and fragments of stone jetted into the dark-grey sky. Soldiers cried out as they tumbled to the street below.

'Why don't they come and fight us face to face?' Charles said. 'Then we'll show them.'

The corporal gave a rasping laugh. 'Reckon they'll smack us around with the guns a bit more first, son.' His smile drained away and he flicked a look at the sky. 'Then they'll send magic to knock through the wall.'

Charles frowned for a moment, then gave a tight grin. 'But we have the Grail. It will come.'

The corporal wiped his forehead. 'Hope it does that soon, son.'

Jack sat with his back to the battlements. The Grail. Did Charles think it would appear at the last moment to save them? Like in the stories?

He gazed across the city as the grey dawn spilt over the roofs and steeples. The sky hurled down squalls of hot metal. Fireballs tumbled to the ground, releasing pulses of flame. Fires seethed everywhere.

Nothing was going to save them.

The Rajthanan guns slackened a little after a few minutes. Jack stood on the fire step and eased his head above the parapet. Charles and Saleem raised themselves beside him.

In the growing light, the fields were more clearly visible, pale beneath a sky thick with black cloud. The ground boiled and smoked and shot up fountains of soil. The enemy artillery sparked from behind rough earthworks and fascines. Other batteries had been set up amongst the buildings outside the city, their muzzles blazing from between the walls of farm cottages. The army swarmed in the distance.

Jack could just make out the quivering purple of the siddha tents.

Round shot bit into the wall, puffing out dust and grit and sending shockwaves through the stone. Spent balls bounced back and rolled on to the plains. Overhead, wisps of smoke from the shells dotted the sky.

Jack saw that William still walked along the wall on the other side of the fissure, shouting and gesturing fiercely with his hands. Jack wondered how much longer he should wait. He only had the rest of the day to get William out of the city. After that it would be too late.

He heard Elizabeth's voice again, crying out in the dark forest.

A gust of cold wind hit him in the face and lifted his hair in a plume behind him. There was a rushing sound, loud enough to be heard over the guns.

'What's that noise?' Saleem asked.

'Don't know,' Jack replied.

'I can smell something sweet,' Charles said.

Jack nodded. He could already smell it – sattva.

The wind grew stronger and his eyes watered. A dark cloud rose from somewhere behind the siddha tents and hung, swirling, in the air.

'What the Devil . . . ?' Charles said.

Jack felt cold.

The cloud moved forward, at first slowly, but then increasing in speed until it was hurtling towards them. It splintered into specks that looked like a mass of flies.

'Keep down.' Jack had no idea what the cloud was, but he didn't like the look of it.

They all ducked. The rushing sound built to a high-pitched squealing.

The corporal next to them stood and looked over the battlements.

'Get down.' Jack motioned to the man.

'What—' The corporal turned, looking at Jack, about to say something. Then the cloud of flies hit. The squealing was deafening. Ten or more thudded into the corporal, knocking him backwards, although he managed to stay standing. Five were embedded in his face. Others had ripped straight through his tunic and blood welled where they'd struck.

He shouted, put his hands to his face. 'Get them off. Get them off.'

Jack tried to hold the corporal still. Tiny steel gnats with long, sharp proboscises buzzed and burrowed into the man's face. Jack tried to pinch one and pull it out, but it wriggled in deeper. Within seconds the creatures had disappeared under the skin.

The corporal gasped, his eyes wide. A line of blood escaped from the corner of his mouth and he gave choking cries.

Along the ramparts, soldiers screamed and clawed at their skin, their comrades trying, with little success, to help them. One man jerked about so violently he toppled over the side of the walkway and fell to the street below.

'They're coming back,' a soldier shouted.

Jack looked up. The flies had reformed into a whirling, squealing cloud, which now came rushing back towards the wall. Jack raised his hands to shield his face. A soldier a few feet away fired his musket into the cloud, which had no effect at all.

A grumble vibrated through the wall and a blast of sattva-scented air hit Jack on the side of the head, unsteadying him for a moment. Five of the Sikhs stood in a wedge on top of the Ald Gate, their arms raised as if praising the heavens. The sattva wind seemed to emanate from them.

The blast struck the flies and scattered them. More than two-thirds sizzled and vanished. Others flew off on random trajectories. But a handful still rushed down, shrilling.

Charles muttered a prayer and made the sign of the cross.

'Cover your face,' Jack shouted.

The flies struck. Jack heard shouts as several soldiers were hit. He lowered his hands. He couldn't feel any pain. He glanced at his chest – no holes in his tunic, no sign of any injury. He looked across at Charles, who huffed and mopped his brow, but appeared unharmed.

The wounded corporal was now still, eyes staring into the black cloud above.

'Jack.' Saleem had his hand on his cheek and when he moved it, a spot of blood was visible.

'No.' Jack rushed to Saleem's side. A fly was burrowing into the boy's face.

'Is it . . . ?' Saleem stammered.

'Stay still.' Jack tried to grab the buzzing splinter, but it was already in too deep.

Saleem gave short, panting breaths.

'Fire. That's the only thing that'll kill it,' said an old, grizzled soldier who was suddenly standing over them. 'Seen them before – out in Turkey.'

The soldier crouched and looked at Saleem's face. 'It's in too far. We'll have to cut it out.'

The soldier drew a knife and Saleem looked wide-eyed at Jack.

'Hold still.' Jack patted Saleem on the arm.

The soldier moved quickly. He slit Saleem's cheek, the lad jumping slightly, and the quivering fly was exposed. He lit a match and thrust it into the cut. The fly buzzed and hissed, then flew off aimlessly.

Jack said a silent Hail Mary.

'Is it gone? Is it gone?' Saleem asked.

'You'll be all right.' The soldier grinned.

When Jack looked along the wall, he saw men shuddering as they lay dying on the walkway, while others were being treated with knives and matches. Stretcher-bearers picked up the gravely injured. The flies had otherwise been destroyed or scattered.

A round shot screamed past. The pounding of the guns continued unabated. Jack glanced in the direction of the Ald Gate and could still see William, a giant rising out of the battle smoke.

Jack's chest started to throb. He took a gulp of jatamansi, then weighed the vial in his hand. It felt empty. He held it up to the light and through the dark glass could just make out a small amount of liquid, enough for one final dose.

He would have to use that wisely.

'What the hell is that?' A private pointed down at the enemy.

Jack and the others looked over the wall. The plains still bubbled and churned from the artillery fire, but there was something else. The fields shivered, as though water were running in streams just below the surface. Jack noticed a glint of metal here and there and the scent of sattva was growing strong again.

'What now?' Charles asked.

Saleem swallowed hard.

The wave of movement reached the ditch surrounding the wall, then thousands of what looked like shining steel snakes wriggled into the ditch, where they collected in a squirming mass, then slithered straight up the wall.

Jack had seen these war avatars once before, but there had been only two of them and they had moved far more slowly than the creatures now rushing up the stonework.

'Men, load!' a sergeant shouted.

The soldiers all loaded their muskets, moving quickly, but without synchronisation. The sergeant didn't shout out the subsequent commands and some soldiers finished before the others.

A shambles. No proper organisation.

What they needed now were Rajthanan officers. But there were no Rajthanans. Just Englishmen – privates, corporals, sergeants.

Charles had his musket loaded and cocked in under fifteen

seconds. But Saleem's hands shook so much he dropped the ramrod. He glanced up at Jack, eyes wide and glassy.

'Take your time,' Jack said. 'You can do it.'

Saleem took a deep breath, wiped away the trace of blood still on his cheek and then retrieved the rod, jammed down the bullet and within seconds was standing with his musket raised and pointing over the parapet. He looked across at Jack, and for once met Jack's gaze without looking away.

'Good lad.' Jack's voice was so soft he wasn't sure if Saleem could even hear him.

And then he looked at Charles, who now grinned back, still with his musket raised and his sandy hair shuffling in the slight breeze. He seemed to have recovered from the blow of his regiment being destroyed and was now as determined as ever to fight for England.

Jack swallowed. He was proud of his two young comrades. He wished things could be different, wished he were genuinely fighting with them for his country. Feelings surged in his chest. 'God's will in England.'

'God's will in England,' Charles and Saleem said back.

Then they all climbed on to the fire step and leant over the battlements.

The snakes were racing up the wall, many already more than two-thirds of the way to the top. The sound of their hissing and clicking was audible even over the din of the guns.

'Take careful aim.' Jack raised his musket to his shoulder, pointed it down and looked along the sights. 'Make every shot count.'

Charles and Saleem took aim as well. Charles fired barely two seconds later – the burst tingled in Jack's ear – but the shot was far too high and missed the snakes and the wall completely. Saleem went next and his shot was better, but it struck the wall well ahead of the closest creatures.

While Charles and Saleem reloaded, Jack focused on the snake nearest to him. It was close enough now for him to see a steel head covered in tiny stalks, and a wriggling body made of metal ribs over mechanical innards.

He squeezed the trigger, heard the familiar crack and felt the butt jab into his shoulder. He moved his head to the side to look around the puff of smoke. The snake gave a metallic shriek and shattered, the fragments coiling as they tumbled back to the ground.

Muskets stuttered all along the wall and the bullets rattled against the stone. Hundreds of snakes fell, but there were hundreds more coming up behind them.

Jack, Charles and Saleem reloaded and fired, reloaded and fired. Jack was getting into the rhythm of it now – it was just like the old days when he'd stood in line with thousands of others, battering the oncoming enemy with round after round. Saleem was getting quicker, and Charles was shouting at the beasts as though he could terrify them.

Charles and Saleem's aims were improving and they both hit several of the creatures. Jack methodically picked off snakes one by one. He was sweating and thirsty. Pain brewed in his chest, but he did his best to ignore it. He couldn't risk using the last of the jatamansi yet.

The ramparts filled with smoke. He found it harder to make out the targets and kept missing, despite the beasts rushing closer. Muskets coughed all around him, but there seemed to be no end to the snakes. It was hopeless.

Soon the first of the creatures reached the parapet and Jack heard shouts as the men tried to fight them off with knives and even fists.

He stopped firing. 'Deploy knives.'

They released the catches on their weapons and the blades clattered into place. The snakes rushed up, their mouths open and glinting with fangs. Jack stood with his legs apart, bracing himself for the onslaught.

Within seconds the first beast was at the parapet, hissing and widening its maw. Jack stepped back, swung his blade and sliced the creature in half. Next to him, Charles jabbed and knocked a second beast over the edge.

More snakes appeared. It was simple enough to dispatch them, but there were so many. Soon Jack had to jump off the fire step and hack at the creatures as they slithered over the battlements.

He felt something tighten about his leg and when he looked down he saw one of the beasts, fangs poised to strike. He stamped down and the creature squealed as it was crushed.

Saleem cried out. Several snakes were entwined about both of his legs, and he was trying frantically to beat them off.

Jack grabbed a pair of the creatures and tore them away. They wriggled in his hands before he threw them over the wall. But there were already more wound about the lad, slipping up over his torso and reaching his neck. Jack grasped another pair and tried to wrench them off, but they held firm this time. One reared up, its body tight about Saleem's neck and its head poised to strike his face. Saleem yelped and tried to knock it away, but the beast swayed like a cobra and avoided his blows. It opened its mouth wider, fangs gleaming—

A sudden, pulverising explosion smacked Jack in the stomach and knocked him off his feet. Stone screamed and dust burst. Something hit him in the arm. He tried to breathe, couldn't, tried again and this time rasped down some dusty air. His chest boiled with pain. When he opened his eyes, all he saw was darkness. He blinked and still saw nothing. His ears were ringing but he could hear groans and screams nearby.

He rubbed his eyes, blinked again, and finally he could see. Still fighting for breath, he sat up. A deep gouge had been knocked out of the wall about twenty feet away and a pile of rubble lay on either side of the fissure, several bodies half buried underneath. Crushed and broken snakes jerked and writhed, but no further creatures slithered over the wall.

Someone beside him was coughing violently. He turned, wincing at the pain in his arm, and saw Saleem lying on his side and spitting out dust.

'You all right?' Jack asked.

Saleem nodded and wiped spittle from his mouth. At least the blast seemed to have knocked the snakes off him.

Jack looked at his own arm. The tunic was torn and there was a bloody cut on his shoulder, but the damage wasn't bad and he could still move the limb.

'Where's Charles?' he asked.

Saleem shook his head. 'Can't see him.'

The dust was clearing. Jack stood and limped towards a mound of smashed stones. Two men lay half buried beneath the pile, one of them moaning and whimpering as he tried to pull himself out. A third figure lay on the walkway, free of the stones and slowly raising himself into a sitting position. Jack ran forward – it was Charles, covered in dust from head to foot, like a miner, but still alive.

'I'm fine.' Charles coughed a few times.

But Jack noticed Charles's right leg was covered in blood. He moved aside a piece of torn trouser leg and saw that half the thigh had been shot off. Through the blood and ripped flesh he spotted an edge of bone.

'What is it?' Charles asked.

'Nothing – just a scratch.' Jack lowered the flap of material. That leg would have to come off. 'You'll be all right.'

'Had me worried there.' Charles laughed a little. He didn't appear to be in any pain.

One of the men buried under the stones gave a cry and Jack rushed over, joined by a pair of stretcher-bearers who came running along the wall. The trapped man was splattered with blood, but it was impossible to tell where it was coming from, or whether it was even all his. The stretcher-bearers pulled away the stones to free him, while Jack went to the second man and saw it was the soldier who'd burnt the avatar fly from Saleem's face. He lay dead, one side of his head crushed.

'He's gone,' Jack informed the stretcher-bearers when they looked over. He made the sign of the cross and closed the man's eyes.

Then he helped to free the trapped soldier and lift him on to a stretcher.

'My friend's also hurt badly.' He motioned with his head towards Charles.

'We'll have to come back for him,' one of the bearers said. 'Unless he can walk down.'

'Hold on.' Jack went across to Charles. 'Can you stand?'

'Reckon so.' Charles tried to raise himself, but the pain seemed to finally hit and his features contorted. 'Might need a bit of help. Leg seems buggered.'

Jack and Saleem helped Charles to his feet and supported him as he limped after the stretcher-bearers.

'Where're we going?' Charles asked.

'To get that leg looked at,' Jack said.

'No. I'm all right. It's not bad.'

'Just need to clean it up a bit.'

'But we have to fight.'

'We'll be back soon.'

Jack glanced along the ramparts as they went slowly down the steps. He made out William, striding through the smoke.

An empty stretcher lay at the bottom of the stairs.

'Get him on that,' one of the bearers said.

'No, I can walk.' Charles winced as he moved.

'It'll be easier if you lie down,' Jack said.

Charles considered this for a moment, sweat beading on his forehead, then nodded. He groaned as he tried to lower himself, finding it difficult with his injured leg. Jack and Saleem helped him down.

'Jack,' Saleem hissed, gesturing to the back of Charles's head without Charles noticing.

Jack looked to where Saleem was pointing. Cold fingers felt up his spine. A piece of shrapnel the size of a fist poked out from the back of Charles's head. Thickening blood oozed from the wound and Charles's skull curved inward slightly.

'Really, I'm all right,' Charles was saying.

Jack swallowed. 'Of course.'

'Follow us,' one of the bearers said.

'Aren't there any other bearers?' Jack looked around.

'No.' The bearer snorted.

Jack glanced up at the battlements. He could see William's large figure silhouetted in the haze between the flashing guns. He couldn't let himself lose sight of his friend now.

'Hurry up,' the bearer said.

'How far's the hospital?' Jack asked.

'What?' the bearer shouted over the roar of the guns.

'The hospital – how far?'

'Not far. We have to go now.'

Jack looked up again. William was his last chance of saving Elizabeth. He couldn't leave now. But there was no one else to carry Charles. The lad would die if they didn't get him to the hospital soon.

Jack felt dizzy and short of breath. The sound of the battle seemed overwhelming.

Damn it.

He picked up one end of the stretcher, Saleem taking the other. He would get Charles to the hospital and then get back to the wall. Saleem could stay with Charles after that.

But he would have to move quickly. He couldn't let William slip away from him now.

18

Jack and Saleem, carrying Charles on the stretcher, followed the bearers down a series of narrow, winding streets. The wounded man on the bearers' stretcher cried out a few times, while Charles lay on his side, saying nothing, more subdued than before. Jack kept glancing at the large piece of metal protruding from Charles's head and shivered each time he saw it.

Round shot whined above. Shells exploded in neighbouring streets and blue fireballs wailed overhead. Many houses had been torn apart and tossed across the road. Jack found himself clambering over rubble laced with pots, lanterns, smashed chairs, rugs. He recoiled at one point when he saw he'd stepped on a child's tunic, but there was no child in sight.

He felt moisture on his face – drizzle. His clothes were already damp. It must have been raining for some time without him noticing. The ground became slick and Saleem slipped and almost fell over a few times.

How far was that damn hospital?

Why was it taking so long?

Why were the bearers going so slowly?

The sound of a man screaming cut through the throb of the guns. Saleem slowed.

'Keep going,' Jack muttered.

The screaming continued. They came to the end of the street and stopped. More screaming. Groans. Cries. The voices of the damned.

They were in a small square surrounded on all sides by stone and timber-frame houses. Tarpaulins had been stretched across more than two-thirds of the square to provide shelter, and beneath these writhed a mass of people. Men lay on tables, drenched in blood, some with their legs or arms shot off, some impaled by chunks of metal, some distorted by greasy burns. Surgeons wielded saws, cleavers and iron tongs. The injured struggled and roared as they were operated on, held down by orderlies in grey, splattered aprons. Blood trickled between the cobblestones and flowed out from under the shelter to be washed away by the rain.

Charles raised his head and took in the scene. He looked back at Jack, eyes widening. 'No. I'm all right. Take me back.'

Jack gripped the stretcher more firmly. 'We have to get you seen to.'

They carried Charles under the tarpaulin. The rain came down harder, drumming on the canvas and running off the edges. Jack steeled himself as he looked at the carnage. Saleem was so pale his ginger beard seemed to shine against his skin.

'Get him up on that table.' A muscular surgeon with a bloody saw strode across to them. His face was locked in a scowl and his hair was dripping with rainwater.

Jack and Saleem lifted Charles on to a red-stained table that smelt damp and salty, the smell of an abattoir.

The surgeon wiped his forehead, leaving behind a trace of blood. He wheezed as he cut away Charles's left trouser leg. The wound looked worse than Jack had first thought. Most of the thigh was gone, leaving just a mess of tendons and gristle. The surgeon then turned Charles's head further to the side and examined the chunk of shrapnel at the back. He sniffed and rubbed his nose with the back of his hand.

He looked at Jack and Saleem. 'Come over here.'

They took a few steps away from the table.

The surgeon pushed his mouth up with his bottom lip, his chin puckering. 'Nothing I can do for him.'

'No,' Jack said. 'You have to.'

The surgeon gave a wheezy sigh. 'That metal in his head – he's finished. It's deep in the brain. Don't know how he's still alive.'

Jack glanced around. What he most wanted to see was a Rajthanan doctor. In the army, the Rajthanans would always handle the most serious cases as European surgeons were in reality little more than medical assistants with limited training.

But there were no Rajthanans.

The rain pummelled the tarpaulin. A trickle found its way through a gap between the sheets and fell on his shoulder.

'I'm sorry.' The surgeon looked down. 'You'll have to move him. Take him somewhere he can rest. Best thing for it.'

'Is there anything you can give him? For the pain.' Jack knew the Rajthanan doctors had drugs that could reduce a soldier's suffering.

'Afraid not. We've got nothing like that here.'

Saleem's eyes were wide and watery. Jack patted him lightly on the back as they turned to the table.

'What is it?' Charles's eyes looked glazed. They rolled about as though he were drunk.

Jack cleared his throat. 'We're just going to take you somewhere – so you can rest.'

'I'm all right, then?'

Jack shot a look at Saleem, then nodded awkwardly.

Charles's eyes focused and he searched Jack's face. 'It's bad, isn't it?'

'Yes,' Jack said.

'Ah . . .' Charles paused for a long time. 'That's it, then.'

'You need to rest.' Jack looked across the square. The rain hammered on the cobbles. He couldn't see anywhere to take Charles.

There were shouts down one of the side streets and men came stumbling through the rain. Some limped, their clothes torn, while others carried wounded soldiers on stretchers. It looked like a large group – perhaps as many as 100 men.

'You'll have to move.' The surgeon nodded towards the approaching troops.

Jack scanned the surroundings again and noticed what looked like a recess in the wall of one of the adjoining streets.

'Come on,' he said to Saleem, and they lifted the stretcher off the table.

They jogged across the square, the rain soaking them immediately, and reached the recess, which turned out to be an archway leading to an inner courtyard. They put the stretcher down under the arch, where it was protected from the rain.

Charles lay on his side, breathing unevenly. He hiccuped a couple of times as he tried to move.

'Take it easy.' Jack crouched and put his hand on Charles's shoulder. He prayed silently that it wouldn't go on for too long, that the lad wouldn't die too hard.

'I need to . . . get back,' Charles said. 'The harvest . . .'

'Just rest,' Jack said.

'Where are . . . ? What day is it?'

Saleem's face was red and he wiped his eyes.

Jack tightened his jaw and looked away. He would have to leave now. He'd already been apart from William for too long – any longer and he might not be able to find his friend again at all. He didn't want to abandon Charles, but he'd done what he could.

He stood up intending to speak to Saleem, then noticed a movement out of the corner of his eye. Something had flickered behind the crack between a set of double doors to the side of the archway.

He rushed over and pushed at the doors. They were locked. Something moved again. He crouched and peered through the crack. At first it was too dark to see anything, but then he made out a woman hunched in the corner of a room. Two children huddled beside her. Her eyes shone in the gloom. She looked afraid.

'Hey,' he called. 'We've got a wounded man here. Have you got anywhere he can lie down?'

The woman edged back into the shadow with the children so that she was no longer visible.

'Please,' he said. 'We're soldiers – English Army. We won't hurt you.'

The woman stayed in hiding.

He sighed. Suddenly it seemed the most important thing in the world to get Charles inside and lying on a bed. The boy didn't deserve to die in the street.

He banged hard on the doors and the bolt inside rattled. 'Open up. Please. We need help.'

There was no response.

'Damn it.' He kicked the door.

Charles groaned. His eyes were open, but unfocused. 'Water.'

Jack looked at Saleem. Neither of them had a canteen or a skin. There was rainwater all around them, but nothing to collect it in. How the hell were they going to get Charles something to drink?

The doors scraped open. The woman stood in the entrance, dressed in a green gown and a white bonnet. She was no older than twenty-five and chewed her lip as she looked at Charles.

'Thank you,' Jack croaked.

They carried Charles inside, going through a front room and into a dim bedroom. They laid him on the wooden bed, on top of the blankets. The room was cool and musty, and faded tapestries hung across two of the walls – it was a wealthy household.

Charles coughed, his brow feverish.

'We need water,' Jack said to the woman, who stood watching from the bedroom door.

She nodded and disappeared. The two children – a boy around five and a girl around eight – came to the doorway and looked in tentatively, the boy with his fingers stuffed in his mouth.

'Come away.' The woman bustled them back into the front room when she returned.

She set a pitcher down on a table in a corner of the room, poured a mug of water and brought it to the bedside.

'Do you want a drink?' Jack asked Charles.

Charles had a look of intense concentration on his face. He managed to nod.

Jack held Charles's head up as he sipped. A little of the water ran into Charles's mouth, but much of it just trickled down his chin and on to his neck.

Jack put the mug on the floor beside the bed. The woman lit a candle and set it on the table, where it radiated a trembling light, but not enough to force away the shadows.

Jack turned to the door. He had to leave now. He'd done as much as he could and the thought of Elizabeth in the cell was stark in his mind.

'Jack,' Charles rasped. 'Saleem.'

Jack turned back, then crouched beside the bed with Saleem.

'Please.' Charles was drenched in sweat that shone in the candlelight. 'Tell my mother . . . and Mary . . .'

'We'll get a message to them.' Jack rested his hand on Charles's shoulder.

'I'll make sure,' Saleem said. 'I'll tell everyone in the village. They'll know you died fighting.'

Charles managed a small nod. 'And you'll fight . . . you'll keep on fighting . . .'

Saleem glanced at Jack, who felt his stomach turn cold as he nodded his agreement.

'Yes,' Saleem said.

'Ah . . .' Charles sighed. 'Good.' He lay back and shut his eyes. 'The Grail will come soon.'

Jack listened to the hushed roar of the rain outside the closed window shutters.

'The guns have stopped,' Saleem said.

It was true. The bombardment had ended.

'Is it over?' Saleem asked. 'Have we beaten them?'

They heard someone running outside in the street. Jack went to the window and squinted through the slats, but he couldn't see anything clearly. More people ran past. More shouting.

'I'm going to take a look,' he said. 'Stay here.'

The children had come back to the bedroom door and now gazed at the wounded man. Jack pushed past them, unbolted the door and slipped outside. He stood beneath the arch. The street was wet and shiny and dotted with puddles. A group of five soldiers ran past, splashing through the rain. Then came a pair of stretcher-bearers carrying a wounded man. Jack called out to them, but they didn't stop.

He stepped out of the archway and peered through the shower. He could still see the edge of the hospital tarpaulin and the figures moving about underneath.

Three soldiers turned the corner and clattered towards him, talking loudly to each other as they jogged along.

'Hey,' Jack called. 'Why have the guns stopped?'

The three halted. One of the men stared at Jack through the rain. 'Haven't you heard? They've smashed through the wall at the Bishops Gate. Some kind of black magic.'

Jack paused. The 9th had been positioned at the gate. 'Any survivors? I mean, from the regiments posted there.'

'How should we know?'

The men went to move on.

'Hold on,' Jack said. 'You know the Ghost? Have you heard where he is?'

'In the Tower. They're making a stand there.'

'Is that where you're going?'

The man paused and glanced at the others.

One of the other men snorted. 'Are you joking?'

They pushed past, splashed down the street and disappeared into the grey haze.

Rainwater ran into Jack's eyes. The Rajthanans were already in the city. He was running out of time.

Saleem wrenched the doors open. 'Quick.'

Jack followed Saleem into the bedroom, where the woman was standing beside the bed. Charles's eyes were closed and he lay still, a slight frown on his forehead, as if he were troubled by a dream.

Jack stared at the woman, a question on his face, but she looked away. He strode over to the bed. Charles had stopped breathing. There was no pulse.

Jack made the sign of the cross. His throat felt hard. There was a trace of pain across his chest and for the first time that day he realised how tired he was. He sat on the side of the bed and rubbed his face. He looked over at Saleem, who just stood there in the half-light, mouth hanging open.

A musket cracked in the distance, the echo rolling up the street.

'They're through the wall,' Jack said. 'The Rajthanans are coming.'

The woman sniffled, put her fist to her mouth and glanced out at her children, who sat huddled in a corner of the front room.

'What should we do?' Saleem asked.

Jack walked through to the front room. He knew where he was going, but he didn't want Saleem to follow. There'd been enough death.

His musket, along with Saleem's, lay on a table. The children crouched in a corner and looked at him as if he were a crazed man.

'Is there anywhere to hide?' he asked the woman.

'The cellar.' She gestured to a rug in a corner.

Jack kicked aside the rug and found a trapdoor underneath. He pulled the door up and looked down into a gloomy, dusty chamber that smelt of old apples.

'Here.' The woman fetched a ladder from an adjoining room.

He lowered the ladder and leant it against the open trapdoor. 'When the Rajthanans come – you and the children, in here.'

The woman nodded, bit her lip.

'They won't harm you.' He tried to sound reassuring. 'They'll be after the men. But all the same, keep out of the way until it's over.'

As Jack spoke, things began to seem clearer. He knew now what he had to do.

He strode over to the table and picked up his musket. Outside, the sound of shots grew closer. He looked across at Saleem, who stood in the doorway to the bedroom.

'Get in the cellar.' He nodded towards the trapdoor.

Saleem frowned. 'Hide? But we have to fight.'

'Get in there. Now.'

'Jack . . . we can't.'

'It's over.'

'How can you say that?'

Jack lifted his musket and pointed it straight at Saleem. 'I'm sorry. Get in the cellar.'

The woman gave a muffled cry and rushed over to shield her children.

Saleem's features drooped like melting wax. He blinked repeatedly. 'What?'

'Move it.'

Saleem walked over to the trapdoor and paused before stepping on to the ladder. 'I don't understand.'

'You will. Take that cross off your chest.'

'No.'

Jack gritted his teeth and looked coldly at Saleem. 'Do it.'

Carefully, deliberately, Saleem tugged away the emblem sewn on to his chest. He now looked indistinguishable from an ordinary European Army soldier.

'Right,' Jack said. 'Get in the cellar.'

Saleem climbed slowly down the ladder. When Jack went over, he could see Saleem standing on the floor looking up at him. Jack pulled the ladder up, leant it against the wall and then went back to the trapdoor. 'I'm leaving you here.'

Saleem shot him an accusatory look.

'It's for your own good,' Jack said. 'The war's over. Forget about it. Stay here until the coast's clear. Get out of that uniform as soon as you can. Then get back to your village.'

'I trusted you, Jack.'

Jack looked away. 'You fought well. You should be proud of yourself.' He found it hard to still the shake in his voice, and he couldn't bring himself to look back down in the cellar. He wasn't betraying Saleem, he was saving him. But the lad wouldn't see it that way.

He slammed the trapdoor shut and the sound rolled through the quiet house. He glanced at the woman, who still crouched with her children. She looked terrified of him. He put the musket on his shoulder, but that didn't seem to calm her.

He took some cartridges out of his ammunition pouch and rested them beside Saleem's firearm. 'I'm going now. Lock the door and don't open it for anyone. When you hear the Rajthanans coming, you all go down in the cellar as well. Take that musket with you.' He gestured to Saleem's firearm. 'The lad down there can use it . . . if it comes to that. Stay down there for a few days. Don't come out until it's quiet.'

The woman nodded, moisture building in her eyes.

'Don't let the lad out of there. If he tries to leave, make him see it's pointless fighting on. You understand?'

'Yes.'

'I'm helping him.' Jack didn't know why he was explaining himself further.

The woman nodded again.

'All right, then,' he said. 'God keep you.'

He left the house and heard the woman draw the bolt across behind him. It was still raining and the light was dim and grey. The street was empty, but he could hear musket fire in the distance. Columns of black smoke rose above the roofs and he thought he could smell sattva.

He had no idea whether Saleem, the woman and her children

would survive. If Saleem obeyed him and stayed put, they would have a chance.

But now he had to go. He had to do what he'd travelled all these miles to do.

He put on his blue cap and secured it under his chin. Then he took a deep breath and stepped out into the road.

19

Was he too late? This thought harried Jack as he ran down the empty streets. Was William already dead, missing, buried under rubble, impossible to find?

His boots splashed and the rain battered his face. From time to time he looked up and saw the white turrets at the top of the Tower in the distance. He wasn't sure of the route and he kept getting lost in the maze of lanes.

His chest tightened and his breath came in icy spikes. If only he could run faster. Damn his injury. Damn his bad heart.

A soldier lay abandoned on a stretcher at the side of the road. His abdomen had been wrenched open and he struggled to hold back the bloody mess of his own innards. He shivered and his teeth chattered as he looked up. 'Help.'

But that wound looked bad, and Jack knew there was nothing he could do to help. He ran on.

'Hey.' The soldier shouted. 'Hey.' He continued shouting even as Jack turned the corner at the far end of the alley.

Then Jack skidded to a halt.

Rebel soldiers littered the street ahead. Most lay still, the bloodied cobblestones around them splattered by the rain, but some moved slowly, groaning, trying to crawl, grasping at the cobbles, choking, retching blood. One man jerked and flapped like a shot bird.

Jack swallowed and trod carefully between the figures to avoid the outstretched arms and clutching hands. The walls to either side were pocked with bullet holes and streaked with blood.

Leaving the dying soldiers behind, he turned left again and went down a covered alley. As he neared the end of the walkway, he heard the trumpet of an elephant. He stopped and shrank into the shadows. The beast ambled past, its sagging skin dark from the downpour. Troops followed, marching steadily with boots squelching in the sodden muck of the road. They were regular European Army soldiers in blue tunics and cloth caps.

Damn. He was running out of time. And luck.

He slipped back to the other end of the alley and glanced around the corner. The Tower was near now, looming above the houses, surrounded by drifts of rain.

Up the street, more soldiers marched past.

He looked at the St George's cross on his chest – he had only to remove it in order to blend in with the other soldiers. He paused for a moment, running his finger over the material. Charles had died for this emblem. Thousands of others had too. More still were prepared to fight for it.

What would Elizabeth want him to do? He guessed that if he could talk to her, she would urge him to keep the cross on his chest and fight for England. But he couldn't do that. He was still a father running through the forest at night trying to find his daughter.

He tore the patch from his tunic and picked away the white threads that remained. He held the patch in his hand, stared at the cross. He was about to throw it away, but then changed his mind and put it in his pocket.

He looked back down the street – no soldiers. He released the catch on his musket and the knife shot out. Then he went forward cautiously. An artillery boom somewhere up ahead made him jump. Footsteps slapped wet cobblestones nearby. He slunk into an alcove and watched as a platoon of European Army soldiers ran across an intersection, accompanied by a Rajthanan officer in a green turban.

There were further rumbles of artillery. The door behind him rattled and dust dribbled from the thatched roof.

He continued up the street. The sound of the guns grew louder. He took a couple of turns, and then the Tower was right before him, floating in a haze of rain and powder smoke.

Guns flared at each other across the empty square where Sir Gawain had given his speech a few days earlier. The Rajthanans had arrayed their light, wheeled artillery across one side of the square, protected only by a low wall of sandbags. The weapons glinted and roared, their bronze bodies hissing and steaming as the rain oiled them. The gunners danced about, sponging, loading, firing, all to the barked orders of Rajthanan commanders. Balls howled through the air. Spent shot littered the square. The outer wall of the Tower rippled with return gunfire, but the ancient stone was weak – in many places the wall was already half smashed and sections continued to burst into dust.

He was too late. The Rajthanans had already surrounded the Tower. Pain stabbed his chest, sharp at first, then settling into a dull, pulsing ache. Elizabeth was slipping away.

Boots tramped behind him. He spun round in time to see a column of soldiers marching straight towards him. There was nowhere to hide, and in any case he was in plain view of the Rajthanan captain leading the troops.

'You there, fall into line,' the captain shouted in Arabic, pointing his scimitar at Jack. He was a thin man with a moustache speckled with silver.

'Yes, sir,' Jack shouted back instinctively.

He went to move to the rear of the column, planning to slip away as soon as he could. But the captain pointed his scimitar again and growled, 'Here at the front, you pink bastard.'

The words stung Jack. Why should he let the captain speak to him like that? But there was nothing he could do about it.

The soldiers came to a halt. They were dark-haired with trim moustaches and goatees, and their captain wore the silver turban of an Andalusian regiment. Jack namasted and tentatively took up a position at the head of the column. One of the soldiers whispered something in Andalusian, which Jack couldn't understand, and he heard snorts of amusement.

'At the ready, men.' The captain strained to be heard over the gunfire. 'We'll be storming the Tower any minute now. Remember, the King is to be spared at all costs. All loot goes to the Prize Masters. Anyone caught stealing will get fifty lashes.'

Jack watched the Tower wither beneath the onslaught. The outer wall was crumbling into a mound of debris and one by one the rebel guns were falling silent. Was William in there?

His throat tightened, not just because he was thinking of Elizabeth. The Rajthanans were destroying the Tower, the ancient seat of the kings and queens of England, built long ago by his people.

His people.

Jhala had betrayed him. Why had Jack thought there was a bond between them?

The Rajthanans had betrayed him. They'd killed Charles. They were destroying London. They'd forced him to kill Harold.

For a moment the image of Robert Salter flashed in his head, the young soldier tied to a tree, waiting for the bullet. Jack shouldn't have stood by and let the lad die like that. He should have confronted Captain Roy, should have stopped it.

Why had he blindly followed army rules?

Why had he blindly followed the Rajthanans?

But there was little point in dwelling on this. He had to put these thoughts aside. Only Elizabeth mattered. And right now he had to somehow get into the Tower and then get William out again.

How could he escape from this Andalusian brigade? He glanced around and saw the captain still standing near to him. It would be impossible to slip away.

An elephant gave a shrill cry as it lumbered into view, partially blocking the end of the street. The creature was draped in a quilted caparison and a siddha in a purple tunic sat atop it, protected from the rain by a batman holding a black parasol.

A team of soldiers wheeled over a spherical wicker cage, inside which squirmed hundreds of avatar snakes, their metal bodies squealing as they scraped against each other. The creatures appeared excited, sticking their heads out of the cage and hissing through steel fangs.

'Release them,' the siddha barked down from the elephant.

The soldiers opened a door on the side of the cage and the snakes spilt out like entrails from a freshly slit carcass. The creatures slithered around the legs of the elephant, antennae flicking.

The siddha held up his hand and spoke words in a language Jack didn't understand. The snakes stopped moving and raised their heads, poised and swaying. Then the siddha spoke a single command and pointed towards the Tower. The creatures hissed and shot off across the square. Jack watched as they reached the far side and slipped into the moat. Soon they were oozing up the remains of the outer wall, pelted by rebel musket fire. Then they disappeared into the chaos of dust and smoke about the Tower.

The Rajthanan artillery stopped completely and the sudden quiet was a shock. Battle smoke clogged the square, but was slowly clearing. The few remaining rebel guns still flashed and sent round shot whistling, but there was no return fire from the Rajthanans.

A horn blared, followed by a second, then a third. The cries were eerie, like wolves baying. Kettledrums pulsed. The sound was familiar to Jack and he felt the hair rise on the back of his neck. He was about to go into battle once again, and there was nothing he could do to prevent it.

The captain drew his scimitar, the metal chiming against the scabbard and the blade shining faintly in the dim light.

The rain streamed down at an angle and hit Jack on the side of the face. He slipped his hand into his pocket, took out the bottle of jatamansi, paused, then swallowed the last few drops.

He said a quick Hail Mary under his breath, then silently prayed to God to let him live, let him survive to save his daughter.

An Andalusian sergeant stepped forward and raised a brass

horn moulded into the likeness of a conch shell – the curious design represented the ancient horns carried by the warriors of Rajthana. The horn blower gave a single, clear note to sound the attack.

'Charge!' the captain roared and ran out into the square.

The soldiers shouted and followed their commander. Jack was forced forward. He ran with the men, reluctant, but unable to avoid it . . . And now he was out in the square, racing ahead with a wave of bellowing soldiers who coursed out of the neighbouring streets. Horns blasted and drums grumbled. Standards swished.

Musket fire crackled across the remains of the Tower's walls, where many rebels were still standing. Bullets whined and sizzled through the rain. Bones cracked, skulls popped and men fell, shouting in Arabic, French or Andalusian. Rain and blood splattered Jack in the face. He tried to slow his pace – he had no desire to be near the front of the assault – but the soldiers were a solid wall behind him. He realised that as he couldn't ease himself back, his only hope, in fact, was to press on as quickly as possible, to get in amongst the walls of the Tower. There at least he would be able to find cover, hide, look for William.

His breathing was shallow and uneven as he gasped down acrid smoke.

A man beside him roared, the cry fading to a gargle. He'd been hit in the mouth and a mess of teeth and blood now rolled down his chin. But he still ran on, a crazed smile on his lips and eyes hungry for the fight. Then he fell, as though sucked up by the ground, and Jack was running on without him.

The moat and the shattered wall were close now. Teams of scalers rushed forward with wooden ramps more than 100 feet long. They leapt into the moat and swam across, floating the ramps beside them. The water boiled with bullets and blood. Soon corpses bobbed everywhere.

Jack reached the edge of the moat. Four ramps had already been laid across, leading to the bank of rubble that had previously been the wall. Soldiers were charging across, spattered by musket fire. Many were hit and tumbled off into the moat. A section of one ramp had caught fire and the flames glinted on the choppy water.

Jack paused for breath, but bullets scythed past him, one tugging at his sleeve. Soldiers were elbowing him out of the way in their rush to get across the moat. He slipped on the muddy bank, struggled back to his feet and joined the mob rushing across one of the ramps.

His feet battered the wooden boards and the storm of bullets shrieked around him and the air burnt his throat. He glanced up and saw the rebels across the top of the broken wall, blasting with their muskets through a mist of rain and smoke. He had to get over that wall, get out of the line of fire. That was the single thought that occupied his mind.

He reached the far side of the ramp and clambered up. The broken stonework was slick from the rain and he slipped numerous times, scraping his knees and hands until they were bleeding. Bullets screamed on the stones about him. The rain pounded down.

The first wave of the attackers was nearing the summit, but the rebels had set up their remaining guns on unbroken sections of wall and now fired grape down the slope. The muzzles flamed, jolted and disgorged hails of balls and metal fragments that flayed the stone. Soldiers fell in groups, as if dropping to their knees in worship before the retching beasts. Jack saw one man race straight at a gun as it fired – his body flew apart in a puff of red.

But the attackers poured on to the summit and hand-to-hand fighting broke out. Men scrambled up to the guns and spiked them, jamming their ramrods into the vents and snapping them off to prevent the weapons being fired.

The rebels were pushed back. As Jack reached the top of the bank, there was no one to oppose him. The attackers were now scuttling down the far side of the shattered wall, where they swarmed up the grassy incline towards the collection of walls and buildings about the White Tower. Puffs of musket smoke revealed that the rebels had regrouped and were defending themselves.

Jack was out of breath and his chest bloomed with pain. He stopped running but a soldier slammed into him and knocked him to his knees. More soldiers bumped into him as they ran past – he was going to be crushed.

He managed to get up again and staggered down the rubble slope. He slipped on the wet stone, fell on his back, slid down a few feet and struck a corpse. Someone trod on his hand and pain shot up his arm.

He got up again and stumbled down the remainder of the rubble, reaching the muddy grass. Instead of running straight up the slope, he managed to dodge his way to the right to where there were fewer soldiers and the wall was less damaged. He got out of the way of the main mass of men and tried to make it over to a stand of trees beside the wall. He felt he was going to pass out and he needed cover. Pools of blackness spread before his eyes. He slipped on the mud, fell and hit his head on one of the tree trunks.

He lay on the ground just within the trees. He was too weak to stand. He heard shouting and the crackle of muskets around him, but it was distant, as if echoing from the far end of a long tunnel. Pain jolted his chest, then flickered down his left arm. He grimaced, gritted his teeth.

Then it got worse. A shaft of fire slammed into his body.

He tried to move and found he couldn't.

Everything went silent.

He realised he'd stopped breathing. He was floating in darkness, drifting away.

He fought for air but no air would come. He tried to shout for help but he couldn't make a sound.

Katelin appeared before him, lying on her deathbed, covered

in sweat, looking at him with glazed eyes. She reached up to touch him and her fingers on his cheek were like a wisp of smoke . . .

The darkness thickened.

'This world is an illusion.' Jhala's words. 'Let go of your will and you'll break through the illusion and then you'll see that you are, have always been, free.'

Perhaps if he let go now he could slip over completely to the spirit realm and be free. He'd been hovering between the spirit and material worlds for so many years. On the trail in Dorsetshire he'd momentarily been whisked outside himself several times, his whole 'self' vanishing for a while.

Perhaps now it was time to give up and vanish completely.

But he couldn't do that. He had to hold on. Elizabeth was depending on him.

He tried to prise open his lungs, but nothing happened. He tried again. The struggle seemed to go on for hours. He was teetering on the edge of a pit of darkness. Just holding on.

But it was no good. He couldn't hold on. He was slipping down. For some reason, he thought of the yantra he'd stolen from Jhala's office. It quivered and circled and glowed on a black background. It would be the last thing he ever saw . . .

Then it flared brilliant white, blinding him.

And warmth suddenly flooded his chest.

He stopped slipping down.

He took a deep, ragged gasp and air plunged into his lungs, so cold it seemed to burn inside him. He took another breath, and then another.

He was alive.

He sat up with a start, rasping and coughing. The vice constricting his lungs eased and the pain slipped back from his arm, although it still bubbled and churned in his chest. The sound of the battle grew louder and sharper. He lay back, opened his eyes and stared up at the shifting leaves of the trees.

He knew instantly what had happened.

The stolen yantra had worked – finally – and the power was holding back the sattva-fire injury.

He flexed his fingers as if feeling them for the first time. He now knew everything about the power – the information appeared in his head as if it had always been there. Although he felt far stronger than before, he understood that the power hadn't completely cured him and he would have to keep reusing it to stay alive. The sattva-fire would remain in his chest, and would always weaken him to a degree, but at least he had something to fight it with now.

But something else gnawed at the back of his mind. Some sort of question. It was as though he were trying to solve a puzzle without even knowing what it was.

Memories tumbled through his head . . .

Jhala had said he'd used a power to save his own life, which was why he was unable to learn new yantras. He'd never said what that power was, though.

Another time, Jhala had said he'd been badly injured in battle, although he'd never said what the injury was.

And now Jack remembered finding Jhala collapsed in his office. Jhala's skin had been like ice, even though he was supposedly suffering from fever. After that, Jack had found the yantra under a cushion – the yantra he now knew healed sattva-fire injuries.

The pieces all came together in his head.

Jhala had never suffered from fever. He'd made that up. His illness was from a sattva-fire wound, which he'd tried to keep secret, perhaps out of shame. He'd had to use the yantra to save his life, and he'd had to keep on using that yantra to stay alive. He must have been using it for decades. He must still be using it.

Jack blinked. Perhaps he should have seen all this before. But how could he have? He'd never known what the power of the stolen yantra was.

And now, a further realisation filtered into his head.

Jhala had told him Europeans couldn't learn the higher powers. He'd also said that once you used a power you could never learn another. And yet Jack was living proof that neither of these were true.

Had Jhala lied to him about all of this?

A bullet shredded the leaves above him, snatching him back to the present. Musket fire. Screams. Shouts. The scent of sulphur and woodsmoke.

He sat up, wincing at the ache that still rolled across his chest. His limbs felt stiff, as if he hadn't used them in days. The world around him was blurry at first, but then, as he rubbed his eyes, it became clearer.

Through the trees he could see up the gradual incline to the main keep, the White Tower, which was now surrounded by attackers. The rebels fired down from loophole windows and from the tops of the surrounding walls, their muskets spluttering and popping. A wooden building away to the left had been set on fire and the flames roared despite the rain.

No one seemed to have noticed him lying near the wall.

He grasped a tree, dragged himself upright and stood leaning against the trunk. He had to find William. And quickly. But how was he going to do that in the chaos, amongst the thousands of men fighting? His friend could be anywhere, might already be dead. He rubbed his face with his hand. There had to be a way.

He spotted the body of an officer lying nearby, green turban stained red. The man's hand still clutched a spyglass. He ran across to the corpse, picked up the glass, then slipped back to the cover of the trees. The attackers still surged up the slope and no one paid him the slightest attention.

He gazed at the battle again. Even with the glass, it would be impossible to spot William amidst the fighting. He would have to use his power . . . his *power*. He was so accustomed to thinking he had just one.

He took a deep breath. He was a siddha now. A proper siddha. As far as he knew the first European to ever learn this much. So he would have to use his *sattva-tracking* power. The first power he'd learnt.

Of course, he couldn't actually track William about the Tower, but going into the trance would at least sharpen his eyesight and hopefully reveal details that he might otherwise miss. He had to try.

He closed his eyes and tried to block out the sound of fighting. After a few minutes he sensed the sattva about him – he was in a weak stream. He concentrated on the yantra and, as usual, it glimmered white on black.

Nothing happened.

It had been strangely easy to meditate as he'd lain dying. Perhaps any distractions had been blotted out.

He tried again, and this time his thoughts skipped and jumped. He saw Elizabeth in the cell at Poole, Jhala sitting in his office and waving the pardon before putting it in the top drawer of his desk, William bursting out of the smoke at the Battle of Ragusa.

He tried to break free of these memories, but they kept building in his mind, as if he were rushing through a dense passage of recollections and images and flashes of sensation.

Finally, he held the yantra still and it blasted him with light. A cool, liquid sensation enveloped him. He was in.

He opened his eyes and everything looked sharp and clear. He could see every leaf on the trees about him, every drop of rain as it hurtled down, each soldier charging up the slope.

He thought about William, recalling his friend's size and shape and the way he moved. Then he stood, raised the glass and began his search. The pale stone and the four turrets of the White Tower leapt before him. Smoke puffed from the windows and dust danced on the walls as they were struck by musket fire.

To the left of the keep lay open ground, across which attackers streamed as they searched for an entrance to the building. To the right stood a wall studded with a pair of bastion towers. Ladders had been raised against the wall and the rebels fought the enemy along the battlements.

He surveyed the first bastion and made out the rebels on the roof firing at their assailants on the wall below. He then followed the wall, where further men fought with knife-muskets and fists, and reached the second bastion. A small group of rebels on the roof shot and hurled rocks down at attackers hidden on the other side of the perimeter wall.

Jack paused and concentrated on the group of rebels. There was a tall man with a shaven head amongst them. Jack watched closely. The man fired down with a musket, reloaded, peered over the battlements, then fired again. Could it be . . . ?

Distantly, Jack was aware that his wound was flaring again. His new healing power had given him only a temporary reprieve and the sattva-fire in his chest would burn brighter the longer he stayed in the trance. His breathing was thin and once again the pain crackled down his left arm. He couldn't hold on for much longer.

He concentrated harder on the tall man in the tower, the figure becoming brighter and clearer, as though viewed through an increasingly powerful glass. The man turned for a moment and Jack made out the face.

It was William.

Jack threw himself out of the trance and the force of the pain knocked him back against the tree. His head hit the trunk and he slid down as darkness roiled at the bottom of his vision. He swallowed down air, fought to stay conscious. As the darkness solidified, he scrabbled with his mind to recall the healing yantra. He saw one part of it, then another, then finally the whole design.

He held the yantra still and immediately his breathing eased. He lay on the ground for a moment, panting. This healing power was going to be useful.

As soon as he was strong enough, he climbed back to his feet, leant against the tree and squinted up at the bastion tower through the glass. Despite no longer being in the trance, he could still see William, although not with the same degree of clarity.

He picked up the musket. The weapon was wet from the rain – the wood and steel shiny – but that wasn't a problem for a percussion firearm. The old flintlocks had needed protecting from moisture – in the rain you had to keep the lock covered with a piece of leather, or hold the weapon under your armpit – but these new firearms were much less vulnerable.

He hung the musket across his shoulder and took a deep breath. This was it. He was going to get close to William and then do what he had to do.

He looked up at the bastion tower again. Somehow, he had to get in there, but he also had to avoid the fighting. The perimeter wall, which bounded the lawns and the keep, ran nearby to the right, and a set of stairs led up to the battlements. If he could get up there, then he could follow the wall to the tower.

He glanced around. There was no one else in this corner of the grounds and no one between him and the steps. He left the trees and ran up the slope, keeping close to the wall. His chest still hurt and he couldn't go much faster than a jog. The spyglass slapped against his chest and the musket bounced on his shoulder.

Breathing heavily, he reached the steps and looked around. No one seemed to have noticed him, but he would be more exposed once he was up on the walkway.

He charged up and crouched beside the battlements. On the far side of the wall was a cobbled street, followed by a further wall, towers, and beyond these the grey expanse of the Thames. About a hundred attackers had made it into the street and were firing up at William and his men in the tower.

Jack ran along the wall, staying hunched. He would be clearly visible to William and the rebels if they looked in his direction. He noticed a small entrance where the tower met the perimeter wall, and he raced towards this, hoping to get inside before he was spotted.

On the far side of the tower, the attackers on the wall had overpowered the rebels and were now trying to batter down a door. Seeing this, William and the others rushed over to that side of the roof and fired down at their assailants. Their muskets clattered and burst and smoke welled around the top of the tower. But the attackers soon had the door open and flooded into the building.

William and his men disappeared from the roof, presumably rushing downstairs to meet the enemy.

Jack reached the archway, breath fiery, dark spots dancing before him, the ground far below reeling and spinning. Should he use the healing power again? No – there was no time.

He paused for a second to clear his head, then peered through the arch. Just inside was a small, empty room. At one end was a stairway, leading down, and at the other end an archway giving access to a dark corridor. He heard the sound of a fight in the depths of the corridor – shouts, cries, chimes of steel.

He slipped the musket from his shoulder, released the knife catch and held the weapon before him as he crept down the corridor. The noise of the fight grew louder. A couple of shots rang out. Footsteps. And then he heard William's voice shouting something he couldn't make out.

He ran to the end of the hall, pressed himself against the wall and looked around the corner. Before him was a long chamber with a high-vaulted ceiling. Pale light spilt in through the windows along one wall and a ghostly lace of rain fell outside. William stood in the centre of the room. About him lay several bodies, both rebels and attackers. A soldier, who appeared to be a Frenchman with his thick beard and shaved head, knelt in front of William, clutching a ripening wound in his belly.

William held a knife that was stained with blood.

The Frenchman tried to stand, but couldn't. He looked up at William and spat. William wiped the spittle from his cheek, then grabbed the Frenchman by the hair and slit his neck as quickly and expertly as a butcher. A line of blood shot out and splattered on the stone floor. The Frenchman gripped his neck and fell to the ground, where he squirmed and moaned.

William now rushed to one of the windows and looked out.

Jack heard the blasts and cries of the battle outside. He raised the musket. His heart battered in his chest and the darkness collected like frost at the rims of his eyes and he was sure he was going to pass out at any moment. But he couldn't let himself pass out, because this was it now. He had a clear shot. He had to do it. Elizabeth was relying on him to pull that trigger.

Only he couldn't do it. He couldn't shoot his friend in the back.

He took a step into the chamber, still with the musket raised.

William spun round and his head jerked back as though he'd been slapped in the face. His eyes narrowed and his grip tightened on the knife for a moment, but then his features warmed into a smile. 'Jack. This is a surprise.'

'I'm sorry.'

'What? Are you going to shoot me?'

'I have to get you back to Poole . . . my daughter.'

'Yes. I remember. Don't be crazy. Put the musket down. We'll fight these bastards, then we'll ride on Poole.'

Jack couldn't help a bitter smile. How did William do it? How did he stay optimistic despite everything? 'It's finished. You can't win now.'

'Who says so?'

'You know it as well as I do.'

William shook his head. 'We can still win. The men will fight to the death to defend their King. We just need to push these bastards back from the Tower and then they'll lose heart.' He looked down for a second, then looked up again and fixed his gaze on Jack. 'And if we don't win, we'll die honourably. Our deaths will be a message to our children and grandchildren to continue the fight, until one day we're free.'

Jack swallowed. William always spoke well. 'If you give yourself up, I can take you back alive.' It was worth a try.

William laughed. 'No.'

'I don't want to shoot you.'

'Then don't.' William took a few paces forward. The knife was still in his hand and the blade had a dull sheen in the light from the windows. 'It's not too late. You can still join us.'

Jack shook his head and rested his finger on the trigger.

'You're really still with the Rajthanans?' William asked. 'You've seen what they've done to this city.'

'No. I'm not with them.'

'Then join us.'

Jack remembered the burnt farms in Hampshire, Charles dead, the old man being beaten on the road back from the market. Elizabeth would want him to fight for England. 'I can't.'

'Thought I knew you, Jack.' There was a slight tremor in William's voice. 'Go on, then. Shoot me.'

Jack clenched his jaw. He blinked. He hated the Rajthanans for what they were making him do. Even now they had power over him. Why should he do what they told him to?

But then he thought of Elizabeth. He was going to do it . . .

William snorted. 'Thought not.' His features softened, the anger draining away. In the grey light, with the falling rain behind him, he appeared lost for a moment.

Jack noticed how old his friend looked, his face criss-crossed by lines and furrows.

'I'm going down there.' William gestured to a set of stairs at the far end of the hall. 'I'm going to keep on fighting. You follow me if you want to.' He turned and began to walk away.

'No.' Jack's voice was thick. He took a few paces to the side, still with his musket trained on William, until he was blocking the path to the stairs. He kicked away a musket lying nearby.

'Out of the way, Jack.'

'I can't let you go.' And yet he couldn't bring himself to shoot his friend – not just like that, after all the years they'd spent together, after William had saved his life at Ragusa. Not really understanding why, he tossed the musket aside and it clattered to the floor. He took out the knife. If he was going to fight William, then at least he would do it fairly.

William's forehead creased. 'There's no need for this, old friend.'

'I'm taking you with me to Poole. One way or another.'

William tilted his head back. His eyes were two dark caves as he slowly nodded. 'Very well. As you wish.'

William bent his knees and stood poised as if to begin a wrestling match. Jack did the same and they began to circle each other. The sound of the battle still rattled and pounded outside, but it seemed far away, as though the two of them were enclosed in a bubble. Jack recalled the sound of the men cheering in the wrestling tent, back when he was in the regiment. He and William had spent endless hours in that tent. He'd even fought William a few times – although his friend had always won easily. William was a strong man and the years didn't seem to have weakened him at all. Jack felt only too aware of the ache in his chest, the shallowness of his breath. He couldn't hope to win in a fight with William. Why was he doing this? Why not just pick up the musket?

They'd been prowling around each other for almost half a minute when William broke the spell and lunged with his knife-free hand, trying to grasp Jack's arm. Jack danced aside and avoided the attack – at least his injury hadn't slowed his reflexes.

'Come on,' William said. 'If you want to fight, then fight. Otherwise let me get on with killing Rajthanans.'

Jack didn't reply. If William was trying to distract and unnerve him, it wasn't going to work.

William lashed out again, but this time, as Jack tried to dodge to the side, his friend lunged in the opposite direction with the knife. Jack had to lean sideways to avoid the blade, and in so doing ran into William's arm. The blow hit him in the chest and he staggered back – not injured, just startled.

William flicked his arm around, the blade flashing straight towards Jack's head. Jack ducked, but he needn't have. William stopped himself from following through, the knife hovering inches from where Jack's face would have been.

Jack slipped under William's arm and was back upright in a second. A film of sweat covered his face and neck.

'You never were a great wrestler,' William said. 'Step aside. I don't want to hurt you.'

Jack struggled to get his breath back. 'Can't do that.'

'You don't look too well. Sure you want to carry on?'

Jack scowled. He was letting William get to him – wrestling was about the mind as well as the body.

He tensed his leg muscles, then sprang forward, jabbing with the knife. It was a desperate move, and he doubted it would work, but he needed to stop William talking.

William, as Jack had expected, stepped back in plenty of time and the knife prodded the air well short. But William kicked up, a move Jack hadn't anticipated. William's boot struck Jack hard in the arm and he almost let go of the knife.

As Jack staggered back, William leapt forward and swung his fist. The blow landed square on Jack's nose. There was a flash and a ringing sound and Jack felt pain spread like hot liquid across his face. He gasped and fell on to his backside.

William towered over him, massaging his knuckles. He'd hit Jack with his knife hand – he could have used the blade if he'd wanted to, and then that would have been the end.

William smiled gently. 'Give up, Jack. There's no point in this.'

But an image of Elizabeth in the cell flickered in Jack's mind and his nerves screamed and screamed. He jumped up and flailed wildly at William with his knife.

William was surprised and fell back awkwardly. Jack gave a guttural cry. His mind was empty. He swung the knife in a loose arc. But William saw the blow coming in plenty of time, moved to the side and grabbed Jack's arm as it swished past. William yanked at the arm so that Jack was flung forward and dashed to the ground. The breath was punched out of Jack's lungs and blackness threatened him. William grasped the arm tightly and wrenched it up behind Jack's back. Now Jack was lying face down on the floor with his knife hand in a painful grip.

'Drop the knife,' William shouted. 'I don't want to break your arm.'

But Jack still clung to the blade and kicked and struggled with all of his remaining strength.

There was a loud crack. William suddenly released his grip and staggered away. Jack flipped over, still lying on the ground. William clutched his shoulder, blood pooling beneath his fingers. At the end of the hall stood a silver-turbaned Rajthanan lieutenant and five Andalusian soldiers. The soldiers had their muskets trained on William, while the officer held a pistol that drooled smoke.

'Don't shoot,' Jack shouted. But his words were drowned out by the tearing, blistering sound of five muskets and a pistol firing.

William jolted, stumbled, tried to stand, slipped to his knees, got up again. It was as though he were balancing on the deck of a ship in a wild sea. Finally, he fell back against the wall, beneath the line of windows. Bullet wounds peppered his chest and abdomen, but he was still alive. He glared at his enemies, then turned his head and looked at Jack, one eye half closed. Jack stared back. There was a light behind his friend's eyes for a moment, then it went out. William's body relaxed as he took his final, long, sighing breath.

'You were lucky,' the lieutenant said in Arabic. 'That bastard would have done you in if we hadn't got here.'

Jack groaned as he tried to move. It felt as though all his ribs had been cracked and a metal peg had been driven into his face.

Bodies littered the slope outside the White Tower. The dead lay contorted where they'd fallen. Those still living sobbed and moaned and writhed like crushed beetles. The rain had eased to a drizzle and fell tenderly on the broken men.

Jack stopped for a moment. The stretcher-bearers had arrived and were carrying away the wounded, but there were so many injured he could tell that most were destined to lie there for hours and eventually die.

He looked back at the White Tower. It stood at the top of the incline, pallid against the dark sky, only slightly damaged by the fighting. The King was still inside, Jack had been told, being held for his own protection now that he'd been 'freed' from the captivity of the rebels. Sir Gawain, apparently, had been taken alive and would be tried within a matter of days. No doubt he would soon be hanging from the gallows.

A gust of wind blew raindrops into Jack's face. Elizabeth was due to be executed in just over two days.

He grasped the stretcher on to which he'd tied William's body, wrapped in a sheet of sackcloth, and staggered forward as quickly as he could. The stretcher bounced over the mud and the twisted bodies, the tortured faces, blank eyes, gleaming teeth, clawing hands.

No one paid him any attention. All those who'd survived the battle were either wounded or exhausted. A private dragging a corpse wasn't anything notable.

He reached the smashed remains of the outer wall and hauled the stretcher up the rubble. At the summit he stopped to regain his breath. Below him was the slope he'd run up an hour earlier. It was covered in corpses, limbs, lumps of flesh, blood, all glistening in the rain. Beyond this was the ruddy moat with the ramps still lying across it, then the square where the bodies formed a carpet that almost completely covered the cobblestones. And on the far side of the square lay buildings reduced to hunched ruins by artillery fire.

The spire of St Paul's rose above the roofs of London, the pinnacle invisible amongst the drifts of rain. At least the cathedral had survived.

He took a deep breath. He would have to leave immediately if he were to have any chance of getting to Poole in time.

As he turned into a narrow lane, Jack spied a horse, a white charger, wandering without a rider. He wasted no time in grasping the reins and then heaving William's corpse, still wrapped in sackcloth, across the animal's back. He mounted and set off in the direction of the New Gate.

Thunder rolled across London and dark cloud toiled above, although the rain had stopped for the time being.

After around ten minutes he realised he recognised the streets and squares about him – he was near the house where Charles had died, and where Saleem was hopefully still hiding. He was in a hurry, but he could spare a few minutes to check on Saleem. He owed the lad that much.

He sawed at the reins and the horse cantered down a side street. Soon the arch to the courtyard appeared ahead. He leapt to the ground, tethered the horse in the courtyard, then strode to the double doors to the house, which swung open when he pulled them.

He hesitated. He'd told the woman to keep the house locked. Had enemy troops been here? Had they found the woman, Saleem and the children?

He swallowed and stepped into the dim, musty chamber. Everything seemed exactly as when he'd left hours earlier. There was no sign of a struggle.

'Saleem,' he called out.

No reply.

He poked his head into the bedroom and was surprised to see that Charles's body had been removed.

Strange.

He marched to the trapdoor, flung it open and stared down into the gloomy cellar. It was empty.

'Saleem!'

He dashed through the other rooms on the ground floor, then hurried up the stairs and searched the top storey. There was no one about. Had they all escaped? Taking Charles's body with them? As he'd ridden across the city, he'd seen thousands fleeing over London Bridge or in small boats across the Thames. Hopefully Saleem and the others were amongst them.

He juddered back downstairs, kicked the trapdoor closed, then turned to leave.

His heart shot into his throat.

A figure in a hooded cloak stood in the entrance, silhouetted against the grey light.

Jack swung the musket from his shoulder and pointed it at the figure. Thunder grumbled in the distance.

'Wait.' The figure raised a hand and drew back the cowl.

Jack blinked a few times. It was Kanvar the Sikh, his orange turban smeared with dirt and his thin face more gaunt than before.

'What are you doing here?' Jack kept the musket trained on Kanvar.

'Following you.' Kanvar stepped into the room, his pallid eyes boring into Jack.

'Following me.'

Kanvar cast a glance about the room, seemingly unconcerned that there was a firearm pointing at him. 'Yes. I sensed you.' He looked at Jack again. 'I sensed what you did.'

'I don't have time for riddles.'

Kanvar stepped closer. 'You broke the law of karma. You used a new power when your learning had already been blocked. You shouldn't have been able to do that. No one's ever done that.'

Jack gripped the musket tighter. It looked as though Jhala had spoken the truth, then – the law of karma really did work as he'd said.

'There's something . . . unusual about you,' Kanvar went on. 'I could tell in Dorsetshire. There was something, but I didn't know what.'

'There's nothing unusual about me. You lot, you siddhas, have been lying to me for years. Why should I believe anything you say?'

Kanvar frowned and stared at his hands for a moment. Then he looked up again. 'You don't trust me. I understand. But I'm here to help. I'll show you.' He reached for something under his cloak.

Jack flinched. 'Stop.'

'It's just this.' Kanvar waved a piece of cloth about twenty inches square. On it was embroidered an intricate circular design. A yantra.

Jack flexed his fingers on the musket. Where was this going?

'Here.' Kanvar held out the cloth. 'It's a new yantra for you to learn.'

'Is this a trick?'

Kanvar shook his head. 'Try it. It'll help you.'

'What's the power?'

'Try it, then you'll see.'

Jack didn't know what Kanvar wanted with him, but he was also tempted by the offer of a yantra. Finally, he lowered the musket and took the cloth. He studied the yantra and was taken aback for a moment – it was far larger and more detailed than the two he'd previously learnt. It would take many months to memorise. Not that this mattered to him at the moment.

'I'll see what I can do.' He stuffed the cloth in his pocket and slipped the musket back on to his shoulder. 'I have to go now.'

'You must come with me.'

'I don't think so.'

'I know where you'll be safe.' Kanvar trod closer and grasped Jack's arm.

Jack shook off Kanvar's hand. 'Listen. I don't know what this is about, but I'm going to Poole and you're not going to stop me. Now, get out of my way.'

Kanvar stepped aside, face solemn. 'Of course, it's your choice.'

'Right.' That had been easy. 'Farewell, then.' He walked to the doorway.

'Jack.'

He stopped and looked back at the Sikh.

'Stay alive,' Kanvar said.

Jack couldn't help smiling at this. 'I'll try.'

20

Jack stopped the horse on a rise, leapt to the ground and collapsed to his knees. The moon was bright and the night sky clear, sobbing stars. The road to Dorsetshire glimmered faintly and the fields of barley to either side swayed.

He clasped his hands before him and bowed his head. He shouldn't have stopped – he had to get to Poole as quickly as possible – but he also knew he had to spare a moment to do this.

Our Father,
you who are in heaven,
may your name be holy,
may your kingdom come.
May your will be done,
on earth as it is in heaven.
Give us today our daily bread.
And release us from our debts to you,
just as we also release our own debtors.
And let us not be tempted,
but free us from evil.
Amen.

He'd been riding almost without stopping for over a day. He'd escaped from London without much trouble and then ridden hard through Surrey and the smouldering, ruined landscape of Hampshire. He'd met soldiers along the road occasionally, but none had stopped or questioned him. The country was only now beginning to recover from the chaos of the mutiny and it seemed that no one was much interested in a soldier like him, wandering the countryside.

William's body still hung across the back of the charger.

'Please Lord, forgive me for what I've done,' Jack said. 'I betrayed my friend. I betrayed my country. But I had to do it for my daughter.'

Sickness rose in his throat.

Our deaths will be a message to our children and grandchildren. William had said that before he'd died.

'William, you haven't died in vain,' Jack whispered. 'Old friend, I'll keep your dream of freedom alive. You will be remembered.'

But first he had to free Elizabeth.

He jumped back on the horse and spurred the animal into a gallop. It was getting late, around ten o'clock. He'd made good time and now there was just the final ride down into Dorsetshire remaining. But he would have to keep up the pace if he was going to get to Jhala before the pardon ran out.

During the long ride, thoughts of the mutiny – the crusade – had swirled and churned like opposing tides in his head. The crusade had failed, as he'd always known it would. But it wasn't the end. It couldn't be the end.

Perhaps there would be a time in the future when his countrymen would rise up again, fulfil William's prophesy of freedom. Perhaps it was possible. But his people would not succeed as they were. They would have to progress.

At one point during the journey he'd seen a band of siddhas subduing a mill avatar. The English would have to learn this skill. They would have to overcome superstition and learn to control sattva and avatars. It was *their* sattva, after all. His people's sattva.

He himself had shown what could be done. He'd become a

siddha, which Europeans weren't supposed to be able to do, and he'd broken the law of karma, which was supposed to be impossible.

He didn't understand how this had happened. But he'd done it all the same.

The horse was tired, but he would ride until daybreak before stopping. He would buy food and water for the charger, but he needed nothing for himself, save a drop of water, which was just as well as he had only a few pennies left in his pocket. He didn't feel hungry. He didn't even feel tired. He was focused simply on getting to Poole and freeing Elizabeth.

It was a clear day as he rode towards the barracks outside Poole, but there was a slight chill in the air and he could smell a trace of salt from the sea. He'd left the main road as it veered off towards the city and now he was galloping down the same dusty lane that he'd travelled along with Jhala and Sengar four weeks earlier.

The barracks appeared ahead, a low stone wall surrounding the main complex. The rickety shanty town of the followers and European soldiers spread out on to the plain to the north. On the edge of the shanty town stood a dusty line of market stalls, where the soldiers would buy their food and what little treats they could afford.

He slowed the horse to a trot. Soon, he would see Jhala. A coal smouldered inside him when he thought about how his guru had betrayed him.

What would he say to Jhala now? By rights he should shoot him in the head. But, of course, he couldn't do that. He would stay calm and get Elizabeth out of the barracks.

Two Rajthanan soldiers in ornate turquoise tunics and turbans stood at the gate. They carried muskets on their shoulders and scimitars at their sides. Jack stopped the horse and the dust rose about him as though he were alight. One of the guards, a young man, looked up.

'I've come to see Colonel Jhala,' Jack said. 'My name's Jack Casey. The Colonel knows what it's about.'

The guard chewed paan slowly, studying Jack's face, then turned and spat red spittle into the dust. He wiped his mouth and glanced at the other guard, saying in Rajthani, 'You know a Colonel Jhala?'

The second guard, a squat man with a round face, shrugged and shook his head.

The first guard looked up at Jack again. 'There's no Jhala here. You'd better be on your way.'

Jack tightened his grip on the reins and the coal inside him glowed brighter. This young man had no respect for him. 'Jhala's the commander of the 2nd Native Infantry. He must be here.'

'The 2nd?' The first guard looked at his colleague again. 'They left a while back, didn't they?'

'Don't know.'

Jack looked up at the row of flagstaffs, searching for the standard of his old regiment – the three red lions running in a circle on a blue background. But he couldn't see it. There were a number of other flags, but they were all for foreign regiments, none of which he recognised.

Why wasn't the flag there? Where was Jhala? The burning coal inside him dimmed, went cold and hard.

'I've got something important here.' He pointed at the sackcloth bundle behind him.

The first guard's eyes narrowed. 'What is it?'

Jack paused. 'Something important.'

'Hey, it's a body.' The second guard had walked along the side of the horse and lifted up a flap of the cloth.

'What?' The first guard swung his musket from his shoulder, saying to Jack, 'You. Get down.'

Jack climbed slowly off the horse. The scent of putrefaction wafted from the sacking and flies began to collect about the corpse.

'Give me that musket,' the first guard demanded.

Jack thought about refusing, then took the firearm off his shoulder and tossed it to the guard. He could still feel the hidden knife against his skin. He would fight these Rajthanans if he had to. They wouldn't stop him freeing his daughter.

The second guard was studying the body more closely. 'Who *is* this?'

'A rebel leader,' Jack said. 'The Ghost.'

'The Ghost?' The first guard frowned. 'I've heard of him. I don't know . . . doesn't make much sense.'

The two guards stepped to one side, but Jack could still hear them speaking in Rajthani.

'Better get it checked out,' the second guard said.

'Could be some sort of trick.'

'He looks harmless.'

'Probably crazy.'

'All the same . . .

'All right. Let's see what Colonel Pundir thinks.'

The first guard turned to the barracks and whistled. In a few seconds a young soldier came running across and was sent off to find the Colonel.

Jack stood waiting beside the horse. The two guards kept their eyes on him, as if he were about to attack them.

He looked through the gate at the square of beaten earth and the low, thatched buildings beyond. Rajthanan soldiers walked about in all directions. He strained to see the prison, but he knew it was too far into the camp to be visible from where he was standing.

The young man returned and spoke to the first guard, who then turned to Jack. 'Come with me.'

Jack glanced at the bundle on the horse.

'You can leave that with us,' the second guard said.

Jack was reluctant to leave William's body – he planned to give William a proper Christian burial – but he could also see that for now he would have to do as he was told.

He followed the guard across the square and between the long wattle-and-daub buildings. It seemed like years since he'd last been here. Nothing had changed, but everything looked different.

They came out at the parade ground and crossed over to the bungalow that housed Jhala's office. On entering the building, Jack saw that the room was largely the same as when he'd last been there. The desk was still in the same position, but behind it sat a Rajthanan who Jack at first thought was too young to be a colonel, until he noticed the braids in the man's turban.

'What's all this about, then?' Colonel Pundir asked. 'You've got a dead body out there.'

'It's the Ghost. He's a rebel leader—'

'I know who the Ghost is, but what makes you sure that's him?'

'I served with him. A long time ago.'

'I see. And you killed him?'

'No. He was killed in London. During the battle.'

'Hmm. A likely story. You know, the Ghost's been spotted all over the place over the last few days.'

Jack went silent. He didn't know what to say.

'That's right,' Pundir said. 'He's been seen in Wiltshire, in Bristol, even up in Newcastle. Everyone's keen for the reward.'

'This really *is* him. I'm not after the reward. I just want . . . I had an agreement with Colonel Jhala.'

Pundir looked down at his desk. 'Jhala isn't here any more. He left with the 2nd over a week ago.'

Jack's heart quickened. He searched Pundir's face. Was the

Colonel going to help or obstruct him? 'Can we get a message to him? The sattva link.'

'I'm afraid that won't be possible.'

Jack tensed and thought about the knife. No one was going to stop him saving Elizabeth. 'It's important.'

'The thing is . . .' Pundir pursed his lips. 'He's dead.'

The room dropped an inch and Jack's breath went shallow. Darkness crept around the edge of his vision.

How would he save Elizabeth now?

'What the . . . ? You look terrible,' Pundir said. 'Sit down.'

'I'm all right.' Jack rested one hand on the edge of the desk and got his breath back. 'How did he die?'

'It's . . . not a pleasant story. You knew him well?'

'Yes. He was my captain – years ago.'

'I see. Well, there's no reason for you not to know. The 2nd was sent up to Bristol a week ago. A small rebellion had started there. But the 2nd mutinied and killed all their officers.' Pundir cleared his throat. 'One of Jhala's servants escaped. He saw Jhala shot down by his own men.'

Jack went silent.

'It must be sad news for you,' Pundir said.

'It is.' Jack was surprised to realise he meant it. Minutes ago he'd been wishing Jhala dead, but now, on hearing this news, he didn't know . . .

For a moment he saw Jhala's face on the day he'd finally packed his things and left the army. Jhala had looked serious and grey. Jack was sure his guru was sorry to see him leave. He couldn't be wrong about that.

'You have been my best disciple,' Jhala had said. 'Farewell, Casey . . . Jack.'

Jack took a moment to compose himself, then stood up straight, taking his hand away from the desk. 'Sir, there's something else. I had an agreement with Colonel Jhala. My daughter's in prison here and due to be executed tomorrow. Jhala sent me to find and bring back the Ghost. In return, he said he'd free my daughter.'

'A strange sort of agreement.'

'Yes. But I'm telling the truth.'

'Well, I don't know. I never met Jhala. He'd left by the time we got here. I don't remember anything . . . Wait a minute. There was *one* thing.' He thumbed through a pile of papers on a corner of his desk. 'Where was it?'

When he didn't find what he was looking for, he stood up and lifted a cardboard box from a shelf. He opened this and went through it. 'Ah, here it is.'

He took out a collection of papers held together by a pin. He scanned through these, running down what looked like hand-written lists with his finger. 'Right, you're in luck.' He looked up. 'Jack Casey?'

'Yes.' Jack straightened. Was there still hope for Elizabeth?

'Jhala did leave me a note about it. Sorry, I'd forgotten all about this list. It's been very chaotic, you understand. Barely been able to get my feet under the desk. Anyway, what he says here backs up your story.'

'You have the pardon, then?'

Pundir flicked through the rest of the papers. 'Hmm. Can't see it here.'

'It was in the top drawer of the desk.'

Pundir opened the drawer and fumbled about for a moment. He took out an envelope and opened it. There was a piece of yellow paper folded inside. He read this, nodding. 'This is it . . . Elizabeth Casey . . . a full and absolute pardon. Well, you're back just in time, Casey.'

Jack breathed out. So Jhala had kept his word.

'We'll have to verify the identity of that body, of course,' Pundir said.

'It's him. Without a doubt.'

'I'm sure you're right. But I have to be certain. We'll have to get a description of him. I'll send a few messages on the link. Come back tomorrow – I'm sure we'll have it all sorted out by then.'

'My daughter will be executed tomorrow.'

'Don't worry about that. I'll tell them to wait.'

Jack wanted to take Elizabeth with him now, not tomorrow. If he couldn't do that, then at least he would be back first thing in the morning to make sure she was spared. He would stay near to the barracks until he got her out. 'Sir, could I at least see her now?'

'I don't see why not. That seems reasonable.' Pundir looked up at the guard, who still stood in the doorway. 'Take him over to the prison, Ghosh.'

Jack namasted – it came so naturally to him, he almost didn't realise he was doing it.

He followed Ghosh across the parade ground, and the stone prison appeared as they rounded a corner. He'd pictured the building so often over the past four weeks that it seemed unreal to be standing in front of it now. There'd been so many times he was sure he'd never make it.

'You going to stand there all day, then?' Ghosh had already gone up the steps to the entrance.

Jack blinked and then allowed himself a small smile. He stepped up into the dim foyer. Two Rajthanan guards slouched beside the door to the cells and a third sat at a rough wooden table, a lantern glowing beside him.

'Colonel Pundir sent him over,' Ghosh explained to the gaoler behind the table. 'Let him see his daughter.'

The gaoler had a sleepy eye that roamed about as he studied Jack. 'What's her name?'

'Elizabeth Casey.'

The gaoler stood and went through an arch into a neighbouring room. He came back with a large register and dropped it on the table. He sighed, sat down and made a great show of leafing through the pages, as though it were an impossibly difficult task. 'When was she brought here?'

'Not sure,' Jack replied. 'She was here four weeks ago. She's in the cell at the end. If you let me through, I'll—'

'No, no. I'll need to find her in here first.' The gaoler continued turning the pages, licking his finger each time. He pored over the scribbled lists and tables. Finally, he stopped and looked at Jack and Ghosh in turn. His sleepy eye jumped about as though following the path of a fly. 'Elizabeth Casey, you say?'

'That's right,' Jack said.

The gaoler tapped his finger on the page. 'Found her here. Bit of a problem, though.'

'What?'

'She was executed three days ago.'

Jack went cold. 'No. The execution's tomorrow.'

The gaoler shook his head. 'It was brought forward. There's a note here that she was long overdue. We normally only hold them for a week.' The gaoler scratched the back of his neck. 'Can't understand why she was kept for so long, to be honest.'

'Are you sure?' Jack whispered.

'Yes. It's all written down here.'

'Let me see the cells.'

'There's no need. She's not there.'

'Let me see!' Jack slammed both hands on the table.

The two guards beside the door stood up straighter.

'I think you'd better go now.' Ghosh put his hand on Jack's shoulder.

Jack shook away the hand and then leapt across the table, grabbing the gaoler by the collar. 'You weren't supposed to kill her!'

Ghosh and the two guards jumped at Jack and held his arms. He wrestled with them, grunting and roaring like a wild animal. He would kill as many of them as he could.

They managed to get him out of the building, but at the bottom of the steps he shook them off. Ghosh was knocked down. The other two guards got hold of him again. Soldiers came running to see what the commotion was about.

Jack got one arm free and lashed out, catching one of the guards on the jaw. Ghosh leapt back to his feet and rejoined the melee. Dust swirled around them as they fought.

'Stop, stop!' The gaoler stood at the top of the steps, waving a small piece of paper.

Jack stopped struggling and Ghosh got hold of him from behind.

'The execution was postponed,' the gaoler said. 'There was a note clipped to the page. I didn't notice it. She's due to be hanged today. She'll be at the gallows now.'

Jack felt a surge of nerves.

Ghosh released his grip and stepped away.

'Where are the gallows?' Jack asked hoarsely.

'Over there.' The gaoler nodded to his right, down a parade between two rows of buildings. 'Hurry and you might get there in time.'

'I'll take you,' Ghosh said. 'Follow me.'

Jack was dazed as he walked beside Ghosh. A couple of other soldiers walked along with them, watching him carefully after his outburst.

But after a few seconds he realised there was no point in walking – why go so slowly?

He sprinted off down the path. Ghosh and the two soldiers shouted and ran after him. He ran faster, his breath scratching his throat, the old ache in his chest building and purplish blots appearing before his eyes.

'Slow down there,' Ghosh called.

But Jack wasn't listening. No one was going to get in his way now. He charged past building after building and soldiers stood and gawped and despite his injury, Ghosh and the others couldn't catch up with him.

'You're going the wrong way,' Ghosh shouted.

That made him stop.

'Down there.' Ghosh panted as he ran up to Jack. He pointed to a path to the right, at the end of which stood a stark, wide scaffold.

Jack shivered, then ran down the path with Ghosh and the soldiers jogging beside him. Three hooded figures dangled from the gallows. Jack's heart jolted. He was too late. He ran as fast as he could but there was no point now. He skidded into the open ground, dust whirling about him. Everything slowed down. The hanging figures swayed and turned in the breeze.

'Father!'

He heard the shout from amongst a group of soldiers to the side of the raised scaffold.

It was her voice.

And there she was, in the midst of the men, her hands bound behind her back, her dark hair ragged across her face and her cheeks gleaming red.

Jack started across the open space. Elizabeth struggled against her captors, but they held on to a rope tied to her wrists and she was unable to break free.

'Father,' she screamed.

'You there,' Ghosh shouted. 'Release her. Orders of Colonel Pundir.'

The soldiers let go of the rope and Elizabeth almost fell forward. She stumbled awkwardly across the square with her hands still bound behind her.

Jack ran up to her, grasped her, squeezed her. She couldn't hug him back, but she dug her face into his shoulder and sobbed and sobbed.

'It's all right.' Tears ran down his cheeks. 'It's all right now. I've come to take you away from here.'

Elizabeth looked up at him, forehead creasing in puzzlement. 'How?'

'It doesn't matter. You're free. That's all you need to know.'

She flung her head back on his shoulder and her whole body shuddered. 'I'm sorry, Father. I shouldn't have got involved. I was so stupid.'

'No,' he whispered in her ear so that no one else could hear. 'You weren't stupid. I'm proud of you. And everyone who fought. I'm proud of you all.'

21

'I thought the Grail would come,' Elizabeth said as she sat on the back of the horse, clinging to Jack.

'A lot of people did,' Jack said. 'At least it inspired them. Maybe a story can be true even if it isn't real. You said that to me last Christmas.'

'Yes, in the church.'

'Did a crusader tell you that?'

'No, Mother. When I was little. I always remembered it.'

Katelin? Jack had never heard her say that.

'I asked her whether the Grail was real and she said it didn't matter,' Elizabeth continued. 'She said that even if the Grail isn't real, the story can still be true.'

Eyes moist, Jack glanced back. There was his daughter – thin, but otherwise well. Her eyes still had that fire within them that he'd always known and her dark hair streamed behind her in ribbons. Thank God she was alive. What would he do without her? He had to face forward again, blinking furiously.

'Where are we going?' Elizabeth asked.

'Shropshire.'

'Why?'

'We need somewhere safe. Where we can start again. Shropshire's a native state. The Rajthanans don't go there, and we don't want anything to do with Rajthanans from now on. Besides, I was born in Shropshire. I still know a few people there.'

His parents were dead and the remainder of his and Katelin's families were scattered about northern England, mostly in service on Rajthanan estates. But he hoped he would still find a few old friends in Shropshire.

Elizabeth had been released that morning. A description of William had come down the sattva link and this had been enough to convince Pundir that Jack really had brought in the corpse of the Ghost.

But Pundir wouldn't hand over William's body, and that still rankled. William should have a proper burial, but there was little Jack could do about it.

A cloud of guilt passed over him. He'd as good as killed William. And he'd murdered Harold. He would never forget that.

His wound quivered, his breath shortened and his head whirled. He tried to recover, but his injury just got worse. He halted the horse beside a stretch of forest.

'What's wrong?' Elizabeth asked.

'Nature calls.'

He swung down and walked as steadily as he could toward the trees. He didn't want Elizabeth to see his weakness. There was no point worrying her.

He plodded into the forest and, once he was out of Elizabeth's sight, let out a deep breath, winced and rubbed his chest. The pain was fierce and worsening by the second.

He eased himself down and sat cross-legged on the forest floor. It took only a moment to recall the healing yantra, and then a few minutes more to hold it still. He reached out with his mind and found he was in a medium stream. He smelted the sattva. Warmth rippled across his chest and he felt lighter, stronger, younger. He breathed deeply, the air clean and sharp.

He slipped out of the trance and sat still for a second. Birds chirped overhead, bees hummed, dappled sunlight hovered about him. He hadn't felt this calm for four weeks. He'd been living on his nerves.

What did the future hold? He didn't know. He'd promised, before God, that he would keep William's dream of freedom alive.

But he wasn't sure yet what that meant. Would he continue the crusade? How?

Would Kanvar's yantra help?

He stood, stretched, rubbed his neck and then walked back.

Elizabeth was safe.

That was all that really mattered.

Acknowledgements

Land of Hope and Glory grew out of my interest in Indian history and was inspired in particular by three books: *The Indian Mutiny* by Saul David, *The Last Mughal* by William Dalrymple and *From Sepoy to Subedar* by Sitaram Panday. The novels of the incomparable Bernard Cornwell also showed me just how much I would have to improve my writing if I was going to have any chance of being published.

I would like to thank both my agent, Marlene Stringer, and editor, Carolyn Caughey, for taking a chance on a new author. Carolyn also provided many insightful comments on the book, which resulted in a much-improved final draft.

Thank you to Dave King and John Jarrold for editorial advice at different stages of the book's evolution, Gail Tatham for the translation of the Lord's Prayer, and Stephen Coulter for information about the Stour River and surrounds.

I owe a huge debt to my family and friends for all their help and encouragement, and for reading various versions of the book. There are too many people to mention but I would like specifically to thank Helena Quinn, Gail Tatham, Harry Wilson, Edward Wilson, Anita Hrebeniak, Blue Quinn, Molly Flowers, Dilraj Singh Sachdev, Renata Huvarova, Chris Tobias, Simon Tobias, Chris Millar, Simon Small, Wayne Tomlinson and Laurence Cooke.

The Straight Razor Cure

DANIEL POLANSKY

Welcome to Low Town. Here, the criminal is king. Here, people can disappear, and the lacklustre efforts of the guard ensure they are never found.

Warden is an ex-soldier who has seen the worst men have to offer; now a narcotics dealer with a rich, bloody past and a way of inviting danger. You'd struggle to find someone with a soul as dark and troubled as his.

But then a missing child, murdered and horribly mutilated, is discovered in an alley.

And then another.

With a mind as sharp as a blade and an old but powerful friend in the city, Warden's the only man with a hope of finding the killer.

If the killer doesn't find him first.